CAPTURE THE SUN

ALSO BY JESSIE MIHALIK

Eclipse the Moon

Hunt the Stars

Polaris Rising

Aurora Blazing

Chaos Reigning

The Queen's Gambit

The Queen's Advantage

The Queen's Triumph

CAPTURE THE SUN

A NOVEL

JESSIE MIHALIK

This is a work of fiction. Names, characters, places, and incidents are products of the author's imagination or are used fictitiously and are not to be construed as real. Any resemblance to actual events, locales, organizations, or persons, living or dead, is entirely coincidental.

HarperCollins books may be purchased for educational, business, or sales promotional use. For information, please email the Special Markets Department at SPsales@harpercollins.com.

FIRST EDITION

Designed by Paula Russell Szafranski
Fox art © Alexdarfox / Shutterstock.com
Title page image © galacticus/Shutterstock

Library of Congress Cataloging-in-Publication Data has been applied for.

ISBN 978-0-06-305110-2

23 24 25 26 27 LBC 6 5 4 3 2

To my dads,
I'm so lucky you're both in my life.

And to Dustin, my biggest cheerleader.

ACKNOWLEDGMENTS

It takes a team to turn my stories into books, and I'd like to thank the following people for their help and support:

Thanks to my fantastic agent, Sarah E. Younger. You're the absolute best!

Thanks to Tessa Woodward, my fabulous editor, whose brilliant insight always makes my books so much better! And thanks to the entire team at Voyager who turns my scribblings into books with what I'm pretty sure is highly skilled arcane magic (and maybe a deadline or twenty), then gets those books out into readers' hands. I appreciate all of your hard work!

Thanks to Patrick Ferguson and Tracy Smith for never tiring of my various complaints when the writing is going poorly and celebrating with me when it's going well. Love y'all!

Thanks to Bree, Donna, Ilona, and Gordon for all of the cheerleading, advice, and encouragement. You've done so much for me, and I appreciate it to the bottom of my heart!

Thanks to Dustin, my incredible husband, who cooks dinner, and reads my first drafts, and is generally an awesome person. I love you!

And finally, thanks to you, reader! It's because of you that I've been able to write these books, and I deeply appreciate your support. I hope you enjoy Lexi and Nilo's story. Happy reading!

CAPTURE THE SUN

CHAPTER ONE

I'd sworn I would never set foot on Valovia again, but I was about to prove myself a liar. That fact had never been in question, but I tried to keep the promises I made to myself. The screen in my cabin gently mocked me, displaying a green-and-brown close-up of the planet while the atmosphere buffeting the ship's hull grew denser as we sank toward the surface.

Valovia had burned me twice already. I usually learned from my mistakes, but once again the promise of money had overridden my good sense. I winced. My former captain, Octavia Zarola, would be so disappointed in me. Tavi had a strict moral compass. Mine was a lot more flexible.

And a lot more lucrative.

Case in point: the sumptuous first-class cabin surrounding me, paid for by Besor Edfo, my contact and potential employer on Valovia. It was an obvious ploy for him to demonstrate that he had money to spare, since I hadn't agreed to take the job yet, only to meet, but it was a nice touch. As was the prepaid first-class return ticket.

Besor had offered me a truly ridiculous amount of money to recover a stolen figurine for him. Apparently, he and a rival had been feuding over the piece of art for close to a decade, and it had switched hands a dozen times thanks to the efforts of a few recovery specialists.

Officially, recovery specialists were experts at tracking down items that had gone missing, whether through negligence or theft. But in reality, we were often the *reason* items went missing.

The latest theft of the figurine had stymied Besor's longtime specialist, so he'd put out a call for an expert.

An expert like myself.

I'd never been able to resist a puzzle, so despite my vow never to return, I was minutes away from touching down on Valovia once again. I just hoped that my curiosity—and greed—wouldn't bite me in the ass.

The ship picked up a subtle vibration as the atmosphere thickened. I checked the suite one last time. The porters had already picked up the trunk containing my clothes and other basics. It would be transferred directly to my hotel by the ship's staff. The trunk's locks were second to none, but I'd placed the few things I didn't want a stranger snooping through into an oversize tote I would personally carry.

Everything else I might need, assuming I accepted the job or at least wanted to research it further, was in a crate I'd shipped before I'd left Fed space—and by *shipped,* I meant *smuggled.* Travel between the Federated Human Planets and the Valovian Empire was allowed, but only under a very strict set of rules and regulations. Crossing the border with a whole lot of illegal tech wasn't something either side appreciated. But if everything had gone according to plan, the crate would be waiting for pickup in a warehouse at the edge of the city.

If not, well, it couldn't be tracked to me. The loss would be a financial hit, but such losses were a part of doing business, which is one of the reasons experienced recovery specialists charged such an exorbitant amount for their services.

Zenzi, Valovia's capital city, grew larger on the screen. I'd tried to move our meeting to one of the other cities on the planet, but Besor was based in the capital, and he'd been reluctant to relocate. That meant I was returning to the very city where I'd spent my previous two disastrous visits.

The same city where I'd met Nilo Shoren—Valoff, hand-to-hand specialist, teleporter, *liar*.

The first time we'd met, he'd flirted with me for a few days then left me waiting for him in a hotel bar like a dumbass while he'd stolen my job. The second time, Tavi had expressly forbidden me from stabbing him, which had saved him a limb or two. After that, we'd settled into a wary détente because rescuing a child had been more important than our petty squabble.

But a mix of anger, embarrassment, and disappointment still burned under my skin. I'd *liked* Nilo, right up until he'd humiliated me, which made the pain extra sharp, like sand in an open wound.

I was traveling under a false name, so even if he was on the lookout for me—which I very much doubted, my hubris wasn't *that* high—he wouldn't know I was back on Valovia.

And Zenzi's population was over two million, so the odds that we would accidentally meet were incredibly slim.

Still, I crossed my fingers to ward off bad luck.

Nilo had his own gravity, much like a black hole, and in this, at least, I was smart enough not to be drawn in a third time—no matter how much I was tempted by his charming grin and sly wit. It was a mask, same as mine. I needed to remember we were more alike than either of us would prefer.

I slid my feet into the nude pumps that added several centimeters to my height, putting me over a meter eighty. Height could be a weapon, and today I wielded it with precision. I expected to meet with Besor as soon as I arrived at the hotel, and with my heels, we'd stand eye to eye. The sleeveless midnight-blue sheath dress accentuated my pale skin and chin-length curly blond hair.

It also made me appear unarmed. I wasn't—I had two knives and a small plas blade hidden under the ruched fabric—but appearances were important.

My makeup was subtle and flawless. I looked poised, expensive, and untouchable. I tailored my look to each client, and according to rumor, Besor appreciated beautiful things. And perhaps if he was dazzled by my facade, he wouldn't pay enough attention to our negotiations, netting me a better deal.

The ship settled onto the landing pad with a barely discernible bump. A few minutes later, someone rang the suite's doorbell, and I shored up my mental shields. Most Valoffs were telepathic, and while they generally didn't go poking around in humans' heads for fun, they *could*.

I refused to have anyone in my head but me.

I opened the door to reveal a young, uniformed Valovian

woman. She bowed shallowly, and her pale skin and ash-blond hair contrasted nicely with the deep garnet uniform. Her eyes were light blue, threaded through with streaks of midnight—a common Valovian trait.

"Ms. Stafford, we have arrived at Zenzi," she said, her tone deferential, as if I really *were* someone important. "If you are ready to disembark, I will show you to your transport."

All of my travel documents and IDs were under the name Alexandra Stafford for this trip, because my real identity—Lexi Bowen—was potentially a little too interesting on Valovia. I didn't know that the empress was on the lookout for me, but I didn't know that she *wasn't,* either. My last trip hadn't exactly ended in an open invitation to return, so a new identity had been prudent.

I'd been answering to my assumed name for a week, so hearing it now didn't bother me. I picked up my tote, did a final visual check to ensure I hadn't left anything behind, then smiled at the woman. "Lead the way."

She bowed again and then swept an arm to my left. "Please follow me."

This passenger liner was large enough that the first-class cabins had their own level, and even the hallway was wide and well-appointed, with light cream paint, polished gold fixtures, and faux marble floors. It also had an elevator to a private external hatch, so VIPs wouldn't have to rub elbows with the huddled masses in the cheaper cabins.

As we waited for the elevator, two more groups joined us, each being led by a uniformed steward. I subtly eyed them. The two middle-aged men—both Valoff—in expensive, complementary suits were obviously a couple, holding hands and making goo-goo eyes at each other while their steward suppressed a tiny smile and politely ignored them. They were adorable.

The human man and woman were *not*. They were older, dressed in designer clothes, and angry at everything. The third time the woman snapped at their steward, who was doing his very best to maintain his placid expression in spite of his clenched jaw, I stepped in.

"What brings you to Valovia?" I asked in Common, masking my annoyance at them behind polite small talk. I could speak Valovan well enough to get by, but most humans preferred Common.

The woman ignored me. The man next to her shot me a contemptuous look, then followed it up with a slow, leering glance down my body. After he realized I was attractive, a lascivious smile appeared, though he had to be at least twice my age. "I'm here for business," he drawled, "but I'm hoping to make time for pleasure, too."

The invitation was impossible to miss, but I pretended ignorance.

The man edged closer, his smile still firmly in place. His eyes, however, were cold and covetous. If he put so much as a single finger on me, he'd learn a harsh lesson in why touching someone without consent was a very bad idea. It was a message I'd be happy to deliver on behalf of people everywhere.

He must've read the danger in my expression because he backed off, but to make himself feel better, he muttered an insult under his breath.

I mentally counted to ten. I was thirty-one, a former soldier, and currently one of the best thieves in the galaxy—dealing with assholes was practically my job description and had been for a long time. And while breaking the man's nose would be eminently satisfying, it wasn't worth the hassle. I was trying to help the steward, not cause more trouble.

Luckily, the elevator arrived before my self-control faltered. As we boarded, the steward dipped his chin in gratitude, which was thanks enough.

We arrived at the transport hub without further difficulty. The passenger liner's gravity matched Valovia's, which was slightly lower than FHP standard, so the transition out of the ship felt seamless. I slipped my steward a tip, then sighed and added a second one. I tilted my head toward the human couple who were still loudly complaining. "Please ensure this goes to their steward. I have a feeling they are going to forget their manners."

The young woman bowed deeply. "Thank you, Ms. Stafford. Is there anything else I may assist you with?"

"No, thank you."

She opened the transport's door. "Your destination is already programmed. Enjoy your stay."

The sleek hotel transport was as nice as the suite I'd just left, with deeply padded seats, a fully stocked minibar, and a panoramic tinted glass window to let passengers enjoy the sights. Aerial transportation was banned in Zenzi, thanks to the Imperial Palace, so the vehicle rose a mere meter before gliding forward and merging with the ground traffic.

I poured myself a glass of excellent Valovian red wine out of a tiny bottle and then watched the scenery slide by. Zenzi was a massive city, and the spaceport was on the edge of it. The Valovian Empire spanned at least a dozen known planets—and probably more we didn't know about. If Valovia was the empire's heart, then Zenzi was its brain.

And Empress Nepru ruled with a gloved fist from her seat in the Imperial Palace.

After a decades-long war, the Valovian Empire and the Federated Human Planets—commonly shortened to FHP or Fed—had finally settled into a fragile peace for the past three years. But a month and a half ago, the last time I'd been on-planet, I'd learned just how fragile that peace truly was, because either the empress or the FHP was actively working against it.

Hell, maybe they both were. Tavi was attempting to track down what was happening, but I'd left her and the rest of the crew of *Starlight's Shadow* behind to pursue my own goals. Guilt filled my chest, but I tried to shake it off. Tavi would be fine. She had the whole crew to look after her.

Of course, I considered half of that crew my family, so it wasn't exactly reassuring that they were all in danger, but at least Eli, Tavi's first officer, would be the voice of reason. And even if things got bad, they had a freaking telekinetic in the crew now, and Torran would protect Tavi with his life.

Tavi would be fine, but *I* wouldn't be if she found out I was on Valovia without backup, which is why I'd neglected to mention this little trip to her. We communicated fairly often, so I'd have to come clean if I ended up taking the job, but I'd cross that bridge when I came to it.

I settled more firmly in my seat and sipped my wine. Outside, the orange sun was low in the sky and sinking fast. Solar days on Valovia were only ten hours long, but rather than working and sleeping in short increments, the Valoffs had combined two solar days into a single *buratbos,* a twenty-hour "day" with two sunrises and sunsets. And because the Imperial Palace was on Valovia, the twenty-hour day became the Valovian standard, much like the FHP standard was twenty-four hours thanks to humans starting on Earth.

The ship had timed it so that we'd arrived in the second half of the *burathos,* which matched up with evening standard time. The transition wouldn't be too harsh, but every time I visited, the Valovian schedule fucked with my sleep. I did fine on planets with extremely long days and nights, but the frequent transition between the two threw off my body's internal clock.

However, never having to wait very long for darkness to descend did tend to make my job easier.

The steady flow of traffic grew heavier, and the interesting architecture of the outer edge of the city gave way to towers encased in glass as we reached the central district. In my experience, cities all tended to look very similar once they reached a certain population density. Zenzi might be a smidgen more beautiful than the FHP's early utilitarian cities, but physics worked the same everywhere, and there were only so many ways to build a skyscraper capable of housing thousands of people.

My hotel was in one of the tallest buildings in the city, a towering monolith sheathed in glittering blue glass reminiscent of ocean waves. I'd picked it for the design alone—and because Besor was footing the bill.

I drained the last drops of wine from my glass, then put it in the sanitizing receptacle. A moment later, the transport glided to a stop at the hotel's covered front entrance. A uniformed bellhop waited for my door to automatically open, then bowed in greeting. "Welcome to Oniatsa Tabr, Ms. Stafford," he said in flawless Common, proving that someone had alerted him about my arrival. "May I take your bag?"

"No, thank you," I said as I exited the transport. "I only have the one. I believe the rest of my luggage was sent ahead."

"It was. It is waiting for you in your room. If you have a comm that works on Valovian networks, then you should already have your room information and electronic key. If not, I'd be happy to direct you to the concierge who will give you a keycard."

"My comm is dual-tech, thank you." I pulled up my room assignment. I was on the thirtieth floor, which should make for a nice view as long as I didn't face the building next door.

The bellhop bowed slightly in acknowledgment. "Mr. Edfo requests that you join him in the Mountain Salon."

I got directions to the room—after waving off repeated offers of a personal escort—and entered the hotel. Inside, a vibrant green indoor oasis, at least three stories tall, flanked the right side of the lobby, and an understated concierge desk hugged the left wall. The main walkway led straight through the room, but clustered seating areas lined each side.

I took in the space with a brief glance. There were a few businesspeople and tourists, including a family with two small children who were doing their best to entertain everyone around them, much to their parents' exasperation. There were also at least three security agents doing their best to look inconspicuous while watching the entire lobby.

All three had noted my entrance.

They had positioned themselves around the room. The fair, blond woman was wearing slacks and a blouse covered by a jacket. She sat on the left side of the walkway, facing toward the path so she could see both the entrance and the exit. She appeared to be reading on her comm, but she spent more time scanning the surroundings than her device.

The dark-haired man with deep brown skin was wearing a charcoal suit and leaning casually against a column while idly scrolling through something on his slate. Every so often he frowned for effect, but his eyes were too sharp to pull off the ruse.

The final man had brown hair and tan skin. He was wearing a navy suit, and he sat at the far end of the walkway, near the hallway that led to the meeting rooms. He was sipping at a cup of coffee—or some other hot beverage in a mug—while lazily surveying the room.

Icy fingers of trepidation stole down my spine, but I kept my expression open and easy as I moved through the lobby. None of my research had indicated that Besor employed personal security while out in the city. They could be security for someone else, but the way they were arrayed gave them the best view of both the hotel's entrance and the corridor that led to the Mountain Salon.

And all three were very carefully not looking at me.

My intuition was finely honed, and right now, it screamed danger. I didn't question it, not even for the lucrative job offer waiting just a few meters away. I'd studied the hotel's map as a basic precaution before deciding on the location, and I knew the meeting room hallway had several exits.

Bolting would draw too much attention. I moved through the lobby with brisk confidence and entered the wide hallway. The door to the Mountain Salon was closed, and no one was visible, but I still couldn't shake the feeling that something wasn't right.

I continued past the closed door without breaking

stride. If this was a false alarm, then Besor would be upset that I'd delayed our meeting, but I could smooth his ruffled feathers once I figured out why all of my internal alarms were rioting.

A glance over my shoulder proved that the Valoff in the navy suit had entered the hallway, his eyes on me. Shit, intuition won this round. If he was a telekinetic, then I was fucked.

With no better options available, I picked up my pace. Escape was far better than a fight, but I still had ten meters before I'd reach the door that led into a labyrinth of service hallways.

A tall, lean man wearing a long, hooded coat appeared in my path, and I jerked to a halt. He hadn't stepped out of a doorway or from a hidden alcove, he'd literally appeared from thin air, something no human could accomplish. A teleporter wasn't as deadly as a telekinetic, but they were much harder to evade.

I slid the hem of my dress up, drew the plas knife strapped to my thigh, and activated it. The ten-centimeter energy blade shimmered into existence, glowing red—the lethal setting. The short blade wasn't a huge threat, but it was better than nothing.

Behind me, a deep voice shouted, "Stop!"

As if I was going to listen to that.

The man in front of me tilted his head, and I caught a glimpse of a familiar one-sided smile. My breath caught. It couldn't be.

He closed the distance between us. The hood shadowed his face, but I would know those striking, gold-streaked green eyes anywhere—Nilo Shoren had found me even though I'd been on-planet for less than two hours.

A maelstrom of emotion arose—annoyance, anger, desire, happiness, and most dangerous of all, hope.

I kept the blade between us. His smile grew wider, and he murmured, "Going to stab me?"

"Depends. Are you going to betray me again?"

Something fleeting crossed his face, but he shook his head. "Believe it or not, I'm here to help."

I didn't believe it, but another shout behind me proved that I didn't have much choice. Nilo stepped closer, and I deactivated the blade. When I stabbed him, it would be because I'd *meant it,* not by accident.

"Take a deep breath," he ordered as his hands clamped around my bare upper arms.

I sucked in a breath to tell him exactly where he could shove his orders, but I didn't get a chance before cold power washed over me and the world disappeared.

CHAPTER TWO

The vertigo was instant and intense. It felt like spinning through zero gravity, where there was no up or down, just endless twists and turns in total, inky darkness. Tavi had tried to explain it, but she'd left out a few pertinent details.

Like how I could still feel Nilo's taut body pressed up against mine, a tiny reassurance in this hellacious void. And how I could feel his power, sharp and cold, swirling around both of us, binding us together.

The glass of wine I'd drank was dangerously close to reappearing when the world popped back into existence. Nilo stumbled and we both nearly went down. He cursed and steadied me for a second, then let go. My stomach heaved, unhappy with the entire ordeal.

"What were you thinking, coming to Valovia—" Nilo started, his tone furious, but I tuned him out.

I closed my eyes, tilted my head back, and took several deep, calming breaths. It helped. I still felt nauseous, but I no longer felt like I would immediately vomit on Nilo's shoes. When I opened my eyes, he held out a reusable bottle. I dropped the plas knife in my tote and accepted it.

Nilo still wore a scowl, but it was tempered by reluctant sympathy. "Sorry," he grumbled. "Humans tend to have a stronger reaction than Valoffs. I should've warned you."

I opened the bottle and took a cautious sip of cold water. When it stayed down, I took a longer drink and looked around. The fading sunlight revealed that we were in a narrow clearing surrounded by a forest of massive coniferous trees. A small house blended into the landscape, with dark brown wooden siding, a curved front wall of floor-to-ceiling windows, and a sloping green roof covered in plants.

There were no other houses nearby. Indeed, with the exception of what was likely a shed or garage, there were no other *structures* nearby. Just trees, trees, and more trees. Nervousness drifted through me like smoke. Despite our squabbles, I didn't *think* Nilo would take me into the woods and murder me, but if he tried, no one would hear me scream.

Of course, if he was stupid enough to try, then no one would hear *him* scream, either.

Bolstered by that thought, I turned to him and gave him the same slow perusal I'd just given our surroundings. At some point while I'd been trying to keep my wine down, he'd pushed back his hood, giving me a clear view, and one thing remained true: Nilo Shoren was an unfairly handsome man.

Not only did he have a bone structure that would make models weep with envy, but he also had dark hair, tan skin, and stunning eyes. Nilo's irises were startlingly green—as deep and vibrant as the forest around us—and streaked through with bolts of gold. Valoffs' eyes always tended to be interesting, but Nilo's were over the top.

I pulled myself away from the magnetic draw of his gaze and looked at the rest of him. He was looking more unkempt than usual. His hair was too long, and several days' worth of dark stubble shadowed his jaw. There was a subtle weariness to his expression that even his usual charming facade couldn't quite hide.

"Are you okay?" I asked with a frown.

That surprised a chuckle out of him. "It's been a long week," he admitted. His humor evaporated, and he leveled a glare at me. "And a lot of that is thanks to you. What were you thinking, returning here?"

I lifted an eyebrow at his tone. "I don't have to defend my decisions to you." Even if those decisions often started and ended with money. "Why did you grab me? Where are we?"

He sighed and swept an arm toward the house. "Welcome to my home."

I glanced between him and the building. It wasn't what I'd pictured for him, in the brief moments I'd allowed myself to think of it at all, but I supposed a teleporter could live anywhere. Envy nipped at me. How much easier would my job be if I could just flit around with a thought?

"I realize it might not be what you're used to," Nilo started, a note of defensiveness in his voice.

I shook myself from my thoughts and interrupted him before he could take offense. "It's beautiful, just not what I expected."

His expression lit in interest. "What did you expect?"

"I figured you'd be closer to the city, probably in one

of the tall buildings in the central district." I could almost picture it—a fancy condo with no hint of personality and furniture that was made for looks rather than comfort.

I'd had a very similar place until I'd realized it was a waste of money when I spent the vast majority of my time away on jobs.

Nilo's mouth twisted into a sardonic smile. "I own a flat on the forty-second floor of the third tallest building," he admitted. "But this is the better option for now."

"Why?"

"Because Empress Nepru doesn't know it exists."

My blood froze in my veins. "Pardon me?"

"You skipped the meeting room—which was the first smart thing you've done this week, by the way—so you had to know something was off, right?"

I ignored the implicit insult as adrenaline poured into my system. My pulse kicked, but danger had always sharpened my focus rather than derailing it. "I saw what I thought were security personnel in the lobby, but they didn't seem to be guarding anyone in particular. That's what tipped me off that something was wrong. Were they actually working for Empress Nepru?" At Nilo's nod, I continued, "How did you know I was here? How did *she*?"

"Besor sold you out. He didn't have your real identity, but when he heard Empress Nepru was quietly looking for a recovery specialist, he gave you up. Your assumed identity was solid, but once a team started digging, they matched your boarding photo to your real identity. The empress ordered a quiet pickup at the hotel. And I only knew you were here because I've been keeping an eye on who *she's* keeping an eye on."

If Besor truly had betrayed me, then his days were

numbered. The risk with hiring recovery specialists was that we were very, very good at getting into places where we weren't wanted.

Like a lying, double-crossing asshole's fancy compound in the expensive part of the city.

My eyes widened as the meaning of the second half of Nilo's sentence broke through the anger. "You have a spy in the palace."

His chin dipped.

"Why would you step in for me and risk burning your source?"

Nilo didn't quite roll his eyes, but I could tell that the desire was there. "Because if you get caught by the empress, then your captain will ride to your rescue, and Torran will accompany her. And the last thing the general needs right now is to be within the empress's reach."

I killed any disappointment before it could form. Of course he was looking out for Torran. And I should appreciate it, because he was right. If I was stupid enough to get caught on Valovia, then Tavi *would* come for me, even at great personal risk.

"Thank you," I murmured. "How far from the city are we?"

"Zenzi is an hour south by transport. There's a lev cycle in the shed in case of emergency, but I would prefer to port you to town to keep the risk of discovery down."

I wrinkled my nose at the thought of future teleports, but I understood his caution. "I don't suppose you grabbed my luggage, did you?"

Nilo shook his head, and I sighed. I still had my tote, so I'd kept everything important, but I needed clothes. This dress was nice, but it wouldn't be if I wore it for a week straight. Luckily, I had additional clothes in the crate I'd shipped. "I have a package that I need to pick up in Zenzi."

"Can it wait until tomorrow? Two more ports today will put me on my ass."

I enjoyed that mental picture for a second, but putting him out of commission for an outfit change probably wasn't the smartest plan if the empress knew I was on Valovia. "Do you have some clothes I can borrow?"

His gaze flickered over me before he met my eyes again. His expression sharpened in interest and a charming grin pulled at the corner of his mouth. "If I say no, will you keep wearing that dress?"

Little pinpricks of heat raced along my nerves. The man was too damn handsome for anyone's peace of mind, but he wasn't the only one who knew how to weaponize attractiveness. I gave him a slow, wicked smile. "If you say no," I murmured, pitching my voice low and inviting, "I'll mutilate your favorite shirt."

The gold in his irises expanded, and his grin bloomed into something hot and sinful. "If you want me shirtless, you only have to ask." When I merely raised my eyebrows, he relented. "I have a few things that should work for you until we can retrieve your clothes."

"Thank you."

Nilo gestured toward the house, and I fell into step beside him. Walking in heels on soft ground covered by tall, thick grass wasn't the easiest, so after a few steps I stopped. "If I take my shoes off, is there anything that's going to hurt my feet between here and the house?"

"I could carry you," Nilo offered with a teasing smile.

"Okay," I agreed, just to shock him. It didn't disappoint—his mouth popped open in surprise and his eyes widened.

But he recovered quickly, and before I could clarify that I'd been joking, he swept me up in his arms, with one arm braced behind my back and one looped under my naked knees, which put his hand dangerously high on my thigh.

His head dipped toward mine and he murmured, "You didn't think I'd pass up an opportunity to put my hands on you without getting stabbed, did you?"

I shivered at the heat in his eyes and the husky note in his voice, but I did my best to ignore the effect. "Who said I wouldn't stab you, hmm?" I asked lightly. I waved an imperious hand toward the house. "Now let's go before it gets totally dark and a bear comes out of the woods and eats us."

Nilo started for the house. "I don't know about a bear, since I am not familiar with the word, but there are *ditbusia,* and they are the reason that the modern Valovan word for demon or 'monster' is *ditbus* . . ."

He trailed off, and I poked him in his very firm, very close chest. "You can't just drop something like that and then not elaborate. What do they look like? Will they attack? What should I do if I see one?"

"Trust me, you'll know one when you see it. They're all teeth and claws and bad attitude. Yes, they'll attack Valoffs, so presumably they'll attack humans, too. They're fearless. And if you see one, it's already too late. They're fast and they can climb, so your best bet is standing still and hoping it's not hungry."

I scanned the darkening forest surrounding us. The sun had dipped below the horizon, leaving us shrouded in twilight. Valoffs had better night vision than humans, so if there was a demon stalking us, Nilo would see it, right?

He caught me staring at the trees and gave me a reassuring squeeze. "Don't worry, I haven't seen *ditbusia* around here in years. They tend to stay farther north."

"That's exactly what someone in a horror vid says right before the scary monster starts eating people."

Nilo's teeth flashed as he smiled, but his tone was serious when he said, "I'll protect you."

My heart quivered, ready to believe him, but his actions always spoke louder than his words, so until he threw himself between me and a clawed monster, I'd take his promises of protection with an appropriately large grain of salt.

Nilo opened the glass door without putting me down and carried me into the house. He set me on my feet and made sure I was stable before he moved away to turn on the lights.

I blinked as I looked around. The entryway opened into a small living room with a thickly cushioned sofa in front of a fireplace. On our right, a tiny wooden dining table with two chairs sat in the corner of the room, next to the wall of glass that made up the front of the cabin. Farther back, a compact kitchen had all the modern conveniences. It was open to the rest of the space, but still separate thanks to a long, narrow island.

Everything was soft and inviting and *cozy*, and it wasn't what I'd been expecting at all.

I slipped off my shoes, set my tote on the floor, and padded deeper into the room—not that there was anywhere to go. The whole building couldn't be more than ninety meters square, and this open living-dining-kitchen area took up most of that.

I glanced at Nilo. "How many bedrooms are in this house?"

"One." He rubbed the back of his neck and looked away. "When I built it, I didn't plan to bring guests."

I bit down on the questions I wanted to ask. Learning more about him was dangerous, because knowledge led to caring, and caring led to heartbreak. This was just another challenge I needed to overcome, and the universe loved to test my self-control. I shook my head and eyed the couch. It looked comfortable enough, and even if it wasn't, at least I'd have a roof over my head and hopefully a blanket or two.

Nilo moved into the kitchen. "Are you hungry?"

"Don't worry about it," I said. "I have a few meal bars that I can eat."

He pinned me in place with a look. "It's a simple question. Are you hungry, yes or no?"

My stomach was still a little iffy after the teleportation, but lunch on the ship had been hours ago. When I didn't answer fast enough, he prompted, "Yes or no?"

"Yes," I admitted. "But you don't have—"

He pointed at the chair. "Sit. Relax. I know you don't want to be here, and I'm sorry that this is how it worked out."

I shrugged, feigning an ease I didn't quite feel. "I'd rather be here than a guest of the empress, so thanks for that."

Nilo dipped his head in acknowledgment, then started pulling out pans and ingredients and whatever else you needed to make dinner. I wouldn't know—I'd spent most of my adult life eating either rations provided by the military or takeout provided by whatever restaurant was closest to my hotel. My time aboard *Starlight's Shadow* was the one exception because Tavi loved to cook, and she always made dinner for the crew.

While Nilo worked on dinner, I checked my messages. Besor had not contacted me despite the fact that I'd missed our meeting. That didn't *necessarily* mean he had betrayed me to Empress Nepru, but it was certainly suspicious considering our frequent communication previously.

I might not trust Nilo as far as I could throw him, but I didn't think he would lie about something like this. Still, I decided to send Besor a note to see if I could get him to give up any more information. I routed it through two proxy servers just like Kee had taught me, so that I wouldn't accidentally lead anyone looking straight to Nilo's hidden house.

That done, I put my comm on the table and stood. Nilo was chopping something that looked vaguely like a long, skinny potato into precision cubes. He held the knife with an easy confidence that made the whole process look effortless.

I leaned a hip against the edge of the island across from him. "Can I help?" I asked, then held up a hand. "Before you agree, you should know that I burn water, but I can chop ingredients."

His smile was warm and soft. It arrowed through me as easily as the knife in his hand would. "I'm almost done with the prep. I don't have any poultry or fish right now, so I thought I'd do an egg and vegetable hash. Does that work?"

I blinked at him. We had never once discussed my diet preferences, but he somehow knew that I preferred chicken and fish over red meat. On *Starlight's Shadow* we'd all eaten entirely vegetarian thanks to Kee's preferences, so he'd gleaned this information based on the handful of meals we'd had together that hadn't been on the ship.

Nilo had a sharp, deadly mind lurking behind his charming facade, and I needed to remember that. Very little escaped his notice, so I would have to be extra careful about what I allowed him to see. I pulled out the easy, friendly smile I used when trying to win someone over. "An egg and veggie hash sounds great, but you can make whatever you prefer. Don't let me mess up your plans."

An unreadable expression crossed Nilo's face, but he just nodded and kept chopping.

I watched him work and waited for the silence to become uncomfortable, but the rhythmic chopping was strangely soothing. I stared at his hands and let my mind drift. The return ticket Besor had provided would be useless now. I'd brought enough hard credits to pay a smuggler to return me to Fed space even if I lost access to my accounts, but finding one who was trustworthy would take time. The team I'd used to ship my crate did not accept passengers.

The delay might not be all bad, though. If I could lie low for a week or two, Besor's guard would drop, and I could pay him a little visit on my way off-planet. But two weeks with Nilo in a one-bedroom cabin was a recipe for disaster.

Hot, sweaty, pleasurable disaster, to be sure, but disaster nonetheless.

Nilo turned to dump the vegetables into a pan on the stove, and I admired the line of his back. He'd ditched his coat, and his gray shirt fit close to his body. He was leanly muscular with broad shoulders that narrowed to a trim waist and a nice ass. He was built like an endurance athlete with no unnecessary bulk, but as he'd proven outside, he was still plenty strong.

And my libido had all sorts of ideas about what, *exactly*, he could do with that strength and endurance. I shook my head at myself and reluctantly dropped my eyes to the countertop. Resisting temptation had never once been my strong suit. If I stayed here, I was doomed.

Pettiness warred with self-preservation. If I wanted revenge on Besor—*and I did*—then I needed a new place to stay as soon as possible. The crate I'd shipped had an alternate set of identity documents, so I should be able to book myself into a cheap hotel without arousing too much suspicion.

And I could certainly survive one night in the same cabin as Nilo, right?

CHAPTER THREE

With the decision made and a rough plan in mind, I glanced up to find Nilo watching me over his shoulder. “Everything okay?” he asked. “Or has my countertop caused you some grave offense?”

I couldn’t tell him I was contemplating my weakness for dark hair and green eyes, so I let my lips twist into a rueful smile. “Just thinking about how I’m going to get home now that Besor’s fancy first-class return ticket is worthless.”

“I can help with that,” he said. “I know a smuggler who can get you across the border undetected. She makes runs to Bastion every few weeks.”

“Is she trustworthy?”

Nilo nodded, but his mouth flattened into an unhappy line. “I wouldn’t send you to someone who wasn’t,” he said. “But, unfortunately, she’s on a run right now and won’t return for at least two weeks.”

"That's okay. After we retrieve the crate I shipped, I can book myself into a hotel for a couple of weeks. The extra time will also allow Besor's guard to drop, which means I can give him a really heartfelt going-away present."

Nilo turned all the way around and frowned at me. "You're not planning to stay here?"

"Your couch is nice, but I need a real bed."

"Stay in my room." He must've caught the surprise in my expression because his mouth curved into a melting smile. "I meant on your own, but if you'd like company, you only have to ask."

I pressed my fingers into the cool countertop and reminded myself why that would be a bad, bad idea. "A hotel is safer."

Thunderclouds gathered on his brow as his scowl grew. "A hotel is *not* safer. Empress Nepru knows you're on-planet. She'll have her Fiazefferia hunting for you. If you return to the city, you will need to maintain your mental shields at all times, even when you sleep. And your shields are not that good."

My nose wrinkled. He was right. My mental shields had barely been good enough to get me through the war, and that was about it. They weren't impermeable even when I was awake, which is why I had to watch myself around Valoffs, because they could occasionally pick up stray thoughts without trying. Shielding while I was asleep was a nonstarter.

The empress's Sun Guardians played many roles in the Imperial Palace, but at their core, they were skilled trackers and assassins—and they were ruthless.

Still, I hadn't been a highly successful recovery specialist for years without learning a thing or two about hiding from hunters. Zenzi was a huge city. As long as I was careful, they wouldn't have time to find me before I'd already moved on.

"You know you are safe here, right?" Nilo asked quietly, his expression oddly intense. "I will not touch you without your express permission." He put his left arm across his chest and bowed slightly. "I swear it."

Personal honor was a cornerstone of Valovian society, but even if it wasn't, I didn't doubt Nilo's sincerity. He might flirt and tease, but he'd never crossed the line. And even when I'd invited him to turn flirting into more during those first, disastrous days, he'd demurred. I hadn't understood it at the time, but now I knew it was because he'd been planning to betray me all along. He could've taken advantage of my ignorance, but he hadn't.

"That's not what I'm worried about," I told him truthfully. "But if the Sun Guardians are hunting me, then it's better if I don't lead them straight to your hideout. I can move around in the city if they get close. I have new identity documents in the crate I shipped, and they're not linked to either my real identity or the one I used to travel here."

Nilo turned to the stove, but I could see the tension in his frame. He stirred the pan for a few minutes, then cracked some eggs over the top of the veggie mixture. My hope that he'd forgotten our argument died when he pivoted back to me, eyes ablaze with gold. "I will stay in the shed if you are uncomfortable sharing the house with me. The city is not safe."

"I know what I'm doing—"

"It's not your skill I doubt," he snapped, then blew out a frustrated breath and ran a hand through his hair. "Fiazefferu are *relentless*. They will not rest until you are found, and the empress has eyes in many places."

"All the more reason for me to leave. You need to stay hidden so you can keep working for Torran, and I threaten that. Speaking of, have you heard anything from Torran or Tavi lately? You haven't mentioned that I'm here, have you?"

Nilo's jaw clenched, and I braced myself for additional arguments, but he returned his attention to the stove and said, "Last I heard, Kee was planning to stay on Bastion for a couple of weeks to dig for info, but that was over a week ago. I haven't had a chance to tell them that you're here, yet."

"I'd rather you didn't mention it," I murmured. "It'll only worry Tavi."

He glanced at me over his shoulder, expression hard. "Do you often keep things from the people who love you?"

I let the stinging wave of anger and pain pass through me without ever losing my easy smile. *This* was the Nilo I was used to, the one who saw too much and didn't pull his punches. But he wasn't the only one with claws. My eyebrows rose as my smile sharpened. "Do you often judge acquaintances you barely know, or am I just lucky?"

"Lexi—"

I waved him off. "Don't bother. Tomorrow I would appreciate a lift to the city, and afterwards I will no longer be your concern. Until then, tell me everything you know about Besor Edfo."

A muscle in Nilo's jaw flexed, and he said, "I will not tell your captain that you're here if you promise that you'll check in twice a day."

"You are not my minder," I scoffed, my tone cutting. "I will not report to you like an errant child, nor will I be blackmailed into it."

"The empress wants you *dead*," he growled, eyes flashing. "It'll be easier to rescue you before that happens if I know exactly when you disappeared."

Part of me understood that what he was suggesting was a reasonable safety precaution, but that part was buried under stung pride and blazing anger. How *dare* he assume I would need to be rescued, as if I didn't know how to do my job.

I held myself still until the anger had burned down into icy calm, then I turned and picked up my tote. I arranged my face into a serene mask before glancing at Nilo. The pan was no longer on the stove, and he was watching me with an inscrutable expression.

"Thank you for the use of your room tonight. I would like to leave at first light." Thankfully, the short nights on Valovia would finally come in handy. In five hours or so, I'd be done with Nilo Shoren once again.

And this time, I'd make sure it stuck.

I was halfway across the room before he spoke. "You're not eating?"

Whatever he'd made smelled amazing, and my stomach protested the thought of eating a meal bar instead, but it would be better for both of us if we minimized our remaining time together. I turned just enough to see him. "My appetite has deserted me. I apologize for asking you to cook."

"You didn't ask, I offered, and you should try to eat a few bites while I change the sheets. I'm not sure how teleportation affects humans, but Valoffs usually feel better if they eat afterwards."

Nilo didn't wait for me to agree, he just pulled out a plate and scooped food onto it. He filled a glass with water and put both on the table. "Please," he murmured, pulling out a chair for me.

My stomach growled, but Nilo didn't comment, he merely waited for my decision. He held himself still, as if I were a spooked animal he was trying to lure closer.

And it was working, dammit.

My temper burned hot, but it cooled just as fast. And now that I was calmer, I could see that while Nilo could've chosen his words with more care, he was trying to look out for me. Just like he'd done by making dinner.

I slipped into the chair, and Nilo let out a breath. "Thank you," he said, as if I was the one doing him a favor by eating.

"Thank you for cooking," I told my plate, not quite ready to meet his keen gaze. "I'm sorry I snapped at you."

"I don't doubt your skill," he said, his voice soft, "and I'm sorry that I made it sound like I did. This week has been difficult."

I glanced up at him and made a decision I hoped I wouldn't regret. "Grab a plate and tell me why. Maybe I can help."

He looked at me for a long moment, as if judging my sincerity, then dipped his head and went to get food. He came back with a plate piled with over twice as much as he'd given me. When he saw me eyeing his portion, he smiled. "There's plenty more if you want it, but I didn't want to pressure you when you said your appetite was gone."

Nilo dug in, and I followed his lead. The potato-looking vegetable was a little spicier than a potato, but it had a similar texture when cooked. There were other unfamiliar vegetables, but they all worked well together with the eggs and the seasoning made the whole dish incredibly delicious.

Nilo must've been watching my reaction because he frowned. "Is it too spicy?"

"No, it's perfect. Nice job."

A tiny, satisfied smiled touched his mouth before he returned to his own meal.

A comfortable silence fell as we ate, and it wasn't until I'd returned to the table with more food that I broached the subject at hand. "So why has this week been so rough?"

Nilo sighed. "Something big is going down, but my informant doesn't know what it is. They are well positioned, but the empress's security has been tighter than usual."

"Is she planning to attack the FHP?"

"Not directly, I don't think. There's been no troop movement reported. But something is happening because everyone is on high alert. Then my contact informed me that the empress was very interested in a certain recovery specialist who was arriving in two days, so I had to scramble for information and a plan. Until last night, I was afraid I'd miss you or fuck up the grab."

"Was Besor actually in the hotel?"

Nilo nodded. "He was in the salon with about fifteen members of the palace security team. They're not as dangerous as Fiazefferu, but they're no pushovers, either."

I contemplated whether or not I could've gotten past fifteen trained Valoffs to stab Besor right in his traitorous face. Probably not, but I would've given it my best effort. "Tell me about Besor."

"He's rich, arrogant, and power hungry. He thinks he's smarter than everyone else, and for the most part, he's right. He has money in nearly every illegal trade on Valovia."

That aligned with what I'd uncovered during my research. Our interactions had been limited to text—and

Besor had been at his most charming in an attempt to secure my services—so I hadn't been able to glean too much, but there were plenty of vids of him floating around, and even in the carefully edited ones, he'd come across as a bit of a pompous asshole.

But rich assholes and their petty rivalries allowed me to live in the style I preferred, so I hadn't thought too much of it. I certainly hadn't expected him to turn me over to the empress, but I *also* hadn't expected her to be actively hunting me.

I'd known that coming to Valovia was a risk, I just hadn't quite realized how *much* of a risk it was.

That was a mistake.

"Do you know what the empress offered him as a reward?" I asked. Besor had been desperate to get his hands on his stolen figurine, so that would've done it for sure.

Nilo shook his head. "But currying favor with the empress is worth a lot, especially when it causes the law to overlook your less than legal businesses. Don't take it personally." When my eyebrows rose in disbelief, he chuckled. "Okay, take it personally, but know that he wouldn't be the only one to take the deal."

"Would you?"

"No," Nilo said with a grin, "but I'm not trying to get on Empress Nepru's good side, either."

I tipped my head to the side. "Your loyalty is so easily swayed?"

His expression lost the teasing edge, and I caught a glimpse of the serious man under the charming facade. "No," he murmured, his gaze intense. "It's not."

A shiver danced down my spine. The words sounded like a vow, but I wasn't sure to *whom*. I tapped the table and changed the subject. "So you don't know what Empress Nepru is planning?"

"No." Frustration sharpened his tone. "But I'm sure I'm not going to like it."

"Any chance it's just some internal political shuffling and not, say, an imminent attempt to start another interstellar war?"

"Could be," Nilo allowed, but he didn't sound convinced.

And unfortunately, neither was I.

AFTER DINNER, NILO INSISTED ON CHANGING THE SHEETS SO I could stay in his room. I told him no less than four times that I was fine sleeping on the couch for the night, but he cheerfully ignored me. Watching him making a bed shouldn't be sexy, but somehow, it *was*.

He folded and tucked the corners with military precision and although the technique was different, I recognized the ritual. He caught me staring from the doorway and grinned, a slow, hot tilt of his lips that I felt all the way to my toes.

His gaze flitted down my body, a light caress I could almost feel. "Feet tucked or untucked?" he asked.

"Untucked, of course. Unless you're a monster."

He laughed, which had been my goal, but the deep, rich sound of pure amusement arrowed straight into my chest. I was in so much trouble.

And I wasn't entirely sure I cared.

Nilo finished the bed and pointed to a door on the wall beside where I was standing. "If you get cold, there are more blankets in the closet. Help yourself."

The bed already had two blankets on it, so I waved him off. "I'm sure I'll be fine."

"The bathroom is across the hall," he said, pointing over my shoulder, "and I'll be in the living room if you need anything." He picked up a bundle of clothes and set them on the foot of the bed. "Hopefully something in here will work until we retrieve your shipment."

"Thanks." I glanced past him. The wall of windows from the rest of the house extended into the bedroom, and thanks to the antireflective coating, I could see the tall, dark silhouettes of trees against the starry background.

I moved closer to the glass. The unfamiliar constellations were bright jewels against the velvet sky. Nilo joined me. "Beautiful, isn't it? This view is the reason I built here, and I never tire of it."

"No matter how often I travel, I'm always enchanted by the night sky," I admitted, my voice soft. "It reminds me how small I am, and how vast the universe is. Some people find that terrifying, but it keeps me grounded. I can't change everything, only myself."

Nilo shifted, and his voice, when it came, was touched with sorrow. "You would've liked my sister," he murmured. "She gave me nearly the same advice fifteen years ago when I was frustrated by how little I could actually *do.* And when I accused her of fatalism, she looked me dead in the eye and told me that it only takes one person to start change. 'Maybe not a *big* change,' she'd said, 'but even tiny changes add up.'"

I smiled wistfully. "I wish I'd met her when I was younger. Of course, I probably wouldn't have listened. I was an ornery little shit before Tavi took me in hand." I glanced at Nilo and gently asked, "What happened to her?"

"She died in combat."

I winced in sympathy. "I'm sorry."

He blew out a slow breath. "Me, too," he said then slanted a look my way. "What about you, any family?"

"Just Tavi, Kee, and Eli." I swallowed the lump in my throat that always arose with the memories of my childhood. "My adoptive parents died when I was nine, which is why I was a little wild when Tavi got me. I'd lucked out with my moms, but the rest of the foster system left a lot to be desired. It was a shock for a kid who'd been raised in a loving home for eight years."

"You didn't have any relatives who could take you in?"

"Nope. Luckily, my parents had a little bit of money, and they'd updated their will to put it into a trust for me, so my foster families couldn't get to it. Of course, neither could I until I turned eighteen, but I made it work." By running away at thirteen and begging, borrowing, and stealing for five years straight.

By the time I'd had to enroll in the mandatory FHP service, I could speak three languages and steal with sleight of hand so subtle that I could take things in broad daylight without anyone noticing. It had taken Tavi nearly a year and an infinite well of patience to break me of the habit of stealing from my fellow soldiers. Sometimes, in the dark of night, I still wondered why she and Eli—and later, Kee—had put up with so much of my shit.

I shoved the memories back into the dark, and asked, "Do you have other siblings?"

Nilo nodded. "A younger brother. He's a corporate lawyer over in Dalo, near our parents. We get together a few times a year."

Dalo was the second-largest city on Valovia, and on the

opposite side of the planet. It was a little colder and harsher than Zenzi thanks to the surrounding mountains. It was one of the cities I'd suggested to Besor as an alternative meeting place.

Wrapped in this cocoon of scenery and sharing, it would be so, so easy to forget how dangerous Nilo really was—both in general, and to me, specifically. He was my every temptation wrapped in a gorgeous package, and already part of me was whispering, *Why not?*

My fingers twitched. With the slightest encouragement, he would likely help me bury painful memories under an onslaught of pleasure. I wavered, then stepped away from temptation.

"Good night, Nilo," I murmured.

He looked at me for a long moment before he bowed his head. "Good night, Lexi. Sleep well."

"You, too."

AS I SLICED THROUGH THE NEAREST ENEMY, I HEARD KEE SHOUT IN pain. I spun, looking for her, but there were too many, and I couldn't see. She cried out again as an explosion lit up the night, then invisible hands clamped around my wrists. I thrashed against the hold, but there was no escape. I was going to die—

"Wake up!" Nilo urged, his voice soft but adamant. "You're safe. I have you."

Reality snapped back into place. I wrenched my eyes open and was met with gold-streaked green. My right hand was tight around the familiar hilt of my knife, but Nilo had pinned both of my wrists to the mattress.

The bedroom lights were on, and Nilo was half sprawled

across me, as if he'd been leaning over and lost his balance. I summoned a smile that I hoped looked better than it felt. "If you wanted to sleep in your bed, you should've said so. I told you I'd sleep on the couch."

Nilo's expression didn't change. "You okay?"

When I nodded, he carefully let go of my wrists and lifted himself off me. I absolutely did not miss his warmth and weight. He hissed as he sat up and my attention snapped back to him. "You're hurt."

"My fault," he said. "I tried to wake you from the doorway, but I couldn't. I shouldn't have gotten so close."

I lifted my hand and brought the short knife into view. I'd gone to sleep with it stashed under my pillow, but I must've grabbed it subconsciously once the nightmare hit. A line of blood smeared the blade's edge, which meant I'd likely ruined his sheets in addition to cutting him. I sat up and carefully set the knife aside. "Let me see the damage."

"It's not your fault," he said, edging away from me.

"How bad is it?"

His mouth quirked into a smile. "I'll survive, but only because I'm fast. Remind me not to underestimate you when you're sleeping."

After much prompting, Nilo directed me to the first aid kit in the bathroom, then peeled his shirt off, revealing a long, shallow cut on his lower right abdomen. I could see where the blade had bit in before he'd jumped away. If he'd been any slower, I might've gutted him.

Guilt clawed at me with sharp talons. I didn't often have nightmares—I couldn't remember the last one, in fact—but when I did, I didn't do them halfway. And the worry for Kee persisted, even as I opened the first aid kit.

Nilo sat on the edge of the bed as I cleaned the area

around the wound. I carefully smoothed medical gel over the slice before closing it with butterfly bandages. Nilo remained still and quiet as I worked, but as soon as the last bandage was on, he caught my hand with gentle fingers. "Do you want to talk about it?"

I shook my head, then admitted, "I was trying to save Kee and couldn't."

"Was it a memory?"

"No, just a nightmare." I met his eyes. "I'm sorry I hurt you."

"As I said, it's not your fault." A teasing smile touched his mouth. "Next time, I'll know that you sleep armed."

"You're lucky I didn't have a plas pistol under my pillow."

His smile widened. "Maybe you wanted me to be able to get close."

I wasn't touching that with a five-meter pole, so I just shook my head. Nilo stood, bringing him close enough that I could feel the heat from his naked chest through the borrowed shirt I was using as pajamas. And now that the adrenaline and worry had faded, I realized I wasn't wearing a bra and the shirt barely covered my underwear.

Danger.

But Nilo's gaze stayed on my face, and his brow furrowed. "Are you going to be okay now?"

I nodded. It wasn't even a lie because I didn't plan to go back to sleep tonight. The sun would rise in a couple of hours, then we could be on our way to Zenzi—and away from temptation.

"Come on, we can watch a vid in the living room. Kee's gotten me hooked on one of her favorite dramas, so I'm sure I have something you'll like."

"Don't let me keep you from sleep. You need the rest."

One eyebrow rose over green-and-gold eyes. "And you don't?"

"Since I'm not teleporting us to the city in a few hours, no."

"If you think I'm going to leave you to sit in the dark and wait for sunrise alone, then you're about to be proven wrong."

My mouth popped open. "How did you—"

Nilo's mouth twisted into a rueful, self-deprecating grin. "You think you're the only one with nightmares?"

CHAPTER FOUR

I ended up on the couch, bundled into what felt like a dozen blankets. Nilo had made me an alcoholic drink that tasted like a boozy chocolate milkshake, then he'd settled beside me in his own fortress of blankets and set the vid screen to a romantic show about a personal assistant who was clearly too good for his boss.

The alcohol finally eased the tension in my muscles. Between the drink, blankets, show, and Nilo's presence, I finally felt safe, even though I'd left my knife in the bedroom.

And with safety came weariness. I set my empty glass aside before I dropped it, then nestled deeper into my blanket cocoon. I fought the pull of sleep, but it was a losing battle. The third or fourth time my head drooped forward, waking me, Nilo sighed and extracted an arm from his own pile of blankets just long enough to pull me over until I was leaning against him.

"Shh," he soothed when I grumbled at him. "You don't have to sleep, but at least stop trying to break your neck."

I recognized the danger, but I didn't have the energy to care. I wiggled around until I was comfortable, then I let the soothing sound of the vid carry me into sleep.

AWARENESS ROSE IN GENTLE WAVES. I WAS WARM AND COMFORTable, still wrapped in a multitude of blankets, which hopefully meant I hadn't tried to kill Nilo again without realizing it. I was sprawled out on my side, leaning up against another person.

Nilo.

The thought didn't bring the panic I expected. I felt . . . good. Happy and relaxed and rested. There would be hell to pay at some point, but for now, I enjoyed the feeling. With the blankets between us, I couldn't feel more than the faintest outline of his body, but something about his breathing made me think he was awake.

I blinked my eyes open to a room filled with dim light. When I lifted my head, I saw that the glass panels had darkened, shading the room from the blazing sun outside. I glanced down at Nilo and found him watching me with an unreadable expression. "What time is it?" I whispered, unwilling to break the fragile peace.

"Midmorning," he replied just as softly.

I hummed an acknowledgment and then lay back down. Nilo froze as my head returned to his shoulder, then he slowly, carefully wrapped his arm around me. I wasn't touch starved, not exactly, but it'd been a while since I'd trusted anyone enough to just cuddle.

Not that I trusted Nilo completely, but I trusted that he wouldn't take advantage of this.

"You don't have to stay, if you want to get up," I murmured a few minutes later. Then I reluctantly added, "I should probably get up, too. We have things to do today."

Nilo's arm tightened around me. "I'm exactly where I want to be. Stay. Just for a little while longer."

I'd expected him to tease me about my propensity for cuddling, especially given our rocky past, but perhaps I wasn't the only one who was touch starved.

We lingered for long minutes as I slowly shook off the last dregs of sleep. Lingering in bed was always a pleasure, though one I rarely indulged in. It was even better when there was someone to share the pleasure with.

Better still when the pleasure turned physical, but I recognized the peril of that particular temptation.

I'd had my fair share of one-night stands and casual relationships because I preferred evenings of mutual pleasure with no strings—or deep emotions—attached. I knew how to protect my heart and enjoy physical intimacy.

I just wasn't sure I could do that with *Nilo*. He effortlessly slipped past every wall I tried to erect between us. Case in point: in less than ten hours I'd gone from vowing to avoid him to being curled up on a couch with him.

I mentally shook my head at myself. I could not be trusted when Nilo Shoren was involved, because even *knowing* that it was a bad idea, I was still so, so tempted to see if he'd be amenable to sharing an orgasm or two before we parted ways.

And that was my cue to put some much-needed distance between us.

I started to sit up. Nilo's arm tightened for a fraction of a second, then he let me go and shook off his blankets. He climbed to his feet, revealing soft, gray pants slung low around his hips and a tight, white shirt that was hitched up just enough to reveal the edge of the bandage.

"How's your side?"

His nose wrinkled in thought as he stretched his arms overhead. "A little sore, but not bad. It should heal in a day or two with the med gel."

"That's good." I dropped my eyes to my lap, troubled. Years of therapy had helped get my nightmares under control, and as far as I knew, I'd never attacked someone while asleep. Both together was unprecedented. And while I didn't really believe the universe sent signs, I also couldn't shake the feeling that I should check on Kee.

Careful fingers tipped my chin up before Nilo crouched down in front of me. "It's not your fault." When I would've protested, he gently cut me off. "I've lived with soldiers for most of my life. I *know* not to get close when someone is in the midst of a nightmare, but I did it anyway. The fault is mine."

"Then we'll agree to disagree. Only one of us was holding the knife, and it wasn't you."

A tiny smile curved his lips, and he leaned in, voice conspiratorial. "Good thing I find women with knives sexy."

"Less sexy when they're stabbing you, I'd imagine," I replied, my voice bone dry.

His eyes glinted. "Not as much as you might think."

That finally surprised a laugh out of me, and his smile acquired a satisfied edge. He stood and offered me a hand up. "Why don't you get ready while I fix us some breakfast?"

I gave him my hand and let him pull me from my tangled nest of blankets. "You don't have to cook," I told him. "I can grab something once we're in the city. But I would like a shower, if we have time."

"We have time. Do you need different clothes?" He heroically did not glance down at my bare legs.

"No, I think I can make something work with the clothes you gave me last night. Thanks for that, by the way."

"You're welcome." He stepped back and swept an arm toward the bedroom and bathroom. "Yell if you need something. Or if you want someone to wash your back."

My mind immediately jumped to Nilo in the shower, hot and hard. I clenched my fists against the desire to reach for him. From the heated look in his eyes, he knew exactly what I was picturing. Well, two could play with fire.

I leaned forward and tilted my face up so that my nose skimmed millimeters away from his jaw. Nilo ground out a wordless encouragement from deep in his chest, but he remained locked in place. "Luckily for me," I whispered in his ear, "I know how to take care of myself." I sank a world of innuendo into the words and Nilo groaned low.

Something flashed in his eyes, and he pulled me up against the firm line of his body, his hold featherlight, but his fingers hot through the fabric on my back. "Let me kiss you," he growled. "Please."

I swayed at the raw desire in his voice. I was self-aware enough to realize I was playing a very risky game with my heart, but just reckless enough not to care. After today, I likely wouldn't see Nilo again for months if not years. Surely one kiss was safe enough, right?

The answer was obviously *no,* but I refused to let something as boring as reality get in the way. And despite the flirtation in our past, I'd never actually kissed Nilo. Maybe he'd be a terrible kisser, and all the desire I felt for him would die a swift death.

I practically *needed* to find out, for science.

My chin dipped, but I clarified, "One kiss."

"One kiss, on my honor," he murmured. His right hand rose to cup my jaw while his left pulled me closer. He met my eyes, ensuring I was still with him. When I nodded again, the gold streaks in his irises expanded, and he closed the distance between us.

As soon as his lips ghosted over mine, I knew I'd made a mistake. Sparks danced across my nerves, scattering my good intentions. How arrogant I'd been, thinking one kiss would be enough.

Nilo tilted my head, deepening the kiss. The first touch of his tongue was an electric shock, and I buried my hands in his hair and pulled him closer, eager to feel it again. Nilo groaned low in his throat and obliged.

The sparks merged into an inferno, and by the time we broke apart, I had forgotten all of the reasons why taking him to bed was a terrible idea. If he could kiss like sin, then what *else* could he do with his mouth?

The gold in Nilo's eyes had nearly swallowed the green, which only made him more attractive. I leaned forward to kiss him again, but he jerked away.

The rejection stung. Perhaps *I* was the terrible kisser. Or perhaps this was just another game for him, and I'd fallen for it *again*.

Nilo caught my wrist before I could retreat. "I can hear you thinking, and you're wrong." At my furious look, he sighed and shook his head. "Not like *that*. I don't need telepathy to read your thoughts when they're written on your face."

My eyes narrowed. "You only see what I let you see."

"Usually, yes, but not right now." Before I could dispute that claim, he continued, "You put your trust in me, and that's not something I take lightly. I swore it would only be one kiss. If I let it continue past that, I would dishonor both myself and your trust." His serious expression morphed into a wicked smile. "But if you would like to renegotiate after you've had a chance to think about it, I'm all ears, *taro*."

I schooled my face into sharp amusement. "Did you forget that I speak Valovan? I'm not your treasure." No matter how much the endearment made my heart race.

His expression softened and his thumb slid over the sensitive skin above my pulse. "Are you sure?"

It took a mighty effort, but I managed to pull my wrist away from his intoxicating touch. "Yes, I'm sure."

"We'll agree to disagree," he said, echoing my words back to me.

I knew a losing argument when I saw one, so I didn't bother to correct him. I stepped around him and headed for the bedroom. "I'll be ready in twenty," I said.

"I'll be waiting."

I LET COOL WATER RAIN DOWN ON MY HEAD WHILE I CONTEMplated what a colossal fucking idiot I was. I *knew* Nilo was a weakness of mine, and yet, the very moment he'd showed the slightest interest, I'd kissed him like his lips were the key to life itself.

It was as if my brain took a vacation every time he looked my way.

The twenty minutes I'd given myself to get ready were

almost up, and I was still hiding in the shower. I gently knocked my head against the dark slate wall. *Colossal. Fucking. Idiot.*

I turned the tap to its coldest setting and sucked in a breath as icy water sluiced over my skin. Where did he get his water, a fucking glacier?

But the shocking cold brought clarity, too.

That kiss hadn't been one-sided. And he *had* kissed me this time, rather than putting me off with teasing touches and sly words. So maybe he wasn't planning to betray me again.

But, in the end, it didn't matter. I needed to focus on getting off Valovia in one piece, and Nilo needed to focus on finding out what the empress was plotting next. The less time we spent together, the better, for a multitude of reasons.

I exited the shower and got dressed. The black pants Nilo had loaned me were loose in the waist and snug in the hips, but the included belt meant they'd stay in place. Nilo's boots were far too big, so I was stuck wearing my heels from yesterday. Even so, I turned up the bottom of each pant leg so it wouldn't drag on the ground, and then checked out the shirts.

He'd given me both a T-shirt and a tunic. I wasn't sure if I was supposed to wear both, but without a coat, the extra layer would protect against the cool air, so I pulled them both on. The green tunic was the same shade as his eyes, and it fell to my knees.

I checked myself in the long mirror on the bathroom wall. It was obvious the clothes didn't fit quite right, but overall, I didn't look too bad. I used a towel to scrunch the last of the water from my hair, then finger-combed the short, blond curls into some semblance of order.

Good enough.

I exited the bathroom to find Nilo dressed in an outfit very similar to mine, but he made it look a million times better. The deep golden tunic accentuated his shoulders and torso.

Did all of his clothes match his eyes?

His gaze flickered over me, and a flash of *something* crossed his face before he smoothed it away. Amusement? Embarrassment? It was impossible to tell, but I'd give my last job's bonus to know what it was.

Nilo silently finished slicing the fruit he'd been working on. He arranged the slices on the two bowls in front of him on the kitchen island, then drizzled an amber syrup over one of them. He pushed the bowl with syrup my way. "Nothing fancy today, I'm afraid, but it's filling."

I picked up the bowl and took the spoon Nilo handed me. A soft, pale-fleshed fruit lay on top of a golden porridge. The bowl was cold against my palm, so whatever it was, it hadn't been heated.

The spoon cut through the fruit and porridge easier than I'd expected. Nilo probably hadn't gone to all this trouble just to poison me, so I popped the bite in my mouth. My eyes widened at the tangy flavor of the fruit, moderated by the sweet syrup. The porridge itself didn't seem to have too much flavor, but it had just enough texture to keep it interesting.

Nilo was watching me from the corner of his eye, so I dipped my chin at him. "It's delicious. Thank you."

We ate standing at the island, like the heathens we were. At least I wasn't the only one who got focused and lost all manners.

I put my dishes in the sanitizer, then went to collect

my things. I tucked the knife in my pocket and stuffed the dress in the tote. It was a moment's work to cinch the plas knife's stretchy thigh sheath tight around my left forearm. The tunic's long sleeves would make it a little awkward to draw, but it was better than nothing.

I checked my comm and found a message from Tavi. She was being careful because this was an open communication channel, so I had to do a little reading between the lines, but it seemed like they were going to attempt to break into the FHP's lunar base on Odyssey.

With my nightmare still firmly in mind, my initial reaction was just *NO,* but if things were far enough along that Tavi had reached out for help, then she was going to do it regardless of what I thought.

Even assuming I risked booking passage with unknown smugglers and left today, it would take me several days to reach them—and finding a ship leaving today wasn't guaranteed. So I sent her all of the information I had, along with the warning that I wasn't close enough to help right away, but if she could wait a little while, then I would meet her next week.

If I made it sound like I was still on Ailved—where my last job had been—without *actually* saying it, then I wasn't technically lying, and what she didn't know wouldn't hurt her. It sounded like she had enough to worry about, and the travel time from Ailved to Bastion was similar to traveling from Valovia.

I flagged the message high priority and paid the ridiculous fee. The upgrade meant Tavi would receive the message in a little over an hour if it transmitted perfectly between comm drones. Even in the worst case, it should arrive within three hours. Normal messages could take twelve hours or more to make the same trip, and I needed to know as soon as possible if I was going to have to find immediate transport.

I checked the rest of my messages, but I hadn't heard from Besor, so I slung the tote over my shoulder and returned to the main part of the house. Nilo was waiting for me next to the door. His eyes skimmed down my body, likely looking for weapons. "Ready?"

"If I needed to leave in a hurry, how fast could I get off the planet and on my way back to Fed space?"

Nilo's expression shifted. It wasn't anything overt, but he went from casual to focused in the blink of an eye. "What's wrong?"

"Tavi may need my help."

"Is she in trouble? Is Torran?"

I sighed. "No, not yet. But they are considering infiltrating an FHP base. I told her that I would help if she could wait until next week."

"Did you tell her that you're here?"

My gaze slid away from his. "Not exactly."

He shook his head but didn't call me on it. "Tomorrow afternoon is probably the earliest I could find you safe transport, and that's pushing it. My preferred contact won't be back for a couple of weeks, and while I have a few others, I don't trust them as much, so I'll need to be careful."

"Are there so few options?" I asked in surprise. I'd done research before I'd agreed to meet Besor, and it hadn't seemed like returning would be a problem.

"Few that I trust not to turn on you," Nilo growled, "especially now that the empress knows you're here."

I waved away his concern. I knew how to stay incognito, and a human looking to quietly return to Fed space wasn't that unusual. "Start thinking about a list. I probably won't get a response from Tavi until late tonight—if she sends it priority—so tomorrow is soon enough."

He didn't exactly look happy about the request, but he reluctantly nodded in agreement.

That settled, I lifted my comm and showed him the address of the shipping company I'd used to smuggle my crate to Valovia. "Do you know where this is?"

Nilo's brow creased in thought. "Yes, but the closest teleport target I have is five blocks away." He looked at my feet. "Will you be able to walk that far?"

These heels were more comfortable than they looked, but five blocks still wouldn't be *pleasant*. "I'll make it work. How do you choose a teleport target?"

"I have to be able to clearly picture the area, and it needs to be somewhere that rarely changes. And because we're trying not to attract attention, it needs to be relatively hidden and not under surveillance."

"Can you teleport somewhere you've never been if you have a clear picture?"

"Yes. Or another Valoff can share a mental image. That's how I teleported your captain to her ship despite not seeing it in person."

"Well, that's useful," I muttered. Teleporters were as rare as telekinetics, which was probably good for Valovia's crime rate, because if I could just pop into a building based on a photo, my job would be far too easy.

Nilo chuckled. "It can be, but teleporting blind is also more dangerous. That's why I'm not risking a new location today."

"I appreciate it. The port itself is bad enough; I don't

want to end up in a wall on top of it. I will happily walk five blocks out of sheer gratitude for surviving."

"Or I could carry you."

I rolled my eyes. "You can't carry me for five blocks."

He tilted his head, his expression unreadable. "Want to bet?" he asked softly, his voice a dangerous lure.

"No. I want to go before it gets dark."

Nilo handed me a lightweight coat with a hood. The weather was cool enough that the coat wouldn't look out of place, and being able to pull up the hood would help me avoid notice. I should've accounted for that before wearing both shirts, but it was too late now.

Nilo donned his own coat, then opened the cabin's door and stepped outside. The sun was sinking in the sky, headed for the first sunset of the day. With just five hours or so of light at a time, it seemed like the sun was always rising or setting. Maybe I'd book a hotel with blackout curtains and then just switch back to standard time. At least then I'd be able to sleep normally.

I followed Nilo outside, then looked back at the house. "Why don't you teleport from inside?"

His eyes glinted in the late morning sun. "Come back with me after we retrieve your things, and I'll tell you."

"You're trying to blackmail me with my own curiosity?" I shook my head. "That's low, even for you."

He chuckled. "'Even for you'? Now who's trying to manipulate whom, hmm?"

I lifted one shoulder, unrepentant. It was worth a shot.

Nilo stepped close and I tensed for the cold bite of his power and the stomach dropping port. Instead, he carefully raised my hood.

"Relax," he whispered.

"Easy for you to say," I griped. "You're not about to lose your breakfast."

"The more you teleport, the easier it gets. And we have time today so you can prepare."

"How do I do that?"

"Close your eyes." When I gave him a narrow-eyed glare, he held up his hands. "You are safe. I would not put you at risk."

The soft words sounded like a promise. Rather than thinking about what it meant, I closed my eyes, but that just amped my tension higher.

"Good," Nilo murmured. "Now, unclench your muscles."

"Or you could just port us, and we'd be there already."

"Trust me in this," he soothed. "I'm going to put my arms around you, but we're not going to port yet."

When I didn't object, he wrapped his arms around me and pulled me flush against his chest. I peeked up at him through my lashes, but his eyes were closed.

Nilo did nothing but hold me and take deep, even breaths. After a few minutes, my adrenaline faded, and I relaxed into his hold.

"If we get eaten by a demon while we're just standing here with our eyes closed, I'm going to haunt you in the afterlife," I whispered against his shoulder.

His body shook with suppressed laughter, but his voice was solemn. "Deal."

A moment later, cool energy rushed over me, and all of my hard-won calm went straight out the window. "Easy," Nilo whispered. "We're not going yet. I want you to get used to the feel of my ability."

"If you poke around in my head—"

He cut me off before I could think of an appropriate threat. "I won't, I swear it."

I focused on my mental shields. It was good practice, and it distracted me from the cool flow of power surrounding me. My shields wouldn't hold against much of an attack, but they would at least let me know if he broke his word.

I'd rarely been so close to a Valoff using their ability when one of us wasn't trying to kill the other, so I'd had only fleeting glimpses of their power. Letting a Valoff get this close during the war would've meant death, and even now, the anxious adrenaline refused to fade.

I needed a distraction, and I latched on to the first thing that came to mind. "Why can I feel your power if we're not teleporting?"

"Porting is a two-part process. First, I picture what I'm teleporting, then I picture where I'm going. This is the first part."

I turned that over, focusing on it instead of the cool touch of his ability. "So you could teleport something you weren't touching?"

"Yes, but it's more difficult unless I know the object very well. Open your eyes."

As I did, his power disappeared from around me. He stepped back and held up his hand. I felt a sharp spike of cold, then a daggerlike knife appeared in his palm. Another spike of cold and the knife disappeared. I frowned up at him. "Are you overextending yourself just to impress me?"

Nilo gave me his signature grin—part mischief, part magnetism, all charm. "*Are* you impressed?"

"Maybe I would be if you explained how it worked."

He laughed, his eyes sparkling. The knife reappeared, and he flipped it around and handed it to me hilt-first. The hilt was a little too big for my hands, but the blade was light and well balanced.

"I made these," he said, "so I know every line and curve. And I've used them for years, so they've become almost a part of me. Teleporting inanimate objects is far easier than people, and the better I know an object, the easier it gets."

The knife disappeared from my hand, and I started in surprise before shaking my head. "That would be handy in a fight."

"Indeed."

"So do people get easier to teleport the better you know them?"

"Yes. I paused to give you time to get used to the feel of my ability, but also to give *me* time to get used to the feel of *you*. That way, if we need to make a quick exit, it'll be less likely to put me on my ass."

I narrowed my eyes. "Could you teleport me without touching me?"

"I could, but it's much more difficult, and the difficulty increases exponentially with distance." His smile heated. "Plus, I *like* touching you."

I liked touching him, too, and that was the problem. I took a deep breath and braced myself. "I'm ready when you are."

His chin dipped, and he once again wrapped me in his arms. Cold power caught me tight, and the world vanished.

CHAPTER FIVE

I wasn't sure I'd call this trip *easier,* but when the world blinked back into view, I knew what to expect. I stood still and let the waves of nausea wash over me until I wasn't in danger of losing my breakfast.

Nilo held me until I opened my eyes, then he stepped back. "You recovered faster," he said.

I gave him a distracted nod as I looked around. We were in a small, dim room that rumbled with the sound of distant machinery. The door in front of us had a sliver of light showing under the bottom edge.

After Nilo confirmed I wasn't about to fall over, he turned and cracked the door open. He paused, listening, then swung the panel wide. Reddish-orange sunlight streamed in, momentarily blinding me.

I blinked the spots from my eyes and followed Nilo through the doorway. The little room we'd arrived in was attached to a tall, featureless warehouse. We'd come out on the side, where the setting sun slipped between the long rows of buildings surrounding us.

Nilo briefly checked his comm then led us toward the street. The wide road had a decent amount of transport traffic, mostly heavy cargo haulers moving containers to and from the spaceport.

There were no other pedestrians.

I pulled my hood lower, hiding my face. It wasn't exactly inconspicuous, but it was better than being instantly recognized by the wrong person—or by someone watching the traffic cameras.

Nilo let me set the pace, and I appreciated the kindness. By the time we'd crossed five long blocks, my feet were definitely unhappy with my shoe choice.

We stopped outside a warehouse that looked exactly like the ones we'd already passed. A small, elegant sign declared that the building belonged to Zenzi Freight Transfer, and a stream of cargo transports were waiting to be loaded.

There were even a few personal transports in the lot as people picked up smaller shipments.

Most smugglers ran legitimate shipping businesses to cover their more illicit activities. The authorities generally knew about it, but they looked the other way for a hefty bribe or two.

Still, it wouldn't do for my face to show up in the surveillance logs.

Nilo adjusted his hood, shadowing his face. He looked at me, then tipped his head to the building in question. "Is this the place?"

"Yes."

"I'll follow you." He paused, then asked, "Will you let me communicate telepathically with you?"

Ice slipped through my veins, and I gave a sharp shake of my head before I could moderate my reaction into something less telling.

He crossed his left arm over his chest. "I swear on my honor that I will stay out of your thoughts. If something happens, being able to communicate will be essential."

"No." My voice came out flat and hard.

Nilo sighed, but he dipped his head in acknowledgment.

I straightened my shoulders and took a deep breath. There was no reason to expect trouble. Even Kee, the best hacker I knew, would be hard-pressed to tie me to this shipment.

I stalked toward the entrance with a purposeful stride. Nilo fell in behind me, a silent shadow. The front door opened to a small, functional lobby. The middle-aged receptionist looked up as we entered. His gaze took in our hooded forms without a flicker of surprise.

"Scan your shipment ID and enter the retrieval code," he said, pointing at a kiosk on the left. "Your shipment will be retrieved momentarily."

I nodded and held my comm to the reader. The machine beeped, then prompted me for the retrieval code I'd set. I had two. One would alert the staff to bring me the crate. The other would prompt them to destroy it and swear it had never existed.

I entered the real code and stepped back to wait at my assigned station. A few minutes later, the small door in the wall slid open and my crate came through, carried by the lev belt. I pulled it onto the workbench and briefly checked the seals—both obvious and hidden—then nodded to Nilo.

"Do you need help carrying it?" he asked.

"No, thank you." I'd traveled enough to know that paying for the upgraded crate with built-in lev was a worthwhile expense, since levcarts weren't always available and my gear was *heavy*.

I pressed my index finger to the tiny, nearly invisible print reader and the crate lifted from the bench. By default, it was designed to maintain its height over uneven surfaces, so when I pulled it toward the door, it didn't drop closer to the floor. I pressed it down until it hovered near my waist, then guided it out of the building.

Nilo followed me, uncharacteristically silent. I had a vague idea of where I needed to go to find a hotel, but mostly I was getting away from the surveillance around the shipping company before I cracked open my crate and changed into more comfortable shoes.

We were nearly back to the street when I caught sight of someone tailing us. "Company," I murmured to Nilo. The person was wearing an outfit similar to ours—a tunic over long pants with a hooded jacket shadowing their face. They didn't look like one of the empress's guards, but they wouldn't have been very good at their job if they had.

"I see them," Nilo said. His jaw clenched, and he reached for my arm, but I shifted out of reach.

"Not yet. It would be better if the nearby surveillance cameras didn't catch us teleporting, and we can handle one person, right?"

Nilo's expression hardened. "I won't play games with your safety."

I slipped the plas blade from my sleeve, keeping it hidden from the person behind us, then flashed Nilo a grin. "Don't worry. I'll protect you."

Nilo grumbled something under his breath. It was probably for the best that it was too quiet for me to understand.

I glanced back, trying to decide whether this was a normal robbery or something worse when movement in my peripheral vision jerked my attention upward. A transport dropped from the sky like a falling meteor.

Since aerial transportation was banned in Zenzi—unless it was imperial business—the odds were good that this was *something worse.*

I had the plas blade and a couple of knives, but my better weapons were locked in the crate. It would take too long to unlock them, so I hoped Nilo was armed.

I lifted the blade as the transport drew level with us. The vehicle didn't have any doors, giving me a clear view of the dozen armored soldiers inside. My plas blade would be more of an annoyance than an actual threat.

My adrenaline spiked. I'd brought a knife to a gunfight, and we were outnumbered six to one. Retreat was the only option, but before I could break and run, Nilo wrapped his hand around my wrist. Cold power rushed over me, then faltered as he grunted.

We remained on the sidewalk, sitting ducks.

The first soldiers hit the ground, and I tried to shake off Nilo's grip so I could take a swing at them, but Nilo held tight and ground out a furious curse. Then an icy wave of power dumped me into the dark.

WE BLINKED BACK INTO EXISTENCE IN THE MEADOW OUTSIDE OF the cabin, and Nilo crashed to the ground. I narrowly avoided vomiting directly onto his body as I spun and lost my breakfast into the grass.

I braced my hands on my knees and breathed through the lingering nausea. This trip had been far worse than any before it, and it had left me weak and shaky.

So much so that it took me a minute to remember that Nilo had hit the dirt as soon as we'd arrived. I turned to check on him and found he hadn't moved. He was out cold but still breathing, so I assumed he was just exhausted and not dead or mortally injured.

I glanced warily at the surrounding trees. It would be dark soon because the sun had already slipped behind the horizon for the first sunset of the day. With his warnings about demons still firmly in mind, I couldn't leave Nilo out here. He'd *probably* be fine, but I'd learned not to count on probabilities.

I reluctantly returned the plas blade to its sheath on my forearm, then set my tote on the ground—well away from where I'd been sick. Nilo had managed to bring my crate along with us, so I deactivated its security and pulled out a pair of socks and boots.

I put the crate into stasis mode, then sat on the lid and eased my aching toes from the nude pumps. I loved these shoes, but right now, I'd be happy not to see them again for at least a day or two.

Once my feet were encased in sturdy, comfortable boots, I contemplated Nilo. He was lean but tall and muscular. My best chance of getting him inside would be to get him onto the crate and let the lev lifters do most of the work.

I crouched and slid my arms under his shoulders, but even lifting him less than a meter onto the crate was an exercise in frustration. I was strong, but his limp body was all dead weight and dangling limbs. When I finally had him carefully—well, *kind of* carefully—balanced atop the crate, it was completely dark, and the trees were ominous shadows against the night sky.

I approached the cabin fully prepared to override whatever security he had, but the door opened at my touch on the control panel. Did he truly not lock his doors?

I guided him and the crate inside, retrieved my tote, and then locked the door behind us. Nilo might not care about security, but I did. By the time I had half rolled, half dropped him onto the sofa, my back muscles ached, and I was ready for a drink even though it was barely lunchtime.

After I'd checked to ensure Nilo wouldn't wake up with a crick in his neck or a body part that had fallen asleep, I sank to the floor and leaned back against the sofa. I blew out a slow breath. That had been far too close for comfort.

Without Nilo's ability, I would've been caught by someone with the authority to fly a transport in Zenzi. A shiver worked its way down my spine as the implications hit.

I pulled out my comm. A quick search brought up the armor most of the guards had been wearing. Sure enough, they were imperial guards—not the famed Sun Guardians but more run-of-the-mill soldiers tasked with protecting the Imperial Palace and the empress.

There was *no way* the empress could've tied me to the shipment, which meant her soldiers had either gotten lucky or Nilo had sold me out. Considering he'd knocked himself unconscious to save me, betrayal was a stretch, but maybe he was working a long con.

He'd said there was a lev cycle in the shed. I could take it and vanish before he woke—and half of me longed to do exactly that. But he'd been kind to me last night, and leaving him defenseless felt wrong. If he'd betrayed me . . . well, I'd deal with it when it became necessary.

CHAPTER SIX

The sun rose and set again before Nilo began to stir. I'd changed into my own clothes and spent the day researching ways to get home. As much as I wanted to give Besor a parting gift he wouldn't soon forget, getting back to the dubious safety of Fed space had taken priority.

I'd eaten a meal bar for an early dinner after I'd poked around in Nilo's kitchen and decided I didn't know what half of the stuff was—and couldn't cook any of it. I'd kept a second bar out in case Nilo needed it when he woke.

Nilo shifted, then groaned. I stood from my place at the dining table. I'd made it one step toward the sofa when Nilo grunted, then sat up in a rush. His eyes swung around the room before locking on me, and he let out a relieved sigh. "You're okay."

"I vomited in your yard, and I think I pulled a muscle

in my back hauling you inside, but otherwise, yeah. What happened?"

He frowned at me and ignored my question. "Did you find something to eat?"

"I ate a meal bar. *What happened?*"

He ran a hand down his face and flopped back on the sofa, disappearing from sight. "They were trying to block my ability to port. They nearly succeeded. Another second or two and we would've been caught."

I moved closer until I could peer down at him. "How does one go about blocking a teleporter?" I didn't bother to keep the interest out of my tone.

Nilo grinned tiredly up at me. "There are several ways, some more effective than others, but in this case, they had a nullifier with them. If they'd gotten a lock on me, we would've been in trouble."

"A nullifier? Is that an ability or an object?"

"It's an ability, like healing or telekinesis."

I absorbed that for a moment before asking, "So a nullifier can cancel your ability to teleport?"

"It's not limited to teleportation, though they can cancel that, too. A good nullifier can cancel out all of a Valoff's natural abilities, including telepathy. Luckily, they are rare, but it's concerning that the empress wants you badly enough to pull one from her guard."

I pinned Nilo in place with a hard stare. "How did Empress Nepru know where to find me?"

Nilo's smile melted into flat nothingness. "I swore you'd be safe with me and yet you think I betrayed you." His voice was as flat as his expression.

"Technically, you swore I'd be safe *here,* and we were

attacked while we were in the city." I knew all about loopholes because I was an expert at using them.

Nilo slowly sat up and climbed to his feet, his jaw set in a hard line. He circled the sofa, and I steeled my spine to prevent an instinctive retreat. He stopped close enough that I could see the streaks of gold in his eyes—streaks that were expanding.

He stared at me for a long moment. "I can't decide if you're *trying* to insult me or if you've dealt with such dishonorable people in the past that you don't expect anyone to keep their word."

"The first time I met you, you flirted with me in order to steal my job, so forgive me if I don't think you're always on the up-and-up."

Nilo's expression shifted, and the corner of his mouth curled into a tiny, devastating grin. "I didn't flirt with you in order to steal the job."

I pressed my lips together and refused to take the bait.

"Nor did I ever lie to you about my purpose."

I clenched my fists hard enough that my nails dug into my palms, causing little pricks of pain, but I kept the furious, bitter rebuttal locked away where it couldn't reveal more than I wanted. I'd stupidly believed that he'd wanted me as much as I'd wanted him, and that was my failure.

Nilo's grin dimmed, so I took a deep breath and smoothed a polite mask across my features. "It doesn't matter. If you didn't tell the empress where to find me, then who did?"

Nilo frowned and ignored my attempt to redirect the conversation. "It *does* matter. Do you think I lied?"

"No," I admitted. He hadn't lied, he'd just worked the loopholes, same as me. Nilo didn't seem convinced, so I waved a hand through the air, brushing the conversation aside. "How did the empress know where to find me?"

Nilo looked like he wanted to continue to talk about the past, but finally he sighed and said, "If I had to guess, I'd say she had people watching every shipper in the city. When they found that your trunk at the hotel didn't have anything interesting in it, they would've guessed that you shipped in your real supplies."

"But there must be hundreds of shipping companies in Zenzi."

"At least." Nilo's eyes narrowed. "I warned you that the empress would be hunting you, and her resources are essentially unlimited."

Anxious prickles raised the hair on my arms. I leaned a hip against the sofa and pretended nonchalance. "Why would she bother?"

"She wants Torran. You would be a useful lever to make that happen."

"But she let Torran go after we rescued Cien."

Nilo shook his head. "She let him go because Torran had already told his sister Feia that he'd rescued her son and had him safely aboard *Starlight's Shadow*. Empress Nepru was not happy about it, and she's even less happy that Torran has decided to stay in Fed space. She's ordered him to return."

My gaze flashed up to meet his. "He's not that stupid, right?"

"No, he's not that stupid," Nilo said, then grimaced. "But she may leave him no choice."

I stiffened in alarm. It was one thing for me to risk myself by coming here, but the thought of Tavi being within the empress's reach made fear-drenched dread crawl up my spine. Empress Nepru was not known for her kind benevolence, and Tavi had interrupted what appeared to be a carefully choreographed plan by rescuing Cien and escaping.

I wouldn't allow myself to be used as bait to trap Tavi and Torran, so I needed to leave Valovia as soon as possible.

Nilo put a comforting hand on my shoulder. "Torran knows what he is doing. He'll keep your captain safe. Speaking of, have you heard anything from her?"

I shook my head, worried. If I hadn't heard from her by tomorrow, I would have to assume she'd been caught, which meant I would need to plan a rescue on my way back to Fed space.

"I'm sure she'll be okay," Nilo said. He squeezed my shoulder, then dropped his hand. "For now, how about some dinner?"

I raised my eyebrows. "Why are you always trying to feed me?"

Nilo flashed me his signature grin. "Maybe I just like watching you eat."

I knew a dodge when I heard one. "Maybe you'd like to give me the real answer?" I demanded sweetly.

Nilo seemed to internally debate something for a moment before his expression sobered. "Our abilities burn calories, so food is culturally important to Valoffs," he admitted. "Providing for those in your care is a basic requirement of honorable behavior."

"I can take care of myself."

He stepped closer, and I instinctively pivoted to face him, leaving me caged between the heat of his body and the sofa at my back. The simmering attraction I always felt when he was close caused my breath to catch.

The gold in Nilo's irises expanded, swallowing the

green, and his voice was a low caress. “I’m not saying you can’t take care of yourself. Two things can be true at once, and it’s my honor to take care of you.”

I wrinkled my nose, desire dimming. Some soft, small part of me had hoped that he was feeding me because he cared, not because his honor demanded it. I was nothing more than an obligation, and I needed to remember that.

Nilo stopped me before I could slide away. His heartbreakingly handsome face filled my vision, but it was his eyes that held my attention. I’d never seen eyes as beautiful as Nilo’s. The gold streaks were like lightning bolts in a green forest, and I could stare at them for hours.

“Food can have another meaning,” he confided, voice soft.

I had to clear my throat before I found my voice. “Which is?”

“Cooking for someone is a way to show interest when you’re not sure if your affection is returned.”

I was swimming in dangerous waters, but I couldn’t help but ask, “And if they *do* return the affection? How can you tell?”

Nilo leaned closer and whispered in my ear, “They will compliment the food—or the chef.”

All this time, I’d been giving Nilo signals that I was interested, and I hadn’t even known. I reared back, stung. “Is this a game for you?” I demanded. “Have you been silently laughing at me because I was ignorant about some random Valovian custom?”

Nilo jerked away and ran a frustrated hand through his hair. His eyes were solid gold, and leashed fury was stamped across his features. “It is not a game,” he bit out, “and even the suggestion is a grave insult, but one I don’t hold against you because *I realize you are human.*" He huffed out an unamused breath. *"Tev acha wur ofu."*

How you test me.

"You test me, too," I growled. In more ways than one, though I was loath to admit it. But his honest reaction soothed my temper. "I apologize for insulting you—that was not my intent. In the future, I will choose my words more carefully."

Nilo nodded slowly, but his eyes remained more gold than green. "Why do you always insist on twisting everything I say, *taro*?"

The jab struck true, and not even the endearment could distract me. If I always expected the worst, then nothing could hurt me by surprise, but this time, I'd hurt Nilo instead. I winced. "I'm sorry."

"I will not lie to you," Nilo said, as serious as I'd seen him.

My gaze slid away from him, and I barely kept my response to myself. There were a multitude of shades of gray between truth and lies, and while I didn't think Nilo would lie outright, I *did* think he would mislead me if it suited his purpose.

Because I would do the same.

But telling him that would probably just insult him further, and I'd promised to choose my words more carefully.

Nilo shook his head, as if he'd heard what I hadn't said. "How do you understand Valovan so well and yet don't understand Valoffs at all?"

"I've always picked up languages easily," I admitted, then sighed. "The Feds didn't want us to get to know you better during the war, unless it helped us win battles, and the information they *did* give us was usually wrong or exaggerated. And there's not exactly a manual, you know."

Nilo spread his arms wide. "Consider me your personal guide to all things Valovian. Ask me anything, and I will answer honestly," he said as he moved into the kitchen and started pulling things out of the refrigerator.

I raised my eyebrows. "Anything?"

He flashed me grin over his shoulder. "Anything. Are you going to shock me, *taro*?"

"I'm not your treasure," I reminded him—and myself.

I crossed the short distance to the kitchen island and leaned against it, gathering my thoughts. I wanted to ask why he kept feeding me, if it was just obligation or if he was indicating his interest, but I wasn't entirely sure I wanted to know the answer. I *should* ask him about his current motivations and loyalties, but instead, I asked, "Why did you steal my job?"

He paused what he was doing and leaned against the island across from me. "Someone was leaking classified information to the FHP, which made Empress Nepru furious and unpredictable. I had reason to believe it was Lady Ottiz. At first, I thought you might be her contact, but I quickly ruled that out. However, I still needed to be close to her to figure out if she was the traitor I sought or not."

I tipped my head to the side. "Was she?"

"No."

"Did you complete the job?"

Nilo's grin was quick and sharp. "Of course."

Lady Ottiz had wanted to acquire a famous painting housed in a rival high-ranking diplomat's private mansion. It would've been a tricky grab, which was why she had been quietly offering a fortune to anyone brave—or stupid—enough to try. Somehow, in a matter of days, Nilo had persuaded her to retract the offer and rely solely on him.

Jealously pricked me—and not just my professional pride. Lady Ottiz was young, rich, and beautiful. She and Nilo would've made a striking couple. The thought of him flirting with me only to turn around and do the exact same thing with her made my heart hurt more than I'd like to admit, but I kept my expression even and waved at the pile of containers on the counter. "What can I do to help?"

CHAPTER SEVEN

Nilo made us veggie and cheese omelets with a side of the potato-looking vegetables—called *loksou*—that he'd sliced thin and fried until they were crisp on the outside and soft in the middle.

I hadn't lied about the meal bar earlier, but after the attack, the worry for Nilo, and then our emotional roller coaster of a conversation, I was hungrier than I'd thought. I glanced at Nilo. "If I tell you this is delicious, are you going to take it the wrong way?"

His mouth curved into a slow, sinful grin that made my pulse hammer. "It depends on how you mean it."

"I mean it politely—nothing else."

"Whatever you say, *taro*."

I huffed at him. "In that case, I'll keep my thoughts to myself. You can just wonder whether I liked it or not."

He laughed, and once again, the sound rippled through me on a wave of pleasure. Nilo was always gorgeous, but with true amusement dancing on his face, he was irresistible.

And why was I resisting anyway? I'd be gone tomorrow, and a marathon sex session was exactly what I needed to ensure my night remained nightmare-free. Plus, even if Nilo was just cooking for me because his honor demanded it, he'd laid an absolutely scorching kiss on me this morning, so he wasn't entirely disinterested.

My focus sharpened as a plan began to form. I'd been going about this all wrong. The forbidden was always far more attractive than the attainable. Banging him out of my system was exactly what I needed to move past my infatuation. We'd both have a pleasant evening, then I'd head back to Bastion tomorrow and ensure Tavi hadn't found more trouble than she could handle.

And this time, I really would avoid returning to Valovia in the future, no matter how much money was on offer.

Plan set, I speared a *loksou* and held my fork out. "This is delicious. Would you like to try mine?"

Nilo stilled, subtle wariness in his expression. But his eyes gave him away as the gold streaks grew. "What are you doing?"

I treated him to the same slow, wicked grin he'd given me. "I'm offering to feed you. I didn't make this food, but I'll still share."

"Lexi—" he growled, something raw and vulnerable in his tone.

"I'm not mocking," I promised quietly. "I'm leaving tomorrow. But I'm here tonight."

Nilo's expression smoothed into his usual playful grin,

but I had the oddest feeling that I'd hurt him somehow and now he was hiding behind a mask. Before I could question it, he wrapped a hand around mine and guided the fork to his mouth. His lips closed around the *loksou* with sensual slowness while his eyes smoldered at me.

Had I imagined the hurt?

"Delicious," he murmured, his voice a purr that tightened my stomach. Desire throbbed through my veins, hot and vibrant.

I withdrew my hand. Nilo let me go, but only after he'd slid his fingers along mine, sparking little flashes of pleasure. It would be so easy to fall into that touch and voice, to forget my worries, but I'd been reading people for a long time, and I trusted my intuition. "What's wrong?"

Nilo's expression didn't even flicker. "Nothing."

But his eyes had shifted back to be more green than gold. And that, more than anything, told me that something was wrong.

"The truth, Nilo. You promised me the truth."

He sighed and ran a hand down his face, erasing the smoldering desire like it had never existed. I sucked in a quiet breath. I'd been burning and he'd been *pretending*. Pain sliced through me like a cut from an unexpected blade.

Nilo frowned at me. "It's not your fault."

"What's not?"

"Food customs are complicated, and you were just working with what I'd told you." At my pointed look, he sighed again and murmured, "You shouldn't offer to share food with someone you're only planning to spend one night with. It would be like telling someone you loved them just to get them in bed."

Humiliation warmed my cheeks, but I kept my expression blandly neutral. "I apologize. I didn't know. It was not my intent to mislead you."

A tiny, rueful smile touched Nilo's lips. "I know."

I returned my attention to the food on my plate and ignored the awkward silence. The mood was broken. I tried to tell myself that it was for the best, that getting closer to Nilo was a mistake, but for a brief, shining moment, I'd truly been looking forward to the night ahead.

After a few minutes, Nilo reached across the table and tapped his fingers on the back of my hand. "Are you okay?"

I summoned an easy grin. "Of course."

He considered me for a moment, then quietly offered, "I didn't say no."

I rolled my eyes at him. "You didn't say yes, either. You might be able to pretend with someone else, but I'm only interested in partners who are with me one hundred percent." I waved my fingers as if I could brush the whole conversation aside—and I wished I could. "Don't worry about it."

Nilo's brows drew together. "I wasn't pretending."

"You absolutely were."

"If you won't believe my words, then let me share my feelings with you."

Ice doused my lingering desire. "No."

Nilo's sharp eyes saw too much, so I changed the subject with zero attempt at subtlety. "Do you have a list of smugglers I should contact? I did some research today, but I don't know who's trustworthy. I still haven't heard back from Tavi. If I haven't received a message by morning, then she's in trouble, and I'll need to leave tomorrow by whatever means necessary."

I wasn't sure Nilo would let the subject change stand,

but after a long, knowing look, he said, "Zenzi has the most options, but it will also be the most closely guarded. If you must leave tomorrow, then we'll likely need to head to another city."

"Can you zap us there?"

"Yes, but it's draining. Taking a ship would be better in case we run into trouble. I have a couple of options that the empress doesn't know about, but she'll be watching the ports, so we'll have to be careful."

I nodded absently, working through various scenarios. "Maybe I should go alone," I said at last. When Nilo started to protest, I cut him off. "I might be a good lever to get Tavi into Valovian space, but *you* would be an excellent lever for Torran, right? That's why you're here." I waved at the cabin surrounding us.

Nilo nodded warily.

"If they catch us both, we're fucked. But if I go alone, I'll blend in easier, and if I get caught, you'll still be available to mount a rescue effort." I let a teasing smile curve my lips. "You *would* rescue me, right? I mean, assuming I didn't get myself out first—which I would."

His left arm crossed his chest, and he bowed his head. "I would rescue you."

"There, problem solv—"

"But I'm not letting you go alone," he finished, interrupting me. He held up a hand to forestall my argument. "It's far easier to mount a rescue if I'm right beside you than if I have to figure out where the empress has stashed you. Even if she doesn't make the logical leap to who's been helping you, she still knows it's a teleporter. She'll put you somewhere I can't reach."

I had an entire litany of reasons why my idea was better,

but by the set of Nilo's jaw, none of them would matter. I dipped my chin. "Okay."

Suspicion chased surprise across his face. "That's it? You're just going to agree with me?"

"Would arguing help?"

"No."

I shrugged. "There you go. I know obstinate when I see it." I tipped my head at his empty plate. "Are you finished eating?"

At his nod, I stood and gathered our dishes. I put them in the sanitizer while I continued to think. I might've decided not to argue, but that didn't mean I wasn't making auxiliary plans. Slipping from the house tonight would probably be my best shot, but I'd have to pass directly by Nilo on the couch unless I could convince him to take the bed.

Or *tempt* him there.

I grimaced at myself. Sleeping with someone to get them out of the way was cold-blooded, and while I might do it for a job, I couldn't bring myself to do it to Nilo.

I tidied up the rest of the kitchen as much as I could since I didn't know where anything went, then returned to the table where Nilo was frowning at his comm. He glanced up at me. "Have you figured out how to leave me behind yet?"

I was torn between wanting to grin and grimace, because *of course* he'd understood what I was up to, the insufferable ass. Instead, I furrowed my brow in puzzlement. "What do you mean?"

He stood, bringing us far too close together. "I find competence very sexy," he murmured, his voice honeyed silk. "But forget whatever you're planning in that stunning brain of yours, *taro*. You won't be rid of me so easily."

I shivered as my desire kindled anew, and the smile

broke through. "And if I was planning to stab you while you were asleep?"

"I'm a very light sleeper."

"Perhaps I'll offer to demonstrate my knot-tying skills, then leave you bound and helpless."

He edged closer. "I'd be putty in your hands," he agreed easily, "but I'm also a teleporter. You'll have to try harder than that."

I looked at him through my lashes and let my voice drop to a throaty purr as I ran one hand up his chest. "Or maybe I'll just ask very . . . *very* . . . nicely."

His eyes went solid gold, and his jaw clenched. "Yes, you should try that," he demanded, voice hoarse.

I slipped my hand around the back of his neck and drew him close enough to whisper in his ear. "Nilo." He made a low sound of pleasure that very nearly derailed all of my good intentions, but I held on to my resolve with both hands. "I *will* find a way to go alone, so you might as well help me do it safely. Please."

His arms wrapped around me, caging me against the heat of his body. "I would do anything for you," he growled, and I smiled in triumph before he added, "but I'm not letting you go alone."

I tried to pull away, but Nilo held fast. I put my hands on his shoulders and leaned back far enough to see his face. Amusement danced alongside desire in his expression, and I huffed out a breath. "Let me go."

Nilo grinned and flexed his arms, drawing me minutely closer. "But I like you here."

And I liked being here, far too much. Nilo's arms were warm and muscular, but he held me carefully, like I was precious.

It was a dangerous feeling.

"Don't make me stab you," I whispered.

His smile widened. "It might be worth it."

Reason, self-preservation, and doubt deserted me. I wanted to taste that smile. I moved before I could second-guess myself, lifting onto my toes and burying my hands in Nilo's dark hair. His arms tightened, and he met me halfway.

His lips covered mine with searing intensity, and I shivered. My stomach fluttered, but I wanted more. I tugged on his hair, and when he hissed in pleasure, I deepened the kiss.

Nilo followed my lead, stroking his tongue against mine, and my knees went weak. He scooped me up with an ease that did nothing to dampen my desire and settled me on the edge of the island, all without breaking the kiss.

I wrapped my legs around his lean hips, and he groaned into my mouth. His fingers slid under the edge of my shirt and found my skin. I arched into his touch, encouraging him, then broke the kiss long enough to lean back and pull my shirt over my head.

At the sight of my delicate, lacy bra, Nilo groaned. "You are magnificent," he whispered, voice reverent. His finger traced a searing path along the edge of the lace, then his mouth followed the same line.

He gently pinched my nipple, and I gasped as pleasure raked me. I tightened my legs. I could feel him against me, stiff as steel. I yanked on his tunic, desperate to get to his skin, and the fabric disappeared from under my fingers in a cool rush.

I started in surprise, then laughed in delight. "That's handy."

He smiled against my skin. "Isn't it?"

I stroked my palms over the warm ridges of his stomach while he murmured wordless encouragement, but when my fingers grazed the bandage, I froze, and the doubts crept back in.

What was I doing? What were *we* doing?

Nilo's hand covered mine. "It wasn't your fault."

When I didn't respond, he lifted his head. His eyes were an endless ocean of gold, flecked with tiny green sparks, and he looked at me like I was his entire world. Longing pierced me. I'd waited my whole life for someone to look at me like that and mean it.

But, like me, Nilo excelled at illusion. I didn't know how he'd guessed my deepest secrets so accurately, but maybe he hadn't. Maybe that was just the look he gave all of the women he seduced.

The thought stung, and that brought me up short. This was supposed to be an evening of mutual pleasure, no strings—or hearts—involved.

His brows drew together. "What's wrong?"

I'd wanted Nilo from the moment I'd first laid eyes on his charming grin and cunning eyes, and now I could have him, I just had to keep my heart safely tucked away. Tonight was about physical pleasure only.

I ran my hands up his chest, and gave him a slow, heated smile. "Nothing."

He didn't look convinced, but I tugged his head down to mine and pressed a tiny kiss against his bottom lip. "I'm sorry I hurt you," I murmured against his mouth. "Maybe I should kiss it better."

"You don't have t—"

I pressed a finger to his lips, then leaned back and grinned at him. "Are you saying you don't want my mouth here?" I touched the skin of his stomach near the bandage, then slid it lower. "Or here?" My fingers dipped under his waistband. "Or maybe here?"

His pants vanished and I laughed in delight. "I thought so."

He rocked against me and when I gasped, he grinned before catching my lips in a scorching kiss. Pleasure sparked along my nerves, and I let it burn away my worries. I wiggled out of my pants far less gracefully than Nilo's teleportation trick, then we were both clad in only our undergarments.

I shivered at the cool counter under my thighs. "Bed?"

Nilo nodded, then scooped me up before I could protest. I wrapped my legs around his waist and enjoyed the friction provided by each step.

Rather than tossing me onto the mattress, Nilo tapped my legs, then set me on my feet next to the bed. "Are you sure?" he asked, his voice deep and rough.

"Yes. Are you?"

He grinned. "Very."

I matched his smile, then gently pushed him backward until he fell back onto the bed. "Then I believe I promised to kiss you better."

I settled between his legs and ran my palms up his thighs before leaning forward and pressing a light kiss to his belly. His legs tensed under my palms, and I smiled against his skin before peeking up at him. "Feeling better?"

Hunger had sharpened his expression into something almost brutal. "I'm getting there," he gritted out.

I took pity on him and tapped his waistband. "Remove this?"

There was a soft pulse of cold, then Nilo was bare before me, thick and tempting. I wrapped my fingers around him, and he groaned as his hips lifted. There would be time for teasing later, but right now, I wanted to drive him past control, past thought and worry, until there was nothing left but pleasure.

Because that's what I wanted him to do to me in return.

At the first touch of my tongue, he hissed out a sound that was somewhere between a plea and a prayer. I hummed in amusement as I took him deeper in my mouth, and his body went bowstring tight.

My muscles clenched as his desire fed my own. I sat up and he groaned at the loss, but when my fingers disappeared under my waistband to glide against the most sensitive part of my body, he closed his eyes and bit out a curse.

When I bent to lick him while stroking myself, he buried a hand in my hair and filled the air with filthy praise that ratcheted my desire higher. When I finally pushed him over the edge, it was with my name on his lips.

Then he rolled me over, and my undergarments disappeared on a cool wave of power. He trapped my hands above my head, then slowly kissed his way down my body. By the time he got to where I wanted him most, I was trembling with need.

The first touch of his tongue drowned the world in pleasure. When he slid one finger, then two into my slick heat, I nearly came undone. Then he proved exactly how talented his mouth could be.

He wound me tighter and tighter until I finally shattered with a moan that might've been his name. I was still basking in the aftershocks when he notched his hard length against me. I shivered as sparks skated over my skin. He met my eyes. "Yes?"

"Yes."

He sank into me with a hard thrust that lit every nerve on fire. I lifted my hips, taking him deeper, and Nilo cursed darkly in Valovan.

We moved together, chasing rapture, until I shifted and he hit a spot that made me gasp. "Yes," he breathed. "Take your pleasure, *taro*."

I did, and I took him with me.

SOMEWHERE BETWEEN ROUNDS TWO AND THREE, WHEN WE WERE curled together in a sweaty tangle of limbs and pleasure, I began to worry that my plan to bang him out of my system wasn't working as well as I'd hoped.

Because Nilo was like the most addictive drug—the more I had, the more I wanted.

When he'd flirted with me before stealing my job, he'd been just as kind and just as charming, but there had always been a subtle distance between us I hadn't understood.

That distance was now gone, and I was dangerously close to losing my carefully guarded heart.

But a relationship between us would never work. Nilo had to stay on Valovia to help Torran evade the empress, and I had to *leave* Valovia for the exact same reason.

Tomorrow I would be on a ship headed back to Fed space, and Nilo Shoren would once again be in my past. So, just for tonight, I put aside my worries and let myself enjoy the pleasure, even though part of me knew tomorrow was going to hurt.

That was a problem for future me, and both current me *and* future me were excellent at ignoring uncomfortable truths.

CHAPTER EIGHT

I awoke sated and sticky and pleasantly sore. Nilo was wrapped around me like my own personal backpack, and I enjoyed the closeness for a moment before my bladder forced me from the bed.

When I returned, Nilo was sitting up with the sheets at his waist, scowling at his comm. When he didn't even look up to watch me walk naked across the room, my instinct for trouble started tingling. "What's wrong?"

"Message from Torran," he said. "You should check your comm."

"Is Tavi hurt?" I asked, diving for my device.

"What? No, sorry," Nilo said, shaking his head. "Everyone is okay, but they're considering entering Valovian space."

"That might be worse," I muttered. I pulled on yesterday's shirt, grabbed my comm, and climbed into bed next to Nilo to read. Sure enough, I had a message from Tavi, but she'd sent it standard priority, the cheapskate. I knew she had enough money now, thanks to the job we'd done for Torran, but old habits died hard.

I read the short note twice, then blew out a slow breath. Tavi had gone ahead with her plan to infiltrate the lunar base, even though the timing meant she couldn't have received my message before she did. From her previous message, I hadn't expected her to move so quickly.

Or for the danger to come from so many directions.

I glanced at Nilo and waved my comm. "Want to compare notes?" At his nod, I ran down what Tavi had told me. "The *Starlight's Shadow* crew went to the lunar base on Odyssey to rescue a fashion maven for reasons that were unclear from Tavi's message. While they were there, they ran into both Commodore Frank Morten and Sura Fev, the Sun Guardian. There was a fight, and Varro was seriously wounded, but they escaped without the Feds blowing them up, which is a minor miracle. But Fev also escaped, and she took Morten with her."

"Torran is fairly sure that Fev is running straight for the wormhole to Valovian space—with Morten. He doesn't know if the FHP will be able to stop them."

"Fuck." I rubbed my face. "I'm guessing that letting the empress get her hands on Morten would be a very bad idea."

"Torran agrees. That's why he's considering following Fev back into Valovian space to try to stop her."

Tavi had left out that tidbit, but if Torran entered Valovian space, then Tavi would accompany him, and I couldn't let either of them get anywhere near Empress Nepru. Desperate plans began to form. I was already on Valovia, and while the empress knew that, she didn't know where I was.

Could I steal an entire person from the very Sun Guardian who'd nearly killed Tavi? Or, barring that, could I eliminate Morten as a threat?

"I have to let Tavi know that I'm here," I murmured, thinking fast. "And that Torran's in danger if he traverses the wormhole. I can deal with Morten and Fev." *Hopefully.*

Nilo ran a frustrated hand through his hair. "And I suppose you're planning to take on Fev alone?" he bit out.

I turned to face him with a frown. "It's better than putting Tavi in harm's way. I thought you'd be happy for Torran to stay in Fed space."

"I'd be happier if you weren't planning to senselessly throw yourself into danger."

My temper woke. "'Senselessly'?" I parroted, my tone glacial. "I am a *legend*. My plans are *art*. *You're* the only person showing a lack of sense here."

He leaned closer until we were nose to nose. "And were you going to include me in these elaborate plans of yours?"

"I was," I bit out, "but now I'm not so sure." When he blinked in shock, I rolled my eyes. "I'm not stupid, Nilo. I know you're currently my best source of information on the planet, and you have an informant in the palace. Not only that, but you are probably the one person on Valovia who isn't planning to betray me to the empress. Why *wouldn't* I use you?"

"I will not betray you," he said, voice soft.

I held his gaze, judging his sincerity before dipping my head in acknowledgment. Even after last night, I still didn't *completely* trust him, but I trusted that he was loyal to Torran and wouldn't do anything to put the former general in danger.

But if it ever came down to a decision between me and Torran, I didn't doubt who he'd choose.

I dropped my attention to my comm. Telling Tavi I was on Valovia without her immediately wanting to come rescue me was going to require a little finesse and a lot of fast talking. I glanced at Nilo. "Do you want me to include a message to Torran in here, so we don't both have to pay for priority delivery?"

Nilo gave me a sly grin. "You should include your message with mine, because I'm using Torran's account."

I laughed. "Deal."

IT TOOK ME THIRTY MINUTES TO COMPOSE MY MESSAGE TO TAVI. Most of that time was spent editing it to just the right tone so she wouldn't instantly head to Valovian space. Once I was done, I sent it to Nilo, who included it with the message he was sending to Torran.

It was only after I was in the shower that the implications of the morning's messages finally sank in. I wasn't leaving today. I might not be leaving *this week*. And I'd just signed myself up to work with Nilo to stop Fev, which meant I couldn't go hide in a hotel room and make my own plan.

There was no way I could keep fucking Nilo without emotions getting involved. Last night had proven that pretty definitively. So no matter how much I still wanted him, I had to keep my hands to myself.

I groaned and rubbed my face. This wasn't going to be awkward at all.

There was nothing to do but face it, so I turned off the

shower and got dressed in plain, sturdy work clothes. I preferred soft, pretty fabrics, and I had a few emergency outfits stashed in the crate we'd retrieved from the smugglers, but they didn't stand up too well to sneaking around places where people didn't want me.

I wrinkled my nose at my reflection. The dark gray pants and black shirt were so *boring,* but that was kind of the point. A thief wearing bright aqua was far more memorable than one wearing black.

Maybe Nilo would loan me another tunic. He seemed like he wasn't afraid of color.

At the thought, my heart squeezed. I was in deep shit. Apparently my heart didn't remember that he'd stolen my job and left me waiting for him like a dumbass, it was just ready to leap in his direction. I had to be more careful.

I painted on my politest, most professional smile, and tested it on the bathroom mirror. Now all I had to do was maintain it for a week or so, kill an elite telekinetic Sun Guardian on my own, and then escape back to Fed space without getting caught—or getting my heart broken.

No problem.

While Nilo got cleaned up, I moved to the couch in the living room and reread the message from Tavi. If the Feds didn't stop the Sun Guardian, she would arrive on Valovia in less than four days, depending on the speed of her ship.

Four days wasn't enough time to plan a grab of one of the empress's most coveted prizes. And that's assuming Sura Fev was even coming to Valovia.

The weight of all the unknowns pressed on my temples. I closed my eyes and tipped my head back. I needed information, and my contacts on Valovia were woefully thin.

But one thing was clear: I couldn't let Empress Nepru

get her hands on Commodore Frank Morten. Morten had been behind the kidnapping of her grandson, and if she was looking for a reason to return to war—and she was—then there was no better candidate than a hated enemy combatant who'd stolen a dear child.

That left me with two options: steal Morten back or kill him. Abducting him from a Sun Guardian would be difficult with weeks to plan. With four days it was all but impossible.

So I'd have to kill him.

I was no stranger to death, and no one deserved it more than Morten. Killing carried weight, but I'd happily bear the burden to see Morten removed from the galaxy, if only so another generation didn't have to face the horrors of war.

"What's put that expression on your face?" Nilo asked, jarring me out of my thoughts.

A grim smile tugged at my lips. "Just contemplating murder."

He stared at me for a moment, his expression sharp and cold. "I will handle Morten. You don't need to be involved. You should return to the FHP as planned."

That was unexpected. I'd been braced for awkwardness, not casual dismissal. His desire to exclude me wasn't exactly a surprise, but the little flare of hurt it brought *was*. And I had no one to blame but myself. I'd known exactly what I was getting myself into when I'd kissed Nilo last night, and now I was reaping the consequences.

I raised a single, sardonic eyebrow. "Did you think that would work?"

His eyes flashed gold. "The empress would be perfectly happy to have you *and* Morten."

"Then she will be disappointed," I snapped. I blew out

a slow breath. Nilo's lack of confidence in me grated, but I'd worked with worse. I smoothed the irritation away behind a smile that was half charm, half threat. "Having a recovery specialist on your team would be a benefit, and you can't convince me otherwise. You can work with me, or I will make my own plan without your input, and we'll see which of us is more successful."

He would win, of course. I didn't have the network on Valovia that I needed to truly be successful, but if he shut me out, I would still try my damnedest.

He must've read the sincerity in my tone, because he cursed under his breath. "I'm going to contact my people in the palace to see if they can find out where Fev is heading. Coming here would be the logical choice, so Fev may have another plan, especially since she knows the Feds likely have people here already."

I frowned in thought. If Morten was important to the Feds, they would try to retrieve him, even if the attempt kicked off another war, which they weren't exactly against anyway. Presumably they were already spinning the narrative: a decorated war hero, abducted by one of the empress's feared Sun Guardians directly from a Fed base. It wouldn't take much to tip the populace into believing that Morten's rescue was worth whatever fallout happened.

"This is a disaster," I muttered. I shook my head. "If Fev doesn't head directly for the Imperial Palace, where is she likely to go?" I mentally crossed my fingers. *Please don't say—*

"Rodeni."

Fuck. I pressed my palms against my eyes. Of course it would be the one planet in Valovian space that I would happily never see again.

"The empire has spent the years since the war turning half the city of Tirdenchia into a huge defensive base called Aburwuk," Nilo said softly.

I'd heard of the city, but thankfully it had fallen earlier in the war and wasn't the one that held my worst memories. But the base name . . . I frowned and asked, "The base is named *Punishment*?"

"Empress Nepru isn't known for her subtlety. She claims it's named for what it will do to any future FHP invaders, but it's also a punishment for the citizens who used to live there and failed to defend the city."

"They were *civilians*. They shouldn't have been there at all."

"It doesn't matter to the empress. They failed the empire and now their homes are gone. I heard a rumor that one of the princes quietly paid each uprooted family, but the rumors were never substantiated by the palace."

As much as I wanted to be shocked, I knew the Feds would do the same thing if they thought they could get away with it.

Nilo continued, "Rodeni is one of the planets closest to the wormhole. It's not quite as close as Bastion on the FHP side, but its goal is similar. In the event of another war, Rodeni will be our front line of defense."

I chuckled without humor. "So I either get to infiltrate the Imperial Palace or the giant Valovian military base on the planet responsible for most of my nightmares. Great."

"You don't have to—"

"Save it," I interrupted with a tired wave. "Which do you think she'll choose?"

Nilo shook his head. "I don't know. It could go either way."

Until his contacts leaned one way or another, we'd have to work on two separate plans, which made the task more difficult. "Do you have a way for us to get to Rodeni without attracting undue attention?"

"It's still populated with civilians, so passenger shuttles run daily. Or I have a few contacts who could take us directly."

I tapped my fingers on my thigh. "Do you have a ship?"

"No, not one designed for long-distance space travel."

I filed that bit of information away. "It's at least a day to Rodeni from here, correct?"

"Closer to two days unless you take an express ship," Nilo confirmed. "And it's a little more than a half day from the FHP gate."

"So we either leave early and risk her continuing to Valovia, or we wait and give her the opportunity to bury Morten so deeply in the base that retrieving him will be all but impossible."

Nilo sighed. "Pretty much."

I took a deep breath and clapped my hands. "Well, it wouldn't be a challenge if it was too easy," I said brightly. "Start working your contacts. I'm going to do some research of my own."

"Don't get caught poking where you shouldn't," Nilo warned.

My lips twitched as a playful grin tried to bloom. "I'll be good. Mostly."

NILO FIXED US A QUICK BREAKFAST, WHICH WE BOTH ATE WITHOUT comment, then we worked in comfortable silence for a couple of hours until the sun sank behind the trees. I stood and stretched with a groan. Digital research was a necessary evil, but I'd much rather scout targets in person. If Kee were here, I'd happily hand off the digital work to her while I went and poked my nose exactly where the empress didn't want it.

Homesickness tugged on my heart. It wasn't a feeling I got often, but when I did, it was always for my time on *Starlight's Shadow*. Tavi, Kee, and Eli were family, and while I was usually happy just knowing that they were somewhere out there, doing well, occasionally I missed them with a fierceness that stole my breath.

"If I go outside, am I going to get eaten by a demon?" I asked.

"No, but take your comm. It's easy to get turned around in the woods."

I laughed. "Oh, I'm not going into the trees, thank you very much. I can get plenty of fresh air on the porch."

"The forest is magical at night."

I shook my head. "I'll take your word for it."

"Give me a few minutes, and I'll go with you."

"No, that's okay," I said a little too quickly. The last thing I needed was to spend time in the dark in a magical forest with Nilo Shoren. All of my good intentions to avoid temptation would disappear faster than our clothes.

I slipped out the door before he could comment. The cool air nipped at my fingers, but I wouldn't be staying long enough for it to turn uncomfortable. The red moon was a sliver in the starry sky, and no matter how much I logically knew that it was only around noon, it felt much later.

I'd been on Valovia for less than two days, and somehow, all of my careful plans were in ruins. Thanks to the Sun Guardian, I no longer had time to plan revenge on

Besor, and it chafed. I knew it was petty, but he deserved some damned pettiness for selling me out.

The door behind me opened, and Nilo approached on quiet feet. He stopped next to me and stared into the darkened trees. "Do you regret last night?"

I would rather risk the demons in the woods than talk about this, but we were going to have to work closely together for the next few days, so a conversation was a good idea, as much as I would rather do literally *anything* else. My emotions were a tangled weave, but this answer, at least, was easy. "No."

"You thought you'd be gone today."

His face was impossible to read in the shadows, but I gave him the truth. "Yes."

He glanced at me, his eyes as dark as the forest surrounding us. "Should I sleep in the living room tonight?"

I squashed the denial before it could make it past my lips. "You need good sleep, since I'm assuming any plan is going to rely heavily on your ability to teleport. I'll take the couch tonight."

Nilo's expression flickered for a moment, but he nodded. "Okay."

Apparently we were on the same page. I should be happy that we'd handled it so easily and with so little drama, but I felt vaguely dissatisfied. It was selfish, and it was mean, but if I was going to be miserable resisting temptation, then the least he could do was suffer with me.

I really *was* the queen of pettiness today.

I shook my head at myself and changed the subject. "Do you happen to have any weapons hidden here? I have a few in my crate, but I'm going to need more before we take on a

Sun Guardian. I'm thinking an orbital missile might do the trick. Got any of those lying around?"

Nilo chuckled and shook his head. "Sadly, I'm all out. But I do know someone who happens to run an illegal arms trade and has a warehouse full of weapons we could liberate. And he's probably hunkered down in his house, worried that you're going to pay him a visit."

I clasped my hands together with a grin. "Is it Besor? Please tell me it's Besor."

"It is. One of his companies smuggles in illegal weapons, a lot of which are military surplus."

I sighed as responsibility overrode vindictiveness. "As much as I'd love to stick it to him, wouldn't it be safer to grab weapons from Torran's house? His armory has enough to get us started."

"Empress Nepru seized all of Torran's assets when he refused to return to the palace. We managed to save some of his sentimental items by moving them before she got to them, but the weapons are gone."

"Damn." I'd never given much thought to what Torran had given up to be with Tavi. I'd just assumed the spat with the empress would blow over, and he'd keep his fancy house and powerful position.

Empress Nepru clearly had other ideas.

"So how does the security at Besor's warehouse compare to his house? Because based on my previous research, his house is pretty well protected, and cracking the same level at the warehouse will take longer than we have."

"The storage location moves around a lot, so he relies on obscurity and muscle more than high-tech security. We won't have any trouble getting in, but getting back out again might be tricky if he's shielded it against teleporters—and he would be stupid not to."

I raised my eyebrows, curious. "How do you shield a building against teleporters?"

"Certain frequencies block our ability to get a stable lock, but the systems are difficult to install and maintain and the signals don't transmit well, so most shielded buildings are only protected at the perimeter, preventing entrance or exit but allowing teleporting inside. It's not quite as secure, but it's far less expensive."

"Is that why you can't teleport into your house, but you can teleport things around inside?"

Nilo nodded. "Even if someone had a visual lock on the inside, they wouldn't be able to port in. But that also means I couldn't get out, so I have a few hidden kill switches if I need to leave in a hurry. Most teleporters do. And we prefer to be able to use our ability inside, even if it is a little less secure."

I thought about it for a second. "So your knives aren't stored in the house, or you wouldn't have been able to summon them while we were out here."

Nilo's eyes glinted. "Correct."

I filed that bit of information away for future research, then turned my attention back to the task at hand. "Do you know where Besor's latest warehouse is?"

"I do," Nilo said with a grin.

I gestured to the darkness surrounding us. "No time like the present. Let me grab a few things, then I'll be ready."

CHAPTER NINE

Nilo teleported us into the city, then paid for a transport with credits he assured me couldn't be traced back to him. We were both wearing coats with our hoods pulled low. After our last encounter with the nullifier, I wasn't looking for a repeat, so we needed to stay off surveillance.

The transport dropped us on a poorly lit street in a run-down part of town. I was armed with a plas blade, a pair of plas pistols, and three knives of varying sizes. Nilo had his own weapons, including a knife that matched the one he'd used to demonstrate his teleportation abilities.

Nilo's research indicated there could be as many as eight guards, so we were aiming for stealth, but we were prepared in case that plan failed—as plans so often did.

After a few minutes of walking, Nilo pulled me aside. Besor's building should be just around the corner.

"I will have to shield for you," Nilo whispered.

"No."

"Then you'll have to stay here. Your mental shields aren't good enough. The Valoffs inside will be able to sense you before you set foot on the property."

I clenched my jaw against the instant, instinctive panic at having someone else in my head. I knew it was irrational, that Nilo wouldn't hurt me, but that didn't make it any less awful. Even if I could force myself to agree, I didn't know if I'd be able to function.

Nilo drew me into a niche of deeper shadow. "What is wrong?"

I shook my head.

"Would it help if I built an additional shield between us? We won't be able to communicate telepathically, but I also won't be able to sense any of your thoughts or feelings, I swear it."

"I don't know," I whispered. "During the war . . ." I trailed off and swallowed, unable to get the words out.

"Many people carry trauma from the war. It is not a weakness," Nilo murmured, his voice quiet but firm.

I chuckled bitterly. "It sure as fuck feels like it."

Nilo pulled me into a gentle hug, and I let myself enjoy the embrace for a moment before I sighed. "Let's try the additional shield. But you have to swear you'll drop it the moment I ask, no questions."

Nilo let go of me to cross his left arm over his chest. "I swear it."

I shook out my arms and bounced on my toes. I felt like I was getting ready to fight, and I was, but my foe was my own brain.

"Let me know when you're ready," Nilo said.

I met his eyes in the dim light. "Don't break my trust."

"I won't," he said, his tone solemn.

"Then let's try it. I'm ready." It was a lie, but waiting wasn't going to make it any better.

I closed my eyes as the faintest hint of cold touched my mind. My pulse skyrocketed as panic took hold. I threw everything I had into reinforcing my mental shields, even knowing that it wouldn't be enough, that the enemy would peel my brain open like an orange. The cold didn't dig any further, but it was a brief respite.

"Lexi, if you don't respond, I'm dropping the shield." Nilo's urgent whisper finally cut through the panic.

"Wait," I gasped, "I'm okay." Another lie, but perhaps one I could make true through sheer force of will.

"You're breathing like a sprinter, and you didn't answer me. I don't need to be able to sense your emotions to know you're panicking. I swore I'd keep you safe, not torture yo—"

I pressed my fingers to his lips and shook my head. "Just . . . give me a second, okay?"

He nodded, and I reluctantly removed my fingers. Now that the panic had receded slightly, I could still feel the coolness of his mental shield. I breathed through the spike of panic. He was not attacking. I was not in danger.

I don't know how long I stood there just breathing, but Nilo didn't rush me. Eventually, I could think past the panic. My adrenaline stayed too high, but I was functional.

I held up my hands, and my fingers were steady despite the anxiety. "This will work," I murmured. Then I blinked and looked at Nilo. "Does shielding this way drain you?"

"It's not as easy as a normal shield, but it is not something you need to worry about today. It may be a concern if we need to infiltrate a military base, but we'll deal with that problem when we get to it."

"Don't overtax yourself."

He grinned at me. "Don't worry, I have plenty of stamina."

I rolled my eyes, but I couldn't quite suppress the shiver of desire. He'd proven that statement true quite thoroughly, and the memory was seared into my mind. I clenched my hands against the yearning to reach for him. We were here to do a job, and I was supposed to be keeping my heart from getting broken.

I was afraid I was going to be quite terrible at it.

I turned to head toward the warehouse without a word, but Nilo stopped me with a light touch. "Are you sure you're okay?"

"I'm okay enough," I admitted. "Let's go get some weapons."

AS EXPECTED, NILO COULDN'T TELEPORT INSIDE THE BUILDING, BUT the security on the side door was laughably bad, so I cracked the lock in under thirty seconds. As far as I could tell, there wasn't any external video surveillance.

"I can sense four people inside," Nilo whispered, "but there may be more who are shielding. The four I can sense are clustered on the other side of the building."

I nodded and drew my plas blade but didn't activate it. It was the only weapon I had that could be set to nonlethal, so I would start with it, because I didn't relish the thought of killing people who were just doing their job—as illegal as that job might be.

After all, I knew a thing or two about taking illegal jobs.

I opened the door just enough to peer inside. The interior was dim, but my night-vision glasses pierced the shadows. Tall shelves would give us a little bit of cover, but it was still far more open than I'd prefer.

I carefully scanned the walls and ceiling for the telltale glow of night-vision cameras. There weren't any. Either Besor had far better tech than my research had indicated, or he really was relying on guards and frequent moves to keep his property safe.

And Nilo's informant had been correct—the shelves were filled with all manner of FHP and Valovian weapons, carefully sorted by type. I eased through the door, Nilo on my heels. I froze as I caught the faint strains of a distant conversation, but it didn't sound like the speakers were moving any closer.

Hopefully the guards would continue talking, which would make keeping track of them easier. I kept one ear on them while I headed left toward a shelf full of rifles. I needed something high-powered and long-range because taking Morten out from a distance would be the safest option.

Whoever Besor's supplier was, they were not fucking around. Many of the weapons looked brand-new, and all of the FHP weapons I recognized were top-of-the-line models.

My boots were specifically designed to be nearly silent on a variety of floor materials, so I quietly crept down the line of shelves until I found a rifle that would make snipers the galaxy over weep with joy. Nilo had stopped a few steps behind me to liberate some more conventional plas rifles.

We'd debated bringing my crate, but we'd decided we would be more mobile without it. We each had a slim bag for smaller items, but otherwise, we could only grab what we could carry. Fully assembled, the sniper rifle was nearly as tall as me, which would make sneaking around a little more difficult, but it was one of the things we'd come for, so I slung it over my shoulder.

Nilo had a rifle over each of his shoulders. We could theoretically leave now, but if Besor had weapons this nice in the most easily accessible part of the warehouse, what else was he hiding?

Subvocal comms allowed humans to mimic the silent telepathy of Valoffs, but they took practice to use, so I'd given Nilo an earpiece but not a mic. He could hear me, but he couldn't respond. "Have the guards moved?" I asked. I could hear them, but the sound was faint enough that I couldn't pinpoint their location.

He shook his head.

"Then I say we see what else Besor is hiding."

Nilo eased closer until his lips brushed my ear. "Be careful," he whispered, his voice barely audible. "This feels too easy."

He wasn't wrong. We could leave now, and we'd have a good start on weapons. But if we were going to break into the Imperial Palace or a heavily fortified military base, we needed all the help we could get.

I swung the sniper rifle off my shoulder and handed it to Nilo. "Stay here and guard the door," I said over the comm.

He emphatically shook his head, his expression furious.

"I'm just going to look around the corner. I won't go any farther without you." I slipped away before he could argue.

The warehouse wasn't large, but the rows of shelves were divided into two halves by a perpendicular walkway.

I crouched at the edge of it and peeked around the corner. The walkway ran all the way to the other side of the building, where three men and a woman were sitting around a folding table, playing cards.

I'd found the source of the conversation.

Two of the guards were facing me, but they were looking at their cards more than their surroundings, and I'd tucked my light hair under a dark knit hat, so it wasn't a beacon in the dim room.

There were a pair of empty chairs, which didn't bode well for my desire to sneak deeper into the warehouse. Another quick glance revealed what looked like a bin of grenades on the shelf diagonally across the walkway. My fingers tingled with the desire to grab a few, but good sense won out. The room wasn't dark enough to hide me crossing an open walkway directly in two people's line of sight.

I was good, but I wasn't *that* good.

But I didn't need to be when I had a teleporter with me. Assuming that Besor had kept his anti-teleporter tech to the perimeter of the building, Nilo should be able to either port us across the walkway or port the grenades to us.

I checked on the guards one more time—they hadn't moved—then eased away from the corner and stood. I turned to go get Nilo and nearly jumped out of my skin when I found someone directly behind me. I was a second away from skewering him with my plas blade when I realized it was Nilo.

Fucking hell, the man moved quietly. And he wasn't carrying any of the weapons we'd picked up.

"What are you doing?" I demanded over the comm.

"I'm watching your back," he whispered.

"I told you to guard the door." I kept using the comm so

at least half of our conversation would be silent. We really needed a better system—one that didn't require telepathy.

Nilo lifted one shoulder in a lazy shrug. "I am. I can see it just as well from here."

I bit my tongue against the need to argue. We didn't have time. "There are four guards playing cards at the end of the walkway. Two empty chairs. Can you teleport in here?"

Nilo tipped his head, then nodded. "But if I do, any nearby Valoffs will likely sense it. Why?"

I hooked a thumb over my shoulder. "There's a bin of grenades over there that I'd very much like to have, but the walkway is too open for me to cross."

Nilo moved up close to me and quickly peeked around the corner. "Is there anything else you want to look for first?"

My eyebrows rose. "I thought you wanted to leave."

"I do. But I'd rather leave with everything you need so we don't have to come back."

"Then let's see if there's a walkway at the other end of these shelves so we can check the next aisle without being seen."

"Quickly," Nilo urged.

I nodded and jogged back toward the door we'd entered through, then past it. A glance over my shoulder proved Nilo was keeping pace with me, his boots as silent as mine.

Nilo was right: competence *was* sexy, dammit.

There was a narrow walkway around the perimeter of the building. I slowed as we approached and listened for the presence of guards. I didn't hear anyone, so I crouched down and peeked around the corner. The walkway was empty.

I eased around the corner and looked down the next aisle of shelves. More weapons, mostly small arms. I crossed to the next aisle. Nilo muttered a curse behind me, but he didn't try to stop me.

We were nearly halfway across the small warehouse. Would Besor put the most valuable items in the center or closer to the guards? From the flimsy look of their table and chairs, I wasn't entirely sure they were supposed to be sitting at all.

I glanced down the aisle and froze in shock. The shelves at the far end, near the center walkway, were lined with at least a dozen different plas cannons, including a large, automated version that was used for base defense. Even the shoulder-mounted versions could punch holes through thick armor and take out small vehicles. There was *no way* they should be in civilian hands.

But since they were here anyway, I might as well grab one.

Or two.

The shelves closest to us were stocked with drones of various sizes, from the tiny room-mapping drones Kee preferred to the large surveillance drones meant to keep an eye on a battle.

I shoved a few of the smaller FHP mapping drones into my bag. I had several in the crate I'd packed, but their life spans tended to be greatly reduced in hostile territory. Beside me, Nilo was adding the Valovian version of the same to his bag.

We crept down the aisle toward the plas cannons. The guards' conversation was loud enough that I could make out some of their words. It was the usual mix of taunting and bullshit that went with card games, and none of them sounded worried.

I stopped in front of the plas cannon I was most familiar with. I hadn't been the heavy munitions expert on the squad, but we'd all had basic training. I could point the correct end at the enemy and hit a big target, but that was about it.

But plas cannons weren't designed to be precision weapons. They were designed to bring maximum destruction in the minimum amount of time—just the thing for breaking into a military base.

Even the shoulder-mounted cannons were *heavy*. This version was more compact than some, but it still weighed over ten kilograms.

I waved at Nilo. "Grab that end," I said over the comm. "Help me lift it down."

We carefully lifted the plas cannon from its stand with only the faintest sound of scraping metal on metal.

I was trying to determine the best way to carry it, since it was missing the shoulder harness, when I heard footsteps. "Guard," I warned Nilo subvocally.

The steps were slow and measured—a guard on patrol, not running to confront the intruders, but they were close, just on the other side of the shelves. If they continued straight across, then we'd have time to retreat before they spotted us, but if they were patrolling only this half then we were about to be in trouble.

We didn't have time to retreat, so Nilo took the plas cannon from me and we flattened ourselves against the shelf. I unclipped my plas blade but I didn't activate it; the glow would give me away. Facing a Valoff with unknown abilities in close combat was a literal nightmare, but the adrenaline drowned out the panic.

I frowned and tipped my head, listening intently. There

were *two* sets of footsteps approaching from opposite directions. The steps across the walkway were lighter and nearly drowned out by the closer guard, but if I took down one person, I'd quickly have another on me.

Nilo tapped my shoulder and held up two fingers. I nodded in agreement.

A shadow moved in the walkway as the guard cleared the shelves. I held my breath. The shadow grew—they were rounding the corner.

"Attack then run," I said subvocally.

There was no time for Nilo to respond. The Valoff saw us before he entered the aisle. I would've preferred to be out of sight of the rest of the guards, but the universe refused to cooperate. I activated my plas blade at the same time I felt a cold spike of power from him.

But he couldn't touch my mind, and that moment of confusion was enough for me to hit him twice. He yelled as he fell, stunned, then there was another Valoff there. Her pistol cleared the holster just as Nilo shot her. She staggered, dropped the gun, and clutched her shoulder.

The not-so-distant clatter of falling chairs meant we had precious little time to escape. "Run," I whisper-shouted at Nilo, then I reached out and smacked the wounded Valoff with my plas blade. She went down. At least that would prevent her from shooting us in the back.

Probably.

I darted after Nilo, who was making good time despite being weighed down by the plas cannon. We rounded the end of the aisle as the first of the additional guards reached the ones we'd downed.

But for all they'd been sitting around playing cards, the guards were well trained. They didn't attempt to chase us down the aisle, which would've given us a few seconds of cover. Instead, they shot at us from the center walkway, and their aim was damnably good.

A plas pulse struck my arm as I crossed the next aisle, and I hissed in pain. The pulse had merely grazed me, and my arm was still functional, but we still had one more aisle to cross before the door. We'd be easy targets.

We stopped at the end of the shelves, using them for the small amount of cover they offered. Soon the guards would split up and we'd be toast.

But we *did* have a freaking plas cannon.

"Give me the cannon," I whispered.

Nilo shook his head. "Too dangerous." His power spiked, and he leaned against the shelves as the bin of grenades I'd wanted appeared at my feet.

"Make good use of them," he whispered.

I clipped the plas blade back into place and crouched down to see what we had. I wasn't entirely sure grenades were *less* dangerous, but they were less likely to punch into a neighboring building—mostly because I couldn't throw them that far.

But with all of the weapons in the building, explosive grenades were still a pretty big risk.

"Any chance they have a telekinetic?" I asked while I pulled two grenades I recognized from the box.

"Unlikely," Nilo said.

That wasn't a no, but now wasn't the time to be fussy. I activated the first grenade and launched it under the shelves toward the center of the room. The sound of the casing on the floor was distinctive, and the guards shouted warnings to each other. I hoped they were retreating.

While they were distracted, I activated the second

grenade and threw it toward the outside door. The smoke grenade shouldn't blow anything up, and it would give us enough cover to get clear in the confusion.

Hopefully.

Nilo jerked me back into cover, and I clapped my hands over my ears as the first explosion punched through the building. A secondary explosion went off that was definitely *not* the other grenade, then the smoke grenade blew, and thick, choking smoke filled the warehouse.

More explosions followed from the center of the building. Plas weapons were not fans of explosions, and this whole room was going to be very dangerous, very soon.

I carefully transferred the rest of the grenades to my bag so I'd have my hands free, then I drew my plas pistol. "Where are the rifles?"

"Near the door."

"Let's go. Follow me."

Nilo nodded, and I eased around the corner. Smoke obscured everything. The guards had gone silent, but unless they had thermal cameras, they wouldn't be able to see any better than I could.

Another explosion rocked the building and the shelves creaked ominously. I nearly passed the door in the smoke, but Nilo tapped my shoulder. I gathered up the three rifles he had stashed earlier, then grabbed another grenade.

"I'm going to blow this place up," I shouted in Valovan. "Run."

Warning delivered, I activated the grenade and tossed it over the shelves toward where the plas cannons had been, then I shoved Nilo out the door.

As soon as we were a few steps away from the building, Nilo gripped my arm and his power washed over me. The world went dark and my stomach wobbled, then the clearing appeared around us. I didn't even feel like vomiting this time. Maybe I *was* getting better at porting.

Nilo let me go and hit the ground on his knees. The coolness at the back of my mind vanished. *"Nidru,"* he groaned as he rested his forehead against the plas cannon he was still clutching.

"Are you hurt?" I demanded, alarmed.

"No, just used too much energy," he murmured. "You?"

I glanced down at my bloody sleeve. The graze had mostly stopped bleeding. "Not really."

His head jerked up, and he climbed unsteadily to his feet. "Where are you hurt?"

"Pulse grazed my arm. It's not a big deal. Do you want these weapons in the house or the shed?"

"Let me see."

"Weapons first, then you can poke at my bloody arm as much as you want. House or shed?"

He stared at me for a long moment, then sighed. "Shed. I have a storage room."

CHAPTER TEN

The shed was smaller than the house, but not by much. Half of the building was a workshop with neatly organized shelves and workbenches. The other half was a garage, complete with the lev cycle Nilo had mentioned.

Nilo stopped me just inside the door and put down the plas cannon. "Stay here." When I nodded, he moved deeper into the workshop side of the room. He waved his comm over a blank section of wall and the floor parted along what I'd thought were merely decorative lines. The panel sank down and slid sideways, disappearing under the rest of the floor and leaving a square opening about a meter wide.

Lights came on in the room below, illuminating a space that looked to be half as big as the workshop area. Secret rooms were my absolute *favorite*. "Is this where you store your treasure?" I asked with a delighted smile.

"Some of it. The ladder is tricky, so let me go down first and you can hand me the weapons."

"That's not your way of trying to keep me out, is it? Because it won't work."

Nilo smiled softly. "If I'd wanted to keep you out, I wouldn't have opened the door for you. I would've left the weapons there and then teleported them into the room after I'd rested for a bit."

I connected the dots. "Is this where you store your knives?"

"One of the places." His eyes gleamed and he gave me a mischievous smile. "You'll have to find the rest for yourself."

I swallowed against the lure of Nilo at his most playful, but I couldn't quite resist the temptation. I batted my lashes at him and let my mouth curve into a seductive grin. "I don't have time to search, but perhaps I could charm it out of you."

The gold in his eyes expanded. "You could try."

My stomach tightened as I fought the desire to do exactly that—not for the secret of any other hidden storage, but because I still wanted Nilo with a fierceness that was its own reminder of why I had to keep my hands to myself.

I dropped my gaze to the hole in the floor, and forced myself to say, "We'd better put this stuff away so we can get back to planning."

I could feel Nilo's eyes on me, but after a moment, he crouched down and lowered himself into the hole using strength alone and skipping the ladder entirely. I heard his feet softly hit the ground, then he called, "Hand me the rifles first."

I handed down the rifles and the plas cannon, then I lowered myself into the room the same way he had, with arm strength and balance. The wound on my arm reminded me of its presence, and I hissed as I dropped to the floor and looked around.

The room was even more neatly organized than the workshop above. Part of one wall had been painted in various-size rectangles of different colors. A single gun or knife hung on custom pegs in each rectangle.

Including the knife he'd teleported yesterday when he'd been showing off.

"Is this so they're easier to port?" I asked with a wave at the wall.

"The colors help with the visualization," he confirmed.

"That's amazing." I turned to survey the rest of the room. He'd leaned the rifles in the corner and put the plas cannon on the ground in front of them. Cabinets with doors took up most of the remaining space, but a small bookshelf against the far wall held a store of paper books with spines in Valovan, Common, and a few languages I didn't know.

And a cot sat next to it. I raised my eyebrows. "I thought you only had one bed."

He grinned, unrepentant. "I do. That is a cot, not a bed. And it's even more uncomfortable than the sofa."

"Do you stay here often?"

Nilo shook his head. "It's here in case I find myself in more trouble than I can handle. I can port here to safely pass out."

"So why didn't we land here when the nullifier attacked?"

"I didn't have time to warn you, and I didn't want you to feel trapped."

He'd risked his safety for my comfort. Warmth curled through my chest, and I ducked my head. "Thank you."

Nilo's gaze snagged on my arm, and his eyes narrowed. "You're bleeding."

"Pulled the wound a bit on the way down. No worries. It'll stop in a second."

Nilo cursed under his breath, then stepped close enough that I had to tip my head back to hold his glare. "I have a first aid kit here, but the one in the house is better. You promised you'd let me look at the wound once the weapons were stored, and they are."

"It's really not that—"

"Get moving," Nilo interrupted, "unless you'd like me to carry you."

The man was barely standing after porting us around all afternoon, but I didn't doubt that if I pushed the issue, he'd try anyway. I raised my hands in surrender. "I'm going."

Nilo and I climbed out of the hidden room, then he closed the hatch. I crouched down and looked at the lines, but even knowing the door was there, it was impossible to tell. "This is excellent work," I murmured.

"Thank you."

I glanced up in surprise. "You did this?"

He nodded. "I had help framing and plumbing the buildings, but everything else, I built myself."

I was beginning to get the impression that Nilo Shoren had more layers than a delicate, flaky pastry, and I wanted to bite into every one of them and discover all of the delicious secrets hidden inside.

I was in deep, deep trouble.

I FOLLOWED NILO INTO THE BATHROOM AND WAITED WHILE HE RETRIEVED the first aid kit. The wound had stopped bleeding again, but my sleeve was stuck to my skin. I didn't have enough clothes to just cut it off, so I peeled the fabric back a little bit at a time. Once it was loose, I eased my arm out of the sleeve then took the whole shirt off.

I had a bra on and Nilo had already seen it all before, so there was no reason at all for my pulse to pick up. But it was slightly gratifying when his eyes widened a bit before he glued them to the wound on my arm.

I sat on the counter, then Nilo carefully wiped away the blood. "I thought you said this was minor," he growled.

I shrugged. The pulse had cut a shallow furrow through the flesh on the outside of my right arm. The wound was a centimeter wide and a few centimeters long, but I'd gotten lucky. If the shooter had hit me a centimeter or two closer to my body, the pulse would've shattered the bone.

Nilo cleaned and bandaged the wound far more carefully than I would've. It was clear he felt somewhat responsible for the injury despite the fact that I'd volunteered to go and it'd been my idea to delve deeper into the warehouse. But I also knew logic didn't always work on emotion, so I bit my lip and let him fuss.

Once he was done, he slid closer so smoothly that I didn't realize I'd parted my legs for him until he was standing between them, pinning me in place. I shivered with desire and my good intentions began to unravel. I clamped my fingers around the edge of the counter to prevent myself from tugging him closer.

"I'm sorry you were hurt," he whispered. "If I'd been faster . . ."

"It's barely a scratch, Nilo. And it's not your fault." I smiled, trying to lighten the mood. "And did you *see* how many of Besor's weapons I blew up? He's going to be furious, and it couldn't have happened to a nicer person." I sobered. "But I hope the guards made it out."

"They were running even before you warned them."

"Then I'd say today was a success." I glanced up at him through my eyelashes and decided to play with fire. "How should we celebrate?"

He stilled, his muscles taut, and the gold in his eyes expanded. A groan tore itself free from somewhere deep in his chest. "Ask for what you want, *taro,* and I will give it to you."

My fingers tightened around the edge of the counter. I tried to remember all of the reasons I should keep my distance, but Nilo's eyes were glowing gold and his hips were between my thighs and I *wanted.*

I swayed toward him, but my stomach growled loudly in the silent room. The tension broke. I chuckled and rested my forehead on his shoulder, which was far safer than my original destination. "I guess we should've stopped for groceries while we were out. I have meal bars."

Nilo brushed his cheek over the top of my head before he drew away. I missed his warmth immediately.

"I still have a few things left," he said, his expression unreadable. "I'll make lunch."

AFTER WE ATE, NILO AND I SPENT THE AFTERNOON CONTACTING smugglers to try to secure passage to Rodeni, because no passenger ship would let us aboard with a plas cannon. None of Nilo's informants knew Sura Fev's plans, so we wouldn't know if she was planning to head to Rodeni or Valovia until after she'd traversed the wormhole. Nilo's spies could track her once she was in Valovian space, but until then, we had to make two plans.

And no matter what Fev did, we'd be starting off behind. It was infuriating.

Just before dinner, I finally found an opening on an express ship that was heading to Rodeni tomorrow afternoon, but we had to pay the exorbitant fee whether or not we ended up needing the seats.

Nilo transferred the credits from one of Torran's secret accounts. Hopefully the former general wouldn't be too upset if we ended up staying on Valovia and wasting the money.

Rather than taking time to cook, I pulled a few meal bars from my crate, and Nilo and I ate them while staying glued to our comms. As the hour grew late, I hoped that the Feds had actually managed to stop Sura Fev on their side of the wormhole.

If not, she'd be traversing the wormhole late tomorrow morning. Until then, we needed rest more than we needed to keep staring at our comms. Especially Nilo. He'd burned a lot of energy today, and I wasn't convinced that he was completely recovered from his run-in with the nullifier.

I stood and pulled him up with me. "Time for sleep." This close, I could see the lines of exhaustion carved into his face. "You should take the bed," I said firmly. "You need the rest."

"And you don't?" he challenged.

"I do, but right now I could sleep on a literal rock, so the couch is fine for me."

He stared at me for a long moment. "We could share the bed." He held up his hands before I could protest—not that I was entirely sure I would. "Just for sleeping." His fingers ghosted over the curve of my cheek. "You have bruises under your eyes and you're injured. You need good rest as much as I do."

I should say no. Getting into bed with him, even platonically, was a dangerous, dangerous game. I'd already proven that I was garbage at resisting temptation, and nothing tempted me more than the man in front of me.

"Nilo—"

"Please," he whispered. "I'll sleep better if I'm not worried about you."

"Cheater," I grumbled without heat, then sighed. "Fine, we'll share the bed. For sleeping *only*. But in case you haven't already figured it out, I'm a cuddler. So if you'd rather not be snuggled to death, I'll stay on the couch."

If I'd surprised him, he hid it well. "I'll take my chances," he murmured, the gold in his eyes growing.

I lifted one shoulder. "Your choice. Don't say I didn't warn you."

CHAPTER ELEVEN

The silky nightgowns I normally wore to sleep were entirely inappropriate for platonically sharing a bed with someone. I twisted in front of the bathroom mirror, trying to determine if I could see my underwear through the delicate, pale green material or if I was imagining things.

I hadn't brought anything else with me into the bathroom, so it was either this or the shirt and pants I'd been wearing, and the pants weren't very comfortable for sleeping. I needed to stop procrastinating and just own it. Nilo had seen me naked, so this wasn't any worse than that. I was decent enough, and despite my earlier threat, I planned to stay firmly on my side of the bed.

I bundled my dirty clothes together and strode from the bathroom with feigned confidence. The bedroom door was open, and Nilo was sitting on the edge of the bed in a tight T-shirt and soft pants. He'd already changed.

He glanced up and froze for a moment before blinking slowly. "I must be dreaming," he muttered in Valovan.

"If you make fun of my sleepwear, then I will kick you to the couch."

His eyes slid down my body, leaving a trail of heat behind. "Why would anyone make fun of perfection?"

My belly fluttered at the husky note of appreciation in his tone. I ignored it. "Is that the side you want?" It was the same side he'd slept on last night, so it was a decent guess.

Nilo blinked at me again, and I smiled softly. If I'd known that a silk nightgown would scramble his brain, I might've tried it earlier.

He cleared his throat. "Yes, I would prefer this side if that's okay with you."

I nodded and moved to the far side of the bed. I dropped the bundle of dirty clothes to the floor. I'd deal with them when I woke up.

Nilo disappeared into the bathroom, and I took the opportunity to slide between the sheets. The bed was enormous, but I stayed on my edge. I hadn't been joking about my tendency to migrate toward my bedmate during the night, but I hoped that exhaustion would keep me in place tonight.

During my time in the military, I'd learned to grab sleep where I could, so I was nearly out when Nilo returned. He turned off the light, then crossed the room and silently slipped into bed. That was almost enough to jolt me back to wakefulness, but my body had other ideas.

Sleep crept over me, and I let it lull me into dreams.

• • •

I AWOKE WITH A WARM WEIGHT ON MY LEFT SIDE. I FELT RESTED, BUT the angle of sunlight streaming into the room meant it was still fairly early. The days on this planet were going to kill me.

"Good morning," Nilo murmured, his voice rough with sleep. His chin was resting on the top of my shoulder, so his voice whispered directly into my ear. I suppressed a shiver.

We were in the middle of the bed. We'd both migrated during the night, which made the embarrassment a little less acute. The sheet was wedged between us, and it took me longer than it should've to realize that he was sleeping on top of it.

"Why aren't you under the sheet?"

"I don't know what you're wearing under that delightful nightgown, and I didn't want to make you uncomfortable if it moved around during the night, especially if we ended up pressed together."

I tried to ignore the warmth that spread through my chest at his thoughtfulness, but it was a losing battle. "Thank you," I said softly.

"You're welcome."

"Have you checked your comm? Any word from Tavi and Torran?"

Nilo shook his head. "I haven't checked, but I set an audible alert on any communications from either of them, and it hasn't gone off yet."

I bit my lip, worried. I would've expected Tavi to contact me by now, even if it was just to yell at me for being dumb enough to return to Valovia. The fact that she hadn't meant that she was busy fighting her own battles—or making her own plans.

Neither option was comforting.

Nilo nudged me. "I'm sure they're okay. Captain Zarola is probably still busy adding threats warning you to be careful—or else."

That surprised a laugh out of me. "Sounds about right."

I stole a few more peaceful moments cocooned in comfortable silence before I shifted and stretched. "I guess we should get started on the day."

Nilo pushed himself up on his elbow so that he was staring down at me with an unreadable expression. "If we must."

Temptation was a sleep-tousled Nilo Shoren. I curled my fingers into the sheet to keep from reaching for him. Losing myself to pleasure would certainly start this day off nicely, but the longer I spent with Nilo, the more I liked him, and my heart was already dangerously involved. Any more would be a recipe for disaster.

"We must," I confirmed, but my lack of enthusiasm caused Nilo's mouth to curve into a tiny, tempting smile that I steadfastly ignored. "How are you feeling? Are you recovered from yesterday?"

He nodded, and his eyes sparkled. "I'm recovered and back to full stamina," he said, his expression too innocent to mistake the innuendo.

I gently patted his cheek. "I'm glad that I won't have to worry about your"—I let my eyes flicker down his body—"*performance.*"

Hunger sharpened his expression, and he tugged me closer, until I could feel the hard heat of him against my thigh. "Would you like a demonstration?"

Yes. I kept the word locked away through sheer force of will, but Nilo had to see the answer in my face. Yet, he didn't move, he just watched me with predatory stillness. If I said yes, all of that focus would be on me, on my pleasure.

The temptation was nearly overwhelming, but I dredged up the last of my willpower and shook my head. The movement was tiny, barely visible, but Nilo backed off immediately.

Regret fought reason, and I slipped from the bed before I could do something reckless. Nilo flopped over on his back and muttered something in Valovan too quiet for me to understand. His eyes were closed, and I realized he was giving me privacy.

Or going back to sleep.

Either way, I grabbed clothes and fled for the relative safety of the bathroom.

I WAS POURING MYSELF A CUP OF STRONG VALOVIAN TEA WHEN MY comm buzzed with a high-priority message. I sloshed the hot liquid over my fingers in my haste to put the cup down and hissed in pain.

I would've ignored it, but Nilo pulled me to the sink and ran cool water over my singed fingers while I looked at my comm with my left hand. When I hissed again, Nilo looked up. "Did I hurt you?"

"No, it's a message from Tavi. The FHP won't stop Fev, so *Starlight's Shadow* is going to chase her through the wormhole," I said, my stomach a tight knot of worry. My eyebrows rose as I kept reading. "I can't believe it; the Feds actually put a bounty on Morten." I read the next paragraph, then leveled a glare at Nilo. "Did you know Torran has a writ of safe passage from the empress?"

"Yes."

Of course he did. He carefully dried my fingers as I read the message again. "Thank you," I murmured, distracted. When I was done, I handed him my comm so he could read. Torran would probably send him a separate message, but mine had arrived first, so it was only fair to share.

Nilo finished reading and sighed. "I hope they know what they're doing."

"I don't know about Torran, but Tavi wouldn't risk it without good reason," I said. "Her crew is family, and she won't lead them into danger unless there's no other option."

I checked the time stamp on the message. It had been sent nearly three hours ago, which meant I *might* have a chance to get another message to her before she traversed the wormhole, for all the good it would do. Tavi already knew I was here, and she planned to put herself and the crew in danger anyway, so either she thought I couldn't take on Fev on my own—true enough—or there were other forces at work she hadn't mentioned.

I looked at Nilo. "If Fev heads for Rodeni, will the empress let *Starlight* follow her?"

He nodded slowly. "Most likely. Torran would be cut off from his allies, which makes the empress's job easier. She'll let him walk into the trap."

"So does that mean Fev is *more* likely to go to Rodeni?"

Nilo paced back and forth like a caged animal. "I don't know. I should've heard from my contact by now."

"Our ride leaves in four hours. We should pack in case Fev chooses Rodeni. Well, *you* should pack. All my shit is already in my crate. Do you have a case long enough for the rifles and plas cannon?"

Nilo stopped pacing. "I do. We should consolidate into a single crate; it'll be easier for us to keep track of it."

"Okay. What do you need help with?"

"I just got an info dump on Aburwuk, the Rodeni military base, if you'd like to start looking at possible entry points. I'm still waiting on more information for the Imperial Palace."

"Could we use the tunnels we found during Cien's rescue to get into the palace?"

Nilo shook his head. "Empress Nepru increased the security after Morten escaped. There's at least two Fiazefferia guarding the palace entrance at all times now."

We couldn't even take *one* Sun Guardian, so taking out two was a nonstarter. But the Imperial Palace would be filled with them, so two might not be so bad, all things considered. If only we could get the empress to leave and take her guard with her, then we'd only have to deal with the normal security.

While I was wishing, I might as well wish that the wormhole would swallow Fev's ship and save us all a lot of trouble, but sadly, wormhole accidents were rare these days.

"Send me the info," I said. "I've sent out requests, too, but I haven't heard back. I'm not expecting much because most of my contacts are human, but maybe we'll get lucky."

Nilo sent me the information, then went to pack. I was deep in the details of the military base, which had been built specifically to keep people like me out, when he returned, scowling at his comm.

"Fev is headed for Rodeni," he said, his face grim. "She traversed the wormhole three hours ago."

"I don't suppose she's going to set down in a nice open field with good sight lines and stay there until we arrive?"

Nilo chuckled drily. "She's on a priority route to Tirdenchia and Aburwuk. She's scheduled to arrive overnight tonight."

"Of course she is," I muttered darkly. "And we won't get there for a day and a half. I have to send a message to Tavi. She probably won't get it until she's already in Valovian space, but maybe I can catch her."

"Send it. I'm going to pack the weapons, then we'll need to leave for the spaceport."

He went out to the shed while I typed up a quick note to Tavi. I attached all of the information Nilo had sent me about Aburwuk. Maybe Kee would have better luck digging up details if she had a place to start, and they were going to arrive before us anyway.

Communication with *Starlight's Shadow* would be a little faster once the ship was in Valovian space, but it still wouldn't be *fast*. That would only happen tomorrow after Nilo and I were through the wormhole that led to Rodeni, because then all of our comms would be local to the system.

Hopefully Tavi would be able to hold out until we arrived, and then we could plan together.

By the time Nilo returned from the shed, I was putting the final touches on the wig I'd donned. He stopped short and stared at me. "You had that in your crate?"

I nodded and patted the wig's long brown hair, then perched a pair of chunky glasses on my nose. The lenses were designed to help foil facial recognition. "Well?"

"It might help deflect suspicion but only at a distance," he said with a doubtful frown.

Sharp disappointment stabbed me. I'd thought Nilo trusted me to know how to do my job. I covered the hurt with an exaggerated roll of my eyes. "You're right, of course," I said, my tone syrupy sweet. "Trying to deflect suspicion at a distance is a waste of time, what was I thinking. Oh, wait, most surveillance is done *at a distance.*"

"Lexi—"

"Never mind." I waved away both the hurt and his explanation. "Let's get everything packed. We need to leave soon so we don't miss our ship."

Nilo looked like he wanted to argue, but finally he said, "I can teleport us directly to their private dock. We won't avoid *everyone,* but it's better than arriving via the public entrance."

"Do they already know you're a teleporter?"

"Yes, I've worked with them in the past."

"Are they going to betray you?"

Nilo's smile was grim. "Only one way to find out."

CHAPTER TWELVE

The dock was a hive of activity as the ship prepared to depart. Both passengers and cargo were still being loaded, giving us a chance to get lost in the chaos. "This way," Nilo urged with one hand on my arm and the other on our lev crate.

It appeared he was prepared to port us out again at the first sign of trouble, which wasn't exactly reassuring.

Leaving our hoods up would've stood out against the sea of dockworkers, so we'd each donned a knit cap instead, but it felt like flimsy protection even with the glasses and wig I was wearing. At least the sun was barely up, leaving the dock steeped in shadow.

Nilo skirted around the edge of the activity, heading for an older man with gray-streaked hair and deeply tanned skin. The man waited until we approached before breaking into a smile. "It's good to see you," he said to Nilo in

Valovan. "I wasn't sure you would make it. You are popular these days."

Nilo's fingers tightened on my arm, but his expression remained friendly. "Is that going to be a problem?" Nilo replied in the same language.

The older man shook his head. "Never cared much for rules, myself," he murmured. "But my people have seen some unfriendly eyes around, so we need to get you on the ship. Follow me."

"He's the captain," Nilo whispered, his voice nearly lost under the din around us. I nodded slightly in acknowledgment as we passed a pair of dockworkers who were moving a tall pile of boxes. The workers carefully avoided looking at us while simultaneously shielding us from view, proving that this wasn't the captain's first time smuggling people who were wanted by the law.

The ship was larger than *Starlight,* but not big enough to be classified as a dedicated cargo hauler. Rather than going up the ramp into the cargo hold, the captain led us to the passenger elevator, which delivered us to the maintenance level.

The captain leaned out the elevator's door and glanced around, then he beckoned us out after him. "Quickly now."

Nilo had to release me to maneuver the crate through the walkway, but we followed the captain until he reached an open section of wall. He looked at Nilo. "The crate will be a tight fit, but I don't suppose you want me to put it in the cargo bay?"

When Nilo shook his head, the captain grinned. "I figured. You'll have to shield for her if we get searched. Can you, or do I need to assign someone?"

"I'll handle it," Nilo said before anxiety could break through my mask of calm.

"We have a few humans aboard as regular passengers, so she won't stand out too much, but shielding for her the entire way would be smarter."

Nilo nodded but didn't comment. The captain ushered us into the smuggler's hold. It was a tiny room with a single narrow bed and a minuscule attached bathroom with barely enough room for a toilet and a sink. The crate would take up most of the open floor space.

"There are rations in the cabinet," the captain said. "Stay here unless it's an emergency. Once we get to Rodeni, I'll find you a safe place to port out. Give the general my regards."

Nilo bowed slightly. "I will." Then he turned to me and said in Common, "Step inside and I'll pull the crate in after us."

I had to go all the way into the bathroom to make enough room for Nilo and the crate. He lowered it to the floor, leaving less than a half meter of floor space. The lid was strong enough to walk on, but the ceiling wasn't that high, so this was going to be an uncomfortable trip. This tiny room was going to be our home for the next thirty hours or so. Good thing I wasn't claustrophobic.

The captain closed the thick section of wall that acted as the door, trapping us inside. Nilo crawled over the crate and settled on the narrow bed with his back to the wall. He patted the space beside him. "Might as well get comfortable."

I leaned against the doorway to the bathroom. "Will the captain betray us?"

"If he was going to, he would've done it already. This room isn't shielded against teleporters, so there's nothing holding us here, and the empress doesn't get anything from allowing us to go to Rodeni."

"Do you think the ship will be searched? Will you have to shield for me?"

"Yes. And the captain is correct that shielding you the whole trip would be safest."

I wrinkled my nose as my pulse picked up. That was not ideal, especially with nothing to distract me.

"It'll be the same as last time," Nilo said, his tone reassuring. "I won't be able to sense your thoughts. I swear it."

"You can't maintain that level of shielding for the entire trip."

His mouth flattened into a hard line and his jaw clenched. "I will."

"You need to be rested when we arrive." I swallowed and dropped my gaze to the floor. "I will deal with it." No matter how much the thought made me feel like crawling out of my own skin.

"I will not torture you." His voice was low and fierce with absolutely no give.

My temper flared. "Well, I'm not going to torture you, either, especially when the problem lies with *me*."

"Come sit next to me. Please."

I took a deep breath. Getting closer to him was dangerous, but we had to figure out the shielding issue. If I could get over the panic, being able to communicate telepathically *would* be a benefit once we started infiltrating the base.

I crawled over the crate and onto the bed. I mirrored Nilo's position with my back against the wall and my feet resting on the crate, but I left a dozen centimeters between us. My muscles were knots of tension as I waited for the cold touch of his mind.

Nilo picked up my hand and traced his fingers over mine, his touch featherlight. "I would like to try something, with your permission."

"What?"

"I would like to extend my mental shield so that it protects your mind, too."

My eyes narrowed. "How is that different than what you did before?"

"Before, I essentially built three shields: one for me, one for you, and one between us. This time there would only be one. I would be able to sense strong thoughts and feelings from you"—I tried to jerk my hand away but he held on—"and you would be able to do the same for me. If I build a separate shield for you, then it'll be much harder for you to sense my thoughts. This will put us on even footing."

Panic fluttered across my nerves, and it was a fight to sit still. He would be in my head. He would see my thoughts. He would *know* how much I wanted him. And I would know if he felt the same.

If he didn't . . .

His fingers squeezed my hand, and I focused on that small touch, breathing deeply. I rubbed the fingers of my other hand against my pants, then the bedding, forcing myself to see and name them as I went.

I fought back the panic, but it left me feeling jittery and unnerved. I took another deep breath. I'd survived the war. I would survive this, too.

My mental shield was as strong as I could make it, though I doubted that it would make much difference. "I'm ready," I said, my voice deceptively even.

"Say the word and I will stop, I swear it," he murmured. When I nodded, I felt a brush of coolness against my mind and squeezed my eyes shut, fighting the rising panic. Nilo would not hurt me. I was okay.

The panic didn't care.

Nilo hissed out a curse and the cool feeling of his mind vanished. I cracked open my eyes and found his jaw clenched and his hand fisted, though the hand that still held mine was gentle around my fingers. "What's wrong?" I whispered.

"You are terrified of me. I swore to keep you safe. I will find another way."

"Is there another way?"

A muscle flexed in his jaw as he clenched it tighter, but he gritted out, "I will find one." He blew out a slow breath. "If only Varro were here." At my questioning look, he elaborated, "Varro is stronger than I am. He could maintain all three shields indefinitely."

Varro might be stronger, but I wouldn't want him in my head, either. There had to be some way for me to overcome my fear, if not permanently, then at least long enough to make the trip. "You said other Valoffs can send you mental pictures that you can use to teleport. Could you do the same to me? Send me pictures of something nice to focus on?"

"I don't think—"

"Please."

Nilo sighed and inclined his head. "When you're ready."

"I'm ready."

The cool feeling of Nilo's mind returned, but before the panic could surge, a picture of a gorgeous flower-filled meadow appeared in my mind's eye, like a daydream I didn't create. The sun was shining brightly overhead and the sky was a brilliant, pale blue. The flowers were a riot of color against the deep green stems, and the whole place had a feeling of untouched beauty.

The flowers dipped in a warm breeze I could almost feel, and I realized this wasn't a picture so much as it was a memory—one that brought Nilo a great deal of peace. "Where is this?" I whispered.

"Near the cabin," he said. "It only blooms for a few weeks in the spring, but it's beautiful when it does."

I could *feel* how much he loved the place, and it was such a warm, joyous emotion that it didn't trigger my panic. I let myself bask in the feeling for a few minutes, then I returned to the task at hand. The cool feeling of Nilo's mind made my pulse kick uncomfortably, but I breathed through it.

I didn't know much about telepathy, but I assumed it was similar to our subvocal comms, which turned loud, intentional thoughts into sound through the magic of technology. I felt silly, but I thought loudly in Nilo's direction, "Can you hear this?"

"Yes." His voice whispered across my mind, so much more intimate than my comm implant. Goose bumps rose on my arms and my mouth tasted metallic. He wasn't hurting or demanding or trying to override my will. This was not the same as last time.

This was not the same.

I locked down the memories, but not fast enough, because I felt a wave of rage that wasn't my own. Rage was better than the small, frightened thing I'd become, so I clung to it and let it drive the panic back. By the time I remembered how to breathe without gasping, I was in Nilo's lap, his arms carefully holding me in a way that would be easy to escape.

The ship had picked up the subtle vibration that meant the main engines were ramping up, and I drew a shaky breath. "I didn't mean for you to see that."

He was quiet for a moment, but a faint echo of emotion flickered across my mind, too quick to name. "If you ever want to talk about it, I will listen," he said at last.

I lifted one shoulder in a half-hearted shrug. "It was war. Everyone has scars, some are just less visible than others."

He opened his mouth to respond, then tipped his head like he was listening to something far away. "They're searching the ship. The captain thinks it's a routine search, but I'll need to reinforce our shield a bit, if you can stand it, and we'll need to stay quiet."

I nodded. I would have to endure, unless I wanted us to get caught before we even left the ground. I straightened and Nilo's arm fell away. I ruthlessly suppressed the stab of disappointment before he could feel it.

I shifted until I was once again sitting beside him as the feeling of his presence increased in the back of my mind. I pulled out my comm. I couldn't risk connecting to the ship's network until we were in space, but I'd cached all of the data I'd collected so far, and I needed the distraction.

Breaking into Aburwuk was going to require all of my skill, and even then I wasn't entirely sure it was doable. Maybe if I'd had weeks or months to plan, I could've found a clever way in, but time was not on my side. Hopefully Kee would turn up something I'd missed, otherwise my plan was going to be some variation of "walk in the front door and bluff."

If we could get past the outer perimeter, then my job became easier—military bases were designed to keep people *out,* not in. It was a subtle but important distinction.

"Have your contacts found anything new?" I thought as loudly as I dared.

"No. But they'll know more once Fev lands."

I wasn't sure I'd ever get used to his voice in my head, but at least I didn't spiral into mindless panic this time. I already had enough adrenaline floating in my veins to power me for the next week or ten.

It took longer than usual to lose myself in the blueprints and schematics Nilo's contact had procured, but eventually the challenge snared my attention. The base was *huge,* far larger than most military installations. Part of the city had been incorporated into the design and part had been razed to make way for new defensive structures.

The outer wall was lined with antiaircraft cannons that would fire on unauthorized transports, and it had only four access points, each guarded by a squad of soldiers. The military spaceport was outside the walls and had underground access to the base, but it was also guarded, and even authorized transports were stopped and questioned.

The only good news—if awfulness could ever be called *good*—was that the displaced citizens had built a ramshackle city around the southern edge of the base. Some of the buildings were the remains of the demolished parts of Tirdenchia, but many of them had been built from whatever materials the builders could scavenge. It would be easy to get lost in such a place, which meant we could disappear after we landed.

But I wasn't sure what Tavi would do. *Starlight's Shadow* wasn't exactly inconspicuous. The Valoffs would be able to track the ship no matter where Tavi landed, and she would arrive before us, so she couldn't count on Nilo's help to get them out unscathed.

Worry compressed my chest. Even a telekinetic as

strong as Torran could be overpowered, especially by other Valoffs. But maybe Tavi would get my message and wait for us to arrive before she landed.

And maybe Fev would voluntarily hand over Morten and apologize for the inconvenience while she was at it.

I shook my head. Tavi was stubborn, but she wasn't reckless. She wouldn't rush in without a plan, so I just had to make sure that my plan was flexible enough to work with whatever she came up with.

If only I hadn't fallen for Besor's offer of piles of money, I could be with her right now, planning together. But then Nilo would be on his own. My heart twisted, and I winced, waiting for him to pick up the thought, but the cool presence at the back of my mind didn't change.

But now that I was paying attention, I could feel faint wisps of worry that weren't mine. Sensing feelings that weren't mine felt strange, but I'd take it a thousand times over glimpsing his actual thoughts, because it gave me hope that maybe he wasn't seeing every inane thought that flitted through my head.

Nilo was staring intently at his comm with a furrow on his forehead. "What's wrong?" I thought in his direction.

It took a second for him to pull his attention away from the comm. "We can talk," he said aloud. "The search is over, and the ship is in the air. The captain is fairly sure that none of the empress's spies are aboard."

"That didn't answer the question."

Nilo sighed. "I'm just looking at Aburwuk, and it doesn't look good. I've got people quietly searching for someone on the inside, but it's a delicate process. Until then, all news has to travel to my contact on Valovia before returning to me, which isn't a very efficient way to plan an attack."

"Have you heard anything from Torran? Do you have any idea what they're going to do once they get to the planet? Or maybe they decided to stay in Fed space?"

"No. He can lean on the guarantee of safe passage, but it remains to be seen if the soldiers will honor it, especially if the empress orders them to ignore it. And once the *Starlight* crew infiltrates the base, safe passage won't protect them. As for staying in Fed space, Torran won't wait in safety for someone else to clean up the problem. He will cross the wormhole, but I'm surprised he's letting Tavi and the rest of the crew accompany him."

I laughed. "I very much doubt he's *letting* Tavi accompany him. If he tried to leave her behind, Tavi would just follow him anyway, and I'm sure he knows that. They're stronger as a team. And do you really think Chira, Varro, and Havil would let him sail off alone? Would *you*?"

He shook his head with a grin. "I'd be first in line to tie him up if he even tried it. Well, maybe I'd let Chira have the first crack at him, but I'd definitely be second."

"Kee and Eli feel the same way about Tavi. So that's how you get the whole ship sailing into enemy territory like they don't have a care in the world, even if it would make our job easier if they stayed away."

Nilo's eyes narrowed on my face. "Did you really expect your captain to stay away while you put yourself in danger?"

"She would've if she knew what was good for her," I growled. At Nilo's raised eyebrows, I relented. "No. As soon as it became clear the FHP wouldn't stop Fev, I knew Tavi would follow her. I'd just *hoped* . . ."

Nilo nodded in understanding. "What have you found so far?"

"We can get in through the gate, over the wall, or through the tunnel from the spaceport. All three have major drawbacks. The gates and tunnel are restricted. Stealing or forging an ID would help, but we'd still be stopped by the guards, and I can't pass as a Valoff, so I'd have to be your prisoner."

"I'm not dragging you into Aburwuk in cuffs," he bit out.

I smiled at his outraged tone. "The cuffs are less of a problem than the lack of weapons. I can easily get out of cuffs, but I can't turn them into a plas rifle."

"And the wall?"

"Monitored, of course. It's designed to prevent climbers, but I could probably bypass the protection given enough time, which we might not have. And the whole base is wrapped in whatever magic current blocks your teleportation ability, so we can't just zap across. However, there is one other option."

"From the air."

I nodded. "If we're lucky, there will be a piece of the base that isn't covered by the teleporter shield, and then we just have to get high enough to get a straight shot at it. If not, then we can jump in the normal way, but I'd prefer to know exactly how sensitive their antiaircraft systems are before we turn ourselves into targets."

"Can you break into their systems?"

"Probably not. I can bypass several types of security, but breaking into military systems is Kee's area of expertise, not mine." I tipped my head at him. "Can you?"

Nilo grimaced. "No, not in the time required."

"But you could, given enough time?"

"Possibly."

That was impressive, and it occurred to me that he

must've been the one who pulled much of the data we'd used during Cien's rescue. Of course, he had failed to share that data with us until Kee had uncovered it for herself, but I hadn't questioned *how* Torran had known about Frank Morten's involvement until now. Nilo was more dangerous than I'd given him credit for.

Nilo shook his head. "I can't tell if you're impressed or upset."

I had actually forgotten he was in my head for a second, and the reminder was an unpleasant jolt. Anxiety crawled along my nerves, and Nilo cursed under his breath. "I'm sorry, *taro,*" he murmured. He ran a hand down his face. "I hate this."

"Well, if it makes you feel any better, so do I."

He leveled a grumpy glare at me. "That does not make me feel better."

"At least we're miserable together, right?"

I grinned when his scowl deepened. It might not make him feel better, but for me, it *did.*

CHAPTER THIRTEEN

We were several hours into the trip when Tavi's message arrived. She'd made it into Valovian space without any trouble, but she hadn't received my message about Rodeni until she was already through the wormhole. She appreciated the heads-up about Fev's destination, even if she loathed the planet itself.

I might've hated Rodeni, but it was so much worse for Tavi, who'd been in charge of our disastrous final mission during the war. The outcome hadn't been her fault—Command had intentionally misled her—but she would never see it that way.

Assuming they didn't get slowed down along the way, *Starlight* was going to arrive on the planet several hours behind Fev and a half day before us. Kee was already at work on the systems, but even Kee was going to be limited by the short time frame. Tavi promised she'd send me everything they knew before they landed.

I'd already given her our ETA and nothing had changed, so I didn't bother with a reply. They would be on the planet before we'd made it through the wormhole separating us, so trying to coordinate an attack with an hour or more delay on every message would be more trouble than it was worth.

With Tavi so much closer to Fev, it was possible that *Starlight*'s crew would find Morten before Nilo and I even hit dirt, in which case we'd have to switch to an escape plan that didn't end up with Tavi's ship in pieces.

I rubbed my face. I loved planning, but I usually didn't have to work around quite so many unknowns. I observed patterns and habits and security systems and entry points and then created a plan to take advantage of each. It was slow, meticulous work, not a slapdash race against time.

As the hour grew late, another problem became apparent: this room only had one bed and it was *tiny*. I could probably make a bunk on the crate if I could find some spare blankets for padding, but it wasn't going to be very comfortable.

Of course, neither was sleeping in my clothes, but I refused to get undressed on a ship where we would be discovered the moment the captain decided to betray us. One more discomfort wasn't going to make much difference.

I slipped into the bathroom to get ready to sleep and enjoyed standing up and walking, even if it was for only a handful of steps. I peeled off the wig and shook out my natural curls. I'd have to wear the wig again tomorrow, but for now I could let my scalp breathe.

By the time I'd finished and slid the door open, Nilo had

moved to sit on the crate. He gestured toward the bed. "I'm going to stay up for a while longer, but you should sleep."

"How do you want to handle sleeping arrangements?"

"You can have the bed. I'll sleep here."

It was exactly what my plan had been, but I hated that Nilo would be the one to suffer. "You can have the bed. You need more rest anyway."

"I'm at full strength. Just take the bed, *taro,* and sleep."

"We could share—" I tentatively started, but Nilo shook his head.

"It's not a good idea when I'm shielding for you." At my raised eyebrows, he elaborated, "It's already difficult to stay out of your head and keep you out of mine, at least as much as possible, and proximity would make it worse." His mouth curved into a slow, teasing grin. "Especially with how close we'd have to be pressed together."

That smile bolted through me like an electric current, and I wanted to lose myself in the pleasure it promised. Nilo groaned, and I felt a flicker of desire that wasn't mine. My gaze flashed to his. His eyes were going gold, but otherwise he held himself perfectly still.

I bit my lip. The reckless part of me that didn't care about future heartbreak was ready to fall into bed with him—with clothes or, preferably, *without.* But with him in my head, all of my thoughts and feelings would be laid bare, and that thought was enough to douse my desire under a wave of anxiety.

But Nilo had been in my head for hours now, and I was functional, mostly. It was going far better than I'd expected, and it was all because of his kindness and care. It still wasn't comfortable and likely never would be, but it was bearable, which made our infiltration plans more likely to succeed.

"Thank you," I murmured.

His head tilted. "For what?"

I debated what to say for a moment before I settled on, "For not breaking my trust or taking advantage of the shielding situation."

His jaw clenched. "You don't have to thank me for that."

I lifted one shoulder in a noncommittal shrug and turned to strip the blanket from the bed. Nilo leaned across the crate and put a hand on the blanket, stopping me. "You don't need to do that."

"I'm going to sleep in my clothes, so I don't need the blanket, and it'll make the crate slightly less miserable for you."

He sighed. "I don't know how much sleep I'm going to get. Fev should be landing in an hour or so, but it'll take twice that long for my contact to get news to me. And after that, Tavi and Torran will be landing."

I pulled the blanket from the bed, then crawled in, boots and all. I moved back until I was leaning against the wall. "Come lie down," I said, patting the spot next to me. "You don't have to sleep or even stay all night, but you have at least two hours to rest, and you should."

"Lexi—"

I fidgeted with the sheets and interrupted whatever excuse he was going to make. "Look, I know you might end up seeing some of my thoughts thanks to shielding for me, and while I don't love that, if you get hurt tomorrow because you're tired, I'll feel responsible, so . . . please."

Nilo was silent for a moment, then he sighed and slid over into the bed. He lay on his side with his back to me, as close to the edge as he could get without falling out of the bed. "If you want me to get up, you just have to say so," he said.

"I'm okay. Wake me up if any new information comes in, otherwise I'll see you in the morning." I paused, then wrapped an arm around his waist and tugged him backward. There wasn't a lot of space, but he didn't need to teeter on the edge of the mattress, either.

Once he'd scooted closer, I started to remove my arm, but he returned the favor by using it to pull me closer. "Lights off," he said in Valovan, and our room was plunged into the total, inky darkness common to deep-space ships.

I waited for the anxiety to come, but instead, all I felt was a gentle calm. I puzzled over it for a second before I realized it wasn't mine. Nilo was practically *radiating* calm. I nuzzled his shoulder and whispered my thanks against his shirt.

NILO WAS NO LONGER IN THE BED WHEN I WOKE, AND I HOPED MY dreams hadn't driven him away. I'd woken several times with a pounding heart, but I couldn't remember *why*. It was probably for the best because anxiety was already churning in my stomach.

The room was still dark, but Nilo's comm produced enough light for me to see that he was standing and leaning against the wall next to the bathroom door. He was scowling at the device in his hand, so apparently he hadn't gotten any good news overnight.

"Lights fifty percent," I said in Valovan, and Nilo's head jerked up.

"You're awake."

"Barely," I said, sitting up. "What's our status?"

"Fev landed on Rodeni, as expected. She had Morten with her, who seemed to be moving under his own power. They are both at Aburwuk."

It was only as he paused that I realized the well of worry I was feeling wasn't *mine.* "What's wrong?" I breathed, my heart in my throat.

"*Starlight's Shadow* disappeared."

"Disappeared how?" I demanded. "What do you mean?"

Nilo shook his head. "I don't know. It happened shortly after Fev landed. As far as my contact can tell, the ship wasn't attacked, but none of the systems around Rodeni tracked it to the planet, either. And I haven't received any messages from Torran."

"Maybe Kee got into their systems, and that's why they don't show up." I wished I had room to stand and pace, but I settled for pulling out my comm and checking my messages.

Nothing.

My worry notched higher. I should've received *something* from Tavi by now, even if she'd sent it standard priority. And if the Valoffs had jammed the ship's communications, Kee should've still been able to get a warning out.

I checked the time. We were still nearly twelve hours from Rodeni and six from the wormhole. I typed a quick message to Tavi asking for a status update and sent it priority. I routed it through a proxy server so it looked like it came from Valovia, but I sent it unencrypted and used a coded, innocent-sounding phrase that required a specific reply.

If someone had Tavi's comm—or forced her to reply—she could leave the phrase out to let me know she was compromised. Kee had designed the system, so only she, Tavi, Eli, and I knew the correct response. It wasn't much, but it was all I could do while trapped in this tiny coffin of a room.

"I sent Tavi another message," I told Nilo. "She can use her reply to indicate if she's being forced to respond. Do you have any theories about what happened?"

Nilo shook his head, then sighed. His voice whispered into my head. "You must absolutely keep this to yourself, but Prince Liang Nepru was on *Starlight*."

"What?" I demanded, shocked. Liang Nepru was Empress Nepru's youngest son. He should've been on Valovia, not *Starlight*.

"He was on Bastion when the station was attacked, then Fev tried to kill him on Odyssey, apparently on Empress Nepru's orders. We all thought the guarantee of safe passage would keep the ship safe, but . . ." Nilo grimaced. "I don't know."

A chasm of agony opened in my chest and stole my breath, but I fought it back. No. *No.* Tavi was fine. She had to be. She and Kee and Eli were my only remaining family. Not only that, but they were some of the smartest, most talented people I'd ever met.

They were alive. To believe anything else was to underestimate a squad that had survived the war against all odds—and that was before they'd added a telekinetic and a healer to their team. I didn't know why one of them hadn't sent me a message, but it wasn't because they were dead. I refused to believe anything else.

"If it wasn't Kee removing *Starlight* from the system," I said slowly, thinking it through, "then it was probably one of the empress's people. If it looks like the ship never landed on Rodeni, then Empress Nepru can deny all responsibility. But it means we might be running a rescue in addition to an assassination slash abduction." I leveled a glare at Nilo. "Are you hiding any *other* information I should know?"

His eyes flashed, and he growled, "Not all secrets are safe to share."

My temper woke. I wasn't stupid, and I wasn't untrustworthy, and I didn't appreciate the insinuation that I was *both*. "Thank you for teaching me such a valuable lesson," I said, my voice perfectly flat. "I had no idea."

Nilo ran a frustrated hand through his hair. "Lexi, I'm sorry, I didn't mean—"

"You meant exactly what you said," I cut in. "Let me know if you hear from anyone on the ship." I turned to my comm without waiting for a response.

It was so easy to forget that Nilo was still the same man who'd smiled and flirted and cajoled me into meeting him at the hotel bar for a date, then stood me up to go steal my job with Lady Ottiz. And he hadn't even had the courtesy to return and tell me the truth. No, I'd learned it from Lady Ottiz herself, another humiliation.

And despite everything, I'd still fallen into bed with him. Maybe I *was* stupid after all.

With nothing else to do, I went back to the data on Aburwuk. Unfortunately, it was clear that I wouldn't be able to get in unnoticed without Nilo's help. I tipped my head to the side—unless I *wanted* to get caught. If I thought getting caught would lead me to Tavi or Morten, I might potentially risk it. But I would have to be sure that they had Tavi, or I would just turn myself into a liability.

Still, I would do whatever it took to rescue the captain. She was the reason I'd survived the war, and I owed her more than I could ever repay.

NILO APOLOGIZED FOR SNAPPING AT ME BY TELEPORTING US SOME real food from the galley, thanks to a telepathic conversation with the captain. I forgave him since I could feel his stress and worry compounding my own. Neither of us were at our best right now.

As we neared the wormhole, anxious energy bled through from Nilo's side of our mental connection. A glance revealed he was sitting on the crate, staring at his comm, but there was a tightness around his eyes that hadn't been there earlier, even after the bad news about *Starlight*. "Are you okay?"

"It's the field around the wormhole," he said. "I'll be better once we're through."

"How did Valoffs ever learn to traverse the wormholes if you all react like this?"

"Carefully," he said with a laugh. "The first anchor existed before our recorded history, so it was just a matter of gaining space travel and sending something through to see what happened. Otherwise, we might've never left our little solar system."

I blinked at him in stunned disbelief. "Wait, *what*?"

It was his turn to blink. "I thought the FHP knew this. It's not a secret."

I shook my head. "We were never taught that. I thought you built yours with experimentation, like we did. Or, if you believe some of the crazier conspiracies, that you stole the technology from us."

"We didn't know about humans until you showed up on our doorstep."

A short alarm rang through the ship. "Wormhole traversal in three minutes," a generated voice said in Valovan. It repeated the message in a few other Valovian dialects I didn't understand then fell silent.

Nilo's knuckles whitened as he clutched his comm. I closed my eyes and focused on one of my favorite memories. My moms had taken me to see the aurora when I was little. The memory was old and faded at the edges, but I would never forget the wonder I'd felt as I looked up into a sky filled with brilliant, glowing light.

"What are you thinking about?" Nilo asked softly.

I steeled myself. "See for yourself."

The feeling of coolness increased a little, but I fought to hold on to the wonder of a sky filled with light. "What is this?" Nilo asked in a reverent whisper.

"The aurora on my home planet. My moms took me when I was young. It was one of the last trips we made before they died." Sorrow rose, but I pushed it back. This was for Nilo.

The engines ramped up, then time stretched and thinned, and even in this windowless room I knew that we'd pierced the plane of the anchor. Nilo's anxiety rose, and I focused on the wonder I'd felt at the changing colors from that night long ago.

The ship shuddered, then we were through. A moment later, Nilo blew out a slow breath. "Thank you, *taro,*" he murmured. His presence in my head dimmed.

"You're welcome."

Now that the wormhole was behind us, we were only six hours from Rodeni, and messages should arrive in a matter of minutes rather than hours. I still didn't have anything from Tavi, but I could start searching for *Starlight*.

I couldn't connect to the ship directly, which didn't surprise me—Kee would've locked everything down before entering Valovian space. But I checked anyway, just in case she'd tried to send me a message that way.

But no matter how much I searched and how deeply I delved into the conspiracy parts of the net, there was no news of *Starlight,* an attacked ship, or any abnormal lights in the sky that might even *indicate* an attack. It truly was like the ship had disappeared into thin air.

Which was impossible, and yet.

The most logical explanation was that they'd been captured by the Valovian military, but that didn't tell me where they'd ended up. Aburwuk would be the clear choice, which meant they might *not* be there. I sighed and rubbed my eyes. We were only hours away, but we still had more questions than answers.

I turned to Nilo. "How far can you teleport? Like if *Starlight* was somewhere on Rodeni, could you port to it?"

Nilo grimaced. "No, not anywhere on the planet, but if it's in Tirdenchia or Aburwuk or somewhere else nearby, then I could port to it as long as it's not shielded."

"Could you tell if it was nearby but shielded?"

"I should be able to, yes. Targets that are shielded generally feel slightly different than targets that are too far away or nonexistent."

Anxiety tightened my chest. What would we do if Nilo couldn't sense *Starlight* at all? I took a deep breath and focused on the things I could control. "Do we have somewhere to stay once we land?"

"No, not yet," Nilo said. He ran a hand through his hair,

leaving it mussed. "I'd been hoping that we could meet up with *Starlight,* but that's not an option now."

"It might be," I said, trying to keep the doubt out of my voice. "But just in case, I'll book us a room. The empress shouldn't be able to trace my new identity, so it'll be safer under my name. Have you found anything else?"

Nilo shook his head. "There's been no mention of *Starlight* in any of the communications my contact has been able to intercept, which means Empress Nepru likely suspects that there is a spy in the palace. I've told them to go dark unless something urgent comes in."

I winced. The empress probably suspected a spy because Nilo had been able to grab me from the hotel, which meant the current lack of information was my fault. I would never forgive myself if Tavi was hurt because of me.

I had to find a way into Aburwuk that wouldn't get us killed, and I had to do it before we landed.

CHAPTER FOURTEEN

As soon as we entered Rodeni's atmosphere, Nilo's power spiked. After a moment, he cursed darkly in Valovan. "I can't sense the ship or any of the crew."

Dread sank claws into my lungs, but I forced out, "Aren't we too far away?"

"Not if they're in Tirdenchia."

"What if the Valovian forces have a nullifier?"

Nilo sighed and it felt as if the weight of the world was in that one exhalation. "Maybe. I've never tried to teleport into a building held by a nullifier, but I expected it to feel like shielding."

I clung to that sliver of hope as I tried to contact Tavi, Kee, and Eli via comm. None of the connections went through, but if their devices had been confiscated, then I'd need to be extremely close to connect directly to their comm implants.

And that likely meant I'd have to be *inside* the Aburwuk military base.

As much as I wanted to storm the gates as soon as we landed, we needed to balance speed and caution. Getting ourselves captured wouldn't do us any good unless it was part of a solid plan—which it might be.

Our room didn't have a screen, so I couldn't watch our approach, but Rodeni was mostly rocky and arid. The main industry was mining, though there were a few pockets of land fertile enough to grow crops. The gravity was slightly higher than Fed standard, which would feel even more so after spending time on Valovia.

Tirdenchia was in an arid part of Rodeni's southern hemisphere, close to several vital mining operations, which is why the military base had originally been built. Those mines—and the surrounding manufacturing facilities—had been a priority target for the FHP, so the city had fallen during the early part of the invasion. Aburwuk was designed to prevent history from repeating, but I felt bad for all of the working-class citizens who'd lost their homes.

The ship thumped down on the landing pad, and I stood and stretched. If nothing else, I was going to be happy to be in a room big enough for pacing. I donned my wig and glasses as we waited for the captain to give us the all-clear.

Standing in the bathroom doorway, I could *feel* Nilo's restless energy, and it ramped up my own anxiety. I no longer panicked—as much—every time I remembered he was in my head, but I was certainly looking forward to the time when it would no longer be necessary.

Nilo stood and said, "The captain is going to check if his office is clear, then we'll port out. He said it'll probably be ten to twenty minutes."

"You still trust him?"

Nilo lifted a shoulder. "As much as I ever did."

"Well that's reassuring," I muttered. I checked my weapons. "I'm ready whenever. I booked us a room in the Riv. It overlooks the base, so we should head there first."

Nilo's expression darkened. "That hotel is used by many of Empress Nepru's diplomats and spies when they visit."

"I'm aware. You'll have to keep shielding for me—sorry about that—but it's our best option for information, and if we're really, really lucky, an ID that'll get us access into the base. A few humans should also be staying there, since it's the nicest hotel in the city."

"It's dangerous," Nilo growled.

"So is going in blind. But I also booked us a second room in the shady part of the city if you would prefer to start there. It's close to Aburwuk's wall, but we would have to leave the lev crate behind because it's too nice not to become a target."

Nilo wrapped an arm around my waist and drew me close. "Don't think I don't see what you're doing," he murmured.

I subtly widened my eyes as I looked up at him, all innocence. "What do you mean?"

"You pretend that you're giving me options when, really, the only viable option is the one you want."

"Viable or not, it's still two options. It's not my fault if one is clearly better."

Nilo's lip ghosted along my jaw, not quite touching, and I clenched every muscle in an effort to stand still and not lean into the touch. Desire flared and I couldn't tell if it was his or mine.

"When you look at me with those wide, guileless eyes

while you manipulate me, it makes me want to do terrible, wicked things to you, *cho afiang ras taro,*" he murmured into my ear.

My tricky little treasure. I shivered in pleasure. None of my lovers had ever seen me so accurately—I'd never *let* them see me so clearly. And I hadn't let Nilo, either, but he seemed to see through all of my masks and schemes.

"Shall I show you?" Nilo murmured, his voice sin and temptation.

I knew it was a terrible idea with every cell in my body, but I nodded anyway. This time, the desire was from Nilo, hot and raw, but he held himself still as the image formed in my mind. I was spread across dark sheets, my arms bound by golden silk ties, and Nilo was kneeling between my bare thighs.

My breath hitched. I hadn't expected a shared daydream, or whatever this was, but at my hesitation, the vision vanished.

"Wait," I protested. My fingers clenched in his shirt, and I realized we were still pressed dangerously close. "Show me."

"Are you sure?"

When I nodded, the vision reappeared, and I closed my eyes and let myself fall into the daydream. I tested the silk around my wrists. It was tight, but not uncomfortable. I instinctively knew that I could undo it with a thought, but I left it.

As connected as we were, I could feel Nilo's reverence as he smoothed a hand up my inner thigh, teasing and worshipping in equal measure. He paused before he reached the apex, and he must've felt my frustration because he chuckled darkly.

"How long could I keep you here, balanced on the edge of pleasure, before you'd beg me, *taro*?" His voice stroked over me. "Minutes?" His fingers crept higher, and we both groaned. "Hours?"

"I think you're overestimating my patience," I murmured. I glanced at him from under my lashes. "Perhaps you'd like to find a better use for your mouth, hmm?"

His eyes glowed gold, but he just stroked me with a single finger. Sparks of pleasure jolted through me, but I needed more. I arched my hips, but Nilo's other hand pinned me down as he kept up the light, tantalizing stroke.

I tried to reach for him, but the silken bonds wouldn't let me, and undoing them felt like cheating. Desire burned away everything except for each tiny movement of his finger. I knew what he wanted, and I gritted my teeth against the urge to give in.

"So stubborn," he murmured. "Is it so hard to ask for what you want?"

Unexpected tears gathered as his words pierced a soft, hidden part of me, and the vision wavered. I opened my eyes to reality and found Nilo looking down at me with a mixture of fierce hunger and gentle understanding. My body was hot and needy, but it was my heart that cracked open.

All of the feelings I'd been trying to suppress made a break for freedom, but Nilo was in my head. Panic joined the maelstrom, and I mentally floundered, trying to shield and suppress at the same time.

"Shh, Lexi," he whispered, running a calming hand down my back. "I will take care of you—if you still want me to?"

My mind might be a mess, but my body was still wound tight. I let his calm bleed into me, then I burrowed my head against his shoulder and dipped my chin. The movement was tiny, but a moment later, the vision returned.

Nilo ran his palms over my legs, stomach, and breasts, slowly building the desire back up to a fever pitch with nothing but touch. And when I was once again burning, he slid two fingers into me while his thumb worked magic, and I tipped over the edge into endless waves of pleasure.

I came back to myself with my head on Nilo's shoulder and my eyes leaking tears. My body quivered with the aftershocks of a stellar orgasm, but I also felt calmer and more grounded. I'd needed the release, both physical and emotional, even if it had been mostly in my mind.

Maybe *especially* because it had been in my mind.

"Thank you," I whispered, wiping my eyes.

Nilo's arms tightened around me. "You're welcome."

I felt a cool spike of power, then he handed me the box of tissues that had been in the bathroom. I accepted them with a watery laugh. "I could've walked the necessary three steps, but thank you."

I wiped my eyes and blew my nose, then used the excuse of returning the tissues to take a moment to rebuild the walls that Nilo had so easily shattered. After my parents died, I'd learned several harsh lessons about what happened when I asked for things I wanted or needed, so eventually I'd stopped *asking* and started *taking*—but only things, never people.

I was a thief, not a monster.

Tavi might've broken me of most of my sticky-fingered habits, but asking for things I needed was still very difficult, and I had no idea how Nilo had figured it out. I felt exposed and vulnerable. My first instinct was to lash out, but I curbed it—barely.

I took another deep breath, then returned to the main room. Rather than hovering awkwardly in the doorway, I stepped closer to Nilo with an easy smile that was only half fake.

If he noticed the mask, he didn't call me on it. "The captain has cleared us to leave. We'll port to his office, then take the service elevator down to the street. I've ordered a transport to meet us."

"Did you try finding *Starlight* and the crew again?"

Nilo's mouth flattened. "I've *kept* trying, but I can't sense them."

I breathed through the spike of fear. Tavi was fine—I just had to find her. And I couldn't do that while trapped in this tiny room, so I gathered my things, then lifted my coat's hood carefully over my wig. I pulled the hood low over my forehead, and Nilo did the same. Rodeni's outdoor temperature was cool enough that most people would be wearing coats.

Once we were ready, Nilo set the crate to hover, then wrapped an arm around my waist. His power rose in a cold wave, and a heartbeat later, we were in the captain's office.

I was so happy to be out of the smuggler's room that I barely noticed the dizzying effects of the teleport. The office was dim, with the only light coming in from the high, narrow windows along one wall. A neat desk sat facing the closed door, but the rest of the office was sparsely furnished, with a large open space in the middle—where we'd landed—and I wondered if it had been left that way specifically for teleporters.

Nilo crossed the room to the door while I checked my weapons. He might trust the captain, but I preferred to be ready to fight, just in case. Nilo cracked the door open and peeked out. He didn't immediately jerk back, so I guided the lev crate closer.

"The hallway is clear," he said, "and I can't sense anyone nearby. The elevator is just to our right."

The key to going unchallenged was to look like you belonged, so Nilo and I strode from the office with casual confidence, but we kept our hoods low. I hadn't seen any evidence of surveillance cameras, but there was no reason to get caught because I'd been overconfident.

The elevator delivered us to the ground floor with swift efficiency, then opened into a room full of chaos. This was clearly an unloading and staging area for the ship's cargo, and people, crates, and boxes were everywhere. The nearest employee didn't look at us as she slowly maneuvered a tall stack of crates between us and the rest of the room.

At least our ridiculous ticket fee was being put to good use, and it was clearly not this captain's first time smuggling people who didn't want to be seen. Nilo and I exited the building without talking to a single person, and as expected, a transport was waiting for us outside.

Private landing pads had the benefit of public street entrances, so customers could easily come and go. It was one of the main perks of renting a permanent dock. It was also nearly a requirement for any captain who wanted to run a smuggling business in addition to legitimate passengers and cargo, because it was far easier to slip away from here than it would've been from the middle of the spaceport.

We loaded the crate into the transport then climbed in after it. I set the destination to a hotel three blocks from the fancy hotel I'd booked, and the transport lifted into the air.

Nilo checked the destination then leveled a glare at me. "What are you planning?"

Transports were rife with surveillance, so I thought as loudly as possible, "I'm going to change clothes, then head to the Riv alone. Once I'm in the room, you can port in with the crate."

His jaw clenched, but to his credit, he didn't immediately start yelling. "Why?" he responded telepathically.

"Because the empress will be looking for both of us, especially if her people track us as far as the ship. You can shield my mind from two blocks away, right?"

"I can, but I'm not going to, because you're not going alone. For all we know, the hotel could be filled with imperial guards, and I can't port you out from that far away."

I doubted it would be *filled* with guards, but if the empress was smart—and she was—then stashing a guard or two in the Riv's lobby to watch for new guests wasn't a bad idea. Especially when she seemingly had an endless supply of people ready and willing to do her bidding.

"Fine," I allowed. "What's your plan, then?" Nilo's eyes narrowed in suspicion, and I suppressed my smile. I could be reasonable—*occasionally*.

"If it were up to me, we'd skip the Riv entirely, but you made a valid point about the type of people who frequent it. There is a secret teleport target on the roof that allows the empress's spies to arrive stealthily, but then we'll have to override the security on the door because normal hotel keys won't open it." His grin was full of mischief. "Feel like a challenge?"

My smile matched his. "Always."

BETWEEN THE WAR AND THE MILITARY BASE EXPANSION, TIRDENchia looked like two different cities that had been stitched together. Near the spaceport, some areas remained nothing but piles of rubble, and even the buildings that had survived still bore scars from the fighting.

Farther south, the reconstructed factories were the only buildings that weren't rubble, and a ramshackle city had grown from around them all the way to Aburwuk's southern wall. Our second hotel room was on the edge of that area, but for now, we headed toward the rebuilt part of the city that was clustered around the military base's main entrance.

Tirdenchia's central buildings weren't that tall, only about a dozen stories, but they were either all new or extensively repaired, shining glass monoliths surrounded by a sea of rubble. The wealthy businesses had rebuilt their haven and left everyone else to fend for themselves.

Beside me, Nilo was tense and quiet. His power rose and fell in waves as he searched for *Starlight* and the crew, but with every failure, his jaw clenched tighter, and my worry ramped higher.

As we approached our destination, Nilo reached for my arm. "Ready?"

"We're not going to land first?"

"No need."

I bit down on the questions and murmured my agreement. Nilo's power rose, and he teleported us and the crate directly to the roof of the Riv. Nilo caught me as I stumbled. I hadn't expected to arrive standing, but it was certainly a neat trick. And I wasn't sure if I was getting used to the effects of teleportation or if having Nilo in my head made it easier, but my stomach only flipped once before settling.

We were in a partially enclosed concrete room big enough that we could've brought two more crates of the same size. Behind us, a large, open doorway led out to the flat roof, but my attention was on the locked door in front of us. It was our ticket into the building, just as soon as I overrode the lock. There was no physical keyhole, so picking the lock—the easiest method of entry—wasn't an option.

"Do you think they'll notice if we kick the door in?" I asked. It was often the second easiest method of entry, if not the subtlest.

"I think they might," Nilo said drily.

I sighed dramatically. "I guess I'll do it the hard way then."

I held my comm to the control panel and set it to cycle through all of the standard override codes I'd found during my research of Valovian systems. The first step of any decent security setup was changing the codes, but people were lazy. This trick worked on private residences better than public buildings, which usually had better security, but it was always my starting point.

The control panel beeped and the door unlocked.

I blinked at it stupidly for a second before trying the handle. It turned easily under my hand. "They need to fire their security company," I muttered, then tipped my head to the side in consideration. "Unless it's a trap, of course. That would be pretty clever."

I waited to see if my internal intuition had anything to add, but my instincts remained quiet. That didn't mean it was safe, but nothing would be gained by standing here, either.

Nilo's hand on my arm stopped me from opening the door. "Why do you think it might be a trap?"

"The default override code worked, which any competent security company would have disabled on installation.

But if someone wanted us inside without making it seem *too* easy, temporarily reenabling the code would be one way to do it." I shrugged. "Or they might just be incompetent. Do you sense anyone nearby?"

He shook his head. The wide door opened outward, so I cracked it open, then used the camera on my comm to peek inside. The interior room was empty, and there were no cameras that I could see. Either some very shady people were regularly using this hotel and didn't want to be seen or hotel security truly *was* terrible.

There was no elevator, but a spacious set of stairs led downward. I'd booked a penthouse suite, so we should only have to go down this one flight of stairs to get to our room. The expense had stung, but the suite had the best view of Aburwuk. The proximity to the roof had also been a consideration. I hadn't known about the teleport location, but a handy exit was always welcome.

I crept down the stairs while Nilo followed with the crate. I used the same override code trick to open the door that led into the main part of the hotel. The hallway was elegantly understated, with polished floors and genuine art on the walls. I knew from studying the hotel layout that the hall was a square wrapped around the central core of the building. There were no windows—those were all in the suites—but careful lighting kept the space from feeling claustrophobic.

This side of the building only had three suites and ours was the one in the middle. I opened the door with the digital key I'd been sent after booking, and Nilo and I eased inside. No one jumped out of the coat closet, so we were off to a good start.

"I'm going to check the other rooms," Nilo murmured in

my mind before moving toward the bedroom on the right. The suite had two bedrooms connected by a large area that was a combination of living room, dining room, and kitchenette. The dining table was a huge slab of quartz balanced on delicate-looking metal legs, and it could seat ten—for all those fancy dinner parties we'd be hosting.

Beyond the table was the main draw of this suite, at least for me: a wide balcony that directly overlooked Aburwuk. I doubted we were high enough to bypass the teleporter shielding, but we'd at least be able to get the lay of the land. And fly a drone or two over the wall to see if we could find anything interesting.

Nilo crossed to the other bedroom while I started searching for surveillance devices with my comm. The suite was surprisingly clean, so much so that I widened the search and tried again. Nothing.

A trickle of unease drifted down my spine. Either we'd successfully flown under the radar and the empress didn't know we were here, or she *did* and her people were doing their absolute best to make us feel as comfortable as possible.

I opened our crate and dug through my stuff until I found the door bar and touch-sensitive alarm. The bar would physically prevent the door from opening and the alarm would let me know if anyone touched the handle. It only took me a minute to set everything up, then I turned my attention to the balcony doors, which would be a little more difficult to secure.

Nilo had thrown the doors wide and was standing outside against the railing. The days on Rodeni were nearly thirty hours long, and the sun was high in the sky, bathing Nilo in bright golden light. He'd left his coat inside, a risk

I hoped he understood, and his dark hair gleamed against his pale blue shirt.

He was still shielding for me, so I didn't let my gaze linger as I joined him on the balcony. The surrounding buildings were shorter, giving us a nearly unobstructed view of Aburwuk's main gate.

"Excellent choice," Nilo said as I drew near.

"Can you teleport in from here?"

He shook his head. "Everything I can see is shielded. We'll need to go higher."

Most of the buildings on the base were only a few stories tall, including several sets of barracks and housing. Estimates varied, but it was safe to assume that somewhere between ten and fifteen thousand soldiers were stationed at Aburwuk, making it the primary defensive base in the sector.

We certainly couldn't defeat that many soldiers, but we wouldn't have to because the size worked in our favor. Once we were inside, it would be easy to blend in.

And I knew just where to start.

CHAPTER FIFTEEN

I changed my wig to a sleek black bob that made my pale skin even paler. My dress was black and unadorned, just a tight sheath that showed my body to its best advantage. I could still hear Nilo pacing and muttering in the other room, but I tuned him out.

He might not like it, but hitting up a hotel bar was always an excellent source of information—it was how we'd met, after all. I winced at the memory as I carefully applied my makeup.

As much as I wanted to storm the base and find Tavi right this second, we *needed* information. Normal soldiers probably wouldn't frequent the Riv's bar—it was too expensive—but officers or other officials might, and they had the kind of access we needed.

And it wasn't like I was *happy* to be leaving Nilo behind. With his charming personality and incredible good looks, he would've had the room eating out of his hand, making my job easier, if only he wasn't so damn easy to recognize. I could alter my looks with hair, makeup, and accessories, but Nilo hadn't brought anything to change his appearance because it wasn't something he was used to doing.

I perched a pair of oversize cat-eye glasses on my nose and checked the mirror. I looked stylish and sophisticated and just a little bored. Careful contouring made my nose look wider and my face look rounder. It was subtle, but it was enough to throw off people who might be looking for me based on a recent photo.

When I exited the bedroom, Nilo stopped pacing to stare at me. Gold lightning streaked across the green of his eyes, and his hands clenched. Worry and longing and desire spilled through the connection before he caught my expression and locked it down.

"I don't like this plan," he growled.

"I know."

"I'm going down with you." He held up a hand to forestall my argument. "I'll stay out of sight, but I'm not staying up here where I can't get to you if you need help quickly."

"Couldn't you just pop in?"

"Maybe, but I'm not risking your safety on a maybe."

Warmth spread through my chest, and I dipped my head. "Thank you."

"Do you have a weapon?"

I grinned and slowly raised my hem until the bottom of the plas knife was visible, high on my thigh. Nilo's eyes went more gold, but he didn't get distracted. "Is that the only one?"

"I have a pistol in my clutch and another knife on the other thigh. I'll be fine."

"You know what it feels like when I'm about to teleport. If you feel something like that, don't let the teleporter touch you. Most won't be strong enough to teleport you without touching. And I'll continue shielding your mind. Mentally shout if you need help."

"Nilo, I'll be fine."

He ran a hand through his hair. "I know. But I still hate sending you into potential danger."

I smiled. "Don't think of me as in danger, think of me as *dangerous*."

THE BAR WAS AS ELEGANT AS THE REST OF THE HOTEL, WITH PLENTY of private tables under softly flickering lights. The high windows were heavily tinted, so the bright sun was muted into a warm glow.

A quick glance revealed two couples, three single men, and a single woman. I couldn't discern who was human and who was Valoff because most of the obvious tells required proximity or movement.

"The older couple is human," Nilo whispered into my mind, "as is the blond man." We'd agreed to keep communication to a minimum unless required, but knowing more about my potential targets was useful.

"Thank you," I thought back.

The humans might be more likely to chat, but they were less likely to have any access to Aburwuk, so I focused on the Valoffs. The woman was working on a slate, a forgotten drink at her side. She would not welcome a distraction.

That left two men: one younger than me and one a few years older. They both looked up when I entered, and they both checked out my figure, though the older man was far more subtle about it.

Neither of them set off my instincts, so I pretended not to see them and headed straight for a seat at the bar. I ordered a glass of wine and waited.

It didn't take long.

The younger man approached first. He had golden tan skin, and his dark hair was cut short, possibly military. He wasn't wearing a wedding ring, but I didn't know enough about Valovian wedding customs to know if rings were normal or not. He was young, in his mid- to late twenties, which meant he probably didn't have the level of access I needed. Still, I'd let him try.

"May I buy your drink?" he asked in accented Common.

I smiled at him and subtly—but not *too* subtly—checked him out. He was handsome and well built, but I didn't feel any particular attraction to him. "No, but I wouldn't mind company. I'm May." The name wasn't tied to any of the identities I'd used.

"I'm Rumus. It's a pleasure to meet you." He slid onto the barstool next to me with an eagerness that told me either he *was* attracted or he just was just desperate to hook up. Maybe both.

"What brings you to Rodeni?" he asked.

I wrinkled my nose. "Business, I'm afraid. I arrived a few days ago, but I've been so busy that this is my first chance to take a break. What about you?"

"I work on the base. I'm enjoying a day off."

I widened my eyes and leaned close enough that he could look straight down my dress—which he did. "So you're a soldier?" I whispered with a touch of awe. "I bet that's . . . *hard*."

Rumus actually flushed, his cheeks turning an adorable pink. Oh, I could just eat him up, and he would let me. "Not a soldier," he clarified, one hand rubbing his neck in embarrassment. "Just a tech."

My instincts whispered a warning. A tech who worked on the base was *too* easy, and I knew a trap when I spotted one. Still, I kept my expression open and interested. "A tech? So you work in a lab?"

He leaned in. "I work on the security systems."

The feeling of unease grew, but I merely wrinkled my nose and turned to my wineglass. "Then you must work with my competitor's system. I shouldn't be talking to you."

Rumus frowned in confusion. He must've expected me to press him for details, assuming he knew who I was. Or he was fishing, and I hadn't played by the script he'd expected. Either way, he wasn't just here to pick up a beautiful woman, but he also wasn't a trained spy. Interesting.

My comm was set to clone any nearby devices—a highly specialized, highly illegal mod that Kee had helped me with—but I needed to be within a meter or so of the target device. He was close enough, so I would have a clone of his comm, including his access keys, but if he was a plant, then using his access once we were in the base would bring the guards down on us.

I needed to get rid of him—and quickly.

"We don't have to talk about work," Rumus said with a smile. "Tell me about yourself."

He practically *radiated* trustworthiness, and I barely stopped myself from confessing everything to him. That was *not normal*. I rarely confessed to people I *loved*. Something was wrong.

"He's an empath," Nilo whispered urgently in my mind. "I'll need to strengthen the shield to block his influence."

My anxiety spiked then melted away, which was fucking terrifying, but I couldn't quite hold on to that emotion, either. "Do it," I silently demanded.

The coolness in the back of my mind increased, and I no longer felt like spilling my guts to the Valoff sitting next to me. Now spilling *his* guts . . . that was still on the table.

But I was an expert at masking my emotions when they weren't being intentionally manipulated, so I gave Rumus a conspiratorial smile. "Can I tell you a secret?"

He leaned closer and I felt a cool wave of power wash over me, but Nilo's shield held. "Of course."

"I hate my job," I whispered. "I don't want to sell security systems to stuffy military people. I want to *sing*." I pouted prettily at him. "Is that strange?"

Once again, confusion crossed his face, then he shook his head and smiled. "That's not strange at all. But I don't want to get you in trouble with your superiors. Enjoy your drink."

Rumus got up and returned to his original seat. Either he'd bought my lie, or they weren't going to pick me up immediately. Leaving would be more suspicious than staying, so I sipped my wine and checked out the other people in the bar.

The older Valoff had sandy brown hair that was graying at the temples and deeply tanned skin. He finished his drink, then glanced at me. I smiled and tipped my head in invitation. He stood and crossed the room with unhurried steps.

If Rumus had been all eager youth, this man was all cool sophistication, from the rich fabric of his navy tunic to the perfect wave of his hair. It remained to be seen if he was round two of the interrogation, but as long as I could keep him close for a minute or two, I'd have a clone of his comm access codes.

Rather than taking Rumus's vacated seat, the unnamed man leaned against the bar, far enough away to be respectful, but close enough to show interest. He was smooth, I'd give him that.

"May I join you?" he asked in Valovan.

I raised my glass. "Until my wine is gone." I glanced at him from under my lashes. "Then we'll see."

He slid onto the adjacent barstool with a smile that didn't quite reach his eyes. "Then I'd better make myself interesting quickly."

I silently wished him good luck, and Nilo's amusement drifted through our connection. I'd much rather be sharing a glass of wine with Nilo than this man who hadn't even bothered to introduce himself, but we still needed information.

"I'll buy you a whole bottle, *taro,* once we're done here," Nilo whispered telepathically.

The man next to me ordered a drink, then turned back to me. "You have quite the interesting mental shield."

"It's designed to keep unpleasant people out," I said, my voice no less pointed for its softness.

"So you are aware a Valoff is shielding for you," he murmured. "I'd wondered." He glanced around. "Where are they?" Before I could lie, he waved the question away. "Doesn't matter. I was here first. Go hunt somewhere else."

Ah, so I wasn't the only grifter in the bar, but I merely raised an eyebrow. "I don't know what you mean. I'm just here for a drink."

"Then once it's gone, you will have no reason to stay. Let me help you out." He picked up my glass and drained it.

My smile sharpened. I would've told him that I was no threat out of professional courtesy if he'd *asked* instead of demanding, but now he'd annoyed me. I let my annoyance grow, along with a healthy amount of fear and anxiety. I leaned away from him and darted my gaze around the room, searching for an escape.

I locked eyes with Rumus, and the younger Valoff frowned as he caught the edge of my emotions. I dropped my eyes and slid from my chair, hurrying toward the exit. As expected, Rumus followed me.

"Wait, May, are you okay?"

I shook my head and dabbed at my eyes. "That horrible man was accusing me of all sorts of things. He claimed another Valoff was shielding for me, just because my company had a Valovian instructor teach me how to build proper mental defenses. Then he told me to 'hunt' somewhere else—I don't even know what that means—and he threatened me after he drank my drink." I shuddered for effect and kept my emotions high. "I just wanted a nice afternoon off," I lamented, sniffing miserably.

"Don't worry. I'll take care of it," Rumus promised. "Do you want me to help you back to your room?"

I didn't know if he was trying to affect my emotions thanks to Nilo's shield, but I slowly let my anxiety bleed away. "No, thank you. You're sweet, but I think I need to be alone for a while. Will you be here tomorrow?"

He shook his head. "I work tomorrow."

"Well, if you get off early, let me know." I fished a card out of the side pocket of my clutch and handed it to him. The only thing on it was a comm address. If he looked it up, it would lead to an anonymous message service that many people used when they wanted to keep their actual addresses private—one that very specifically did not keep any logs.

He took the card with a smile. "I will. How long are you in town?"

"Just a few more days, unless we get the contract, then maybe a month." I leaned in. "Personally, I'm hoping it falls through because then I'll get to go home for a few weeks. But don't tell my boss."

Rumus laughed. "Your secret is safe with me."

I HEADED TO THE ELEVATOR WHILE RUMUS RETURNED TO THE BAR. I hoped I'd sown enough seeds of doubt that if the grifter tried to out me, Rumus wouldn't believe him. I'd also learned a few interesting things, though none of them were good news.

"I'll meet you in the room," Nilo said telepathically.

"Where are you?"

"Near the bar. I'm going to see what your empath does when he returns."

"Be careful."

"You, too," he said, then he went silent.

The penthouse elevator was empty when it arrived, and no one else was waiting. I stepped inside and let it whisk me upward. None of the cameras I'd set up in the suite had gone off, but that didn't *necessarily* mean the room was still safe.

If the empress already had people sniffing around the hotel, then we'd have to move sooner than I would've liked, especially since Nilo hadn't had any luck finding *Starlight* or the crew.

The elevator door opened. I listened for a moment before stepping out into the empty hallway. Now would be an excellent time to snoop in some of the other rooms. It was midafternoon, so most people would likely be out. If they weren't, then I could feign drunkenness.

I held a hand to my head and stumbled into the nearest door. I let my head thump against the surface, and the knock echoed into the room beyond.

Nothing stirred inside.

It was a moment's work to pick the lock, while looking like I was just fiddling with the handle. The door opened and I stumbled inside. "Riccardo, I'm back," I trilled.

Only silence answered, but a quick scan showed that it was because the suite was currently unoccupied. I returned to the hall and found two more empty suites before the fourth suite returned a result.

Unfortunately, that result was someone yanking open the door while I was leaning against it, which overbalanced me. I fell backward into the room before an invisible force clamped around my body.

Cold terror whited out my thoughts, and Nilo demanded, "What's wrong?"

His voice in my mind was enough to jolt me back to myself. "Telekinetic. Not a fight. I'll shout if I need help."

The telekinetic set me back on my feet and let me go. "Can I help you?" a brusque female voice asked in Valovan.

A brusque, *familiar* female voice.

Tavi's message had included all of the information Kee had pulled on Sura Fev, the Sun Guardian, including footage of their fight on Odyssey. This was the woman who'd nearly killed Tavi and who'd used Kee as a shield. Fev was in the fucking hotel, just around the corner from our own suite. I wanted to turn and stab her with every cell in my body, but I'd never connect. She'd kill me before I touched her.

"Fev is here?" Nilo demanded, his mental voice icily calm.

My thoughts were bleeding through our connection, but I had bigger problems right now. "Yes. Stay off our floor," I thought back, then I half turned to Fev, hiding my face behind the waterfall of my black bob. "What're you doing in my room?" I slurred in Common. "How'd you open my door?"

"You must be mistaken," she replied in unaccented Common.

"Noooo, I'm in two-two . . . two . . . two?" I counted on my fingers, staring at them as a reason to keep my face averted. "How many twos is that?"

"Useless human," she muttered in Valovan before switching back to Common. "Twenty-*one*-twenty-two is down the hall. Twenty-two-twenty-two doesn't exist. This room is neither."

"Are you sure?" I squinted up at her through my hair, confirming her identity. "My room has this same tile."

"*Every* room has this tile," she ground out.

"Oh." I waved a hand. "Sorry." I giggled and whispered, "I had wine with lunch. I think it went to my head."

Sura said nothing, so I teetered out of her room, one hand on the wall, the other wrapped around my clutch with a white-knuckled grip. If she stopped me, I *might* have enough time to draw my pistol before she crushed me.

Her door clicked closed, but I didn't dare turn around to see if I was alone. There was absolutely no way that she wouldn't have recognized me if she was expecting me to be in the hotel. My hair might be different, but that wouldn't be enough to fool someone trained in protection. And if one of the empress's personal guards didn't know I was here, then neither did Rumus.

So who the fuck had *he* been expecting?

The question plagued me all the way back to the suite. Rumus had definitely set off my instincts, but if he hadn't been searching for me, then his ID would still be useful. So would Sura Fev's, assuming she'd had her comm on her.

Nilo yanked the door open as soon as the control panel beeped. "Are you okay?" he demanded. He pulled me inside without waiting for an answer, then closed and bolted the door behind me.

"I lost several years off my life, but otherwise, yes."

"You're sure it's Fev?" His jaw was clenched, as if he expected the telekinetic to appear at any moment—and maybe he did.

"Yes. How do we use this?"

"We don't. We need to leave, *now*."

"But she knows where Tavi—"

"What do you think is going to happen when she realizes that we're on-planet? She's going to immediately check the hotel registrations, if not the rooms themselves."

He wasn't wrong, dammit. The information we needed was tantalizingly close, but getting it would be incredibly dangerous. And as much as I thrived on danger, taking on a telekinetic without backup was a little *too* dangerous, even for me.

"No luck finding the crew or the ship?"

Nilo silently shook his head, and despair tried to drag me under. What if Tavi really *was* gone, and I hadn't gotten to say good-bye? Pain sliced through me at the thought of never again seeing the captain sitting on the bridge with

Luna curled up in her lap, or Kee's sunny smile, or Eli's stupidly handsome face. Did they know how much I loved them, despite the fact that I was terrible at admitting it? I would even miss Luna's incessant demands for food. For all of our grumbling about it, the whole crew adored that mischievous little fluff ball.

Wait . . .

"What about Luna?" I asked, mind racing. "Could you find her? She's probably still in the ship unless Tavi was worried about her being caught." I swallowed. "And if something happened to the ship, maybe she escaped."

Nilo tipped his head in thought, then frowned in concentration. "Maybe," he murmured. His eyes went distant as the frown deepened.

I paced as Nilo searched. It was that or pepper him with a million questions, none of which would help him find the little burbu. Tavi wouldn't release Luna unless things were truly dire, but if we could find the burbu then we'd at least know that Tavi had made it to the ground.

And I desperately needed that reassurance.

My hope began to wane as the minutes dragged on. I couldn't feel any change in Nilo's power, but sweat broke out on his forehead and he grimaced.

"Can I do anything to help?" I asked.

He silently shook his head. The color slowly bled from his face, leaving him pale and clammy. Just as I was about to tell him to stop before he hurt himself, his frown disappeared, and he gave me a weary, triumphant grin.

"I found her."

CHAPTER SIXTEEN

Relief overwhelmed me. If Luna was alive, then Tavi had made it to the planet. It didn't explain why *Starlight* had disappeared from all of the tracking systems, but at least it wasn't a million particles floating in space.

"Where is Luna?" I asked.

Nilo sighed. "My connection to her is faint, and communicating with a burbu isn't as straightforward as communicating with a person," he said. "Most barely know how to communicate at all. Because Luna has spent so much time with Tavi and the crew, she's a little better, but it's still not much."

"Can you find her? Is she in the ship?"

"I can sense her, but it's not a precise location. She's that way"—he waved an arm toward the base—"but I'm not sure how far. I'm trying to teach her how to share a picture of where she is, but mostly I'm getting images of her empty food bowl."

I smiled despite myself. Tavi fiercely loved the fluffy little burbu and spoiled her rotten, but Luna still demanded that her food bowl be full at all times or it was clearly a disaster. At least that much hadn't changed.

"She is . . . outside," Nilo said after a few more minutes. "She must be on the base, because I can't teleport to her."

"The soldiers won't hurt her, will they?"

Nilo shook his head. "Burbus are protected. If someone sees her, they will be far more likely to feed her than hurt her."

That was one less thing for us to worry about. Tavi would be inconsolable if anything happened to Luna—as would Eli, Kee, and I. Luna had been our companion for years, so losing her would be like losing part of the crew. If she was out of the ship, then we'd have to find her before we made our great escape.

But first we had to find a way *into* the base.

"Are you feeling well enough to go do some recon?" I asked Nilo.

He gave me a slow smile. "If you would like a demonstration of my stamina, *taro,* then I would be happy to assist."

I grinned at him and shook my head wryly. "I don't know about stamina, but you certainly have arrogance in spades."

He bowed slightly, his left arm across his chest. "Telepathy isn't my strongest skill, but I can still teleport us out of danger if needed. I would not put your safety at risk, not even to find Tavi's treasured pet."

Nilo was rarely serious, but when he was, he was *deadly* serious. I stepped closer until he met my eyes. "I don't doubt your skill," I said, my voice soft and sincere. "Thank you for looking out for me."

He pulled me closer, wrapping his arms around my back. "When I felt your terror, I wanted to tear down the building," he whispered into my hair.

"After I got over the initial shock, you have no idea how much restraint it took not to turn around and stab her."

His arms tightened. "I'm glad you didn't attempt it. I've sparred with Torran enough to know that fighting a telekinetic is a losing proposition."

I leaned back until I could see his face. "Can you teleport out of a telekinetic hold?"

"Yes, but it takes a lot of energy. If she caught us both, it would pretty much wipe me out to teleport us to safety, and that's assuming we were touching. I don't know if I could port you out of a telelock without touching you."

His eyes went distant and a furrow wrinkled his brow as he imagined it, so I touched his jaw, drawing his attention back to me. "Don't borrow trouble. Fev didn't recognize me. I'm okay."

"You got lucky."

"*So* lucky," I agreed easily. That seemed to throw him, and I laughed. "Nilo, I'm not afraid to admit that a telekinetic would kick my ass. I have many surprising, delightful skills, but winning a fight against a highly trained telekinetic Sun Guardian isn't one of them."

"Surprising and delightful, hmm? Do tell."

I slid my hand along his jaw, angling his head toward mine, and hunger filled his expression. I tipped my head up and whispered, "If I told you, it wouldn't be a surprise."

His lips covered mine, and I groaned my approval. When I'd been sitting in the bar, flirting with another man, the only thing I'd wanted was to get back to Nilo. He was liable to break my heart, but the longer I spent with him, the less I cared.

I would rather have the experience *and* the heartbreak than not have him at all.

Desire shivered through our connection as I licked his bottom lip, and I gave myself over to the feeling. I clutched Nilo's shoulders and plastered myself against him. He made a low sound of pleasure that curled my toes. He tilted his head and deepened the kiss, exploring my mouth with a heated thoroughness that made my stomach clench.

When I broke the kiss to take a shuddering breath, Nilo's eyes were shades of glimmering gold. I watched, mesmerized, as the colors grew and shifted against the green of his irises in a breathtaking kaleidoscope. "Your eyes are incredible."

He smiled softly and touched a gentle finger to my cheek. "So are yours."

My hazel eyes were a mixture of brown and green and gold that *was* pretty—for a human. But they were plain in comparison to the dazzling extravagance of Nilo's eyes.

He grinned at my doubtful expression. "Shall I compliment you until you believe me? Your eyes are like looking at a hidden summer forest bathed in golden sunset."

I blinked at him in astonishment. I'd never had my eyes described so poetically before, but now every time I looked in a mirror, I would remember his voice whispering compliments in my ear. "Thank you."

He pressed a chaste kiss to my lips, then stepped back. "I suppose we need to get back to our task. You mentioned something about recon?"

I wrinkled my nose, but I knew he was right. "If we get closer to the base, can you get a better lock on Luna?"

"Maybe. It wouldn't hurt to try, and I'd like a closer look at the gate and wall."

"Sounds good. Let me change and then I'll be ready."

I CHANGED OUT OF MY DRESS AND INTO STURDY, NONDESCRIPT clothes that would let me blend in rather than stand out. I kept the wig and glasses. On our way out, I was going to stop back by the bar and see if Rumus was still lingering, because if he wasn't a trap, then he could be incredibly useful.

I strapped a full-size plas blade to my right leg, but I tucked my pistol into a pocket. Carrying a blade for protection was fairly common, but a pistol was less so—at least in this part of the city. Once we crossed over into the shanties, more visible protection would become a boon.

I returned to the main part of the suite to find Nilo standing by the balcony windows. He was outfitted in a deep green, nearly black, tunic and charcoal pants. His plas blade was in a holster on his back, as was one of the knives that he could teleport with barely a thought. He wasn't carrying any visible guns, and a close look didn't reveal any obvious hiding spots. "No gun?"

He waved to his pocket with an impish grin. "See for yourself."

Never one to back down from a challenge, especially not one delivered with such charm, I crossed the room and slid my hand into his pocket, only to pause in surprise when I met a pistol grip. The small plas pistol slid easily from his pocket. The holster was part of the design of his pants and clever tailoring kept it from being obvious.

"Is this a custom design?" When he nodded, I asked, "Do you think they could make something like this except in a dress?"

"I don't know, but I'd be happy to introduce you when we get back to Valovia."

I replaced the pistol and waved my fingers at him with a grin. "If those pants go missing this trip, I don't know anything about it."

"I have another pair you're welcome to borrow."

I considered it, then shook my head. "It wouldn't work as well for me because my hips are curvier, but the designer could probably make something else for me. Are you ready to go?"

"Yes. Do you have a destination in mind?"

"I'm going to stop by the bar and see if Rumus is still there. He was waiting for *someone* and if it wasn't me, then I'm interested to know who it was. He works on the base, so his help would be hugely beneficial, if we could get it."

"Who do you think he was meeting?"

"I don't know, but whoever it was, he was eager but cautious. I can find his contact information if I need to, but if he's still in the bar, that's even easier. Next problem: How do we get past Fev's room without accidentally running into her? Does a Sun Guardian take the stairs?"

Nilo rubbed his face. "The stairs are probably safer, but it would be saf*est* to change hotels."

I pointed out the window at Aburwuk. "I'd like to get a drone over the wall tonight, and that'll be easiest from here. After that we can move."

"You do realize I can just port us onto the roof later?" he asked in exasperation.

And truthfully, I *had* kind of forgotten. I was used to

working alone, but that needed to change and fast. "Is that wise?" I asked. "I figured you would need to conserve your strength in case we really needed it later."

"Shorter ports are easier, as is porting less stuff. Unless we're planning to infiltrate the base tonight, porting us to the roof and back won't be a problem."

I looked longingly around the luxurious suite I'd barely gotten to enjoy. I'd had plans for that ridiculous dining table that didn't involve eating—or at least, not the usual kind. I knew this wasn't a vacation, but having a safe space was important and our next hotel was going to be far, far worse.

Of course, it probably wouldn't be home to a telekinetic Sun Guardian, so it had that going for it.

"Fine," I agreed with a sigh. "We'll swap hotels, then you can port us back later tonight if we don't find a better vantage point. But that means we'll need to take the elevator because of the crate. Do you have a hat or anything to make yourself look less like"—I waved my arms at him—"you?"

"You can take the crate down in the elevator, and I'll take the stairs. If Fev spots you, I'll port you out."

I took one last, wistful look at the floor-to-ceiling windows then went to repack my stuff.

I CAUGHT RUMUS AS HE WAS LEAVING THE BAR. OR, RATHER, *HE* caught *me*. The short hallway between the bar and lobby was empty, giving us a hint of privacy. "I thought you were staying for a while longer?" he asked, glancing questioningly at the crate at my side. Nilo was lurking somewhere nearby, but I mentally told him to hang back.

I lifted one shoulder in a half-hearted shrug. "Change

of plans. What about you? Did you meet the person you were waiting for?"

He tensed and looked adorably wary. "Who said I was waiting for someone?"

"Weren't you?"

His eyes slid away from mine. "Of course not."

"My mistake. Well, it was nice to meet you, Rumus."

His shoulders slumped, and he admitted, "My name isn't really Rumus."

I leaned in with a smile. "Funny, because my name isn't really May."

He gaped at me for a moment, then stared at my face. Adrenaline danced along my nerves. This was a big gamble. If he really was working for the empress, then I'd just handed my presence to her on a silver platter. I didn't doubt that I could elude the man in front of me, but escaping from Fev would be trickier.

"Would you mind if I asked you a silly question?" Rumus-who-wasn't asked.

I surreptitiously checked to ensure the hallway remained empty, aware that he could be telepathically calling reinforcements even now. When no one jumped out to attack, I said, "Go ahead."

"If you spotted a single rainbow alone in the forest, what would you do?"

I froze in shock. The question was undoubtedly from Kee—it was one of our coded phrases, and one she wouldn't use with someone she didn't trust, at least a little. And she'd predicted that I would head to the bar at the fanciest hotel in the city. Kee might be occasionally scattered and terminally optimistic, but when it came to information, she never missed anything.

I stepped closer and whispered, "I'd give it a hug."

Remus-who-wasn't didn't move, and for a moment I wondered if he'd somehow randomly guessed the exact phrasing of Kee's question. But then he took my hand in his, and I felt the small object he'd palmed. For someone who wore his emotions so visibly, he was surprisingly good at sleight of hand.

He lifted my hand to his lips and pressed a light kiss against my skin. "Good luck," he whispered, his voice barely audible even from directly in front of him. "It was nice to meet you."

I casually slipped the palmed object into my pocket without looking at it. There would be time for that later when it wouldn't potentially compromise one of Kee's assets. "You, too," I murmured. Louder, I continued, "I wish I'd been the person you were looking for."

He sighed wistfully. "Me, too." He bowed slightly and continued past me to the lobby.

I let him get a head start, then I followed him. When I passed the stairwell, Nilo slipped through the door and joined me. "What was that?"

"That was hopefully a gift from Kee," I thought loudly, unwilling to mention the system engineer's name aloud.

Nilo dipped his head in acknowledgment, and then inserted himself between me and the crate. He cupped my elbow, ostensibly to escort me through the lobby, but I knew he wanted to be touching me in case we needed to port.

I stepped into the lobby with all the confidence of a person who knew exactly where she was going. There were a few people scattered around, but none of them looked up at our arrival. Ten meters and we'd be outside.

We were nearly across the room when a door behind

the concierge desk opened and Sura Fev stepped out. She was talking to a dark-haired woman, who, based on her clothes, was likely a hotel employee.

Fev only had to turn her head a degree or two and we'd be right in her sight line. I kept my pace slow and steady, so we wouldn't draw her attention. "Do you think she knows we're here?" I thought loudly.

Nilo turned his head toward me to help shield his face. "I don't know," he responded telepathically. "But if I port us out, she definitely will. Let me know the moment she starts to look this way."

I laughed quietly, like I didn't have a care in the world. "Let's try for the door. Just keep looking at me."

The distance to the door shrank with every step, but it still felt like it was light-years away. I had to concentrate to prevent myself from getting tunnel vision, but I'd had years to practice acting natural when the situation was anything but.

Then, less than two meters from the door, Fev looked up. From the corner of my eye, I saw her gaze sweep over us without pausing, and I thought we were in the clear. The outside door slid open, but before we could step through, Fev's head snapped back toward us with a frown.

Everything else was lost as Nilo's power spiked and the world vanished.

CHAPTER SEVENTEEN

Once the world stopped spinning, I rounded on Nilo. "You ported us too soon. She might not have recognized us, but now she *knows* we're on-planet. And if she checks the hotel's surveillance, she'll know I met with Kee's contact, too."

Nilo's eyes flashed with temper. "I told you that I would not risk your safety. If she'd telelocked us, I might not have been able to get us out at all."

It was a valid concern, but losing the element of surprise hurt. I'd bumped directly into Fev, more or less, and she hadn't recognized me. That wouldn't happen again.

But I let the argument go. Neither of us was going to budge, and we had more important things to worry about—like what Kee's contact had given me. I looked around. We were in a noticeably more working-class part of town, somewhere between the shining buildings of downtown and the shanties along the southern edge of the city.

The surrounding buildings were only a few stories tall, and most of them showed signs of wear. They had all been meticulously repaired, but many of the materials didn't quite match the originals.

"Where are we?"

"You weren't the only one making plans, *taro.* I've rented a building for us nearby."

"Why didn't you tell me?"

"As much as I hated it, your plan was a good one. I was going to tell you once we left the Riv. Which we've done, and I have."

"Har-har," I grumbled. "What's in the building?"

"Not much, but it did come with a lev cycle, which will help with mobility." His eyes went distant. "I can no longer sense Luna, so she must be farther north or west."

"Aburwuk's spaceport is on the western side of the base. Maybe *Starlight* is there, but you can't sense it because something—or some*one*—is blocking you. As soon as I can get a drone in the air, I'll do a sweep. The spaceport is outside the main walls. It has decent security, but it should be easier than getting into the main base."

Nilo nodded, then guided me through several blocks of back alleys and hidden paths until we ended up at the building he'd rented. It wasn't much to look at, just a squat, two-story gray rectangle, but it was on a corner lot and only shared one wall with the building next door.

Rather than going in the front door, we circled around to the back of the property where a normal entrance door stood next to an oversize garage door. The reflective windows gave no hint of what was inside, but Nilo approached the door without hesitation. He swiped his comm over the control panel and the door silently unlocked.

A closer look revealed that while the control panel appeared as old as the building, it was actually a recent, top-of-the-line model with hardened security. I could crack it, but it would take a lot of time, effort, and specialized tools. Whoever owned the building didn't want any uninvited guests, which made me feel marginally better about stepping into the unknown.

Nilo pulled the crate through the door, and I followed. The ground floor was a large, open area with what appeared to be a small office partitioned off at the front door. The promised two-person lev cycle was a Valovian model I'd only flown a few times, but it appeared to be in good repair. Far more interesting was the workshop that surrounded it. There were enough tools and 3D printers that we could make just about any part or tool we might need.

"I hope you spent Torran's money on this," I murmured. The former general could certainly afford it. I'd done a little digging while we'd been working for him, and his assets made my own comfortable luxury pale in comparison.

"It was not cheap," Nilo agreed with a laugh. "And as it happens, I *am* using one of Torran's untraceable accounts."

I gestured to the stairwell. "What's upstairs?"

"Just the living quarters: four bedrooms, a kitchen, and a pair of bathrooms."

It was too bad that we wouldn't need to share a room—or a bed. And the building seemed to have decent climate control, so we wouldn't even need to snuggle for warmth.

I blew out a breath and returned to reality. If everything went according to plan, we'd be too busy infiltrating Aburwuk to worry about sleeping tonight, especially now that Fev knew we were here.

The clock was ticking.

"Is this space secure?" I asked Nilo, even as I started scanning for cameras and trackers.

"It should be," he said.

Once the scan came back clean, I pulled out the object that Kee's contact had given me. It was actually two objects: a keycard and a datachip. I might trust Kee, but I didn't trust the empath enough to insert an unknown datachip into my main comm. That was a good way to end up with a compromised device.

Instead, I dug my dummy comm out of the crate. I had several cheaper comms that I could use as burners, but the dummy comm had no networking capability at all. Data had to enter and leave the device through datachips alone. Neither the burner comms nor the dummy comm were tied to any of my accounts, so if they were compromised, the attacker wouldn't gain anything. It was overkill, since remotely compromising a device without any network connections was nearly impossible, but it kept me safe.

Nilo watched me with undisguised interest, so I explained what I was doing, then I took a deep breath before I inserted the datachip. As expected, the only file on the chip was encrypted, but Kee and I had been exchanging encrypted messages for a long time. I set the decryption to run with her custom algorithm and my private key.

"This will potentially take a while," I told Nilo, "depending on how much data is included."

Neither of us moved.

The file decrypted faster than I'd expected, only taking a few minutes. It was a compressed archive, so I expanded it to reveal a handful of files and folders, including a video file named "LEXI_OPEN_THIS_FIRST!!!!!"

"Which one do you think we should open first?" I asked Nilo wryly.

"Kee is many things, but subtle isn't one of them," he said with a laugh.

I opened the video file and Kee's face filled the screen. "Hiya, Lexi," she said, then grimaced. "It's weird talking to the camera like it's you when I don't even know if you'll see this." She shook her head, tousling her pale, rainbow-colored hair. "Since you haven't responded to any of our messages, I'm going to assume that they're blocking either us or you. I've gotten messages to Rodeni, so I'm guessing it's you."

I frowned at the screen. I'd *also* gotten messages to Rodeni. So why hadn't I gotten Kee's messages?

"I have a contact on Rodeni who's promised to try to pass this along, but while my encryption is good, it's not unbreakable, hence the video file." She waved then switched to signing. Kee had learned sign language as a kid because her dad was deaf, and she'd taught Tavi, Eli, and me during the war. She signed using a relatively unknown dialect, so it was more secure than spoken words.

Even so, she was being intentionally vague. She wasn't finger spelling anything, so everyone got a nickname that she could sign.

"What's she saying?" Nilo asked.

I backed the video up to where she started signing and translated for Nilo. "'The general and the captain'—Torran and Tavi—'are planning to do something stupid and heroic and the rest of the crew is trying to talk them out of it, but you know how the captain gets.'" Here, Kee rolled her eyes, and I'd never related to a gesture more.

"'The weapons expert and the prince are going to try to

hide our approach—with a little help from yours truly—but we're not sure how successful we'll be. Our target coordinates are in the archive, but they're reversed and encoded, so be sure to invert and decode them before you come find us.'"

I paused the video. "How would Varro and Prince Liang be able to hide an entire ship?"

Nilo's eyes narrowed in thought. "Varro is an extremely strong telepath, but hiding a ship is a monumental task. Liang must be either an amplifier or unusually strong."

"A telepath can *hide* a ship? Like turn it invisible?"

"Sort of. They make you think it's not there even when it's right in front of you. Not many Valoffs are strong enough to trick other Valoffs, but Varro is—at least for a little while."

I breathed through the spike of panic. I already knew Valoffs could make a human see things that weren't there, so it wasn't too much a stretch to believe the opposite, but not being able to trust my eyes sent anxious prickles skating along my nerves.

I returned to the video and kept translating. "'Once we're on the ground, we're going radio silent, but *Starlight* will be passively receiving messages on our secure band, so switch your comm. The captain, general, healer, handsome, and silver'"—it took me a second to work out that she meant Tavi, Torran, Havil, Eli, and Chira—"'are heading for Aburwuk while the mechanic and I watch over the other two and the ship.'"

Nilo paused the video. "If Varro and Liang did manage to hide the ship, they would both be exhausted afterwards, likely for hours. Can Kee and Anja hold the ship?"

"It depends on how much trouble they want to cause, but yes. *Starlight's Shadow* has an excellent defensive system.

But I don't think Tavi would take Luna into the base if the ship was safe, so if Luna is outside, then something must've happened."

Nilo nodded, and I unpaused the video. "'In case you can't find us or if we get caught, my contact is supposed to be getting you a keycard to help once you're in the base, but you'll have to find your own way in. And you *had better* stake out the fanciest hotel bar in the city or all of this prep is going to be for nothing, and I'm going to be so mad at you.'"

Even signing, Kee managed to convey the emphasis just fine, and her attempt at a grumpy scowl was enough to make me smile.

She sobered. "'The Feds asked us to neutralize the commodore by whatever means necessary. He knows something vital they don't want the empress to find, and whatever it is will undoubtedly lead to war again, so if we fail, it'll be up to you. Love you, cat.'"

Even my nickname—which was derived from *cat burglar* to my eternal amusement—couldn't distract me from the quiet finality of the statement. Coming from someone who was normally so upbeat and optimistic, it sent shivers down my spine. They *hadn't* failed. I wouldn't believe it until I had no other choice.

But I *would* find *Starlight*.

AFTER DAYS ON VALOVIA, IT SEEMINGLY TOOK THE SUN *FOREVER* TO set. By the time true darkness arrived, I'd nearly worn a path in the garage's concrete floor. Kee hadn't included much additional information except for the landing coordinates of the ship, which pointed to a hilly area north of Tirdenchia.

Hiding a ship of *Starlight*'s size in the open would be nearly impossible, even with help from the terrain. Choosing an open area instead of a city meant Tavi had decided they would likely need to fight their way out. It was not an encouraging sign.

And something else was going on, too, because Nilo had confirmed—repeatedly—that he should be able to port to the location. So either the ship wasn't there, or he was being blocked.

I was fully kitted out in all black camouflage, including thin gloves and a balaclava that I would pull down to cover my face and neck once we got closer. My pale skin and blond hair glowed in the dark, so everything had to be covered. My night-vision glasses had special lenses that were designed to reduce reflections.

Basically, once darkness hit, I became a shadow.

I openly carried my blade and pistol, and I was planning to take the sniper rifle, too. I'd considered the plas cannon, but Tavi would never forgive me if I blew up her ship, so it was staying behind tonight. I also had a case of the tiny drones we'd grabbed from Besor's stash. If we didn't find *Starlight* at the expected coordinates, then I'd do a sweep of Aburwuk's spaceport.

Nilo emerged from the staircase in a thin, stretchy bodysuit. I raised my eyebrows. "That's one option," I mused. I let my gaze slide down his body. "Not much protection, though."

His grin was filled with mischief. "Did you wonder why the crate was bigger than it needed to be?"

In truth, no. I'd had a few other things on my mind, and all of my stuff had been neatly stored on top of the weapons.

I shook my head, and Nilo *tsked* sadly. "How am I supposed to impress you when you don't even notice my cleverness?"

"Were you trying to impress me?"

He grinned. "Always." He opened the crate and waved me over. "Help me with this, if you would."

We unloaded the weapons and gear, and once the crate was empty, it was obvious that it had a false bottom. Well, maybe it was obvious *to me,* who knew how to look for such things, but it really was cleverly fashioned. Nilo pressed several hidden buttons in what I assumed had to be a specific order, then lifted the lid out, revealing a full set of Valovian armor.

I sucked in an awed breath. "You *are* clever, dammit."

Nilo laughed. "Unfortunately, this is my personal set, so it'll be too tall for you or I'd give it to you. And I tried to get my hands on another set before we left but it's more difficult than you might expect."

"I believe you. I tried for a set after we were on Valovia last time, and it was impossible to find. Apparently the empress looks the other way on weapon smuggling, but her people crack down hard on armor smuggling. Stealing it from the military is basically the only way to acquire it." A thought dawned. "You stole the armor we used during Cien's rescue."

Nilo's lips twitched. "I don't know what you're talking about. I *may* have borrowed some extra armor, temporarily. But if I did, the soldiers never even noticed that it was missing."

I bowed playfully. "Consider me impressed with your cleverness."

I helped Nilo into the synthetic armor that covered him from neck to feet. He could've done it himself, but it was faster with two people, and I hardly needed an excuse to put my hands on him.

I did a final check of my weapons and gear while Nilo did the same. Every time I caught his armor out of the corner of my eye, I got a jolt of adrenaline. I *knew* it was Nilo—and he wasn't even wearing the helmet so I could *see* that it was him—but years of war had equated that armor to death.

He looked up and caught my eye. "You're uncomfortable."

"You would be, too, if I suddenly turned into a nightmare." I waved off the inevitable offer I saw on his face. "Keep the armor, Nilo. It makes you damn near indestructible, and we're going to need every advantage. Taking it off because I can't control my fear would be the height of stupidity."

"Being afraid isn't stupid," he said softly.

"But letting that fear override good sense *is*. I'll be okay. Are you ready to go?"

At his nod, I waved to the lev cycle with a grin. "I'll pilot."

MY GRIN GREW WHEN I FOUND THAT THE LEV CYCLE HAD A BLACKout mode that turned off all visible light, *and* someone had removed the altitude limiter. I didn't know who Nilo had rented the building from, but apparently the owner wasn't above a little sneakiness.

They seemed like my kind of person.

Nilo and I strapped the rifle case to the cycle, then I straddled the seat, and Nilo climbed on behind me. This model didn't have an outer shell, just a windscreen, so we'd be exposed to the elements, but the night was clear, if cool.

I ran through the start-up sequence and the safety clamps closed around our legs, securing us to the vehicle. The restraints weren't required, but by using them, I could push our speed and still be relatively sure that neither of us would fall off.

We'd decided to rely on telepathic communication, since Nilo's helmet and my comm didn't talk to each other. "Ready?" I thought loudly.

"Yes. Do you have the route?"

"It's on my comm," I confirmed. "We'll stay lowish while we're in town, then go high and dark once we're out of the populated area. Hold on."

He wrapped his armored arms around my waist, and I eased the lev cycle from the ground and out through the garage door. I waited for the door to close, then headed north. There was a steady stream of transports higher up, so I stayed closer to the ground. Lev cycles were typically ground-based transportation because they were small and often unenclosed, but their lev engines were just as capable of altitude as the transports.

They weren't as safe as transports, but they were *incredibly* fun to fly. I hoped Nilo had a strong stomach.

Traffic thinned as we reached the edge of the city, and I shut off the cycle's light. From here on out I'd be depending entirely on my night-vision glasses and comm for navigation.

I wasn't sure what we'd find at the exact coordinates Kee had given me, so I'd scoured satellite images and topographical maps to find a few potential vantage points that were far enough away from the ship for us to stay undiscovered.

Hopefully.

I'd switched my comm to the secure channel Kee preferred and turned off all other connections. Nilo had also turned off his comm's networking access. If we got caught, it wouldn't be because we were broadcasting our location.

Darkness closed around us as we left the lights of the city behind. There were a few mines out here, but mostly it was undeveloped. Just in case the Valoffs really hadn't found *Starlight* yet, my flight path wasn't a straight line. We'd be heading toward a mine that was slightly east of our true destination, then I'd use the hills and valleys for cover as we got closer to the landing coordinates.

I opened the throttle and the lev cycle jumped forward. Nilo's arms tightened around my waist as we pulled into a shallow climb. The lev cycle was fast and responsive, and flying it was a pleasure, even with the worry tightening my stomach.

We passed the mine, and I dropped our altitude until we were just skimming a few meters above the ground. Nilo's arm tightened in warning as a sheer cliff loomed in front of us, but the routing on the comm had already warned me. The lev cycle roared upward, clearing the top with at least a meter to spare.

"You're going to be the death of me," Nilo growled in my mind.

"Relax, I've got this. I used to race these things as a kid. You won't find a better pilot on the whole planet."

He squeezed my waist. "I trust you."

Warmth filled my chest. Few people trusted me, especially once they got to know me. But Nilo had already seen all of my flaws and problems and weaknesses, and he'd still decided to put his trust in me. I silently vowed that I wouldn't do anything to make him regret that choice.

We rode in silence until we neared the first potential vantage point. "Do you sense anyone nearby?" I thought loudly.

I slowed the lev cycle while Nilo searched. After a moment he said, "No, but the area around where the ship is supposed to be is just kind of . . . blank. It's *odd*."

"Nullifier?"

"I don't know. Like I said before, I haven't had much experience with nullifiers because they're rare and nearly all of them are drafted for secret military projects or Fiazefferu."

I set the lev cycle down on a flat spot a half dozen meters from the summit of the hill between us and *Starlight*'s landing coordinates. The ship was still nearly a kilometer away, but we were high enough that I hoped we'd be able to see something.

Nilo swung his leg over the saddle and stepped off. I left the vehicle in standby in case we needed a hasty exit, then I followed him. We crept up the rocky hill, and once we got close to the top, we both flattened ourselves to the ground and belly crawled the rest of the way.

I carefully scanned the surrounding hills, searching for lookouts. I didn't find any, but I also couldn't see *Starlight* from here thanks to a narrow ridge that hadn't been clear on the topo map.

"Do you sense anything?"

Nilo shook his head. "But that blank feeling is definitely coming from where *Starlight* is supposed to be."

"How long could a nullifier block an entire area like that?"

Nilo considered it. "Maybe a few hours if they were strong and no one was fighting them."

"What are the odds that Aburwuk has multiple nullifiers just sitting around?" I asked.

"Actually, there probably are at least two attached to the base, but I'd be surprised if they had them both babysitting a ship this far out. Especially if Torran hasn't been caught yet. The typical methods to take down a rogue telekinetic include massive damage, a lucky hit with an immobilization pulse, or a strong nullifier."

"So a nullifier could take down Fev?"

Nilo turned toward me, but I couldn't see his face through his helmet's visor. "Technically yes," he said telepathically, "but don't count on one defecting. They are fed duty and honor from the moment their ability manifests."

Personal honor was deeply important to Valoffs, but money was important to everyone. Nothing might come of it, but it was worth considering. For now, though, we needed to move.

I took one more look around, then shimmied backward until I was low enough to stand up without making myself a target. Nilo followed me. "Next stop?" he questioned.

"Would it help if we circled the landing zone first?"

"It might, but it's a risk. The next stop is closer to where the ship is supposed to be, right?" At my nod, he continued, "Then let's head there. If we still can't see anything, we'll do a loop."

We returned to the lev cycle. I eased us into the air but stayed close to the ground as we circled the hill. The next point had a tricky approach through a narrow ravine and up a steep rise, but it was the only way to get close while staying relatively hidden.

Nilo was silent as I navigated through a gully that was closer to a crevasse than I would've preferred. The lev cycle squeaked through with only centimeters to spare on either side. By the time we were out, Nilo's arms were locked around my waist in a grip just shy of painful.

When I set the lev cycle down, he didn't move. "Are you okay?" I mentally asked.

"Give me a second," he said. "I don't know how you did that."

I chuckled quietly. "Ravine racing was good money, if you could do it."

He let go of me and swung off the vehicle. "Let me guess," he said, his mental voice dry, "you excelled at it."

I grinned at him. "Of course. Bravery and stupidity are two sides of the same coin, after all, and when I was young, I had both in ample supply."

I hopped off the lev cycle and checked the hills around us. There were no obvious spotters, and no one took a potshot at us, so I started up the short, steep climb. I focused on the burn in my quads and ignored the gnawing worry in my stomach.

When I couldn't climb any higher without turning myself into a target, I hit the dirt on my belly. I said a prayer to anyone who might be listening, then eased up to peek over the ridge.

The valley was empty.

CHAPTER EIGHTEEN

I blinked, sure that I was mistaken, but no matter how much I squinted, the valley remained empty despite the glowing target on my comm that indicated where *Starlight* should be. We had a perfect view, but there was *no ship.*

"What the fuck?" I breathed.

"We knew it was a long shot—" Nilo started.

"Do you still sense the blank spot?"

Nilo's helmeted head turned back toward the valley. "Yes."

"Is this a Valovian ability?"

"None that I know of," Nilo said. "Maybe if a nullifier and a strong telepath worked together, but even then, a nullifier will usually cancel out everything around them. They *can* nullify specific targets while leaving others alone, but it's more difficult."

"Can you sense any Valoffs nearby?"

Nilo shook his head. "I can't sense *anything* nearby, but that doesn't mean there isn't a squad of soldiers down there. The whole bottom of the valley is blank."

That was not ideal. I took out my comm and sent a short request for acknowledgment on Kee's secure channel. There was no response.

Either the ship truly wasn't there, or their comms were being jammed. I was going to have to get closer to figure out which it was. I opened the drone case and pulled out the smallest, quietest drone. It easily fit in the palm of my hand with room to spare. This type of drone was usually used inside to map unknown rooms, but it could work outside as long as the wind was low—which it was.

I reenabled the short-range networking chip on my comm, then plotted a flight path for the little drone. Rather than flying straight for the valley, it would sweep around and approach from a ravine on our left.

That done, I set it aside and unpacked the sniper rifle. The drone was so small I needed the rifle's scope to keep an eye on it, even with the help from my night-vision glasses.

Nilo retrieved his own rifle. Once we were both situated with a good view of the valley, I sent the drone off. It transmitted a stabilized video back to my comm, but the vid wasn't showing me anything I couldn't see with my own eyes, so I focused on the drone itself.

Keeping it in the rifle's sights was tricky, so I swung the scope to the place where it would pop out of the ravine, and a minute later, it zoomed into view, heading for *Starlight*'s location.

Between one breath and the next, it disappeared, and the video on my comm died.

The drone hadn't been hit; it had just *vanished* into thin air.

"Did you see that?" I asked Nilo while I scrambled to check the last few seconds of video on my comm.

"It's impossible," he breathed.

The vid didn't appear to show anything until I slowed it down. There, at the end, was a single, blurry frame that truly *was* impossible. A mini camp had been set up around *Starlight*. It was difficult to tell, but the ship looked intact and the cargo bay door was closed.

Were Kee and the others still inside?

Nilo pointed at a vertical column on the screen. "That's a temporary comm tower," he said. "Standard military issue."

I eyed the valley. "How tall are they?"

"Ten meters."

I should've brought the plas cannon after all, but it was too late now. I overlaid the drone's photo on the terrain then used our distance from the landing site and our relative elevations to work out approximately where the top of the comm tower would be.

"What are you doing?" Nilo asked.

"I'm going to shoot it—actually, I'm going to shoot *at* it. Then I'm going to see what happens."

Nilo was silent for a beat, then said, "In that case, you should be aiming for the box at the base of the tower. It houses all of the electronics."

I grinned at him. "See, this is why I brought you along." I checked the photo again and adjusted my calculations. Shooting into the unknown was highly unsafe and irresponsible, but so was running headfirst into an unknown situation, which was our other option.

The sniper rifle had the latest and greatest targeting assistance, so with just a few inputs, it spit out the place to aim in order to hit what was hopefully the comm tower's control box. I carefully lined up the shot, then asked, "You ready for some chaos?"

"Remember that I'm wearing armor," Nilo said. "Stay behind me and don't be heroic."

"While I appreciate that you think I'm heroic, I'm also very invested in staying alive. You've got a point; I've got your back. Unless you can teleport once the tower goes down. If so, port us into the ship."

"I will, but if it's too dangerous, I'll port us back to the garage."

I nodded and once again marveled at how much easier my job would be if I could just port away at the first sign of trouble. It was probably best that I didn't have the ability because I would abuse the hell out of it.

I snugged the sniper rifle into my shoulder and checked the aim one last time. I took a deep breath and let half of it out before I gently squeezed the trigger. The gun spat out a plas pulse that was visible in the dark, but nothing happened. I adjusted my aim and fired again. And again. And again.

A soldier in Valovian armor appeared. "Friend or foe?" I asked Nilo, but the question was answered when they started shooting at us.

"Foe," Nilo confirmed.

The sniper rifle's targeting computer had identified the threat, so it was a moment's work to adjust my aim. Valovian armor was damn near impenetrable, but this rifle had been designed to punch straight through—and it did.

The soldier collapsed, and triumph warred with regret.

I had hoped that I was past the days of war and death, but if I didn't rescue Tavi and stop Morten, far more people than me would suffer, so I returned to aiming for the hidden control panel. It took three more shots, then it exploded.

Violently.

Nilo covered my body as the shock wave rushed over our hill. Maybe that hadn't been the control box after all, but whatever it was, destroying it had worked. When I looked up, I could see *Starlight*. What was left of the camp was on fire and a few figures were rushing around, seemingly leaderless.

Kee's voice crackled through my comm implant. "Lexi, please tell me that's you."

"Kee!" I shouted, as if that would help my subvocal mic pick up the word.

"You have no idea how happy I am to hear from you," she said. "Have you heard from Tavi?"

"No. And Nilo hasn't been able to contact Torran, either."

She cursed emphatically enough that her subvocal mic picked it up. "Okay, our current plan isn't working, which means I can light these assholes up. Are you out of the danger zone?"

"We're half a klick away, so have at it."

Starlight's ground defense system made short work of the few remaining soldiers. Once we were sure that the way was clear, Nilo and I approached on the lev cycle. The makeshift camp was in ruins, and as far as I could tell from what was left, I'd hit some sort of generator instead of the control box.

By the time I had landed the lev cycle near *Starlight*, Kee had the cargo bay door open. She rushed out while Anja stood guard. They were both in lightweight, flexible armor, but Kee wasn't wearing the matching helmet. Instead, she had on some sort of metal crown looking thing wrapped in wires.

She threw her arms around me and squeezed. "I'm so glad Rul found you."

"Who?"

She let me go and frowned. "My contact? If you didn't meet him, how did you find us?"

"Ahhh, *that* contact. He was using an alias, but yes, he found me. How did you know I'd be in the Riv's bar?"

Kee rolled her gaze toward the sky, highlighting the dark smudges that marred the pale skin under her eyes. She hadn't been getting enough sleep again.

"Give me some credit, Lex. Finding information is kind of my thing, and you aren't as mysterious as you'd like to believe."

I clutched a hand to my chest. "How dare you."

Kee laughed, then sobered as she looked at the smoldering camp. "Do you know what they were using to jam signals? I couldn't get anything in or out, nor could I connect to it. I've never seen anything like it." Her nose wrinkled. "It was incredibly annoying."

"It's worse than that," I said. "Nilo couldn't port through it, and we couldn't even see through it. I didn't think that the Valoffs had optical camouflage that advanced."

Kee shook her head. "They don't."

"They do now."

"There was also something blocking my telepathy," Nilo said. He'd opened his visor, so I could see the way his eyes narrowed. "And it didn't completely go away until you took out the remaining soldiers."

"Maybe one of them was a nullifier and the tower was an artificial amplifier?" I asked. "Is that a thing?"

"Not that I know of." He turned to Kee. "Are Varro and the prince still aboard?"

Kee's expression dimmed as she nodded. "They're in the medbay, and they're both still out cold. They burned through a lot of energy on the way in."

I tapped her crown. "What is this?"

"One of Morten's inventions," she said. "It makes it harder for Valoffs to sense humans. Morten used it to ambush me and Varro when we were on FOSO I."

I waved a hand at the ruins of the comm tower. "Somehow, I don't think he came up with that technology on his own. No wonder the FHP wants him back or dead—they're protecting both the secret and their mole. And the empress wants him for the same reason."

Kee nodded. "But the secret isn't *that* secret. Anja and I cobbled together another helmet that works almost as well. Of course, she's brilliant, so there's that."

I set aside my questions and focused on the current issue. "What's the plan?" I asked. "Are we going to move the ship or do you want Nilo to port you back to our base? I can take you—and maybe Anja, if we squeeze—on the lev cycle while he ports Varro and Prince Liang back."

"I'm not leaving you behind," Nilo ground out.

"Can you port all of us *and* the lev cycle? Because we still might need it."

His jaw clenched and he refused to answer, which was answer enough.

Kee tapped her chin, her eyes distant. "I've spent the last twelve hours scouring the satellite data I pulled down before they blocked my connection. There's nowhere to hide *Starlight* that they won't find in a matter of hours. Our backup plan was to move to Tirdenchia, so if Tavi escapes, she'll check there before heading here."

Kee looked at Nilo. "If we move to Tirdenchia's spaceport, can you teleport Liang, Varro, and me out? Because I'd rather not deal with the authorities, assuming I can keep us off their trackers until then."

Now it was my turn to protest. "I'm not letting you fly off without me."

Nilo's eyebrows rose, and his voice whispered in my mind, "Not so easy when the tables are turned, is it?"

Kee waved her hand at me. "You and Anja are going to be the distraction."

Nilo's smile lost its satisfied edge. "What?" he demanded.

Kee ignored him. "I've created a transponder that mimics *Starlight*'s signature. You'll buy us some time by heading away from the city and dropping it somewhere difficult to find. Meanwhile, I'll fly the *Hisi Las* here"—she hiked a thumb at *Starlight*—"into Tirdenchia and magically appear at the spaceport."

"You're forging a Valovian registration? Can you do that?"

Kee shrugged. "It won't hold up to a deep dive, and I haven't been able to get access through the FHP–Valovian wormhole, so we'll have to switch back at some point, but it might buy us a day or two."

"Okay, let's move," I agreed. "How big is the transponder?"

Kee headed back up the cargo bay ramp. "It's a small case. Anja can hold it while you fly. Do you need me to disable the altitude limiter on your lev cycle?"

I grinned. "The owner already beat you to it. But I'll grab some armor while you grab the box."

Kee gestured to the lockers at the front of the cargo bay. "Help yourself."

I hesitated. The Valovian armor the soldiers had been wearing would be far more protective, but stripping it from their bodies would take time, and someone was going to notice we'd taken out their camp sooner or later—probably sooner.

Plus, it just felt *wrong* to defile the dead.

I hoped that I wouldn't come to regret my bout of sentimentality, but I entered the ship and found the extra armor Tavi kept for bounty hunting jobs. Nilo helped me strap on the lightweight protection. This type of armor wouldn't deflect a close shot, but it was better than the fabric under it.

"Be careful," Nilo murmured when we were done. "I'll stay in contact with you. If you need me, I'll get you out."

"Thank you." I pressed a quick kiss to his mouth. "Just in case," I whispered.

He snagged my waist and drew me closer, then kissed me with a slow, thorough intensity that made the world disappear. When we came up for air, his eyes were blazing gold. "You *will* mentally shout if you need help, and you *won't* take any unnecessary risks. Promise me."

I swallowed. "I promise. Keep Kee safe."

He bowed his head. "I will. See you soon."

"Soon," I agreed.

ANJA CLUNG TO MY WAIST AS THE LEV CYCLE SKIMMED UP THE HILL at a speed just shy of reckless. We'd attached the transponder to the vehicle with a quick release, freeing Anja's hands, and she had a rifle strapped to her back in case we ran into trouble we couldn't outrace.

Not that it would do much good if they sent a ship after us.

I'd only worked with Anja during our previous short trip to Valovia, but she'd proven herself steady and dependable, even when things went sideways. She was exactly the kind of person I wanted guarding my back when I was doing something stupid—like pretending to be *Starlight* with nothing but the air around us for protection.

Unfortunately, the lev cycle wasn't really equipped to track incoming ships until they were almost on top of us, so we were relying on *Starlight*'s sensors, but the more distance we put between us, the less reliable they became.

I was following a flight path that sent us north and east, toward the next largest city in the area, and away from *Starlight*'s route to Tirdenchia. We were moving far faster than *Starlight,* which was built for spaceflight rather than atmospheric flight and lumbered through the air. Kee was having to keep the speed down in order to stay close to the ground without accidentally hitting an inconvenient hill.

So even though my and Anja's flight path to Tirdenchia was more than twice as long as *Starlight*'s—thanks to us playing decoy—we *should* arrive in the city about the same time as Kee, Nilo, and the rest of the crew because they were taking a more direct route.

We descended toward a wide, flat plain surrounded by distant hills, and I pushed the throttle wide open. Anja's arms tightened as the lev cycle jumped forward. The ground blurred under us, but my eyes were already on the horizon. The extra speed was nice, but being in the open set my teeth on edge.

We were halfway across when Kee's voice echoed over the comm. "Two ships heading for the landing zone," she said. "They are rapidly approaching from the south. ETA five minutes. Based on their current speed, they will overtake you in fifteen minutes if they continue north."

"Copy," I acknowledged.

We wouldn't make the next city in fifteen minutes, but at least we'd be out of the plain. Kee and I had plotted some very rough escape points along the route—places where it wouldn't be immediately obvious to the ships following us that *"Starlight"* was just a box with a transponder. The next one was twelve minutes away, which was cutting it dangerously close.

But I needed to buy the real *Starlight* as much time as possible. "How close are you to your destination?" I asked, leaving out the city name just in case someone was listening in.

"Twenty-five minutes."

I swore silently as I did the mental math. The chase ships were moving nearly six times *Starlight*'s speed. Once they started searching, they could fly a circular pattern and *still* find Kee before she made it to Tirdenchia's spaceport.

"Fly faster," I urged. "I'll do what I can."

I veered slightly to the west. It would put me closer to the chase ships, but it would draw them farther away from Kee. I kept the throttle pegged even as we rocketed up the first hill. I had less than ten minutes. "Hold on tight," I told Anja.

She squeezed my waist in answer.

Adrenaline sharpened my reflexes as I dropped us into a valley that wasn't narrow enough, but it was better than the plain. The hills would reflect the transponder signal up and away, granting us a few extra seconds. I'd take every one I could get.

I got my wish as the valley narrowed. Flying headlong into an unknown ravine was sheer madness, but I didn't let a little thing like reality stop me. The rocky walls flashed past us as the space narrowed. Instinct and skill took over, and all of my focus was on keeping us in one piece as the ravine twisted along some invisible fault.

Ahead, the ravine cut sharply left. Rather than following, I pulled us up and out. Might as well give the chase ships something to chase. "How much time?"

"Five minutes," Kee answered immediately.

"Let me know when it's sixty seconds."

Lights in the distance drew my eye. The only thing out here were mines, but that might work. The chase ships wouldn't know what *Starlight* looked like. I just needed anything vaguely ship-like. Or a building big enough to hide a ship. Or literally anything helpful—I wasn't in a position to be too picky.

The seconds ticked by faster than I would've liked, but eventually the lights resolved themselves into a mine. And, even better, a mine with a *lake.* It was the first surface water I'd seen, so it was likely an artificial cooling lake.

But how deep was it?

As I neared, it was clear that there would be no convenient ships I could toss the transponder at, but the lake appeared deep enough to hide a ship of *Starlight*'s size. And if it wasn't, I doubted the pilots would know that.

"Chuck the box in the lake," I told Anja. "I'm not slowing down, so you'll have to time it carefully."

"I've got it," she replied, her voice calm.

And she did. The box hit the water just as Kee warned, "Sixty seconds."

I pulled the lev cycle hard to the right, racing for the nearest hill. We crested the top and dropped over the other side at maximum speed. I scanned the surroundings for a place to hide. A rocky overhang wasn't ideal, but it was the best I could find, so I slid under it with a hard stop. I put the lev cycle on the ground and killed the engine. Without the rushing air, my breathing sounded incredibly loud.

"Are you okay?" Kee demanded.

"Shhh," I replied subvocally. A pair of small, sleek ships streaked past high on our left, and I held my breath. If they were searching with thermal cameras, I wasn't sure the overhang would be sufficient to hide us. They swept around to the left, making another pass over the lake.

Anja and I sat in silence for twenty minutes while one of the ships hovered over the lake, presumably trying to determine why *Starlight*'s signature was coming from the water when their sensors couldn't find the ship itself. The other ship made increasingly wide search passes, coming dangerously close to our hiding spot.

When both ships finally moved on, I let out a tiny, relieved sigh.

Anja chuckled quietly. "Yes, that."

"Kee, are you at the spaceport?"

"Yep. I paid for a berth and everything. So far, no one has shown up demanding our heads, so we'll stay in the ship and keep an eye on the sensors until you get close, then Nilo can port us out. It looks like your friends are finally moving off, but they're running searches between us. Head north, then sweep around to the east. I'll let you know if they change course."

"Thanks, Kee." I looked over my shoulder at Anja. "Ready for more?"

She nodded, but added, "Will you think less of me if I told you I spent most of the flight with my eyes closed?"

I barked out a laugh as I started up the lev cycle. "I'd be more worried if you hadn't."

CHAPTER NINETEEN

The trip back to the building Nilo had rented in Tirdenchia took twice as long as it should've, but it was otherwise unremarkable. I landed the lev cycle in its spot in the garage, and as soon as the restraints released, Anja climbed off with a groan.

"Thank you for not killing me," she ribbed good-naturedly.

"My pleasure." I glanced at Kee who had changed out of her armor and was currently scowling at her slate. "Where's Nilo?"

She tore her attention away from the device long enough to roll her eyes. "He's upstairs with Varro and Liang. They both woke up just before the port. The three of them are probably making some sort of ridiculous heroic plan that involves us"—she waved at the three of us—"staying here while they go storm the gates. I thought I'd broken Varro of that habit, but the other two are a bad influence."

My eyes narrowed. "Nilo had better not try to leave me behind."

Kee perked up and a playful smile tugged at her lips. "Don't think I didn't see that kiss earlier. Anything you'd like to share with the class?"

Anja held up her hands with a grin. "Leave me out of it. I don't want to be enemies with anyone who can fly a lev cycle like that."

Kee's attention turned to her. "Or maybe you just don't want to answer any questions about a certain prince, hmmm?"

Anja's light brown skin flushed a shade darker, but she attempted to brazen it out. "I have no idea what you mean."

Unfortunately, Kee's focus jumped back to me, and she raised her eyebrows expectantly. I loved Kee like a sister, but it was still difficult to quietly admit, "I like him."

She nodded as if she'd known it all along and didn't press for more details, which made me love her all the more. She gestured at her slate. "I'm working on Aburwuk's security, but I haven't been able to find Tavi yet."

"Why did she take Luna?"

Kee grimaced. "We weren't sure we'd be able to hold the ship, and we didn't want to leave Luna potentially trapped inside. She's a decent scout, and she's happiest with Tavi, so the captain took her along." Kee frowned and tilted her head. "How did you know Tavi took her?"

"Nilo briefly sensed her. He can't contact Tavi or Torran, but he did find Luna."

"Where?" Kee demanded.

"Somewhere north. It was while we were at the Riv,

and he can't sense her from here, but he thought Varro might be able to."

Kee's eyes went distant almost exactly like a Valoff's would when they were communicating telepathically. After a moment, she said, "He's not fully recovered, but he's going to try."

"Is he constantly in your head?" I asked. I could still feel the cool press of Nilo's presence in the back of my mind, and while I was *starting* to get used to it, every time I noticed it anew, it sent my pulse racing before logic reasserted itself.

"Most of the time," Kee confirmed.

"And that doesn't bother you?"

She lifted a delicate shoulder. "I love him," she said softly, as if that explained it all. And maybe it did.

I pulled her into a gentle hug. "I'm happy for you."

She squeezed me tight, then let go and bounced on her toes. "Now, who wants to make a plan that'll make the Valoffs upstairs apoplectic?"

The three of us grinned in unison.

KEE, ANJA, AND I WERE DEEP IN DISCUSSION WHEN NILO, VARRO, and an unknown Valoff with silvery hair and light golden-tan skin emerged from the stairwell. Prince Liang Nepru—for it could be no one else—was an exceedingly handsome man, even if I could see exhaustion in the line of his shoulders.

We had clustered around one of the worktables where we could all see Kee's slate, and the group of Valoffs crossed the room toward us. Nilo's eyes traced the lines of my body, ensuring that I was okay. I'd shed the armor, but I was still in camouflage. Nilo had changed into a gray tunic and black pants, and I did a similar visual inspection of him. My relief at seeing him uninjured was probably leaking through our connection, but I couldn't help it. Knowing that he was okay and seeing it were two different things.

Liang stopped in front of me and bowed with fluid grace, all charm. "Liang Nepru, at your service."

I eyed him warily. I knew a mask when I saw one. "Lexi."

When I didn't add a surname, Liang's eyebrow crept up and a tiny smile pulled at his mouth. *"Kitfev kite."*

A beautiful mystery. I kept my expression perfectly neutral, no matter how much I wanted to roll my eyes at him.

"Should we warn him that Lexi speaks fluent Valovan or let him find out for himself when she flattens him?" Kee mused aloud.

I cut an exasperated glance at her, but she just grinned in response and held up her hands. "I'm just trying to save his life. He's kind of important, you know."

"Not to me," I muttered subvocally.

Her grin widened, and she looked at Liang, who was watching the exchange with interest. "You owe me." He lit up and her nose wrinkled. "Wait, I take that back. You Valoffs and your debts," she grumbled. She shook a finger at him. "Be nice. Lexi is like my sister, and if you annoy her, I'll *help* her flatten you."

Liang nodded, then turned back to me. "I believe I have you to thank for our rescue."

I didn't need Kee's pointed sigh to know I should tread carefully. "I just flew around. Kee and Nilo did all of the hard work."

"Thanks a lot," Kee said over the comm.

Liang's eyes narrowed and he gestured at my clothes. "I very much doubt you had so little involvement."

Ah, so he had brains behind all of that beautiful charm. I gave him my widest, emptiest smile, but Nilo must've sensed the danger, because he appeared beside me. "Varro can sense Luna," he said, diverting my attention.

Varro was the most muscled of the Valoffs on Torran's team. He looked like he could break me in half, and he probably could. He had tan skin and short, dark blond hair, but even though his hair had grown out some since the last time I'd seen him, he still very much looked like a professional soldier.

The big Valoff was standing next to Kee. *Looming* might've been a better word, but it was a protective loom. I had no doubt that Kee was currently the safest person in the room.

"You can sense Luna from here?" I asked.

Varro nodded but didn't elaborate. Kee huffed and nudged him with her elbow. "She's outside," Varro added. "I caught a few images of the buildings around her, and we were able to work out her general position based on satellite imagery."

"Is she on the base?"

Varro nodded again, and Nilo held out a slate. "She's in this area," he said, indicating a cluster of buildings in the northeast part of Aburwuk.

I set the slate on the table so everyone could see what we were looking at.

"Do we know what those buildings are?" Anja asked. She pointed at one of the larger structures. "That looks like a workshop, possibly mechanical."

Nilo shook his head. "We're not sure, but we know that's not where prisoners are generally held."

"Torran is a telekinetic," I said, thinking aloud. "If that building really is a workshop, there would be thousands of potential projectile weapons just sitting around for him to use. Even if they have a nullifier, why tempt fate?"

"We don't know," Nilo said. "Telekinetic prisoners are usually kept in special cells for exactly that reason."

I glanced at Liang. "You're part of the imperial family. Do you know what technology they were using to hide *Starlight*?"

"I was more of a 'charming playboy' imperial than a 'military secrets' imperial."

"The two aren't mutually exclusive."

His grin grew and he tipped his head in acknowledgment. "True, but unfortunately, I wasn't that smart. And now, if my mother gets her way, I won't survive to correct the mistake."

I considered him for a moment, then took a stab in the dark to see how he'd react. "I don't believe you. Someone paid off the families that were displaced by the expanded base. It was you. That speaks to compassion *and* insight."

A perfect, charming mask fell across Liang's face wiping away any hint of his emotions. "Why do you think it was me?"

"Why *was* it you?" I challenged.

He held my stare for an uncomfortably long moment, but I didn't back down. "They didn't deserve to be turned out of their homes," he admitted quietly. "But I didn't know about it until after the fact—hence the payments. If I'd been paying more attention, maybe I could've done something better."

"What are you talking about?" Kee asked.

"When Empress Nepru expanded the military base, she authorized the takeover of residential sections of Tirdenchia," Liang said. "The residents were turned out with little notice and no help. I found as many of them as I could and gave them a small payment to help them resettle. The empress was furious when she found out."

I wasn't sure if Liang was trying to distance himself from the empress or her actions, but it was telling that he was using his mother's title rather than her name or simply *mother*.

Liang added, "Any access to military secrets that I might've had before were immediately forfeit. Most of my sources refused to speak with me or my people. I was told in no uncertain terms that my job was to be a pretty ornament that did not cause trouble."

He waved a hand at us. "As you can see, that's going quite well."

"Are you *officially* banned from, say, military bases, or is it more of an unspoken rule kind of thing?" Kee asked.

"Counting on my credentials to get us in would be incredibly foolish."

"So you *could* get us in?" Kee persisted.

"Yes, as long as you'd like a personal greeting from Sura Fev immediately afterwards."

Anja spoke up. "The empress wants Prince Liang dead. Delivering him straight to a military base would only benefit her."

Liang frowned. "I'm not staying behind—"

"You are," at least half the room agreed.

Kee looked at Anja. "And so are you."

The mechanic scowled. "I know I'm new, but I thought I'd proven myself."

"You have," Kee interrupted gently. "Which is why you and Liang are our emergency fail-safe. If we can't get to Tavi or if we get caught, it'll be up to the two of you to stop the war, if you can. Before we leave, I'll show you how to release all of the data I've collected so far. And having an imperial prince at your side won't hurt, assuming Liang is willing."

He sighed and rubbed his face. "I don't know how much sway I have, but I'll try."

"That's all I ask," Kee said with a smile. "Now, we'll need someone to *look* like Liang. Nilo is about the right build. As long as they don't have biometrics, we could probably make it work." She turned to Varro and wiggled her fingers. "Could you make Nilo look like Liang instead of a ghost?"

Varro studied Liang and Nilo for a moment, then shrugged. "Briefly."

"Enough to get us through a military checkpoint?"

"Tonight? Maybe. Tomorrow would be better."

"The longer we wait, the more prepared they'll be," I warned. "Sura Fev already knows that Nilo and I are on-planet, and now that *Starlight* has moved, she likely knows that we're all together. They'll be on high alert. And while they're welcome to do their worst to Morten, they also have Tavi and the crew. Morten is such a slimy weasel, he's probably singing like a lark in an attempt to save his ass."

"Sura won't alert the whole base," Liang said. "That's not how Fiazefferu work. It's also likely why Torran is being kept in an unusual building. She's waiting for backup to arrive."

I shook my head. "Sura might be waiting for backup, but she has *someone* watching Tavi and the crew, because she has a suite in the Riv."

"What?" Kee demanded.

"I ran into her when I was doing a little snooping in the penthouse suites. She didn't recognize me, but she saw us when we were leaving, and since we vanished into thin air, it wouldn't be too hard for her to put it together."

"She might have commandeered a small team to help guard, but she's still likely waiting for additional backup from Valovia," Liang argued.

"Then that's even more reason to move sooner," I said.

Kee sighed. "That doesn't give me time to get into their systems."

"What about your contact?" I asked. "He said he worked in security."

"He's already helped as much as he's going to," Kee said. "I offered him an obscene amount of money for direct access and he turned me down. Apparently the empress has a strict 'traitors are horribly murdered' policy, and he wasn't willing to risk it."

I frowned. "What about the keycard?"

"He claims he has plausible deniability for it, but I don't know." Kee checked her comm. "What about just before dawn? That'll give us another nine hours or so to rest and prep."

"And worry," I grumbled.

"And worry," Kee agreed.

EVERYONE SEPARATED TO RESEARCH OR REST. WE WERE GOING TO reconvene in eight hours, which would give us an hour of prep time before we needed to head for the base. Four bedrooms, which had seemed like a lot when Nilo and I had first arrived, soon became too few. Liang and Anja each took one, and Kee and Varro picked one together, leaving one for Nilo and me to share.

Kee waggled her eyebrows at me but otherwise didn't comment as she disappeared into her room with Varro.

I was planning to sleep for a few hours before getting up early to do a little recon on the lev cycle, but my nerves were wound so tight that sleep was looking exceedingly unlikely. I knocked on the open door of the room Nilo had picked, and he waved me in.

"I can sleep on the couch if you want," I offered.

He gave me a searching look. "Is that what *you* want?"

I swallowed and silently shook my head. His eyes bled gold, but all he said was, "Good."

I closed the door and moved deeper into the sparse room. A large, plain bed and a tall wardrobe were the only pieces of furniture, but we were in the one room that had its own bathroom. I raised an eyebrow at Nilo. "You snagged the best room."

"Did you expect anything less?" he asked with a grin.

"Nope." I set the bundle of clothes I'd grabbed from the crate on the bed, then stretched my arms overhead as I tried to let go of some of the stress I was carrying. "I'm going to shower and then attempt to sleep for a few hours. What's your plan?"

Nilo frowned. "Why only a few hours?"

Of course he'd caught that. "Because I'm going to recon the base before we get together for the final plan."

"And were you planning to take anyone with you?"

"I hadn't thought that far ahead," I hedged. "But you're welcome to come along if you'd like, unless you have something else planned."

"I was planning to see if I could get high enough to port

into the base," he said. "We can do that and recon, if you don't mind."

"Works for me." I picked up my clothes and headed for the bathroom. "I'm going to shower and change."

I closed myself inside the tiny bathroom before Nilo could offer to wash my back again, because I wasn't sure I'd turn him down. But when I saw the shower, I chuckled. I wasn't sure *I* was going to fit in it, what more two of us, so any lingering thoughts I had about sexy shower time were promptly forgotten.

The warm water released some of my tension, but the quiet gave me plenty of time to think about everything that could go wrong tomorrow. I hated the thought of taking Kee into the base, but I was happy to have her skills. Between the two of us, we should be able to open any door we found.

But my main concern was for Tavi. Luna would be able to sense Tavi—if not smell her—so it was extremely likely that the buildings Varro had seen were in fact where they were holding the captain and crew.

And if whatever they were using to keep Torran locked down also affected Nilo and Varro, then we would be flying blind. It could be a building full of Sun Guardians for all we knew.

Not that that would stop me from trying to rescue Tavi and Eli—and by extension, everyone else. It wasn't that I didn't care about the Valoffs, I did, but they hadn't kicked my ass until I became a halfway decent person. Tavi and Eli *had*.

I shut off the water and finished getting ready for bed. Nilo had already seen my nightwear of choice and hadn't seemed to mind, so I slipped the silk nightgown over my head with a shrug.

When I reemerged into the bedroom, Nilo was nowhere to be found. The overhead light was off, and the bed was turned down. I left the bathroom light on and the door cracked so Nilo would be able to see when he returned. I suppressed the urge to go ensure that the lev cycle was still in the garage—but I would if he didn't reappear soon.

I set an alarm on my comm then climbed into bed. The sheets were scratchy, but they smelled clean, so I'd take what I could get. But if I died tomorrow, and I'd spent my last night alive on scratchy sheets, I was going to lodge a complaint with the management.

Nilo slipped into the room with two glasses of amber liquid. I sat up and he handed me a glass, then sat down next to me. "For luck," he whispered.

"For luck," I echoed and touched my glass to his.

I took a sip and smooth, smoky alcohol burned pleasantly down my throat. I hummed in pleasure and Nilo smiled. "I thought you might like this."

"It's no milkshake, but I'll take it. Did you bring it with you?"

"No, Torran had it on *Starlight*. I just borrowed it. Permanently."

"Is he going to forgive you?"

He chuckled. "Eventually. Saving his ass will probably help. Saving Tavi will help more."

"Are we stupid to rush in without enough information?" I asked, my voice soft. In the dim light, it was easy for doubts to grow.

"It's a delicate balance," Nilo said. "Go too soon, and we put ourselves in danger. Wait too long, and we put the rest of the crew in danger."

I nodded. "I'm usually good at balancing risk and reward, but I feel like I've been playing catch-up from the beginning."

"We both have," Nilo agreed, "but we've done all right." He clinked his glass against mine again. "We don't know what their plan for *Starlight* was, but we stopped it—or at least delayed it."

I smiled and sipped my drink. "And we're still here to annoy Fev, so that's something."

Nilo hummed a wordless agreement.

We finished our drinks in companionable silence. When Nilo reached for my glass, I decided that I wanted sleeping on scratchy sheets to be my only regret if I died tomorrow.

"Take me to bed," I murmured.

His expression heated, but his smile had a teasing edge. "You're already in bed. You'll have to clarify if you want something else."

I stood, then took his glass and set it on the floor with mine. I gathered my courage. If I slept with him again, it wouldn't be purely physical—at least, not from my side. My emotions were already dangerously involved, and I hated being vulnerable because it gave another person the ability to hurt me.

Nilo had, once. And there was no guarantee that he wouldn't do it again.

Trust was so incredibly difficult. I trusted him with my body, but trusting him with my heart was far harder. His hands fisted in the sheets as I stopped in front of him. His gorgeous face was turned up to me, and the green in his eyes was slowly being swallowed by gold. He was so still I wondered if he was holding his breath.

I grazed my hand along his stubbled jaw. "Nilo," I whispered, then my throat closed up. I swallowed. Asking for what I wanted was a different kind of vulnerability, but in this, at least, I trusted Nilo wouldn't hurt me. "Nilo, I would very much like to fuck you tonight, if you are interested."

Nilo's eyes blazed with hunger, then he turned and pressed a kiss into my palm. He grinned up at me. "I would be more than happy to help you try to break this bed." His hands slid up the bare skin of my leg and disappeared under the hem of my nightgown. When he found that I wasn't wearing underwear, he groaned.

I lifted a shoulder, unashamed. "It's more comfortable this way."

"Oh, I agree," he breathed. "What do you want, *taro*?"

"I want to lose my mind. And make you lose yours."

His hands slid down the backs of my thighs. "If I continue to shield for you, our emotions are likely to spill across the connection. Will that make you uncomfortable?"

Panic fluttered through my pulse. If I lost myself in pleasure—and I hoped I would—Nilo would get an unfiltered view of my emotions. I wouldn't have anywhere to hide. The panic notched higher, and my breathing picked up.

The cool feeling at the back of my mind vanished. I was once again alone in my head, but it didn't bring the relief I expected. My emotions were a tangled web, but as long as I was attempting to be vulnerable, I might as well go big. "Wait. I want to try."

Nilo shook his head. "I could feel your panic."

"I know. I can't control it, but I still want to try." My smile was wobbly. "Think you'll be able to distract me thoroughly enough that I'll forget to panic?"

He looked at me for a long moment, then the cool feeling in my head returned, and his expression sharpened. "Are you challenging me, *taro*?"

"What if I am, *omazas*?" Nilo stared at me in shock, and I smiled and gently patted his jaw. "What, did you think you were the only one who got to make up pet names? If you don't like that one, then I guess I could go with *zasso*, but that seems a little too literal."

I couldn't feel anything through our connection and his expression didn't give me any clues, either, but I continued to offer him tiny, hidden pieces of my heart. "Or maybe you'd like *hich*? Then again, I didn't get to pick my nickname, so maybe you're stuck with *omazas*."

A breath shuddered out of him and his eyes blazed gold. He wrapped his arms around my hips and buried his cheek against my stomach. "Call me whatever you like: precious, lover, or . . ." His breath hitched. "Or hope. I accept."

I threaded my fingers through the soft strands of his dark hair. I couldn't make sense of the jumble of emotion leaking through the connection, but it made me feel warm and bubbly, so I hoped that meant Nilo was happy. "Now, about that challenge, *omazas*. Think you're up for it?"

Nilo's arms tightened, and he stood, lifting me as he rose. I laughed and wrapped my legs around his waist. "Show-off."

"Oh, *taro*, I haven't even started." His hands cupped my bare ass, pulling me tighter against him. "I've dreamed of peeling you out of this nightgown," he whispered. "Or taking you just like this, shrouded in silk."

I wiggled as my desire rose. "More doing, less talking."

Nilo turned and dropped me on the bed. I bounced, then sat up with a laugh. Nilo already had his tunic half off, so I ghosted my hands up his legs in order to help with his pants. Except I got distracted cupping him through the fabric, and he groaned low.

The fabric disappeared, and I raised an eyebrow even as I continued stroking him. "Shouldn't you be conserving your strength?"

"Worth it," he gasped.

Oh, I liked that sound very much. I licked him and the gasp melted into a moan, which was even better. I used the distraction to guide him down to the bed. I crawled up to give him a lingering kiss, then took my time exploring the planes of his body, from the muscles of his shoulders, down over the low slope of his chest, across the gently rippling expanse of his abs, and lower still, until he shuddered and hissed and his pleasure cascaded across our connection.

The shared pleasure was so intense and unexpected that it only took a few strokes of my fingers before I tipped myself over the edge with a shiver. Our combined pleasure echoed between us, underscored by deeper emotions that I refused to evaluate. I flopped over next to him, happy and sated.

Nilo groaned and heaved himself onto his elbow, so he could peer down at me. "You're dangerous."

"I warned you," I said with a laugh. "It's not my fault that you didn't listen."

"I had plans for you."

"Oh?"

"Yes." He traced a finger over the silk of my nightgown, circling ever closer to my nipple. "Many plans." My nipple beaded, pressing against the silk, but Nilo ignored it, and I had an idea of what his plans might entail.

But then his hot mouth closed around the silk-encased flesh, and pure pleasure burst through my veins. I arched against him as my desire reignited. “I like your plans,” I moaned.

“Good.”

He drove me toward orgasm slowly, inexorably, and I could feel *his* pleasure mixing with my own. When he finally slid into me with a thrust that left me gasping and shaking, he held me close and then started the climb again.

And, true to his word, he distracted me so thoroughly that any panic I felt was quickly submerged under endless waves of pleasure.

Happy and exhausted, I fell into a dreamless sleep tucked securely in his arms.

CHAPTER TWENTY

I was already awake when my alarm went off. I silenced it and nudged Nilo, who snapped to alertness with enviable ease. "It's time to get up," I whispered.

I retrieved my camouflage clothes then retreated to the bathroom for a quick shower. By the time I emerged, Nilo was already dressed in his armor. "We're not the only ones who made early plans," he said. "Varro and Kee are already gone, and Liang and Anja are getting ready."

"Damn overachievers, every one of them," I grumbled. "Did Kee take the lev cycle?"

"No. She and Varro took a transport. They're near the main gate. Kee is attempting to lift some access codes."

"Of course she is." I shook my head, but I couldn't really blame her for not telling me, since I'd done the exact same thing. I handed Nilo a meal bar and grabbed another for myself. I missed his cooking. When he grinned, I realized I'd missed it a little too much, and he'd caught the thought.

I scowled at him, but he just pulled me close and nuzzled my neck. "I'm glad you like my cooking."

"You're supposed to be staying out of my thoughts," I grouched.

"I am, mostly. But your love of my cooking was just too great to contain."

I playfully smacked his shoulder and he kissed me until I forgot what we were arguing about. When we broke apart, I brushed my fingers over his cheek. "Be careful today. Don't do anything stupid and heroic."

"I could ask the same of you," he replied.

"I'm never heroic," I teased, but his expression didn't lighten at the joke. "I'll be careful."

"I will do the same."

I nodded. That was all I could ask. I did a final check, then headed out of the bedroom. I found Liang and Anja in the kitchen. Liang was cooking while Anja was frowning at a slate. "Breakfast?" he offered.

"No, thanks. We're heading out."

Anja looked up. "Do you have plans for that plas cannon in your gear?"

"Not exactly, why?"

"With all the equipment downstairs, I think I can make a little remote trigger in case we need a big explosion as a distraction. But we'll need to decide if you all want to try to smuggle it into the base, or just leave it somewhere that points at the base."

"Ask Kee," I said. "If we're still planning to enter as Liang's guard, carrying an FHP plas cannon probably won't work."

Anja nodded. "That's what I figured. We'll find somewhere to stash it."

"Sounds good. We're heading out to do some last-minute recon. We'll be back an hour before dawn. I have my comm and Nilo can communicate with the other Valoffs, so keep us posted if you go out."

"We will," Liang said, and Anja nodded in agreement.

Nilo and I headed downstairs to the lev cycle. I checked the rifle and its case. I hoped we wouldn't need a long-range weapon this early, but leaving it behind was as good as inviting the universe to fuck with us.

I swung a leg over the seat, and Nilo settled in behind me. I started the lev cycle and the safeties engaged, then I opened the garage door and eased out into the night. The air was cold against my exposed face.

"How high do you need to be?" I thought loudly at Nilo.

"I'm not sure. Let's do your recon first, then we'll try to find a port location."

I nodded and headed for Aburwuk's wall. I kept the lev cycle close to the ground, where it would normally hover if someone hadn't overridden the altitude limiter. The streets were empty and quiet, which meant I didn't have to dodge traffic, but we also wouldn't be able to get lost in a crowd.

A wide avenue ran alongside the wall in this part of the city. The street was separated from the wall itself by a strip of undeveloped land. I had no doubt that if I crossed into that three-meter zone that an immediate alert would pop up in a security office on the base.

The wall itself wasn't that high, under four meters, but the top meter was a razor wire structure designed to prevent climbers and the entire wall was monitored. I could get over the razor wire, but not before I set off the alarms.

I'd been hoping that the builders had cut some corners that weren't evident on the schematics I'd studied, but the wall was a smooth, solid surface. There weren't any drainage holes or any other access points that could be exploited. It was over or nothing.

"Try to get a port lock through the main gate," I thought loudly.

"I tried from the hotel room without success, but I'll try again," he responded.

It didn't surprise me that the gate was protected, but I wish the builders had been just a little less thorough. How was I supposed to exploit their mistakes when they hadn't made any?

The main entrance had two sets of gates that worked like an airlock. We'd have to present our identification to be allowed through the first gate, then it would close behind us while the soldiers verified our access. The inner gate would only open if we were authorized. If we failed the check, then we'd be arrested or attacked, depending on what came back from security.

The plas cannon could make a hole, but that would bring the entire base down on us.

And even if we made it through and found Tavi and the crew, we'd still have to go through the same two-gate arrangement on the way out. Maybe Kee would be in their system by then and could open the gates for us, but counting on maybes made me nervous.

I flew past the gate as slowly as I could without becoming suspicious. A handful of soldiers were visible, but no one was entering or exiting. I didn't see Kee or Varro anywhere, but I doubted they would be standing in the open.

"I can't port through the gate," Nilo said telepathically. "Which means I won't be able to port *out,* either."

"Unless we take down the system powering the shield."

"It'll be on an emergency backup. But making a hole in the wall with the plas cannon might work, if we position it right."

I nodded and continued north, but it was more of the same. Continuing past the edge of the city was risky, but it was possible the rest of the base wasn't as protected. Outside of the city, the base had a hundred-meter no-fly zone at ground level. The distance expanded as the altitude rose, so if we wanted a peek over the wall, we'd have to move even farther out.

I made sure we were well out of the restricted zone then increased our altitude enough that I wouldn't have to worry about hitting a stray boulder. It meant I couldn't see the wall as well, but that was the trade-off for being uninteresting to station security.

As we swept around the north side, it was obvious that this was the original wall before the base had been expanded. But even so, it was in good repair and had the same razor wire topper as the rest of the base.

Knowing that the empress had razed half a city to expand the base as punishment for failing to hold off an invading force was apparently a good motivator for keeping up with maintenance. No telling what she would do to the base itself if it ever suffered a breach.

I winced. I guess we were about to find out.

The wall around the spaceport was actually taller than

the rest of the base and it was topped with a battery of anti-aircraft cannons. They could protect the entire base from here, but there were a few additional units scattered around in case these became targets.

Stealing a ship—which was incredibly difficult in the best of times—would be a nonstarter. They'd shoot us out of the sky before we made it a hundred meters.

It was only as we approached the south that we saw the first hint of neglect. It was clear the soldiers had attempted to keep people from building right up to the walls, but they had not been very successful. The southern gate had additional barriers to protect the entrance, but there was only a narrow alley through the ramshackle buildings that wasn't even large enough for a lev cycle.

The whole area was a warren of narrow paths and rickety buildings. From above, it looked like a solid sea of rubble with only an occasional opening wide enough to see the path below. Getting lost in there would be easier than I'd expected.

But the gate was perhaps even more heavily guarded than the main gate. Six armed and armored soldiers stood just behind the outer barricade, facing outward. The gate had the same airlock design, which meant more soldiers probably waited inside.

Some of the people here must work on the base and they didn't want them to overwhelm the main gate. Otherwise, there was no reason to keep this gate open.

Disappearing might be easy in this part of the city, but moving through it wouldn't be fast or straightforward. We'd trade speed for obscurity. It might be a worthwhile trade, but it depended on exactly how we ended up getting *out* of the base in the first place. If we had to go over the wall, this wouldn't be the worst place to do it.

When we returned to our starting point, frustration warred with disappointment. I'd hoped to find something that meant we wouldn't have to rely on walking in the front door, but I'd failed.

Nilo squeezed my shoulder. "It's not a failure," he whispered into my mind. "Now you know what the rest of the base looks like, and that information is valuable."

He was right. Seeing it was better than looking at schematics, but I still would've preferred an open, unguarded door, or at the very least, a nice, person-size drainage gate.

"Where would you like to try to teleport from?" I asked.

"How high can we fly?"

"The no-fly zone starts at a kilometer in the city. If we want to go higher, we'll have to move farther out."

"I'm not sure a kilometer will do it, but I'll try. Head north."

I nodded and pulled the lev cycle into a steep climb. We rose rapidly, and I kept an eye out for other transports, both visually and on the sensors. We were still running without any lights, and I doubted we were the only modified lev cycle in the city.

And there was no better time to get up to no good than in the early hours before dawn.

I leveled us out just under the no-fly zone and headed north. I felt Nilo's power spike and ebb in a rolling wave. As we neared the edge of the city for the second time, I could feel his frustration bleeding across our connection.

"It's not your fault that they're not incompetent," I said.

"It feels like it," he growled.

I knew that feeling all too well, so I just reached down

and squeezed the arm he had wrapped around my waist. "Do you want me to fly higher?"

"No. I would likely have to be directly over the base, and while I know you are an excellent pilot, it's not worth risking the antiaircraft cannons."

"So we're waltzing in the front door after all," I said with a sigh.

"It appears that way."

My stomach flipped before settling. Time to break out my best performance ever.

I PARKED THE LEV CYCLE IN THE GARAGE AND WAITED FOR NILO TO dismount before I did the same. Anja was bent over one of the workbenches, welding a bracket. Liang, Varro, and Kee were gathered around a slate, pointing at the screen, but Kee waved as I approached. "Did you find anything?"

"Nothing useful. The outer wall is well protected and there aren't any easy ways inside. What about you?"

She grimaced. "Varro's not sure he can get us through the gate undetected unless I can shut down the surveillance. I managed to get rough access overnight, but if I shut down the cameras, they'll know something is up. However, I did get a pair of access codes while we were watching the gate, so it wasn't a total waste."

"Any sign of Fev?" I asked.

"No."

Nilo pointed at the maintenance building on the slate. "If Fev is staying in the Riv, then she trusts whoever is in there watching Torran and the crew enough to leave the base. It may only be one team who switches out with Fev, or it may be multiple teams working in shifts."

"Hopefully Fev is planning to sleep to noon today," I said. "I know if I'd just spent several days with Morten that I wouldn't be in any hurry to get back to him."

We all stared at the slate as we contemplated the unlikeliness. It certainly would help, but we'd have to plan as if she *and* a team were guarding Tavi.

Anja joined us, carrying the metal bracket she'd been working on. "I still need to override the plas cannon's safety, but the switch and bracket are done. You should be able to trigger it from anywhere you have comm access."

"Ooh, very nice," Kee said, then frowned in consideration. "Where should we aim it?"

"The Riv's roof has a nice view of the main gate," I said, "but civilians use that gate, too, and we're not the fucking Feds. Plus, we don't want to give Empress Nepru any excuse for war."

Kee nodded her agreement. "We need somewhere that'll cause a lot of drama without a lot of death—and ideally, something that could be blamed on an accident."

"Aim for the generators," Varro said. "The stored fuel will make a large explosion, and they generally aren't crewed unless it's an emergency. They are purposefully stored away from everything else."

Nilo zoomed out on the satellite image on the slate, then scrolled until he found the generators in the northern part of the base. He spun the image until it was like we were looking at it from the Riv. I tilted my head, calculating the angle from the roof. "Oof, it'll be a tricky shot," I said.

"I could hit it from the lev cycle," Anja offered.

Kee immediately shook her head. "Too risky. Ideally, we wouldn't be tied to the weapon at all."

I looked at Anja. "Can you engrave something on the cannon itself?" When she nodded slowly, I said, "Then please add, 'Courtesy of Besor Edfo' in the biggest letters you can."

Nilo laughed, but the rest of the room looked lost, so I added, "He was my contact on Valovia. He sold me out to the empress, so we stole a few guns and blew up his warehouse in retaliation. The plas cannon was one of the weapons we stole."

"He is trading in *plas cannons*?" Kee asked in disbelief. Then she shook her head and pointed at me accusingly. "And you were going to *work* for him?"

I had no defense, so I just lifted a shoulder and said, "Yes."

Kee frowned. "If you need money—"

My heart twisted, but I cut her off before she could stab the knife deeper. "Kee, most of my clients are not exactly good people. I'm *a thief.* You don't hire a thief when the law is on your side."

"I know that," she said, her tone equal parts defensive and disappointed. "I just thought . . ."

Her disappointment made *me* defensive. "I'm careful about which jobs I accept. I don't take any jobs where people are going to get hurt. Well, except for me, maybe, but that's always a risk." I waved my hands dismissively. "But that's neither here nor there. We need to decide where to put the plas cannon then get moving."

Kee sighed but dutifully turned back to the slate. "The generators are a good target, and I happen to know that the Riv's rooftop cameras are on a loop for at least the next six hours, thanks to Rul."

"I hope you paid him a boatload of credits," I said.

She grinned at me. "A *big* boatload, all untraceable thanks to Torran."

I met Anja's gaze. "Can you and Liang handle the plas cannon placement while we're working our way through the front gate?"

"I can't speak for the prince, but I can do it."

"I will go with you," Liang immediately offered. "If Fev is in the building, it will be better if I shield for you."

Anja inclined her head in agreement.

"Hopefully, Fev is still asleep, but don't give her any reason to be suspicious," I said. "If something looks weird, get out. The plas cannon is a last resort, but we can plan around its lack. I happened to snag a few grenades that'll have a similar effect if we need it."

Kee grumbled something under her breath that thankfully even her subvocal comm didn't pick up.

I stared at the slate. "So Varro is going to make Nilo look like Liang, and we'll also presumably have Liang's access codes." At Kee's nod, I waved a hand between her and me. "How are we going to explain our presence? Even with Nilo shielding for me, I doubt I read as a Valoff."

"It's close," Varro said. "I will help shield, and you both should pass."

"Once we're past the gates, we can use the anti-telepathy helmets," Kee said. "If anyone gets too close, they'll notice something wrong, but from a distance we won't register as anything at all."

"I hate that fucking helmet," Varro growled.

Kee patted his arm. "We'll leave them off unless we need them, but it's better to have them, just in case."

I'd take any edge we had, so I nodded my agreement

and met Liang's eyes. "So the rest of us are your assistants? Guards? Hangers-on?"

"Surprise inspection crew," Liang said. "That'll get them to ask the least amount of questions."

"How does one usually address a prince? And how pushy can I be to get them to let us in?"

"My title is His Imperial Highness Liang Nepru. And you can be *exceedingly* pushy. The imperial family is a specter that no one wants to annoy, so most people trip over themselves to get out of our way."

I grinned. "I'll try not to let the power go to my head." I turned to Kee. "I need an official-looking inspection document with the imperial seal, if there is such a thing, prominently displayed. When I wave my comm around and start demanding names, I want it to be very clear that they'll be going into a report that they would rather not be in."

She grabbed her slate. "Give me five minutes."

I tapped the table in thought. "Let's say Fev *has* alerted the base to look out for us and has painted Liang as a traitor. What's our backup plan?"

"If we can fight through the gate, Varro can shield us while we find Torran," Nilo said, and Varro nodded in agreement. "Then we'll make a big explosion to distract everyone and extract through whichever gate is closest."

If I'd had more time—or if I'd been on my own—I never would've proceeded with such a flimsy plan full of so many potential holes, but time wasn't on my side. I sighed. Plans often didn't survive first contact, anyway, so flexibility was key, but this was pushing it.

"I sent you the form," Kee said. "It has lots of scary looking fields, like 'dereliction of duty' and 'recommend retraining.'"

"Perfect, thank you." I looked at the rest of the group. "We'll meet at *Starlight*. If anyone can't get to the ship, find somewhere to lie low and wait for backup. If the ship is compromised, we'll meet here. Kee has a secure comm channel setup, so be sure you're using it, especially if Kee and I are going to be in helmets that block telepathy."

"Let me know if you need a temporary comm," Kee said. "I brought a few extras."

"Any other questions?" I asked. Everyone shook their heads and their expressions started morphing into the serious, focused look soldiers wore into battle. I absolutely hated seeing Kee's glowing happiness dimmed, but I couldn't afford to leave her behind.

I pointed to Kee and Anja. "Stay with your partners. The Valoffs know their military bases and customs better than we do." I turned my gaze to Varro and Liang. "Keep them safe." It was an order, and though they didn't have to follow my orders, both Valoffs bowed with their left arms across their chests.

"No orders for me, *taro*?" Nilo asked, all innocence.

Kee couldn't contain her grin at the endearment, and I shook a finger at her. "Don't encourage him." I slanted a glance at Nilo. "I figured you'd be glued to my ass, but if you'd like for me to order you around, just ask nicely."

His eyes blazed gold and his hands flexed at his sides. The rest of the group smothered their laughs and found somewhere else to be.

"Do your final preparations and meet back here in fifteen," I called after them. I wasn't sure how I'd turned into the team leader, but I'd happily give the responsibility to someone else.

"You're doing great," Nilo murmured.

"It feels like I'm groping my way forward in the dark," I admitted. "I don't know how Tavi does this all the time."

"She has a team to help her, and so do you. Do you really think this group would follow you if we thought you were incompetent? We've all been soldiers. Well, except for the prince, but he's fought his own battles."

I grimaced. "That doesn't make it any easier."

Nilo wrapped his arms around me. "I'll help you. And you *know* Kee is on your side, but every group needs a leader, someone to make quick decisions in the heat of the moment. And I think you're better at it than you're giving yourself credit for."

"Yes, but I'm usually only risking myself." And that was the crux of the matter. I had no problem risking myself, but when it came time to risk someone else, I was far more hesitant. And that was no way to lead an infiltration into an enemy base. Every single person needed to pull their own weight, and I needed to let them.

"Is this going to work?" I whispered against Nilo's shoulder.

"You'll make it work," he said. He gently kissed away my protest. "I believe in you."

And I could feel the truth in those words. I basked in his confidence for a moment before finding my own. I *would* make it work. There was no other option.

CHAPTER TWENTY-ONE

Kee, Varro, Nilo, and I took a transport to the main gate. The added feel of Varro's mind shielding my own sent my panic spiraling. I breathed through it while Nilo held my hand. I wasn't sure I would've been able to handle it without having had him in my head for the last few days. I was getting better, but panic wasn't logical—and it still felt like failure.

Fortunately or otherwise, I didn't have time to dwell on it. I checked on the others one last time as the transport slid past the first gate. Tying Liang's ID to the transport itself was a risk if Fev was looking for him, but it allowed us to skip the outer security check. They wouldn't demand further authentication until we were trapped between the two gates.

I channeled all of my nerves into my mask. The poor soldiers outside didn't have any inkling of the storm I was about to unleash on them.

Nilo squeezed my hand, then it was showtime. All of us were required to exit the transport for inspection, but I was going to try to head that off. I climbed out and left the others inside. "Who is in charge here?" I demanded in Valovan.

A small gatehouse was off to my right, and an armored young woman emerged from it. "I am. Please ask everyone to step out of the vehicle." She wasn't wearing the standard combat helmet, so I could see her face, and so far, she looked more uneasy than suspicious. The gate area was lit up with spotlights, but thanks to my night-vision glasses I noted at least four armed and armored soldiers on the surrounding walls.

I scoffed at the request. "Why is His Imperial Highness being subjected to search?"

"I apologize for the delay, but it's base policy," she responded.

"His Highness *makes* policy; he doesn't bend to it." I lifted my comm with Kee's made-up form clearly visible. "And you are?"

She swallowed and her eyes flickered to the soldiers on the walls then back toward the gatehouse. So at least one more soldier was hidden inside.

None of them responded, at least not verbally. "Let me just contact General—"

"We are here for a surprise inspection of the base, including the headquarters," I interrupted, all scathing impatience. "Do you know the meaning of the word *surprise*?" When she nodded meekly, I let acid drip from each word. "Then you know that if you *contact* the general, it will no longer be a *surprise* inspection, will it?"

When she shook her head, I knew that I almost had her. I lowered my voice and stepped closer. "Look, I know you're just doing your job, but Prince Liang has had a very trying morning, and he hates getting up early *and* inspections, so he's in an absolute *mood*. You would be better off to let the general deal with him."

The woman's fair skin paled even further. Apparently imperial moods were something to be feared. And right on time, Liang's voice rang out from inside the transport. "What is *taking* so long?" he demanded. He was linked in via comm because the fewer senses Varro had to fool, the easier it was for him. It wouldn't work when speaking face-to-face, but for now, it kept the difficulty down.

"Just a moment longer, Your Highness," I called back, my voice both soothing and a little fearful. "I'm afraid you have quite the fan out here, and she's overcome that you've graced the base with your presence. You wouldn't mind meeting one of your people, would you?"

"Bring her to me."

"I suggest you get your visual ID while the prince is feeling benevolent, then let us continue on our way," I whispered to her as I pulled her toward the transport's door.

"This is against—"

"Pretend," I advised, then shoved her in front of the door.

"Who are you?" Liang demanded. Even though I *knew* Varro was tricking my brain along with everyone else's, it was a shock to *see* Liang sitting across from him rather than Nilo. Varro's ability was scarily powerful.

"I'm . . ." She paused and reconsidered giving her name. "I'm head of gate security, Your Highness."

Nilo perfectly mimicked Liang's pretty pout. "I thought you were a fan." His gaze shifted to mine. "You told me she was a fan." There was a deadly soft threat in the words.

Varro somehow made Nilo sound exactly like Liang, and I shivered in fear, which luckily worked with the act.

"Are *you* the reason we're being delayed?" the faux prince demanded, switching his attention back to the soldier. When she floundered for a response, he looked at me again. "Get her name and get us moving. This is unacceptable." He pointedly sat back and turned his attention away from the door—a monarch dismissing a peasant.

I pulled the soldier out of view and lifted my comm. "What is your name?"

"Please don't report me," she begged. "I was just doing my job."

I narrowed my eyes. "*You* were supposed to play along," I hissed. "Now he thinks I lied to him, and I'll have to deal with that for the rest of the day. Why should *I* help *you*?"

"I'll clear you through the gate," she said. "And I won't tell General Do you're coming." She shivered and muttered under her breath, "He deserves the surprise."

I considered her for a moment, then nodded. "But if I get reprimanded for this, I'm going to make sure you go down with me."

She sagged with relief. "I will ensure your transport is approved for direct access to headquarters. You will not be stopped again."

I bowed with my left arm over my chest. "Thank you."

She mirrored the gesture, then I returned to the transport. The door closed and Varro sighed in relief. A moment later, the inner gate opened and the soldier waved us through. The transport slid forward under Nilo's manual control.

"I can't believe that worked," Kee whispered.

"No one wants to cross the imperial family if they can avoid it," Varro said. "And Lexi played it perfectly."

"I just channeled every obnoxious asshole I've ever met," I said with a shrug. "Will she truly not report us?"

"It depends on how much she respects her chain of command," Nilo said. "But it sounded like General Do isn't her favorite person, so she might not, at least for a little while."

"Can either of you sense Luna?" I asked.

Both Valoffs nodded. "She is still north of us," Varro said. "But I still can't sense any of the others."

"And Tavi isn't answering her comm," Kee added, her brow furrowed with worry. Even if the soldiers had confiscated Tavi's physical device, her comm implant should've been able to connect at this range.

I tapped Nilo's arm. "Can you teleport?"

His power rose, then he nodded. "Some places. A few of the buildings are too close together or have better shielding. And I can't port out."

"The plas cannon is in position," Varro said. "Liang and Anja are now going to check on *Starlight*'s status."

"Tell them to be careful," Kee said, and the weapons expert inclined his head.

Nilo briefly landed in front of the headquarters building. Varro grunted, but if he was using his ability, I couldn't tell. Nilo jerked the transport into the air and headed farther north until he found a building with several other transports waiting. He landed in the middle of the cluster.

"Make note of our location," I said. "If we get separated, we'll meet back here. If the transport is missing or compromised, everyone is on their own for extraction. But let's not get separated."

The others nodded, then the Valoffs donned their armored helmets while Kee handed me one of the metal crowns. "The power switch is in the back," she said. "Red light means it's on. If you're wearing it, it'll be very difficult for Nilo and Varro to communicate with you, so turn it off if you need help. And leave it off for now so Varro can partially hide us."

I nodded and put the helmet on. A padded metal and wire band wrapped around my head, but the top of the helmet was mostly open, so it wasn't much protection. But I trusted Kee, and she thought the helmet's ability to hide us from Valoffs made the trade worthwhile.

Varro and Nilo wore their standard-issue Valovian armor, while Kee and I had on the armor the *Starlight's Shadow* crew used for bounty hunting. It looked distinctly human, so Varro was going to work some telepathic magic on it to make us less interesting, but he wasn't going to obscure us completely, which took more effort, unless there was no other option.

"Let's go get Tavi," I said subvocally, testing our comms. Kee, Varro, and Nilo nodded.

We left the transport and started north. Nilo was on my left, and Kee and Varro were side-by-side behind us. Varro and I had rifles in addition to our plas pistols while Kee and Nilo only carried sidearms and plas blades.

But if it came to a fight, we would be quickly overrun by an entire base full of trained soldiers, so we were aiming for a fast grab and then a hasty escape.

We moved quickly and purposefully, like we belonged but were running late. There were a few other people out, but mostly the base was quiet as the first hint of dawn smudged the horizon. Ideally, we'd be long gone before the sun fully rose.

We were halfway to the maintenance building where we thought Tavi was being held when a white blur chirruped and launched itself from atop a stack of crates. I spun as Kee caught Luna with a happy exclamation.

Kee petted the little burbu and cooed nonsense to her for a moment before asking, “Do you know where Tavi is?”

Luna tilted her head and blinked her big eyes, then a picture of an empty food bowl appeared in my mind—and Kee’s too, if her snort was anything to go by.

“At least you’re consistent,” Kee grumbled before fishing in a pouch on her waist for a bite-size piece of jerky. “You’ve probably had every soldier on this whole base feeding you, but here you go.”

Luna scarfed down the dried meat then looked pleadingly at Kee. “No more until we find Tavi,” the systems engineer admonished. “The captain is in trouble.”

Luna chirped and wiggled until Kee let her go. As soon as Luna hit the ground, she darted off toward the north, presumably heading for the building she’d shown Varro. We resumed our trek. The Valoffs could probably sense her, but we humans couldn’t, and Luna seemed to know that because she circled back for us whenever we fell too far behind.

We were almost to the large maintenance building when Nilo whispered, “Stop.”

I stopped and Nilo guided me into the deeper darkness between two buildings while Varro did the same for Kee. “I feel it, too,” Varro confirmed.

“What?” Kee and I asked simultaneously.

“It’s the same blank feeling that was hiding *Starlight,*” Nilo said, “but this one is far more subtle. If I hadn’t been looking for it specifically, I might not have noticed.”

Kee looked at Varro. “Can you sense anything through it?”

Varro shook his head.

I grimaced. "So we have no idea how many people might be inside—or what kind of weapons they might have. Fuck." I took a deep breath. "Let's circle around the outside, then Kee and I will enable our helmets before we enter."

Kee started to protest, but I cut her off. "We don't know if the field is being generated by a nullifier and a synthetic amplifier or just a synthetic nullifier, but either way, Varro won't be able to hide us from whoever is inside because the whole area seems to block telepathy. If we're already not going to be able to communicate telepathically, then these helmets might at least let us surprise whoever is inside."

Her nose wrinkled, but she nodded in acknowledgment.

Luna followed us around the building until we came to an unmarked door on the north side. When we would've continued on, Luna sat next to the door and chirruped at us. Kee cooed at her and fed her another piece of jerky. This must be where they'd brought Tavi in. I didn't see any cameras, but that didn't mean they didn't exist.

The building was two stories tall and while I hadn't seen any roof access from the ground, there was a conveniently placed drainpipe right next to the door. I'd climbed worse, but the trip down would be harder than the trip up.

"I'm going to look at the roof," I said over the comm. "Varro, can you hide me while the rest of you continue around the building?"

"I can port you," Nilo said telepathically.

I shook my head. "Save your strength. I can climb."

"It'll be harder to hide you if you're not with the group," Varro warned.

"Don't strain yourself. I'm good at staying hidden, and the darkness will do most of the work."

Nilo squeezed my hand. "Be careful."

"You, too."

Climbing in armor wasn't the easiest feat, especially because my legs were stronger than my arms, but I'd worn my soft, flexible boots. I pulled on the pipe to ensure it was secure, then gripped it and leaned back slightly, using leverage to anchor my feet to the wall. When nothing came crashing down, I climbed upward.

The climb only took a few seconds, but the transition to the roof was trickier. The pipe ended at a drain hole below the top of the wall, which meant I'd need to lift myself up and over the edge to get to the roof.

Once I was as high as I could climb, I gripped the pipe with my feet and carefully pushed myself up until I could reach the top of the wall. Doing a pull-up with the amount of weapons and armor I was carrying wasn't happening, so I dangled from the wall while I raised my feet to the top of the pipe. The new location gave me enough room to stand again and get my torso on the wall. Then it was just a matter of wiggling over onto the roof.

I really hoped the others had moved on because this wasn't the most dignified way to climb, but it worked for me.

The roof was flat, and the short outer wall ran all the way around the building. There were no obvious doors, but part of the roof was obscured by ducts and ventilation equipment. My night-vision glasses didn't pick up the telltale shine of a camera, so I moved toward the middle of the building.

There were no skylights on top of the building that I could use to see inside, but on the far corner from where I'd climbed up, there was a square hatch that was used for maintenance access.

The door was locked and had neither a physical deadbolt nor a visible control panel, but there had to be a way for a technician to get inside if the door accidentally closed while they were on the roof—I just had to find it.

And the most likely option was the keycard I'd gotten from Kee's contact. I slid it from my pocket and paused. "Kee, how much do you trust this keycard?" I asked subvocally.

"Did you find a door?"

"Roof hatch. Electronic lock, but the control panel is inside."

She thought for a moment. "The keycard may not work, but I don't think anything bad will happen if you use it. Should we come up there?"

"Let me see if I can get the door open first."

"Focus on something around you so I can get a visual lock," Nilo said.

Rather than thinking about exactly *how* he would be getting that visual lock from something I was looking at, I focused on a section of roof a few meters away that had two intersecting ducts that would hopefully work for uniqueness. I noted the cracks in the roof sealant and the marks on the ducts until Nilo said, "Got it."

A shiver worked its way down my spine. I wasn't sure I'd ever get used to knowing that a Valoff could pull an image from my brain, but I didn't have time to worry about it because I needed to get this hatch open.

I knelt down and swiped the card over the top of the door opposite the hinges. About halfway up, I heard a faint beep and the lock clicked open. Hopefully Rul had tied this keycard to a maintenance worker or someone else innocuous or we were about to become very suspicious.

I turned the handle and lifted the hatch. It opened easily and a peek inside revealed a steep staircase down to a small, dark room. My night-vision glasses revealed a typical maintenance closet.

The closet would offer us some cover, but retreating up the stairs would not be quick or easy. Still, it might be better than entering one of the main doors.

"I'm going to see what's inside. Stay put for now," I thought to Nilo as I started down the stairs.

"Lexi, I don't think that's a goo—" Nilo started, but the feeling of his presence in the back of my mind disappeared as soon as my head cleared the roofline. I didn't dare try my comm, but the fact that Kee wasn't yelling at me was a pretty good indicator that comms didn't work, either.

It was strange to miss something that still gave me panic attacks, but I'd gotten sort of used to having Nilo just a thought away. Being on my own after days of togetherness felt odd.

The closet door was not locked—it didn't even *have* a lock. I carefully cracked the door open, but all I could see was the wall at the end of a dim hallway. The door swung the wrong way, dammit.

I listened carefully, but I couldn't hear anything except a low-level buzzing that could be fans or electronics, so I opened the door wide enough that I could peek the other way. A line of windows overlooked the main part of the building and they continued around the corner out of sight.

But the thing that caused me to freeze in place was that the maintenance closet was tucked into the corner behind the security office.

The *occupied* security office.

I could only see a soldier's uniformed arm from this angle, and the monitor above it showed a line of empty cells. I leaned a tiny bit farther out, but the rest of the monitor didn't reveal anything else. There was at least one more monitor in front of the soldier, but peeking at it would be risky.

And getting caught by a Valoff with unknown abilities was a good way to end up dead. Unless the nullifier was blocking their abilities. Or maybe the soldier *was* the nullifier?

As much as I wanted to press forward and find the answers, I had a team counting on me, and I couldn't leave them in limbo forever. And while I could *probably* take one soldier with surprise on my side, if there were two or more then the odds changed—and not in my favor.

The soldier stretched and started shuffling things around, but they didn't look my way, so I carefully eased back into the maintenance closet and silently closed the door.

I turned for the hatch and my instincts kicked in at the sight of someone in Valovian armor crouching on the roof. I reached for my pistol, but before I could draw it, Nilo opened his face shield, which saved me from having to explain why I'd shot him.

It *didn't* explain, however, why he was on the roof.

He motioned me up the stairs, and I climbed with my heart hammering. Once my head cleared the roof, Nilo's presence returned to the back of my mind and my comm reconnected in time to hear Kee murmur, "Thank the Lady."

"What's going on?" I asked. "I told you all to stay put."

"Two unknown soldiers just entered the building," Nilo whispered. "We were coming to warn you."

CHAPTER TWENTY-TWO

Luna was perched on Kee's shoulder, and Varro loomed behind the two of them. I looked at Nilo. "Did you port up here?"

He shook his head. "We climbed the pipe."

"*They* climbed," Kee said pointing at Nilo and Varro. "They basically tossed me up, and Luna rode on Varro's shoulder."

"And no one noticed any of that?" It was dark, but it wasn't *that* dark.

Varro shook his head. "I was shielding."

"Any chance that one of the arriving soldiers could be Fev?"

Nilo shook his head. "They were in uniforms, not armor. One was a woman, but it wasn't Fev."

"Okay, that's good," I said. "When I entered the building, my connection to Nilo was severed. And I'm guessing you tried to contact me over the comm and couldn't?" When Kee nodded, I continued, "Then we have to assume it's the same technology that was used on *Starlight*—no comms, no telepathy, and maybe no visuals."

"That is annoying," Kee complained. "How am I supposed to do anything if I can't even get a connection?"

"This hatch leads to a maintenance closet, but there's no way out without going past the security office. The office has windows into the main part of the building and there was at least one soldier with a monitor showing empty holding cells. I couldn't confirm if Tavi, the crew, or Morten were inside."

Kee's eyes lit up. "I can work with a security office."

"I originally planned to take down whoever—or *whatever*—was acting as a nullifier so that Torran could hopefully help with the escape, but the extra soldiers change things. Preventing them from using their abilities or telepathically calling for backup is a huge advantage for us."

"It's a risk," Nilo argued. "Because we don't know *how* they're suppressing abilities. If they're using a synthetic amplifier, then the nullifier will be able to selectively allow the other soldiers to use their abilities, assuming they're strong enough. And we won't be able to communicate or use our abilities, either. We don't know how many soldiers are inside. If even one escapes, we'll have the whole base on us followed shortly by Sura Fev."

"The arriving soldiers might be a shift change," I said. "So there might only be two inside, and I'll take two normal soldiers over Sura Fev any day, even if one of them is a nullifier. Fighting a telekinetic in an enclosed space is a nightmare."

Kee shivered and paled. "Yeah, we already tried that,

and it didn't go well." Luna butted her head against Kee's, and Kee absently reached up to pet the little burbu. The fight on FOSO I had left its mark.

Nilo sighed. "Fev wouldn't leave guard duty to soldiers who were incompetent. If one is a nullifier, then it's likely that the other one is a telekinetic. That way if anything happens to the nullifier, the telekinetic can take over."

I grimaced. So we were back to fighting a telekinetic after all. "Which would you put in the security office?"

"The telekinetic," Nilo and Varro answered together.

I breathed through the spike of adrenaline. I had been a few meters from a potential telekinetic and hadn't known it—assuming our guesses were correct. Once again we didn't have enough solid information for a plan, but we had to move forward anyway.

"Something shady is definitely happening in this building, and Luna tagged it as well, so we have to check it," I said.

Kee nodded. "If nothing else, it may let me get deeper into their security system."

I pulled off my helmet, found the power switch, and flipped it on. A tiny red light pulsed inside the headband. Good enough. When I put the helmet on, the cool feel of Nilo's presence disappeared completely from my mind, just like it had when I'd entered the building.

And wasn't *that* telling. Morten *definitely* had someone in the Valovian military feeding him information—or he was giving Fed research to the Valoffs, which was a whole other level of traitorous for someone trying to restart the war.

Nilo cursed under his breath, and Varro grimaced in sympathy. Apparently neither Valoff was a fan of this technology.

Kee turned on her helmet, and I reminded everyone, “Stick together and move quickly. We find Tavi, the crew, and maybe Morten, then we get out.”

They all nodded and Nilo closed his face shield. I let the adrenaline steady into sharpness, then led the group down the stairs into the maintenance closet. Kee brought Luna along, and while I was worried for the burbu, leaving her on the roof wouldn’t be any better.

Once we were all inside, I signed to Kee, “Can you get a connection?”

She poked at her slate for moment before shaking her head. Our comms were out, too, so we’d have to rely on sign language, pointing, and whispers.

I waved everyone into a close huddle, then turned to Nilo. “Can you telepathically communicate with Varro now that we’re inside?” I asked, my voice barely audible.

Nilo’s forehead wrinkled, and he silently shook his head. So whatever was suppressing their abilities covered the whole building, not just the perimeter like teleporter protection.

“I can’t sense anyone, including all of you,” Varro murmured with a wave at the group.

He was a strong telepath, so hopefully if he couldn’t sense anyone else, then they couldn’t sense us, either. The only wild card was the nullifier. Hopefully these helmets were as good as Kee claimed or this would be a very short trip.

“The security office is to the left,” I whispered to the group. “The guard was sitting with their back to us, but I don’t know if that’s changed.”

“Armor?” Nilo asked.

When I shook my head, he drew one of his knives. A

blade had the potential to be quieter; it also had the potential to go horribly wrong. But I had to trust that Nilo knew what he was doing because for all of his playfulness, he had survived the war, same as me.

"I will go first," he whispered.

I pointed at Kee and Varro, "Stay here unless we run into trouble. We'll signal when it's clear."

"Lex—"

"Kee, I love you, but you are not stealthy."

She made a disgruntled face at me, then reluctantly nodded.

I drew my pistol and waved Nilo toward the door. I'd let him take the lead, but I'd be right behind him.

Nilo silently opened the door a crack, and we all held our breath as we listened for movement. When nothing happened, Nilo peeked around the corner then slipped from the room as silent as a wraith. I followed him, my boots soundless on the metal floor.

We stayed low and away from the windows. I could see the guard, a tan woman with dark hair. She was watching the screens in front of her, unaware that death approached. If Tavi and Torran weren't here, then she was about to be killed for nothing, and it would be my fault.

Nilo was as lethal as he was silent. The woman died with barely a gurgle of sound, and he quietly eased her to the floor away from the desk. No one else was in the office, but three monitors showed the rest of the building.

There were more cells than I'd expected and many of them were filled. It took me a breathless second to find Tavi. She was sitting with her arms on her knees and her face was turned away from the camera, but I would recognize her anywhere. She was wearing what looked like her own clothes, but she had no weapons or armor.

After that, it was easier to find Eli, Torran, Havil, and Chira because while they were all in individual cells, they appeared to be grouped together away from the rest of the prisoners.

I sagged in relief. We'd found them.

Nilo went back for Kee, Varro, and Luna while I scanned the monitors. Three male soldiers were clustered together near a tall garage door and a smaller entry door. They appeared to be casually chatting, so I hoped two of them were from the previous shift and would be leaving soon. One soldier was wearing a helmet that was eerily similar to the ones Kee and I had on.

If there were any other guards, they were somewhere without surveillance.

Kee settled into the dead guard's chair with Luna and nudged me out of the way. "Let's see what we have here," she murmured. She touched Tavi's video. "Thank the Lady," she murmured.

"Can you open the cells?" I asked.

"Probably, give me a second."

I glanced at Varro. "Is the nullification field still active?"

His chin dipped, and he pointed at the guards on the monitor. "Those are Dravowuia uniforms—Special Forces."

Of course they were. The Special Forces attracted soldiers with some of the strongest and most dangerous abilities—assuming the Sun Guardians didn't snag them first. During the war, entire squads of Special Forces soldiers had been sent out occasionally with devastating effect, but it was more common for one or two to support a platoon or company.

They were loyal and well trained, so it made sense that Fev had tapped them for guard duty. The soldiers might've thought it was beneath them, but I doubted they'd say as much to a Sun Guardian's face.

But perhaps we could use that arrogance against them.

I was contemplating exactly how that might work when two of the soldiers exited the building. The remaining soldier—the one in the helmet—pressed a button on the wall, and his voice came through the speaker on the desk. "I guess I'm going to go check on our guests. Let me know when the tea is ready."

Fuck, they were using hardwired comms. We all looked at Kee who was scowling at the screen in front of her. "I've got nothing," she whispered furiously. "I have no idea what the guard sounded like."

But the soldier didn't seem to expect a response because he moved deeper into the building at a leisurely pace. He didn't even have his weapon drawn.

I swung the rifle off my back. "I will take care of the guard. You keep working on the cells."

Kee nodded absently, already absorbed with the data on-screen. Luna slipped from her lap and started nosing around the room, but Varro was keeping an eye on her, so I crossed to the door that led out of the office.

"There's not much cover," Nilo said from his place against the opposite side of the doorway. "The stairway is exposed to most of the building."

A peek revealed what he meant. We were in the upper corner of the building. Two stories of cells lined the walls, each with a thick, opaque plexiglass front wall and door.

The grate walkways led to this corner, which made it easy to ensure the prisoners stayed put, but it made it hard for us to leave the security office without being seen. Even the stairs to the ground floor were wide open to the rest of the room.

A large garage door was at the far end of the left wall, and the door next to the pipe I'd climbed was in the opposite corner from where we were now. Neither exit was super convenient.

In the middle of the building, a separate square island included closed-in rooms on the ground floor and more cells on the upper levels, reachable by a separate stairway. That might be where they were keeping Tavi and the others, but the opaque glass made confirmation impossible.

Nilo pulled me farther back into the security office and gestured toward the floor. Everyone except Kee complied. She hunkered behind the monitors and kept working.

I heard the footsteps a moment later, approaching from below us and to our left. The soldier crossed under us and kept going. There was an additional stairway at the end of the line of cells. If he continued his current path, he would climb up to our level at the far end, and I would have a straight shot at him.

I waited for the footsteps to move away, then lay in the doorway with my rifle on the floor. The safety railing had only two crossbars between each post, so I would be able to shoot through it. I aimed for the top of the stairs and breathed slowly.

It took an age for the soldier to reach the far end of the building, then an additional decade for him to climb the stairs. My nerves were wound tight, but my hands were steady. He put one foot on the upper-level walkway, and my shot caught him in the middle of the chest. He collapsed back down the stairs with a crash.

Nilo cursed and pulled me to my feet. "What's wrong?" I demanded.

"The nullification is gone, and now it's very loud in here, telepathically speaking. We need to move."

Our comms were still down, so the nullifier hadn't been the only thing protecting the building. Or maybe the amplifier also worked to jam comms. "Kee, how are you doing on the doors?"

"Almost there," she murmured. "They require a higher level of access than this soldier had. You want them all open?" A loud crash rang through the building. "Well, Torran just let himself out, so do you want the rest open?"

I circled the desk and leaned over her shoulder. "Is Morten here?"

"I haven't seen him."

"He's here," Varro said. "Lower level, in the middle."

Kee scowled. "None of those rooms have surveillance."

"Fuck." I weighed our options. "Open all of the cells. I don't know if the rest of the prisoners are here for real crimes or not, but chasing them down will hopefully keep Fev busy, and maybe we can escape in the chaos. And if Morten makes a run for it, it'll give me an excuse to shoot him."

Kee flashed me a grin, then tapped out a few more commands. The locks clicked open throughout the building. The sound was loud enough to wake up any of the prisoners who hadn't already awoken thanks to the nullification failing.

"I'm going for Morten," I said. "Get the comms up."

Kee nodded and kept working. I looked at Varro and he

nodded solemnly. He would watch her back in case any of the prisoners made it this far.

"I'm going with you," Nilo said.

If he expected me to argue, he was going to be disappointed. I was happy to have him at my side when there were a bunch of unknown Valoffs roaming around. I met him at the door and we slipped from the room with Luna following us.

Tavi waved from the second-floor railing of the middle island. "Lexi, you have no idea how happy I am to see you," she yelled.

I waved back, while Luna chirruped and darted down the stairs, arrowing for Tavi.

"Torran is gathering the rest of the crew," Nilo said. "They're going to meet us on the ground floor." His head tilted. "And Morten just moved for the first time."

"Where is he?"

Nilo took the stairs down to the ground floor. "Follow me."

We hit the bottom of the stairs and were moving toward the middle cluster of rooms when someone staggered out of one of the open doors. Commodore Frank Morten had the bleary look of a person under heavy sedation.

I brought my rifle up. He wouldn't feel a thing, which was more mercy than he deserved.

"Stop!" Kee commanded, her voice echoing from speakers throughout the building. "He has to stand trial."

My finger hovered on the trigger. "You expect us to risk our lives to get this piece of shit back to safety just so the Feds can slap his wrist and let him go? No thank you."

"Kee's right," Tavi said from behind me. "Stand down."

For the first time in many, many years, I considered

disregarding one of Tavi's orders. Frank Morten was a garbage human, and the universe would be a better place without him in it.

"Lexi, please," Tavi said softly. "Trust me."

I might ignore a command, but I couldn't ignore a plea. *"Fuck."* I blew out a slow breath and eased my finger away from the trigger.

"Thank you," Tavi said.

"You're not welcome," I grumbled.

Luna was clinging to Tavi's shoulder, but the captain laughed and pulled me into a side hug anyway. "I missed you, Lexi. Thanks for coming for us."

I glanced at her, uncertain. "I hope you knew I would."

"I did."

Morten was still trying to stumble away from us, but he wasn't making much progress. "For the record, I reserve the right to shoot the asshole the minute he so much as breathes wrong. He can stand trial with a bullet wound or two. Or ten."

"You won't hear any arguments from me," Eli said. He looked tired and he had a black eye, but the most concerning part was that he had an unconscious Havil draped over his shoulders.

"What's wrong with Havil?"

"Just exhaustion," Eli said. "Torran took some damage, and Havil healed him."

It took more than "some damage" to exhaust Havil, but now wasn't the time for questions. I looked in the room that Morten had emerged from. It was set up like a standard medbay, albeit one with everything locked down. Even the IV pole was bolted to the wall.

I jerked back as a hellacious metallic screeching noise

echoed from above us, and a moment later, Kee's voice came over the comm. "Torran took care of the synthetic amplifier. I'm still working on a couple of things, but comms are back up."

"Excellent work," I replied at the same time Tavi said, "Good job."

I laughed and bowed to her. "Your command, Captain."

Torran and Chira joined us on the ground floor. It seemed that most of the other prisoners had been on this level. A few were peeking out of their cells, but only a couple had braved the open. They weren't attacking, so we ignored them.

"Enemies incoming," Kee warned just as the outer door started to open. "It's the Special Forces soldiers that were here earlier."

The door slammed closed, and Torran grunted as the metal shrieked. "Another telekinetic," he warned aloud.

Tavi cursed and waved at the block of rooms next to us. "Everyone behind cover. Eli, grab Morten and stay out of sight." She looked at me. "Got an extra gun?"

I handed her my rifle and drew my plas pistol as we jogged around the corner. The cover wasn't great, especially with Morten yelling at Eli, but it was better than standing right in front of the door when the telekinetic came through.

Once we were in position, Torran must've let go of the door because it flew open with a bang, then tore from the hinges. The telekinetic used it as cover as the two soldiers entered the building, leaving us with no shot—not that we didn't try anyway, but none of them connected.

Nilo groaned. "The nullifier is back, but they're not as strong without the amplifier."

"Get back in your cells!" an unfamiliar male voice yelled in Valovan. "Anyone out of a cell will be killed." A scream punctuated that statement as the telekinetic jerked an escaped prisoner over the second-floor railing and let him fall to the ground. Torran's power caught the prisoner just above the floor, but only for a second before the nullifier canceled his ability. Hopefully it had been enough to break the fall.

"So the nullifier is strong enough to selectively choose targets even without the amplifier," I muttered. "That's handy for them."

"Selective nullification is draining," Nilo said. "They will focus on general telepathy—to prevent us from communicating—and threats."

Torran's voice rang out from the other side of Tavi. "I am General Torran Fletcher, and I have a writ of safe passage from Empress Nepru. Stand down immediately."

"Threats like that," Nilo said with a sigh.

CHAPTER TWENTY-THREE

"You are a traitor to the empire," the soldier told Torran. "Your writ is void. If you have any honor remaining, you will turn yourself in."

I winced. Questioning a Valoff's honor was a grave insult, and if the thunderclouds gathering on Torran's brow were any indication, that soldier was about to be in for a rough time—assuming the nullifier didn't wipe out Torran's ability.

But the soldiers didn't need to capture us, they just needed to contain us long enough for more backup to arrive. Time wasn't on our side.

"My helmet prevents Valoffs from sensing me, right?"

Nilo shook his head. "Whatever you're thinking, forget it."

"We have, *at most,* ten minutes until Fev shows up. And probably less than that until more Special Forces show up.

So I'm going to sneak around the other side of this block, and once I start shooting to distract them, you and Tavi and Torran are going to shoot them in the face and/or smush them into paste. Got it?"

"Your helmet won't prevent the telekinetic from smashing *you,*" Nilo growled.

"Which one is the telekinetic?"

"The shorter one," Chira said from behind me. When Nilo grunted at her, Chira added, "Lexi is right. We need to move, and they won't expect a human they can't detect. But give me your gun and go with her. Between your shield and the nullifier, they likely won't be able to sense you, either. And if it gets too dangerous, you can port her."

"Unless the nullifier locks me," he argued.

"I'm going," I said calmly. "You can stay here or come with, but decide now."

Nilo handed Chira his pistol. "Don't miss."

She bowed with her left arm across her chest. "I won't."

We worked our way around the middle island as Torran and the soldier continued to trade insults. The fact that the telekinetic hadn't pushed farther into the building told me that their job was containment rather than capture—and that we needed to leave.

Tavi must've come to the same conclusion because her voice echoed through my comm implant. "Kee, wrap up whatever you're doing."

"I need five minutes."

"You have one. Make it count."

Kee's curses came through loud and clear, but she didn't argue.

"We're in position," Tavi said. "Whenever you are ready, Lex."

I peeked around the corner. I still didn't have a shot. The soldiers had holed up behind a column supporting the upper level. Between it and the door, they'd found one of the only pieces of cover in that part of the building. I had to flush them out, but trained soldiers wouldn't give easily. A grenade would do it, but with two telekinetics and a nullifier, it was anyone's guess where it would end up, and I couldn't risk hitting our side.

Which meant I'd have to leave cover myself.

"This is such a bad idea," I muttered.

"I won't let you be hurt," Nilo said.

I briefly squeezed his fingers then calculated the place that would give me the best angle for a shot. A prisoner peeked out of a cell along the wall. I waved her back. If she stepped out, she was going to get caught in the crossfire because I was aiming for exactly where she was standing.

"On my mark," I said over the comm. "Go!"

I darted across the open space and vaulted over the walkway railing that separated the cells from the rest of the building. I had a split second to decide which Valoff was shorter, then I pulled the trigger. The pulse hit and the soldier went down, but an invisible force locked around me with bruising pressure.

I'd chosen wrong.

My lungs refused to expand, and I couldn't do anything except hope that the nullifier was too busy bleeding to lock down Nilo's power. If Nilo wasn't able to port me to safety, then he'd do something stupidly heroic despite his promise, and I'd have to yell at him.

But I had no doubt Nilo would save me, and *that* thought brought me up short.

It had been a long time since I'd trusted someone new to

watch my back and bail me out when things went sideways. Tavi, Kee, and Eli were the only other people I was that close with, and I loved them for it.

And now Nilo.

This time, the pressure in my chest had nothing to do with the telekinetic power wrapped around my body. Joy and fear and hope swirled into an impossible jumble.

A heartbeat later, the telekinetic's hold tightened, and I wheezed out what little breath I had left. Nilo's power rose, but before he could port us, cool power spiked on my *left,* where the prisoner had been, and the entry door smashed into the telekinetic.

I hit the walkway as the door spun away and several well-placed shots hit the soldier in the chest. He went down and didn't get up.

Nilo helped me to my feet. His face shield was open and his expression was unreadable, but his hands shook as he ran them down my arms, checking for injuries. "Please tell me he didn't hurt you," he whispered.

"He just gave me a little hug," I lied. I shoved my wild emotions back into their boxes. There would be time enough to examine them later, once we weren't in the middle of an escape.

Nilo's eyes flashed, but an unfamiliar woman asked in Valovan, "Are you okay?"

I turned to her. She was leaning against the door, breathing hard. She had long red hair and skin nearly as pale as Chira's. "You're telekinetic?" I asked warily.

"Not a very strong one, but yes." Her head tilted. "And you're human."

"I am. Thank you for your assistance."

"I'm not sure I helped. I believe the general had it under control, but I did what I could. If you're escaping, can I come with you?"

"We have a Sun Guardian after us," I said, "so you might be better on your own."

"I'll risk it."

My eyebrows rose, but my questions were forgotten when Kee thundered down the stairs with Varro behind her. "We need to go," she said as the group started to gather near the outer door. "A transport just requested priority clearance to come over the wall, so you know what that means."

"Fev." Tavi spat the name like a curse. "Do you have a transport?"

"Technically yes," Kee said, "but it's linked to Liang's ID, so Fev probably knows about it."

Tavi looked at me. "Tell me you have an extraction plan."

"I do, but you're not going to like it. We can remotely detonate their generators, then slip away in the confusion."

Tavi scowled. "So your plan is to put the base on high alert?"

"I told you that you weren't going to like it. But it's not like we had a multitude of options. The base is shielded. Nilo can't port in or out."

Eli dragged Morten closer and the commodore's eyes landed on Tavi. "Octavia Zarola, we meet again," he sneered. "Tell this brute to get his hands off me."

"I don't think I will," Tavi said, her voice calm and cool.

"Listen here, you little bi—"

Torran stepped in front of Morten, his glare cold enough to freeze a star. "Think very carefully before you finish that sentence," he growled. "Your bounty only pays half on proof of death, but it's a sacrifice that I am more than willing to make. Tavi is the only thing standing between you and an extremely painful end."

Morten scoffed. "There's no bounty."

Kee grinned with obvious delight. "That's where you're wrong." She held up her comm with an alert showing a picture of Morten in uniform.

"You could've mocked that up in two minutes," Morten said with a careless smirk. But there was new tension around his eyes.

"Yep, I could've, but I didn't. Every comm at Bastion got the same alert, and we were given a million-five contract for you. But as Torran said, it only pays half for proof of death. Still, half of one point five million credits is a lot of money, and as a bonus, we wouldn't have to deal with you all the way back to Fed space."

Morten paled, but his expression turned vicious. "I should've kill—"

Torran knocked the commodore out with one well-aimed punch, and Eli let Morten's body collapse to the ground. "Oops," he said without a hint of remorse.

Tavi rolled her eyes. "Let me guess, your hand slipped."

"I was going to let it slip straight into his jaw, but Torran had already handled it."

"And how are you going to carry him *and* Havil, smartass?"

"I guess I'll have to drag Morten," Eli said with obvious relish.

Eli was strong—and vengeful—enough to do it, but Varro handed Torran his rifle, then bent down and pulled Morten over his shoulder with far less care than Eli was using with Havil. "I will carry him," Varro said.

"Thank you," Tavi said. "Now let's get out of here."

As we moved toward the door, the telekinetic prisoner spoke up, her voice soft. "If we can get to the southern gate, I might be able to get us out," she said in Valovan. "There's a tunnel—or there was, but it was weeks ago. Sometimes they find them and shut them down, especially if we can't afford the bribes."

"And you are?" Tavi demanded after Torran translated. He repeated her question in Valovan.

"I'm Nia. I worked in the kitchens until I got caught stealing food and they figured out I was telekinetic. They sentenced me to six months of 'helping' with their research."

Tavi waved toward the door. "Everyone out. It won't do us any good to let Fev land on top of us."

Luna led the way out of the building. Tavi stopped at the downed soldiers and grabbed their weapons. She passed a pistol to Nilo and one to Eli.

"Wait, I almost forgot." Kee sprinted across the building and came back with the first soldier's helmet. "We think this was helping to amplify his ability. Anja can help me analyze it when we get back to the ship."

"Good, now let's move," Tavi said.

The horizon was brightening with the coming dawn, but the darkness was still deep enough to give us some cover. "Turn off your helmets," Varro said to Kee and me. "I will shield."

The moment I removed my helmet, I felt Nilo's presence return to the back of my mind. And maybe it was because I was already running at maximum adrenaline, but for the first time, I felt more relief than panic.

We jogged south. "What was your extraction plan?" I asked Tavi over the comm.

"Surprise attack on the main gate," she admitted.

Ha! I wasn't the only one who had shitty extraction planning.

"Hug the walls," Kee said and pointed to the building on our left. Varro must've relayed the order to the Valoffs in the group because everyone crowded against the nearest building and froze in place. A moment later, the whine of a transport's engines passed overhead. Thanks to the angle, we couldn't see the transport itself, which hopefully meant they couldn't see us.

"Two guesses who that was," Kee said. She tapped something on her comm. "I killed the power in the building, which might buy us a few more minutes, but we need to move."

We picked up the pace. Nia led us through the base, choosing unused paths and smaller alleys. She didn't have night-vision glasses, but the dim predawn light didn't slow her down. Kee was quietly verifying the path on her comm, but so far, the telekinetic hadn't led us astray. We were almost to the southern gate when she jerked back against the building we had been about to pass.

Tavi peeked around the corner and cursed. "Troop transport just landed. Four soldiers in full Special Forces combat armor. No sign of Fev."

The lack of Fev was the only good news. Surprise wouldn't work this time because the group knew we were somewhere on the base. And if Fev was smart, she would've told them we'd killed their fellow soldiers, so they'd be out for blood.

"Where is the tunnel?" Tavi asked.

Torran translated, and Nia pointed ahead to a building

with a pile of crates next to it. It was the building closest to the wall. "It should be there, out of sight of the gate, but the opening is narrow. Only one at a time."

It might've been out of sight of the gate, but it wasn't out of sight of the Special Forces soldiers. We had over five meters of open ground to cover between us and the next building, and they would be on us before we could disappear into the tunnel—assuming it was still there.

"I can shield our presence at this distance, but they're likely too strong for me to shield us visually," Varro said.

The group was in no shape to fight, not against four elite soldiers with unknown abilities. I moved closer to Tavi. "Nilo and I can circle back and cause a distraction while you get to the tunnel. Then Nilo can port us back here." I glanced at him. "Assuming he's willing."

Nilo nodded, but Tavi shook her head. "Splitting up is dangerous."

"We can use the plas cannon to blow the generators," I offered, "but if Fev sent the Special Forces soldiers, then they likely won't move even if we do, and we'll just alert the rest of the base. Then we'll have to fight even more soldiers while carrying two people and short on weapons."

Tavi cursed. "Do *not* do anything risky," she ordered. "I don't want to have to break back into this damned base to rescue *you*."

"We'll be careful," I promised.

Tavi, who knew me well, narrowed her eyes. "I'm serious, Lexi. We only need a few seconds of inattention. Draw them away, then get back here."

"I will keep her safe," Nilo promised.

Tavi's eyebrows rose, but she just said, "Good luck."

"You, too," I said. "See you soon."

Nilo and I turned back the way we'd come. "Should I turn my helmet on?" I asked.

"No, I will shield for you. We're far enough away that my shields should be sufficient. And since I don't understand your signed language, having a way to silently communicate is valuable."

"I can teach you, if you'd like. Not now, obviously, but once we're safe. Or I'm pretty sure Kee is teaching the rest of the crew—she's the one who taught me."

Nilo's head tilted, but I couldn't see his expression thanks to his helmet. "I would prefer to learn from you."

He was as much as admitting he wanted to spend more time with me, and a little thrill of excitement danced through my belly. Maybe this time, whatever was growing between us would work, and I wouldn't be left embarrassed and alone.

Hope filled my chest, but I ruthlessly squashed it. Now was not the time to lose focus. The butterflies would have to wait until we were safe.

Nilo and I slipped through the shadows like wraiths. The third time I looked over my shoulder to ensure he was still there, he chuckled. "You won't lose me that easily, *taro*."

I shook my head in mock concern. "I'm just ensuring that I'm not moving too fast for you, *omazas*."

Nilo's hand flexed at his side, and he took a step in my direction before jerking himself to an abrupt stop. "If we weren't in the middle of a dangerous situation involving Fiazeffere, I would show you *exactly* how fast I can move," he growled, his words a dare and a promise.

I shivered but managed to ask, "So a dangerous situation *without* a Sun Guardian would be fair game?"

He stepped closer and opened his face shield. "Yes."

I bit my lip and his gaze arrowed to my mouth. The butterflies moved lower. "Then let's get out of *this* dangerous situation and find one more . . . *accommodating*. Try to keep up."

"I'll be right behind you," he said before snapping the face shield back into place.

I took him at his word and stopped checking on him. I darted between buildings and through alleys until we'd circled to the far side of the gate.

"Can you port from here?" I asked.

Nilo's power rose a tiny bit. "Yes."

"What are the odds that they have *another* nullifier?"

"Low but not zero," Nilo said, which is what I'd assumed, but I'd hoped I was wrong.

"How do you want to do this? We can shoot them, but our pistols aren't going to punch through their armor unless we get really lucky. And we need them to think that everyone else is with us."

"We need them to catch us sneaking between buildings."

"Agreed." I nodded to the building in front of us. "After you."

"You wouldn't be trying to put yourself in the more dangerous position, would you?" Nilo demanded softly.

"Of course not," I lied because that was *exactly* what I was doing. "I'm clearly human and you could just be a soldier out for a stroll. You'll get their attention and I'll hold it."

"I'm in armor," Nilo argued. "You get their attention and *I'll* hold it."

I could argue, but every second counted. "Fine. I'll go first. You will follow. We'll shoot at them a couple of times so they know we're serious, then we'll make a break for it.

Once we're far enough away, you'll port us back to Tavi and the others."

Nilo dipped his head in agreement.

I peeked around the corner. None of the soldiers were looking this way directly, but they should still catch the movement out of the corner of their eyes, assuming they had night-vision enabled on their helmets.

I darted across the opening to the next building, moving slightly slower than I usually would. I expected shouts or maybe shots, but what I didn't expect was for two armored soldiers to appear in front of me in the blink of an eye.

I had just enough time to realize they had a teleporter before one of them grabbed me and jabbed a gun against my belly. I felt a spike of cold behind me.

"Move or port and she dies," the soldier holding me said.

The coolness dissipated.

"Get yourself out," I thought at Nilo. "Tell Tavi not to worry about me."

"I will not leave you," he said.

My heart twisted. Stupid, stubborn man.

"Where are the others?" the soldier on the left demanded.

"I killed them," I lied blithely. "There was a million-credit bounty. Let me go and I'll share it with you. What do you say? Ninety-ten? That's a cool fifty thousand each just to look the other way for a few minutes."

"Hold her," the soldier on the left said, then a spike of ice drove itself into my head, shattering Nilo's shield and breaking through my own like it had never existed.

Tavi stood in front of me, a worried frown on her face. "Where are the others?" she asked softly.

"You're not real," I whispered.

She cupped my cheek. "I don't want to hurt you, Lexi, but I need to know where the others are. It's very important. Where did you see them last?"

Pictures from the building where we'd rescued Tavi rose without my permission, and I couldn't stop them. Panic flared but it was whisked away and replaced with calm. I tried to remember why I couldn't tell Tavi what she needed to know. She was my captain; I could trust her.

"Yes, you can," she whispered.

But it wasn't trust I was feeling—it was terror. And Tavi would never threaten to hurt me. That knowledge was just enough to remind me where I was. I focused hard on *not* thinking about Tavi's words about attacking the main gate, which of course meant I thought of nothing else.

"Octavia Zarola plans to escape through the main gate," an unfamiliar voice said through Tavi's mouth.

Horror washed through me, and I jerked in the soldier's grip, willing to do anything to escape.

"Take her back to the holding cells," the voice said. "I'll deal with the teleporter."

Nilo's voice whispered through my mind as a well of icy power swept over me. "You are my heart, Lexi. I'm sorry I didn't tell you sooner. Forgive me."

Then dizziness stole me away and I knew nothing at all.

CHAPTER TWENTY-FOUR

I came to with Tavi and Kee shouting at me over the comm. I blinked at the ceiling, unsure why I felt bereft and panicky and *furious.* A glance around confirmed that I was in the bedroom Nilo and I had shared last night.

Nilo.

Memory barreled through my system like a freighter and I jumped up. "Where are you?" I demanded over the comm.

"We're in the southern part of the city. Where are *you*? Is Nilo with you?"

Anxiety cut like a blade. "He's not with you?"

Damning silence was answer enough. I reached for my connection to Nilo, but there was no cool presence in the back of my mind. There was nothing at all, just endless echoing emptiness.

Despair tried to rise, but I drove it back with fury. When I found him—and I *would*—I was going to yell at him until I lost my voice. We were supposed to be a team. He was supposed to trust me.

We were *supposed* to work together.

"He told Torran he was getting you out, but now neither Varro nor Torran can reach him," Tavi said. "We thought he was with you. Are you still on the base?"

I looked around the room again. I touched the rough sheets that still faintly smelled like sex. If this was an illusion, it was the best one I'd ever seen. "No. I was caught. He wasn't close enough to touch me, but somehow, he ported me out. He is not with me. I'm in the garage."

"Got it," Kee said. Then, quieter, "We'll get him back."

Tears filled my eyes and as much as I wanted to pretend that they were *furious* tears, they were not. Guilt and despair and horror leaked from my eyes one drop at a time. I buried my face in my hands. A Valoff had rifled through my thoughts, and then Nilo had sacrificed himself for me. Whatever was happening to him right now was my fault.

Assuming he was still alive.

Surely Sura Fev would realize Nilo was more valuable as a hostage than a corpse, but that didn't mean the soldiers would feel the same.

I took a deep breath and pieced myself back together. Nilo was alive and I was going to find him and kick his ass. But I didn't need to drag the whole crew into it.

"You all should continue to the ship," I said over the comm. "I will retrieve Nilo and follow you later."

"Did you really think that would work?" Tavi asked.

"It's safer—"

"I'm not leaving anyone behind," she said, steel in her tone. Then, more softly, "We'll get him back, Lex. Together."

"It's my fault," I whispered. "If I hadn't been caught,

then we wouldn't be in this situation. It's my responsibility to fix it."

"And you will—*with us.* Liang and Anja are staying on the ship since they managed to sneak in without getting caught, but the rest of us will meet you in an hour or so, once we're sure we've lost any potential tails."

"Be careful," I said.

"You, too. Don't do anything rash."

Part of me wanted to charge directly back into the base, which merely proved that Tavi knew me well. "I won't. See you soon."

Tavi closed the connection, and I bit my lip against the renewed urge to cry at the captain's unconditional support. Tears wouldn't get me anywhere, but action *would.*

I stood, intending to do just that when Nilo's last whispered words replayed in my memory. Had he really told me I was his heart or had that been the work of the empath in my head? I fiercely wanted it to be true—which made it more likely that the empath had plucked the idea straight from my mind.

Nilo had somehow wormed his way into my heart, and I wasn't above trying to steal his in return.

And I was an excellent thief.

BY THE TIME TAVI AND THE CREW ARRIVED, I'D DEVISED A DOZEN ways to get Nilo back, depending on where he was being held. I hoped that Kee or Varro could help with that part of the plan or I was going to be doing *a lot* of sneaking around tonight, and while the nights on Rodeni were far longer than on Valovia, they weren't *that* long.

Varro was leading a sullen Morten by the upper arm and Eli still had Havil on his shoulders. The medic appeared to be wavering in and out of consciousness, so hopefully he'd be okay after a bit more rest.

After a nod of greeting, Eli and Chira disappeared upstairs to settle Havil into one of the bedrooms. Tavi pointed at one of the chairs in the middle of the room. "Morten, sit your ass down and keep your mouth shut. Move and I'll let Torran knock you out again."

Morten glared at her, but he did as he was told.

"Did he give you trouble?" I asked subvocally.

"Surprisingly, no," Tavi responded. "But he knows he's fucked here, so he's using us to escape. I don't expect his good behavior to last."

"What are we going to do with him while we rescue Nilo?"

"I'll leave someone to watch him—the rescue crew will have to be small anyway."

I nodded. That aligned with my plans, most of which involved just Varro and me. I hated taking him away from Kee, but if he could shield us from prying eyes, that would be invaluable during a stealth mission.

Chira and Eli returned and everyone joined me at the table. "Tell us what happened," Torran said.

The underlying command let me separate the events from my emotions, so I briefly explained the chain of events, including the teleporter and the empath and how they'd made me think Tavi was the one questioning me.

All of the humans in the group winced in sympathy.

"Why did they think we were going to leave through the main gate?" Torran asked, his voice surprisingly gentle.

"Tavi told me that was her plan, so I focused on *not* thinking about that memory, which let the soldier home in on it immediately. They didn't press for more."

Varro grunted. "Many Valoffs can't fool an empath," he said. "You did well."

It didn't feel like it, but I didn't argue.

"After that, they were going to take me back to the detention center, I think, but Nilo's power sent me here. It knocked me out for a few minutes. I woke up to Tavi and Kee shouting at me."

The Valoffs shared a worried glance. "How far was Nilo from you?" Chira asked.

"Maybe five meters. I'd just crossed a gap between buildings. Why?"

When none of the others spoke up, Chira sighed. "It's very difficult for a teleporter to port a person without touching them, and distance makes it more difficult. If you were also being held by another Valoff, that makes the difficulty worse as well." She slanted an unreadable glance at Torran, then said, "We likely cannot reach him because he is unconscious."

"What aren't you telling me?" I demanded quietly.

"He may be in a coma," Varro said. "And there is a tiny possibility that he used so much power that his body shut down."

It took a second for the meaning to sink in. "You mean he could be *dead*?" My voice broke on the last word, but I couldn't bear repeating it.

"Nilo is strong," Varro said, "so it is unlikely. But it is possible."

"We need to work on your bedside manner," Kee muttered, rubbing her face.

Varro lifted one muscled shoulder. "She deserves to know."

If that jerk had killed himself to save me, I'd . . . I'd do nothing, because he would be dead.

I gripped the edge of the table. There wasn't enough air in here. Why couldn't I breathe? My lungs heaved, but I was still suffocating. Luna jumped up on the table and chirruped at me. When I ignored her, she batted at my fingers, her claws little pinpricks of pain.

I scooped her up and buried my nose in the downy softness of her fur. She rubbed her face against my shoulder and purred, a deep reverberation that I could feel in my chest. I focused on breathing and nothing else, until it no longer felt like I would pass out.

When I could focus on more than Luna, I found Kee rubbing my back and everyone else mysteriously absent. Shame burned through me. "I'm sorry," I said. "I should've handled that better. And the soldiers. I froze and Nilo had to risk himself because of my failure. If he's dead, it'll be my fault."

"He's not dead," Kee said with total conviction. She took a deep breath. "Did you know that Varro was injured when we were on FOSO I?" When I nodded, Kee grimaced. "I lost my shit. Went into a full meltdown right in the middle of the mission. I barely remember most of it."

"That's diff—"

"If you try to tell me it's different, I'm going to use one of the knives you so adore to stab you."

I chuckled weakly and gently rubbed Luna's head. "I'd probably deserve it."

"Eli gave me a pep talk that opened my eyes, so now I'm going to give one to you, even though I'm terrible at it. We all carry trauma, but it doesn't make us weak. It makes us *survivors.* And today's been a lot. You're allowed to break. You have a whole team who will have your back until you're ready to go again. And not one of us is judging you, so stop judging yourself."

Tears spilled over my lashes, and Kee wrapped me in a tight hug. "We love you, Lexi. We're your family. We'll *always* have your back."

"Thank you," I whispered, pulling her close with the arm that wasn't holding Luna. "And you're not terrible at pep talks at all."

She laughed. "I don't believe you, but you're welcome." She met my eyes, her expression surprisingly shrewd. "Do you love him?"

"I don't know," I admitted. "Probably." I wiped my eyes. "I think I was half in love with him the first time I met him."

She smiled gently. "I'd wondered. It's not like you to let someone get under your skin so thoroughly. Does he know?"

"No."

"When we find him, you should change that."

I grimaced. "What if he doesn't feel the same?"

"What if he does?"

I had no response, but hope fluttered through my chest. *What if he did?*

Kee patted my back. "Tavi is making breakfast when you're ready."

"I'll be up in a few."

Kee nodded and left me to my thoughts. I scratched Luna under her chin. "Thank you, too," I whispered.

She purred in response, then a picture of an empty food

bowl appeared in my mind. I laughed. "I know you're missing breakfast for me. Let's fix that."

She hopped down and led the way upstairs.

THE KITCHEN WAS TOO SMALL FOR ALL OF US TO SIT AT THE TABLE, so we scattered into the living room. The fridge had been stocked with basic ingredients including eggs, so Tavi had made us a veggie scramble for breakfast.

The food was warm and delicious, but I couldn't help wishing that Nilo had been the one to make it. Worry for him sat like a stone in my belly, but I forced myself to eat. Surviving on meal bars was possible but not preferred, and I wouldn't do Nilo any good if I was too tired and hungry to mount a proper rescue.

By some unspoken agreement, we all talked of inconsequential things while we ate. The familiar routine soothed my jagged edges, and when Eli jumped up to do the dishes, I went to help him. We shooed everyone else out of the kitchen.

"How's Havil?" I asked.

Eli smiled fondly. "Grouchy."

With his deep brown skin, warm brown eyes, and striking cheekbones, Eli was one of the most beautiful people I'd ever met. He was also strong and fast and brilliant. People routinely underestimated him, despite the fact that he was packed with muscle and never missed anything.

"Medics make the worst patients, but I'm sure you and Chira will get him patched up in no time."

I'd kept both my expression and tone completely innocent, but Eli slanted an amused glance at me. "You're not as clever as you think you are."

It was clear he was head over heels for the normally soft-spoken medic. Eli flirted with everyone—it was one of his favorite interrogation techniques—but he'd put special effort into Havil, Chira, and Anja.

I hoped the mechanic wasn't going to break his heart.

"I disagree," I said. "I'm *exceptionally* clever. And if you didn't want people sticking their noses in your business, you joined the wrong crew."

"Isn't that the truth," he muttered, but he couldn't quite suppress his smile.

I stacked the last of the dishes in the sanitizer and decided to poke my nose a little deeper. "So Havil. And Chira. What about Anja?"

"The universe doesn't need sculptors anymore because you and Kee and Tavi could wear down stone with nothing but your questions," he groused.

I laughed and nudged him with my shoulder. "You don't have to tell me. I just want to make sure you're happy, and I don't get to see you that often."

"You know you're always welcome on *Starlight*."

I blinked back tears at his immediate, unconditional offer. "I know, but the universe's most valuable objects aren't going to steal themselves."

"True enough. The whole recovery specialist market would probably collapse if you retired." He gripped the back of his neck and sighed. "I was so worried for him," he admitted softly.

I hugged him. "I'm glad Havil's okay."

"Me, too," he breathed. He squeezed me then let me go. "As for Anja, I believe she has her eye on a certain mouthy prince."

"You're not upset?"

"Things never got serious between us, so I'm just glad she's happy. But I *will* break his face if he hurts her."

"So that just leaves . . ."

"You're a menace," he growled. Then he sobered and sighed. "If I tell you, will you keep it to yourself?"

"Of course."

"Chira is . . . conflicted. As Torran's first officer, she's technically Havil's superior, so there's tension there. Mostly it's been her and me, or him and me, but I want it to just be *us*. And Havil isn't opposed, but Chira is afraid of overstepping."

"Do you want advice or just a sympathetic ear?"

"Lay it on me, oh wise one."

"Communication, trust, and ironclad boundaries are your friends. Along with time."

He smiled. "And here I'd thought you would have some miracle solution."

"Afraid not, unless you'd like me to accidentally lock the three of you in a room together." I waggled my eyebrows at him.

Eli laughed and shook his head.

"I have faith that you'll work it out. And I'm glad you're happy."

"Are you happy?" Eli asked carefully.

I bit my lip as the worry I'd been carrying grew heavier. "I will be."

"Good."

Tavi poked her head in the room. "I've locked Morten in a closet and we're meeting downstairs to plan whenever you're done in here."

I pouted at her. "A closet? And you didn't let us watch? That's cruel, Captain."

Tavi's smile had a satisfied edge. "You should've seen his expression. I think Kee took a picture."

"It would be a shame if that leaked to the media," I deadpanned.

Tavi shook her head ruefully. "Kee is *way* ahead of you."

We followed the captain down to the ground floor. I felt better. My worry for Nilo was a constant presence, but I could think past the panic now. I'd needed the break, and just as Kee had predicted, the crew had my back.

Tavi looked at Kee and me. "So how are we getting in?"

"The tunnel is the obvious choice," Kee said. "Assuming Nia doesn't rat us out, that's our best option."

I nodded in agreement and asked, "Where is she now?"

"She helped us through the city, then returned to the shanties," Chira said. "We gave her enough credits to get her family out of Tirdenchia. She was planning to leave immediately, but even if she doesn't, I believe she will remain loyal."

Kee tipped her head in thought. "Thanks to the security office, I'm deeper in their systems than I was before. Given time, I could get us access to waltz in the front door, but Fev probably expects it. If she hasn't alerted the whole base, she'll at least have people watching the gates."

"Or we could ambush Fev in her hotel room," I said. "She might not tell us where Nilo is, but taking her out of the picture makes our jobs easier."

Tavi blinked. "You know where she's staying?"

"I ran into her at the Riv. It's possible she's moved since then, but I doubt it. She's too arrogant to think of us as a threat."

"Please tell me you did not literally run into her," Tavi said.

"I didn't." But Tavi's sigh of relief was cut short when I continued, "I was trying to break into her room and she was inside." Tavi's eyes narrowed dangerously, and I held up my hands. "I didn't know she was even in the hotel. I'm not *that* stupid."

"It's unusual that Fev isn't staying in Aburwuk," Torran started, but he was interrupted by a loud thud from upstairs. The former general smiled. "Commodore Morten just learned the hard way that I am reinforcing the closet door."

Eli snorted. "Maybe he broke his neck and saved us a lot of trouble."

"I could go check," I offered with my sweetest smile.

"Somehow, I doubt he would survive your tender care," Tavi said.

"He'd *survive,*" I assured her. "He just might wish he hadn't."

"As tempting as that thought is," Tavi said, "we need less torture and more planning. Every minute we linger is more dangerous than the last."

I sighed. She wasn't wrong. "You should take Morten and go before more Sun Guardians show up. I swear I will get Nilo out." *Or die trying.*

I kept the second part to myself, but Tavi looked like she'd heard it anyway. She opened her mouth to no doubt tell me where I could shove my idea, but Torran said, "Lexi is right. You should go. All of you."

Tavi rounded on him, eyes flashing. "And where will you be?"

"Varro, Chira, and I will retrieve Nilo then follow."

Tavi took a deep breath and pinched her nose. "I *know* your honor is pushing you to protect me, and I'm trying to be understanding, but I'm not leaving you behind. I will *not* leave anyone behind—not on *any* planet, but especially not on *this fucking planet* that has already stolen so much from me."

The streaks in Torran's eyes dimmed and he bowed his head. "Forgive me, *cho akinti,*" he murmured. "I did not think." He gathered Tavi in his arms and the rest of us found the other table highly interesting—so interesting that we all needed to move to it, immediately.

With everything that had happened, I'd not had time to think about our last visit to Rodeni. But Tavi had a soft heart, and this planet had nearly broken it—and her.

I pulled out my comm and checked my messages. The odds that Nilo had messaged me were infinitesimal, but it also gave me something to do while Tavi took a moment. Everyone else was doing something similar, and no one looked impatient or upset. My heart squeezed. None of us were family by blood, but we were still family.

I would do everything in my power to protect each and every one of them.

Most of my inboxes weren't interesting, but I'd received a new message at the address I'd used to communicate with Besor. Had he finally responded? I opened the message and my breath caught.

The short note was unsigned, but it didn't need a signature because the two sentences spoke for themselves:

I will trade Nilo for Morten, tonight at sunset, on the roof of the Riv. Come alone or Nilo dies.

CHAPTER TWENTY-FIVE

The world tilted sideways as I read the note a second time. It *had* to be from Fev, but what was she up to? I hesitated for a heartbeat, then two, torn. It was certainly a trap, but if I went alone, then at least I would be the only one falling into it.

And then Tavi would hunt me down in the afterlife and murder me twice over for being so stupid.

"I got a message from Fev," I said, my voice a bare whisper.

It was enough. Kee's head whipped my way. "What?"

I handed her my comm with fingers that trembled. Fev had Nilo. Of course she did, but the confirmation *hurt*. Was he okay?

Was he alive?

"I'll track the address," Kee said, "but it looks like an anonymous service. It probably won't help us."

"The meeting is a trap," I said. "It has to be."

"Of course it is," Kee agreed. "But that doesn't mean we can't turn it to our advantage."

I shook my head as the shock started to wear off. "I have to go alone. I won't risk Nilo's life."

"We won't risk his life," Tavi said, "but you're not going alone."

"I am," I said, my tone unyielding. "I will take all of the help you can give with respect to planning, but I *will* go alone." I swallowed. "I would never forgive myself if Nilo died because of me."

"And how do you think *we'd* feel if we let you go off alone and *you* died, hmm?" Kee asked. "Would you let me go off to rescue Varro on my own?"

No. "Of course I would," I lied.

"Riiiiight," she drawled, unimpressed.

"Focus," Tavi said. "If Fev is using the roof of the Riv, she doesn't want the base involved and she thinks she can keep Nilo from porting, which means she either has a nullifier or Nilo will be unconscious. We'll have to plan for both."

"Or she won't bring Nilo at all," Eli said.

Unfortunately, Eli and I thought a lot alike. That would be the worst-case scenario because I would be risking myself for no chance at rescuing Nilo.

"We'll plan for all three," Tavi corrected with a sigh.

"The plas cannon is still on the roof of the Riv," I said. "At least, as far as we know. It's pointed at the generators on the base, but we could retrieve it for an attack on Fev."

Kee shook her head. "We have to assume that she already has the roof under surveillance."

"Can you get access to the cameras?"

"Maybe. Rul had access before, so there must be some sort of security flaw, assuming he didn't patch it up."

"She'll have someone watching from the surrounding buildings," Chira said.

"Kee, start working on the cameras. Everyone else, start pulling up satellite images and brainstorming ideas. We're on a tight deadline."

I SWUNG A LEG OVER THE LEV CYCLE. WE'D SPENT THE DAY GOING over every possible plan, contingency, emergency, and alternative. None of the Valoffs had been able to contact Nilo, and despair hovered, waiting for a moment of weakness.

I wouldn't give it one.

Despite a lengthy, heated argument, I was going to arrive on the Riv's roof alone. I was wearing the same lightweight armor I'd worn into the base. It was better than nothing, but it wouldn't protect me against a telekinetic—or even a close shot.

I had two of Nilo's knives strapped to my thighs—along with two of my own—plus a plas blade and pistol. I also had a shortcut button strapped to my wrist that would trigger the plas cannon, assuming it was still in place. It was a pitifully small armament for fighting a telekinetic, but more weapons would not help. For that, I needed the rest of the team.

Chira and the sniper rifle were already hidden on a nearby building with a good line of sight, while Varro and Kee were making their way up the Riv from the inside. Tavi and Torran were responsible for taking out any backup, then helping with Fev. Eli was responsible for moving Havil, Luna, Morten, and the rest of our stuff to the ship. The medic was wobbly but capable of moving on his own, which was good because Morten was likely going to give them trouble.

Taking the commodore along had never been part of the plan. If I hand-delivered Morten, then Fev had no reason to keep me *or* Nilo alive. Of course, the whole thing could just be her attempt to fish for more hostages, so we were both playing risky games.

Liang and Anja were on standby in *Starlight* in case things went completely sideways.

I flipped the power switch on Kee's prototype helmet and put it on. It cut me off from telepathic communication, but it would hopefully let me get closer to Fev before she noticed me.

If not, this was going to be a very short, very painful mission.

I eased the lev cycle from the garage. Sunset was still thirty minutes away, but I couldn't sit still any longer. I would fly a circuit of the city before heading to the Riv. I had a trio of trackers on me—including one tucked into my bra. If Fev did get her hands on me, at least Kee would know where to find the body.

Traffic was fairly light and nothing set off my instincts. As far as I could tell, there were no troop transports waiting to swoop in. That didn't mean Fev hadn't already packed the hotel with troops, but Kee hadn't spotted any on the cameras.

"I'm on my way," I said over the comm.

"We're in position," Chira said. She was far enough away to risk communication, but everyone else would maintain radio silence unless it was an emergency or they had vital information. "Fev has not arrived yet. Good luck."

You, too, I thought silently. My stomach tightened. We'd expected Fev to arrive early. If she hadn't, then maybe I had a sliver of a chance of surprising her.

I dropped from one of the main transport flight paths to the back corner of the Riv's roof fast enough to make my stomach swoop. A dozen meters from the roof, I jerked the lev cycle to a halt.

The roof was *not empty.*

But I could almost see why Chira thought that it had been, because the figures seemed to be wavering in and out of sight. They had another one of those fucking portable synthetic amplifiers they'd used on *Starlight,* the kind that also blocked comms and vision. That meant they probably *also* had another nullifier who was getting a ridiculous power boost.

Fuck me.

"They are shielding the roof," I said over the comm. "Tell Varro to grab this mental image if he can."

I focused as hard as I could on the roof and on Varro. We'd found he could briefly override my helmet as long as I helped.

"He's got it," Chira said, and I shivered. I'd felt nothing.

"If shit goes to hell, get the image from Varro and shoot the box with the antenna—that's the amplifier. I likely won't have any comms or telepathy once I land on the roof, so you'll be on your own to determine when that is. Try not to shoot me."

"I won't be able to see you," she hissed.

"I'll try to stay out of your way."

I lowered the lev cycle the rest of the way to the roof without waiting for a response. Sura Fev stood in Valovian armor with one of the crown-like metal helmets on her head. She was using Nilo as a shield, with her back to the concrete stairwell room. There were two Valoffs in Special Forces armor with her, one of whom was also wearing a metal helmet rather than the combat helmet. The odds were good that he was the nullifier, but it didn't really matter. I wasn't a match for any of them.

I slid from the lev cycle and crept around an air duct until I could see the synthetic amplifier. This was a different version than the one they'd used on *Starlight*. It appeared to be custom-made for urban environments, because everything was smaller and lighter. The telescoping antenna was only three meters high, and the whole thing was built into a square crate a meter across. Assuming it was a lev crate, one person could easily manage it.

So far, none of the soldiers had spotted me, and I wondered if amplifying a nullifier still had some significant downsides or if they were just arrogant enough to assume I'd waltz in the front door. Unfortunately, I didn't have a clear shot at Fev, and any attempt was likely to glance off her armor and hit Nilo.

I focused on Nilo. They'd stripped him out of his armor and under layer and put him in plain gray clothes that looked like a prison uniform. He was standing on his own, but he didn't exactly look stable. If Fev wasn't holding his arm, I wasn't sure if he would be able to stay upright.

That wasn't great, but at least he was here and alive. I could worry about everything else once I'd rescued him.

This half of the roof provided a decent amount of cover, but the area closer to the stairwell was far more open. Once I fully crossed into the amplifier's field, I'd be on my own.

I worked my way closer, and even though I knew approximately where Anja had placed the plas cannon, it still took me several seconds to spot it. She'd done an excellent job hiding it in the maintenance framework surrounding it.

Getting it down quickly would be a real challenge, though, so my backup plan to use it as a weapon died an abrupt death.

The sun slipped below the horizon, and my time was up. I circled around until it looked like I'd come from the building's front corner, then I strode into the open with easy confidence. The hair on my arms rose as I crossed into the amplification field. The wavering vision cleared, but my comms died.

Luckily, no more soldiers appeared, so that was the first win.

Now I just needed about a dozen more and we'd be good.

When Nilo caught sight of me, his eyes widened in horror and he jerked in Fev's arms. "Lexi, get out," he yelled, his voice hoarse with anguish.

"Stop," Fev said, shaking him. "You, too," she added, pointing at me. "Where is Morten?"

I smiled and spread my hands. "He's somewhere safe."

She hadn't telelocked me. Was she trying to get me to let my guard down, or was the nullifier affecting her, too? It could go either way, and until I knew which, I had to be careful.

"That was not the deal," she said.

"You mean the deal that you made up that was entirely in your favor? Yeah, that was a bad deal for me, so I changed it."

The two soldiers with Fev started moving my way. I drew my pistol and plas blade. "Why don't you just stay over there with your boss?" I asked conversationally.

"What's your plan here?" Fev asked with what sounded like true curiosity.

"It's nice that you assume I have a plan," I said. "It took me most of the day to grab Morten and give Tavi the slip. Then I had to find somewhere to stash the commodore where he wouldn't escape, and now here I am." I waved the plas blade at the roof. "Plan complete."

I looked around. It was clear that seeing *out* of the nullifier's field wasn't much easier than seeing *in*. Too bad I couldn't let anyone outside know thanks to the lack of comms and telepathy.

I gestured with the pistol. "Give me Nilo and I'll tell you where Morten is."

Fev shook her head. "I don't think you understand how this works." She yanked Nilo's head back and pressed a pistol to his temple. "Tell me where Morten is or Nilo dies."

"Wait," I shouted. "Give me your word that you'll let us go if I tell you."

She laughed. "No."

I gritted my teeth. I needed her to let go of Nilo, and I needed her to do it *soon*. "You have five minutes until Tavi receives an automated message with Morten's location." I holstered my pistol, switched the plas blade to my right hand, and pulled out a keycard. "I'll give you the key in exchange for Nilo. If you're fast, you can beat her there—or ambush her."

"You would turn on your captain so easily?"

"Not easily," I disagreed, "but for Nilo, yes. And the message does warn her that I am meeting with you, so she won't be entirely unprepared."

Fev tipped her head to the soldier in front. "Get the keycard."

I backed up and raised my blade. "Do these two know that you attempted to murder Prince Liang?" I asked Fev.

"Because I saw an extremely damning vid, and it would certainly be a scandal for Empress Nepru if it leaked—which it will, if Nilo and I don't walk away from this."

"Not entirely stupid after all, are you?" Fev asked. "How annoying."

She swung her gun around and shot the other two soldiers without batting an eye. My pistol might not make a dent in their armor, but hers did, punching straight through. As soon as the Valoff in the metal helmet died, Fev's power clamped around my body in a crushing grip—he'd been a nullifier after all, and his ability had affected Fev, too. She must be down to less powerful soldiers who couldn't selectively target. The thought brought me a vicious sort of satisfaction, but I feared I wouldn't have long to enjoy it.

Fev dropped Nilo. He stayed down.

Comms were still out, but I wasn't sure about telepathy. With the helmet on, no one would be able to reach me, so I was on my own for a bit longer.

"Where is Morten?" Fev demanded. When I stayed silent, the fingers gripping my plas blade opened without my permission until I dropped the weapon then kept spreading. Tears sprang to my eyes, and I whimpered in pain as my first finger dislocated.

"Tell me or I'll start breaking bones." Nilo grunted from the ground, and Fev pointed at him. "Starting with his."

I held out for a heartbeat longer, until Nilo groaned in pain. "I don't have Morten!" I shouted. "I couldn't sneak him away from Tavi. But I know where he is."

The helmet lifted from my head and crumpled into a ball with a screech of metal. "Let's see if you're still lying, shall we?"

The mental attack felt like an ice pick straight through

my head, and I moaned in agony. I couldn't think past the pain, which might've been the only thing that saved the plan.

The door to the stairwell exploded open, and Fev whirled around. A plas pulse bit into the roof where she had been a moment before. She jerked me toward her and used me as a shield as she pushed Varro back into the stairwell and slammed the door closed. Then, for good measure, she brought the whole concrete room down into a pile of rubble.

I screamed in wordless anguish. Kee was in there with Varro, and my stupid fucking plan had just gotten her injured or killed.

Fury burned away every thought except revenge. I turned toward the telekinetic, my mind racing for a new plan, one that ensured Nilo would walk away—and Fev *would not*.

My eyes narrowed. How powerful *was* she? She'd been strong before, but nothing like this. Her helmet and the amplifier must be boosting her power, just like they had for the nullifier.

Well, fuck.

"Tell me where Morten is, and I'll make your death quick," Fev said.

"Port out," I whispered to Nilo.

Fev laughed. "He's not going anywhere. I had to pump him full of stims just to get him on his feet long enough to lure you here."

When I didn't speak, she twisted my hand until something in my wrist snapped and white-hot agony lanced up my arm. My jaw clenched and I groaned out a curse.

She kept going.

A ragged scream tore itself from my throat despite my intention to suffer in silence. Every nerve in my arm throbbed with fiery agony and tears blurred the world around me.

Fev dragged me to the edge of the building and let my toes just brush the short, narrow wall surrounding the roof. Then she dropped me. I scrabbled for balance, but she'd positioned me in such a way that it was impossible. I tilted backward and knew I was lost.

I'd failed.

I wouldn't rescue Nilo, wouldn't avenge Kee, wouldn't do anything at all except die a stupid, pointless death. I'd made peace with death long ago, but bitterness filled me that *this* would be my end.

I would die and Fev would still have Nilo. Fury and anguish fought for control.

I looked for him, but Fev's body blocked my view. I hadn't told him what he meant to me. I hadn't gotten the chance to see if he felt the same. And that, more than anything, felt like a knife to the gut. I didn't *really* believe in an afterlife, but I silently vowed to haunt Fev for the rest of her days for taking that opportunity from me. If nothing else, I'd use my dying breath to curse her name.

But even if it was a fool's hope, I wasn't going to die without a fight. My right wrist was shattered, but my left could hold my weight for a little while. Maybe long enough for Tavi and Torran to arrive. Maybe long enough to survive.

Maybe.

I bent at the waist, hastening my fall, and strained toward the edge of the building. It was too far. I knew it the moment I shifted, but I reached for it anyway, hoping for a miracle.

Fev snorted, then her power clamped around me and jerked me back up onto my toes. It wasn't the miracle I'd wanted, but I'd take it. I wasn't dead yet.

"Tell me where Morten is or next time, I'll let you fall." She peeked over the edge. "Your armor might protect you enough to make for an excruciating death."

I couldn't move, locked in her power, but I felt the minute shift of weight as one of Nilo's knives disappeared from its sheath. Maybe I could buy him enough time to make it out.

"Tavi is planning to return Morten to Fed space," I sobbed. "He has a bounty, and she wants the payout."

"Where is he now?"

I blinked slowly, like the pain was making my brain foggy. It was barely an act. "On his way to the ship with Eli."

Fev growled and twisted my broken wrist. My bones ground against each other and spikes of torment overloaded my nerves. My brain shut down and tears made my vision blurry, but perhaps that was for the best. No one needed to stare their death in the face.

"Where is the ship?" Fev asked, every word bitten off in frustration. She shook me out of my stupor.

"South of town," I gasped. "Twenty klicks." My thoughts briefly settled on the coordinates Kee had shown me before skating away again.

Fev's lips curled into a smug smile. "I'll give your captain my regards." Her power tightened around my body, but rather than crushing me to death, she gasped in pain and her hold loosened.

Nilo jerked his bloody knife from Fev's neck at the same time the synthetic amplifier exploded in a shower of sparks.

Fev's hold disappeared, and my body lurched, looking for balance on the narrow ledge. I had just found it when two more Special Forces soldiers appeared on the roof.

Nilo tackled me and we tumbled over the side of the building together.

CHAPTER TWENTY-SIX

A bright flash lit up the twilight sky, and the ground was both too far away and too close. It rushed up at us with terrifying speed. Hopefully my comm would survive long enough to upload the vid I'd been recording, or Kee was going to be mad, assuming she was okay. Of course, she was probably going to be mad about my death, but there wasn't much I could do about that.

I focused on Nilo and tried to push him away. "Save yourself!"

He scowled and pulled me closer, then his power crashed over us in an endless, dizzying swirl. When the world reappeared, we landed on something soft that gave under our weight then collapsed further with a loud crash.

"Are you hurt?" Nilo demanded from beside me, his voice slurred. "Where is Havil?"

"I'm okay," I gasped. "I think." I looked around. I'd landed beside Nilo on our bed from last night—the same place he'd sent me earlier. Luckily, we'd only fallen for a few seconds or even the mattress wouldn't have saved us. I turned to Nilo with wide eyes. "What was your backup plan if we'd fallen farther?"

He was barely conscious, but he grinned and whispered, "A lake."

I huffed. "Did it occur to you that swimming in armor isn't easy?" He blinked at me, and I was pretty sure that it *hadn't* occurred to him.

"Can you port us to the ship now?"

I felt a tiny flash of coolness, then Nilo shook his head. "Not safely. I'm too drained. If it wasn't for the stims, I wouldn't have made it this far."

"Save your energy. I'll see what we have to work with."

My arm throbbed with unrelenting agony every time I took a breath. Sitting up was an exercise in torture, but we needed to move. It was possible that Fev had pulled this location while she was poking around in my head. And while I could hope that Nilo's knife attack had been fatal, she'd had a teleporter on the roof to rush her to a medic, so I doubted it.

"Lexi, where are you?" Tavi demanded over the comm.

"At our start point," I said. "Nilo is here, too, but we're both in rough shape."

"The soldiers ported Fev out after you set off the plas cannon and blew up the base's generators."

I paused my attempts to wiggle toward the edge of the bed without jostling my arm. "What? I didn't set off the cannon." I risked a glance at my wrist—my mangled wrist.

Acknowledging the damage only made it hurt worse, and I closed my eyes as my stomach heaved.

"Fev must've tripped the switch when she was breaking my bones," I whispered. "Then once my comm came back online, it sent the signal."

"How bad?" Tavi demanded, her voice quietly furious.

"My right wrist and arm are worse than useless," I said. "I can shoot left-handed, but not well. Nilo is barely conscious."

"Officially, Aburwuk has grounded all transports in Tirdenchia while they investigate the cause of the explosion," Tavi said. "And with all traffic being diverted down, everything is gridlocked. But Fev likely told them that it was an attack rather than an accident because the city is on lockdown until further notice."

"The spaceport?"

"Still running, for now."

"Are Kee and Varro okay?" I asked hesitantly, refusing to consider the alternative.

"We're okay," Kee said, and the relief at hearing her voice nearly put me under. "The stairs protected us from most of the rubble."

"You and Nilo took the worst of it," Tavi confirmed. "Can you meet us somewhere or do you need extraction?"

I nudged Nilo. "Can you walk?"

"Not far," he said. "The stims are starting to wear off. When they do, I'm going to go down fast."

"We need to get out of this building, so we can meet you, but we won't make it to the ship without help. Kee, can you still track my location?"

"Yes."

"I have to wrap my arm, then we'll head toward the spaceport. Meet us where you can."

"We're going to be on foot," Tavi said, "unless the traffic clears up, so we'll be at least half an hour behind you."

"The lev cycle is still on top of the Riv, assuming Fev didn't find it."

"Kee and Varro grabbed it and the plas cannon just before the authorities showed up. Varro is shielding them, but they're stuck in the gridlock. If you can get a transport, take it."

"Will do," I said. I let the connection go, then continued to ease my way to the edge of the bed. I swung my legs to the floor and a million tiny needles stabbed their way from my wrist to my shoulder. I held my breath until the feeling passed, but I needed to immobilize my arm if I was going to have a chance of making the ship.

I stood and blood rushed from my head, darkening my vision. That was . . . not good. My wrist was swollen and purple and who knew how many blood vessels had been ruptured. I needed a hospital or a medic. If I could make the ship, the autostab would be able to keep me going until Havil healed enough to mend me.

Assuming Havil *also* made it to the ship.

"Nilo, get up," I said. He groaned but didn't move. "Please, Nilo. I need help."

He blinked open bleary eyes and crawled from the bed. When he saw my arm, his face went completely blank.

"Help me bind it and make a sling for it," I said.

His jaw clenched. "I will port you to the ship."

He reached for me, but I jerked back with a pained hiss. "Don't even think about it if it's going to hurt you," I growled. "I'm still mad at you about earlier. Varro said porting me from that distance could've killed you!"

A shadow of his usual playful grin touched his mouth. "Only if I didn't know you as well as I do, *taro*."

I flinched. "I'm serious, Nilo."

"As am I," he said quietly, losing the playfulness and giving me a peek at the soldier underneath. "I vowed to keep you safe. Getting you out was the best I could do in the situation."

"I spent the day wondering if you were even alive to rescue."

"I'm sorry," he murmured. His gaze dropped to my swollen wrist. "And now you've been hurt because of me anyway. You should've left me."

"Do you know that Torran tried that same tactic with Tavi earlier? It didn't work for him, either. We don't leave people behind. So get your ass in gear and let's go."

Nilo bowed in acquiescence. The bathroom's limited first aid kit didn't have anything that would work for my arm, so Nilo cut the sheets into strips and wrapped my wrist while I bit my lip. Tears leaked from my eyes, and based on the anguish on Nilo's face, he wasn't enjoying this any more than I was, but it had to be done.

Once my wrist was bound, he fashioned a sling for me, then bound the sling to my torso. I would be all but useless in a fight, but at least I could move without feeling like I was going to pass out.

Mostly.

The two of us weren't exactly inconspicuous, but at least night was falling and the shadows were getting longer. We left the garage to find that the transport gridlock wasn't restricted to the city center. Many of the occupants had abandoned their rides and decided to walk, which made foot traffic far higher than usual.

I watched for a moment, but none of the transports moved. We could easily get one, but then we'd be just as stuck as everyone else.

I tilted my head toward the nearest alley. "This way."

The narrow alley was mostly empty. A few locals were using the shortcut, but most of the pedestrians were understandably wary of slipping into the dark between buildings in an unknown part of town.

I still had my pistol and some of my knives, but I'd lost the plas blade, so my only nonlethal weapon was gone. Anyone stupid enough to start something with us would be getting a decidedly lethal knife to the face.

Nilo and I staggered onward. We weren't making *good* time, but at least we were making progress and putting distance between us and the garage. At this pace, it would take us over two hours to reach the spaceport, and that was only if Nilo could continue for two hours, which seemed unlikely with the way he was moving. His jaw was clenched and his face was set into granite lines of pain and determination.

The traffic on the next street wasn't any better, so I kept us to the shadows. With the city in lockdown, people would be looking for someone to blame, and a frustrated group could turn into a mob far too easily.

We'd been traveling for nearly fifteen minutes when Nilo stumbled and fell. He landed on his hands and knees with a pained groan. "Are you okay?" I asked.

"Leave me," he said.

"You know I won't, so get your ass up." I hissed in pain as I tried to help him up with my good arm. Bending of any kind was intensely agonizing, but I pushed through it.

"Looks like you are having trouble," an unfamiliar male voice said in Valovan from deeper in the alley. Without my night-vision glasses, I saw his shape and not much else, but the glint of a blade was unmistakable.

"I'm having a shit day," I told him in Valovan. "And I'd be happy to take it out on you. Go find easier prey."

He laughed. "You look easy enough to me. Give me your valuables and weapons and I'll let you go."

I snorted. *Sure.* I drew my pistol as Nilo climbed to his feet. "Stay behind me," I ordered. When he made a sound of protest, I quietly added, "I'm still wearing armor."

"I don't suppose you know anything about why the city is in lockdown?" the man asked. "I believe the authorities would be interested in a Valoff traveling with an injured human—"

I shot him. My left-handed aim wasn't great, but he was only a few meters away. He collapsed with a gurgled curse, and I closed my eyes against the guilt. If it was him or us, it was going to be *us*.

I wrapped my good hand around Nilo's arm and urged him onward.

BY THE TIME TAVI AND TORRAN FOUND US, NILO WAS LEANING heavily against me and it was all I could do to keep us moving forward. When Torran took Nilo's weight from me, I nearly cried in relief.

Tavi's face swam into my vision. She swept a glance over me and her jaw clenched, but when she met my gaze, her eyes were kind. "Can you walk?"

"Not fast," I said with a quiet laugh.

She nodded and we moved out at a pace I could maintain. She looked at me out of the corner of her eye. "Did you run into any trouble?"

I swallowed. "Yeah." I didn't elaborate and she didn't ask.

With Torran practically carrying Nilo, we made much better time. When we got far enough out that the traffic thinned, Torran ordered us a transport and bundled us inside.

Sitting was excruciating, and Tavi hissed in sympathy. She looked at Torran. "Will Havil be healed enough to help?"

"He should be able to stabilize her," he said. "Unless . . ." He trailed off. Unless someone was hurt worse than me before it was all said and done. *Starlight* only had a single autostab. It hadn't been a problem when there were just four of us because we usually didn't take jobs that were so dangerous we all took life-threatening injuries. But with a bigger crew and more dangerous jobs, that was changing.

And based on Tavi's expression, she knew it, too.

The transport was faster than my pained shuffle, but it wasn't *fast*. The surface roads had been designed for a city that relied on aerial transportation, so they weren't meant to handle the entirety of the city's traffic. Even here, on the outskirts, intersections were clogged with vehicles.

Chira had scouted ahead while Kee and Varro were a little behind us, but we were all approaching the spaceport. True night had finally fallen, shrouding the city in darkness.

Torran's head tilted like he was listening to something far away. "The main entrance is closed," he said.

Eli had gotten Havil and Morten to the ship with a few careful lies and a large pile of credits. The underpaid workers at the cargo checkpoint had been more than happy to look the other way for a few minutes since Eli was gorgeous, charming, and seemingly rich—or at least rich enough to make it worth their while.

Unfortunately, with the lockdown, that plan wouldn't work for us. And if *Starlight* attempted to pick us up outside of the spaceport, the ship would immediately become a target for the same reason. If only Fev hadn't broken my damn wrist and triggered the plas cannon, my life would be a lot easier right now.

"There's a smuggler's entrance on the far side," I said with a sigh, "but we won't be able to take the transport—too obvious."

Tavi raised her eyebrows. "How do you know that?"

"Figured we wouldn't be leaving through the front door. There's also a human-friendly smuggler in Ving that might be able to get us through the wormhole for the right price."

"And you're just now telling me?"

I sucked in a deep breath as the transport lurched into motion and jarred my arm. Once I could think again, I asked, "Would you willingly leave *Starlight*?"

Her expression hardened before her smile turned rueful. "I suppose you're right. How far is the smuggler's entrance?"

"Couple of klicks," I said. "Over rough ground. It's going to suck."

Her eyes drifted from my face to my arm before she turned to Torran. "Can Varro sneak us through the main gate? Or hide the ship long enough for a fast pickup?"

"He's expended a lot of energy today, so hiding the ship is out," Torran said. "As for the gate, it depends on how many are guarding." His eyes went distant for a moment, then he shook his head. "Chira says it's at least a half dozen, and that would be pushing it."

I fumbled my comm from my pocket and pulled up the entrance's location. "Get us as close as you can on the road."

Tavi studied it for a second before altering the transport's destination. She held up my comm to Torran and pointed at a place on the map. "Tell Chira, Varro, and Kee to meet us here. Anja and Eli are quietly getting the ship ready to launch."

Nilo's eyes were closed, and he hadn't spoken for several minutes. He'd pushed himself too far and worry was my constant companion, like a rock in my shoe. I'd forget about it for a moment, then it would stab me somewhere soft and tender.

The transport dropped us on the north edge of the spaceport. Chira arrived a few minutes later, then Kee and Varro arrived on the lev cycle. Kee hopped off, still clutching the plas cannon. Her gaze flickered over my bound arm. "Are you okay?"

"No, but I'll live," I said. I looked at Varro. "Can you give me a lift then come back and ditch the lev cycle?" When he nodded, I frowned in thought. "Actually, maybe you should take Nilo."

"Nilo is in no state to defend himself," Torran said. He tipped his head toward Chira. "She can take you, then Nilo, then catch up to us on the ground."

Chira bowed in agreement, and Varro climbed from the lev cycle. I stared at it while trying to gather what little determination I had left. This was going to hurt like hell, but it would be far faster than walking over uneven ground in the dark.

Once Chira was in position, I gritted my teeth and approached. Torran stopped me with a brief touch on my good shoulder. "If you would allow me, I will help you."

Getting telelocked again sounded like the worst idea ever, but so did climbing on the lev cycle on my own. I nodded. His power wrapped gently around me and somehow avoided jostling my arm at all. He lifted me and set me on the lev cycle with apparent ease.

"Thank you," I murmured. "That was amazing."

Torran smiled and bowed slightly. "You are welcome."

"Hold on," Chira said. The safety system engaged, and I clutched Chira's shoulder with my good arm. She looked back at me. "I will fly carefully, but let me know if it is too much."

"Thanks, I will."

The lev cycle lifted from the ground and Chira eased us forward. We left the road behind as we circled the spaceport's outer fence. True to her word, Chira piloted the lev cycle gently, and we arrived at the culvert that served as a smuggler's entrance without any additional pain.

Chira set the lev cycle down and the restraints released. "How can I help?" she asked.

I sighed. "I'm not sure." I gripped her shoulder and carefully stood. Pain lanced through my arm as I swung my leg over the seat. *Fuck, that hurt.* Tears gathered in my eyes, and I paused long enough to blink them away.

Stepping down to the ground was another lesson in agony, but I clenched my jaw and breathed through it. When I was sure I could stand on my own, I let go of Chira's shoulder.

My fingers were stiff from the amount of force I'd used, and I shook out my hand. "Sorry. I didn't mean to hurt you."

"You didn't. I'm just impressed you made it off without swearing."

I laughed in surprise. "That just proves that you weren't in my head. It was just a constant litany of swearing."

She chuckled, then peered at me. "Will you be okay on your own?"

I drew my pistol and found a convenient large rock to lean against. "With the mood I'm in, I *dare* anyone to start shit."

She nodded. "I will be back shortly with Nilo."

I waved, and she engaged the lev cycle, then disappeared into the dark. The night was clear and quiet. Here, a little farther from the lights of the city, it was easy to see the unfamiliar stars in the sky. Rodeni didn't have a moon, so the only light was from the stars themselves.

I heard the quiet whir of the lev cycle before it became visible. Even with my eyes adjusted to the dark, I only saw it as a slightly darker shadow. I lifted my pistol in case it *wasn't* Chira.

"Don't shoot. It's me," she whispered into my mind. She parked the lev cycle near me, and I heard the safety restraints release. "Nilo, time to move," she said.

Nilo grumbled something too low to catch. I moved closer. "I can help," I said. I was close enough to see their silhouettes against the lights of the city.

"Stand back," Chira said. She twisted around. "Nilo, get up, now," she commanded sharply.

Nilo jerked up and nearly toppled from the vehicle. Only Chira's quick grab saved him, but he obediently swung his leg over the seat and made it to the ground.

Where he promptly collapsed.

"Stim's gone," he slurred.

"I know," Chira sympathized. She climbed off the lev cycle and helped Nilo lean against my rock. "But you have to hold on a bit longer. Lexi is going to watch over you until I get back, but she's hurt, so don't cause her trouble."

"She's my heart, and I failed her," Nilo whispered, so low I barely caught it.

"She's also right next to you," Chira said drily. "So you haven't failed her yet." With that, she climbed back on the lev cycle. "I'll be back as soon as I can."

"Thank you," I said. "I'll keep him safe."

"Don't be surprised if he passes out," she warned. "But if he starts convulsing or anything else unusual, let us know over the comm."

"I will."

Chira nodded, then she and the lev cycle retreated back the way they'd come.

Nilo groaned, and I moved until I could gently pat his head with my good arm. "Stay with me."

"I will," he whispered. He drifted into silence and I thought he'd fallen asleep or lost consciousness when he surprised me by mumbling, "You're hurting. I hate it."

I blinked, taken aback. I couldn't feel his cool presence in my head. "How can you tell?"

"Your breathing."

As I drew another short, sharp breath, I realized that he was right—and that I'd been listening to his breathing in return. Nilo's head tilted back against the rock, and he sighed as if the weight of the world pressed on him. "Should've ported you."

Now wasn't the time for an argument, but I couldn't let that statement stand, either. "No."

He hummed his disagreement, but his breathing was deepening. A moment later, he slipped into what I hoped was sleep rather than unconsciousness, and I silently vowed to keep him safe.

Despite my worry that we weren't the only people trying to exit the planet in a hurry, the night stayed quiet. Quicker than I would've expected, Chira's voice whispered into my head, "We're nearly there. Don't shoot us."

"Okay," I thought back. Valoffs had slightly better than human night vision, so perhaps she could see me despite the fact that I couldn't see her at all, and there was no telltale glow from a comm.

A few minutes later, I finally heard the faint sound of footsteps on rocky ground. I nudged Nilo. "Time to wake up."

He grumbled at me, but I caught the gleam of starlight reflected in his eyes, so he was awake.

Three silhouettes approached and I frowned. "Tavi?"

"I'm here," she responded, her voice grouchy. The shadows stopped. Clothes rustled, then feet hit the ground, and the silhouettes grew to five. "Torran and Varro carried me and Kee while Chira scouted," she said. "Kee and I can't see shit, and I didn't think a light was a good idea."

From her tone, she wasn't happy about being carted around like baggage, but she'd done it because she knew it was the best option.

"It's been quiet here," I said. "The culvert is just ahead, then the ground should be smoother."

Footsteps moved off, then Chira said, "Is the fence monitored?"

"I can't say for sure, but I would be surprised if it wasn't."

"You're not going to enjoy this," she said. "You'll have to crouch to make it through."

I lifted my hand from Nilo's head and held it out to the darkness. "Let's get it over with."

Warm fingers closed around mine, too large to be Chira's. "I will take you and Nilo through," Torran said.

Nilo grumbled something incomprehensible, but otherwise didn't object, which told me exactly how exhausted he was.

Torran's power wrapped around me. "Relax," he said. "I'm going to tilt you over, but don't tense or you'll hurt yourself. I won't let you fall."

"Easy for you to say," I groused, but I did my best to remain limp as he tipped me over until I was horizontal, staring at the sky. This was freaky as hell, but my arm didn't hurt any worse than before.

A gentle wind blew around my head, and I realized we were moving. My inner ear was convinced I was stationary, and the difference made my stomach roil. I closed my eyes, determined not to vomit on Torran in return for his help.

The culvert was cool and Torran's soft footsteps echoed down its length. Rusty hinges squeaked as he opened the gate that was supposed to stay locked but never did. Then we were through and he set me on my feet.

"Thank you, again."

"You're welcome." He blew out a deep breath, and I wondered how tired *he* was. He went back for Nilo, then the whole group joined me on the inside of the spaceport's fence.

"Follow the cairns," I said. "They'll keep us off surveillance."

"I'll take point," Chira said. No one contradicted her, so she took off, and we stumbled into motion after her. The pain was getting worse, but I clenched my jaw and kept moving.

I was so focused on following that I nearly ran into Chira's back when she stopped. I looked over her shoulder. *Starlight* was fifty meters ahead, dark and quiet. I couldn't see anyone around, but there were plenty of places to hide.

Chira looked back at me. "Keep heading for the ship. I'm going to scout ahead."

I wasn't sure I was in any shape to lead, but I nodded. Chira disappeared around the edge of a nearby ship, and I continued forward. "Are the ship's sensors picking up anything?" I asked Kee over the comm.

"No, but they're running in stealth mode. Still, there's no one close."

Opting for speed over stealth, I kept us on a fairly straightforward path. We were nearly to *Starlight* when the cargo ramp began to lower and Chira reappeared.

"It looks clear," she whispered, but her forehead was furrowed with worry.

"What?"

She shook her head. "I don't know." She switched to telepathic communication and told the group, "Stay on guard."

I glanced back. Kee was directly behind me. Varro and Torran were helping Nilo, who was on his feet—barely. Without Eli to watch our backs, Tavi had taken over as rearguard. Everyone was looking a little ragged, but it was much worse for the Valoffs.

We needed to be on board, now.

I drew my pistol and followed Chira as she eased around the side of *Starlight,* sticking close to the edge of the ship. She took a defensive position in front of the cargo ramp and waved me inside. Instead, I joined her to offer a little protection to Kee and the rest.

So I had a front-row view when cold power spiked and Sura Fev ported in with four soldiers in Special Forces armor. All four pointed high-powered rifles at us and telekinetic power wrapped around me. Based on Kee's gasp, the whole group was locked in place.

Fev was missing the top half of her armor. A piece of the base layer had been cut away at her neck. Her skin was still bloody, but she'd made it to a healer in time. Unfortunately.

Her mouth curved into a vicious smile. "By order of Her Imperial Majesty the Empress, you are commanded to lay down your arms and surrender quietly. Refusal will be met with death."

CHAPTER TWENTY-SEVEN

The telelock wasn't painful, which made me think it wasn't Fev who had me locked. But I couldn't move at all, and even if I *could,* our group was too tired to fight four highly trained—and presumably fresh—soldiers in addition to Fev. Using *Starlight*'s defensive system to kill them would bring about a whole new host of problems, and we still needed to make it through the wormhole and back to Fed space in one piece.

"What are the charges?" Torran asked.

Fev's smile turned smug. "High treason."

"Show me the writ," Torran said. "Because Empress Nepru promised me safe passage, so if you are claiming that she is breaking her promise, then I am allowed to verify it for myself."

"That is not how this works," Fev scoffed. "You are responsible for the death of six soldiers. You have been deemed an immediate threat. Attempt anything and you will be executed for the safety of the empire."

The lights came on in the cargo bay, and the hatch into the ship unlocked. I didn't know who stepped out, but Fev's fair skin paled further before she fixed her face into an expressionless mask.

The soldiers around Fev stared for a moment, then bowed as one, their left arms across their chests. Fev didn't move, but her jaw clenched.

"Sura Fev, we meet again," Liang said, his voice quiet but laced with authority. "I had the most *illuminating* conversation with the empress earlier today. Apparently, she had *no idea* that you'd tried to kill me."

The Special Forces guards shifted uneasily.

"Or even that you'd taken it upon yourself to attack Bastion and FOSO I. Mother," he said, for once emphasizing his relationship to the throne, "was *furious.* I believe you already received the recall notice."

"Lies," Fev spat.

"Then you'll have no issue with showing me the writ for the capture of General Fletcher, I presume."

Fev's eyes swept across our group before landing on me. She jerked me forward, breaking the other telekinetic's hold, then held me in front of her like a shield. She turned until I was between her and everyone else, including the Special Forces soldiers. She held up something I couldn't see. "This is an active-pressure grenade. Give me Morten. Now."

I swallowed. Active-pressure grenades were last-ditch weapons. The control lever had to be continuously pressed. If the holder let off the slightest pressure—like when they died—the grenade would immediately detonate.

No delay, no warning.

And the best ones—or the most dangerous, depending on which way you looked at it—were biometrically locked to the person wielding them, so a telekinetic like Torran couldn't just snatch the grenade away and apply the same pressure.

Sura Fev was determined to either walk away alive or take me with her to hell.

The soldiers she'd brought with her didn't seem to know what to do with themselves. None of them attacked Liang, but they also kept their rifles trained on Tavi and the others.

"Why are you so desperate to get your hands on Morten?" I asked. I had an idea, but I wanted to see if she would confirm it.

"He kidnapped Prince Cien," she snapped.

"I wonder how he found out about the tunnels under the palace," I mused aloud.

My jaw slammed shut hard enough that I worried my teeth would shatter. "You will stay silent," she hissed.

Tavi's voice crackled through my comm implant. "Don't risk yourself."

I wasn't sure it was an order I could follow, not with everyone else also in danger.

"Answer the question," Liang demanded. If he could hear our group comm conversation, he didn't show it.

Fev scoffed. "How should I know how a Fed traitor gets his information? Perhaps it was from *you*. Maybe you are taking out the competition."

Liang laughed. "I have three older siblings and two of them have children. I will never be the emperor, and I prefer it that way."

While Fev focused on keeping my mouth shut, the rest of the telelock loosened slightly. Her breathing was elevated, which could be from stress or anger, but it could *also* be because Nilo had stabbed her in the neck after she'd expended a great deal of energy. And healing wasn't only exhausting for the healer. Though the patient expended *less* energy than the healer, it wasn't zero—especially for such a serious wound.

Fev must be running close to empty.

Hopefully she was, or I was about to do something very stupid.

Fev was gripping the back of my collar with her left hand, leaving her right hand free to hold the grenade. I still wasn't sure what I was going to do about that explosive little issue, but that was a problem for future me.

Present me needed to work a knife very carefully from the sheath on my left leg. The sheaths were blocked from Fev's view by my body, and my left side was facing away from the soldiers, so only Tavi and the others might be able to see what I was doing.

My arm was mostly immobile, trapped by the telelock, but my fingers carefully slid sideways until I felt the cool metal of the hilt. It was one of my smaller, thinner knives, but I'd take what I could get. My arm wasn't in the *best* position to draw a blade, but with a little luck, I might be able to accomplish it.

I curled my fingers, easing the knife from the sheath a millimeter at a time while Fev and Liang traded barbed insults.

Nilo, who was leaning against Varro and looked barely conscious, was the first to notice. His eyes narrowed and he minutely shook his head. The fact that he couldn't communicate telepathically told me exactly how exhausted he was.

He whispered something, and Varro's eyes slid my way. "What are you doing?" the weapons expert asked telepathically.

"Getting ready to cause a distraction. Can you take advantage of it?"

"The captain told you not to risk yourself."

I wasn't sure how he knew that unless he was in everyone's head—mine included—but I didn't have the time or energy for panic.

"Enough," Fev snarled, shaking me hard enough that I lost my grip on the knife's hilt and a bolt of agony from my shattered wrist whited out my thoughts.

"Bring me Morten, immediately, or I will start breaking her bones." She laughed harshly. "*More* of them, anyway. How many can she endure before she goes into shock?"

"Let her go and walk away," Liang ordered. He leveled a hard glare at the soldiers Fev had brought. "Lower your weapons."

Two rifles dipped toward the ground and Fev growled. "The empress has ordered me to capture the traitors, and Prince Liang does not have the authorization to change that order. As he said, he's far down the succession—more decorative than useful."

I swallowed my pain and once again reached for the knife's hilt. My arm had shifted slightly, which made the grab a little easier this time. I eased the knife from the sheath as Liang laughed.

"You have no such orders," Liang said with such scorn I almost believed him. Had Fev really been acting without the empress's knowledge? I'd thought she had been feeding Morten information on the empress's orders, but perhaps it went deeper than that.

Or maybe the empress had decided to cut Fev loose in an attempt to cover her own ass.

Either way, it was becoming increasingly obvious that Fev didn't have a good way out of this situation, and that would make her desperate and dangerous. I needed to act before she did.

"I have proof," the prince said. He held up a slate and Empress Nepru's face filled the screen. *Holy shit.*

"Sura Fev is a traitor to the empire," the empress said. "I have every confidence that Prince Liang will bring her to justice, and he speaks with my voice on Rodeni."

There was a moment of stunned shock, then everything went to hell.

Fev snarled and jerked me backward as the soldiers turned and pointed their rifles at us. "Don't hurt the hostage!" Liang yelled.

I gripped the knife with white-knuckled determination. If I dropped it, I'd be fucked. I was likely fucked anyway, but if I was going to die, then I would take Fev with me.

"I will die for the empire, human, so unless you want all of your friends to die with me, I suggest you convince them to let me go," Fev growled.

"What is your endgame?" I asked. The telelock on my jaw was gone, and the one holding me in place was weakening. A little more and I could act.

"I serve the empress," she said with the fervor of a true believer.

"Then why betray her?"

"I didn't," she snapped quietly. "She knew exactly what

I was doing and approved every step. But now she requires death, so I will deliver as many as I can."

Well, that sounded ominous. I was out of time. Fev had stopped retreating and the cool feel of her power was rising. Whatever she was about to do would hurt more than just her and me.

"Be prepared," I warned the group over the comm.

"Lexi, no—" Tavi started, but I was already in motion.

I wrenched myself forward and almost stumbled in surprise at how far I'd been able to move. Fev cursed, and her power shifted, but rather than making a run for it, I spun in place. Her confusion only lasted a heartbeat, but it was enough.

I drove the knife up toward her abdomen. The thin blade easily pierced the stretchy base layer fabric and sank into her flesh. She jerked back with a pained gurgle and blood painted her lips. I'd hit a lung. It wouldn't be immediately fatal, but I also wouldn't have time to escape the coming explosion.

As if to prove my point, she held up the grenade with a macabre smile. "For the empire," she whispered.

I let go of the knife and reached for her hand in desperation, but I was too late.

Her grip loosened and time slowed.

Off-balance and reaching, there was nothing I could do. I wouldn't get to explore my feelings with Nilo, but at least he'd be alive—as would Tavi and Kee and Eli.

That wasn't a bad legacy, all things considered.

My moms would've been proud.

I heard the click as the lever sprang free, and my heart twisted in regret. Then cold, dizzying dark swept me up.

I landed on the cargo bay floor screaming in denial.

CHAPTER TWENTY-EIGHT

My stomach heaved while someone in armor crouched nearby. As soon as I was sure I wasn't going to vomit, I croaked, "Nilo?"

"I don't know," Liang said. "I sent him what energy I could, but amplifiers are inefficient at a distance. Are you okay?"

No. But I nodded and climbed to my feet with Liang's help. Everything hurt, and tears blurred my vision. I tried to blink them away, but more just kept appearing.

I ignored them.

It was hard to see past the cargo bay door, and I was thankful for it. Torran was issuing orders to the soldiers, some of whom seemed to be wounded. I looked for Fev, but it was too dark to make out more than a deeper shadow on the ground.

Varro had Nilo in his arms. He and Kee were rushing up the cargo bay ramp while Chira and Tavi waited for Torran. Nilo had blood on his face, and Varro's expression was grim. He dashed past me, but Kee stopped.

"He's going to the medbay," Kee said. "Havil is already there."

I swallowed. "Is Nilo . . ." I trailed off, refusing to voice any of my fears.

"He's alive," Kee said, but her mouth was pressed into a hard line.

Tavi, Chira, and Torran climbed the ramp. The four soldiers were retreating. "Eli, get us in the air," Tavi commanded over the comm.

"On it," Eli said.

Tavi's eyes swept over me. "Did Fev hurt you?"

"More than my wrist?" I asked, then shook my head. "No, I'm just as hurt as I was before, no more."

"Good, because now I don't feel so bad about being furious at you. What were you thinking?" she demanded.

"Fev was going to kill you all. I don't know how, but she was gathering her power, and she as much as told me. Better me than all of you." Tavi's eyes flashed, but I held up my good hand. I was momentarily silenced by the blood on it, but I rallied before Tavi could berate me. "Don't tell me otherwise, because you would do exactly the same thing."

Her nose wrinkled, but she didn't disagree.

Starlight's engines rumbled to life. Eli was wasting no time getting us off this godforsaken planet, a plan I wholeheartedly agreed with.

Liang held out his arm. "Come on, I need to go help Havil, and you need some medical attention as well. I'll escort you."

I gripped his arm with bloody fingers. "Did you really talk to the empress?"

His mouth tightened. "I did."

"And what did she say?"

"To stay out of Fev's way, more or less. Mostly less, but the sentiment was there."

When I gaped at him, a tired grin touched his mouth. "The video was a clever fake that Kee started making for me before we arrived. It wouldn't stand up to a close critique, or even a close viewing, but it worked tonight."

"So is she going to let us go through the wormhole?"

Liang's expression hardened. "Yes. I truly don't think she knew that Fev had decided to kill me. That surprised her, but it wasn't enough to shake her confidence in Fev, so that tells me my loss wouldn't be the great wound I'd hoped it would be. But it *would* be highly embarrassing if it got out that one of her elite Fiazefferia tried to kill a member of the imperial family. And if I don't make it, the vid will automatically release."

The door to the medbay slid open. Nilo was in one of the normal beds, not in the autostabilization unit. That had to be a good sign, right?

Havil was bent over him, a frown on his face, and Varro was slumped on the next bed over. I dropped Liang's arm and eased forward, being careful to stay out of Havil's way. "Is he okay?" I asked.

"He will be," Havil said, "but it was close. Without Liang's help, he probably would've killed himself, and likely you in the process." Havil shook his head. "But as it is, there's no lasting damage, just exhaustion. He will remain unconscious for some time." Havil squinted at my bound arm. "What happened to you?"

"Sura Fev," I said.

A cool wave swept over me, and Havil's frown turned into a worried grimace. He looked at Liang. "I'll need your help, if you are willing and able."

Liang bowed slightly. "I am at your service."

Havil pointed at the bed behind me. "Your arm needs immediate attention."

I glanced at Nilo and hesitated. "If you're too tired, it can wait. Nilo needs—"

"Nilo risked his life to save yours. Your wrist is bleeding internally, and it will go septic without intervention. Dying is no way to repay his sacrifice. Get on the bed."

Liang helped me climb up. I felt bruised from head to toe, but I grabbed Havil's hand as he reached for my improvised sling. "Don't overdo it. I can wait to be fully healed."

Havil blew out an exasperated breath, but his dark eyes were kind. "I won't tell you how to do *your* job if you will refrain from telling me how to do mine. Deal?" Before I could press him, he relented. "I will not exhaust myself to the point where I can't help the others."

"Thank you," I whispered meekly.

He inclined his head. "Unfortunately, I don't think we can wait for the autostab to put you under, so I'm going to give you a strong shot of pain medication. Let me know when it starts working."

He waited for me to agree, then jabbed me with something that burned slightly. It didn't take long for the floaty, disconnected feeling to distance me from the pain. I could still tell that everything hurt, but I no longer cared.

Havil leaned over the bed and looked at my eyes. "How are you feeling?"

"High," I said, or thought I said. My lips didn't quite

work right. *Did I even have lips?* I frowned and tried to remember.

Havil gently drew my attention back with a tap on my shoulder. "I'm going to start. Let me know if it becomes too much." His mouth hadn't moved. How could he speak without a mouth? Some distant warning rang, but I was too relaxed to care.

Then he cut the sling away and unwrapped my arm. The pain broke through the fog and I groaned. Yeah, that didn't feel very nice.

"You're doing well," Havil whispered.

Was I? A staticky burn started in my arm, and I tried to jerk it away, but nothing happened. Tears streamed from my eyes, which was annoying because it meant I couldn't see. The burn intensified until I could feel nothing else. I whimpered. Why was Havil hurting me?

"I'm sorry," Havil said. "We're almost done. Have strength."

I tried, I really did, but my body had other ideas. My mind shut down, and I fell gently into the waiting arms of unconsciousness.

CHAPTER TWENTY-NINE

I woke to the familiar hum of the engines combined with the quiet beeping of the autostab. Strong painkillers lingered in my system, so either I hadn't been out for very long or Havil was dosing me with the good stuff.

Opening my eyes took far more effort than it should've. The lights in the medbay were dimmed, and I frowned at the ceiling. This was not the bed where I'd started.

I was in the autostab.

I wiggled my fingers and toes. Everything seemed to be accounted for and functioning, so why was I in the autostab when Nilo needed it more?

Worry propelled me up, but lightheadedness put me right back down. I closed my eyes and waited for the nausea to recede. Okay, that might've been a bit too fast. If I fell out of bed and gave myself a concussion, Havil would scowl at me, and I didn't want to make the easygoing medic mad.

The medbay door slid open and someone rushed in. "You're awake!" Kee whisper-yelled.

"Barely," I said with a groan. "How long was I out?"

"Only about an hour. Havil and Nilo are still asleep, but Havil got you hooked up to an IV before he conked out. He said you can remove it when you wake, but that you need to drink plenty of fluids. Apparently, you lost a decent amount of blood."

"Help me up."

Kee pulled me up into a seated position and supported me when my head went light again. "Maybe you should stay here a bit longer," she suggested quietly.

She wasn't wrong, but I shook my head stubbornly.

"Are you sure? Because I know for a fact that Tavi is planning to yell at you, and so is Eli. The only reason *I'm* not yelling is because you look like you're about to fall over even though you're sitting down."

I smiled at her. "You're too nice to yell."

"Ha! Shows what you know. I'm getting quite good at yelling."

"Good for you," I said, and I meant it. Kee was one of the smartest people I knew. Now that she was gaining the confidence to trust her instincts, she'd be unstoppable.

"Let me shut off the IV drip," she said, "then I'll help you remove it."

"Thank you." Needles and I had an uneasy relationship. I probably *could* remove my own IV, if I had to, but I would vastly prefer for someone else to do it.

Kee fiddled with the autostab's control panel for a moment, then gathered some supplies and got to work. I looked away, but she was fast and efficient. We'd all learned the basics after Tavi had acquired the autostab. The machine did a lot of the work, but it still needed an operator.

Kee bandaged the small wound, then put away the supplies. While she did that, I held out my right arm. My wrist was still mottled with deep bruising, but a lot of the swelling had gone down. I clenched my fist and let it go. It ached, but it was a lingering pain, not an acute one. Havil truly was a miracle worker.

I swung my legs over the side of the bed, then carefully slid to the floor. My legs held and while my head was still too light, the nausea was tolerable. I crossed to Nilo's bed. Someone had covered him with a light sheet, and his chest rose and fell with reassuring regularity.

"Havil said he probably won't wake until tomorrow. Hopefully we'll be nearly to Bastion by then."

My breath caught. If Nilo wanted to immediately return to Valovia to continue gathering information for Torran, that would give us so little time together.

Kee caught my expression. "Did you tell him?"

"No. There wasn't time."

She made a noncommittal sound, but I could hear the doubt in it. And she was right. I *could've* made time. After all, confessing hardly took any time at all.

It was the fallout that I was worried about.

The medbay door slid open again, and Eli entered. Relief crossed his face when he saw me standing, but it was swiftly chased away by a scowl. "What were you *thinking*?" he demanded.

"Tavi already yelled the exact same question at me," I grumbled. "You can ask her."

Eli's eyes flashed. "I'm asking *you*." He didn't often

break out his first officer's voice, but when he did, my spine automatically straightened in response, and I started looking for a handy shadow that I could use to slip away.

Sadly, the medbay had a distinct lack of handy shadows. "It was me or all of us, so I chose me," I said.

"You all are giving me gray hair," he complained. I looked at his shaved scalp and raised an eyebrow. He shook his finger at me. "Just because I cut it off doesn't mean it's not there."

"I, for one—" Kee started, her tone impish.

Eli turned his glare to her. "Do you want to be on bathroom cleaning duty for the rest of eternity?"

Kee mimed locking her lips.

Eli sighed and ran a hand down his face. "I'm glad you're okay," he said. "Even if you scared a decade off my life."

"Did you have any trouble getting us away from Rodeni?"

He shook his head. "We're still running under Kee's false registration. They let us go. Tavi is debating how long to wait before we switch back."

I nodded. There was a Valovian battleship guarding this side of the FHP–Valovian wormhole. *Starlight* had decent weapons and armor, but a battleship would turn us into tiny particles of dust without even needing to break out their biggest guns.

Eli crossed the room to check on Havil, then carefully tucked the sheet more securely around the medic. Kee and I shared a secret grin. Eli flirted like it was his job, but when he was truly gone for someone, he showed it with tiny, thoughtful actions that most people might not even notice.

My heart twisted. Nilo had been doing the same for me

since I'd arrived on Valovia, and I'd been so hurt and wary, I'd thought he'd had some ulterior motive.

But what if he *hadn't*?

I squeezed his hand in silent apology. Sex was easy, but intimacy was not, and while I would rather exit the ship sans spacesuit than admit my feelings, Nilo deserved honesty.

Decision made, I started toward the door, my gait a little wobblier than I would've preferred. "I'm going to grab some food in the galley, then I'll see if Tavi needs me for anything."

Eli stepped close and scooped me up. When I started to protest, he scowled at me. "Breaking your neck on the stairs because of your pride is a stupid way to die."

"I could've made it." Probably. Maybe.

Eli shook his head and muttered, "Gray hair."

I subsided and let him carry me upstairs. Sending him to the ship earlier with Morten and Liang had been the best plan, but I knew it chafed him to not have been part of the rescue, especially when I'd gotten hurt. He, like Tavi, took his responsibilities far too seriously.

Eli put me down next to the table in the galley. "Stay there," he ordered, pointing at my usual chair. "I'll make you some dinner."

I tossed him a jaunty salute, then sank into the chair before my legs could give out and embarrass me. Kee slipped into the opposite chair and pushed a plate of cookies across the table. "Have one. Varro made them a couple of days ago, but they're still delicious."

Eli set a glass of water in front of me with a stern look, and I nodded my thanks. I also snagged a cookie because the sugar would give me an energy boost if nothing else. But the sweet and spicy gingersnap cookie *was* delicious, so I grabbed a second one. "Tell Varro that he's hired," I said.

Kee grinned. "I tell him all the time. This was a new recipe. I think he nailed it."

"He did."

I'd just finished the second cookie when Eli put a plate of what looked like Tavi's favorite tomato and chickpea curry in front of me. Humans weren't so different from Valoffs after all—we showed care with food, too.

I blinked away tears and dug into my food while Eli went back to clean up. "Leave it," I called. "I'll do it once I'm done."

"It's only the one pan I used to heat it up. Just eat."

I did. The food was warm and filling, and I felt better with every bite. Eli joined us at the table. He and Kee gossiped about the latest vid drama Kee was obsessed with and the scandal a popular celebrity was causing while I finished eating. They were keeping the conversation light and entertaining for my benefit, and love filled my heart.

Once I was done, I reached across the table and squeezed their hands. "Thank you," I murmured.

Kee smiled softly, and Eli dipped his head. "You're family, Lex. Never forget that."

I blinked away a fresh wave of tears, then stood and took my dishes to the sanitizer. I barely even wobbled, but Eli watched me like a hawk.

I tipped my head toward the bridge. "I need to talk to the captain. You two might as well come, too, because Fev got chatty at the end."

The three of us made our way to the bridge where Tavi, Torran, Chira, Anja, and Liang were talking quietly. Varro was nowhere to be found, but based on how exhausted he'd looked earlier, he was probably asleep in his bunk.

Or Kee's.

The thought made me smile.

Liang and Torran were also looking a little rough around the edges, but everyone on the bridge had at least had a shower and a change of clothes since the last time I'd seen them. Luna was sprawled on Anja's terminal, and the mechanic was absently petting her, a distant look on her face.

Tavi looked up from her place at the captain's terminal. Her gaze swept over me from head to toe, and she didn't miss the bruising on my wrist or the bandage where the IV had been. "Should you be up?"

"Probably not, but that's never stopped me before." I slipped into my usual seat at the operations terminal and checked the screen. We were on course for the wormhole and no one was targeting us, which were both wins.

Eli joined Chira at the tactical terminal and Kee took her usual place at navigation. With Anja at engineering and Torran at communications, we nearly had a full bridge. We were only lacking Havil at the medical terminal.

"Did Fev tell you anything?" Tavi asked.

"She claimed that she hadn't betrayed the empress. She said the empress knew about all of her plans and had approved them, but I don't know exactly how *much* she'd told the empress. 'I have a plan to take down the FHP' is a lot different than 'I'm going to kill your son.'"

Liang flinched, and I winced in sympathy. "Sorry."

He waved off my apology. "Not your fault." He sighed. "I think it's a bit of both. I think the empress *did* know what Fev was doing, at least at a high level, but I believe

Fev may have been withholding details or altering reports to support her cause. She was one of the empress's closest advisors, so her opinion held a great deal of sway."

The prince glanced at Torran. "That's why I advised you to draft a full, exact accounting of everything that's happened, starting with Cien's kidnapping. I will ensure it is delivered directly to the empress."

"What about you?" Kee asked. "You can't mean to go back, can you? The empress—*your mother*—was okay with your death. That's just wrong."

Liang's eyes slid to Anja briefly before he shrugged. "I have to go back. I'm always in some type of danger, I just didn't expect it to come from inside the family. But now I have a little insurance against a sudden accident."

Anja looked away in disappointment but not surprise. She'd already known he was planning to go back. Luna chirruped and butted her head against Anja's hand. The little burbu's presence with Anja instead of Tavi suddenly made a lot more sense.

"Where is Morten?" I asked just to change the subject.

Tavi rubbed her face. "He's cuffed and locked in the cabin we use for bounties. Torran is keeping a telepathic eye on him. The last thing we need is for him to become a martyr."

"Do you really think the Feds will convict him?"

Eli shook his head, but Tavi just sighed. "I hope so. If not, we'll raise hell. Then *two* massive governments will want us dead."

"I can do it," I said. "It'll be easier for me to disappear than all of you."

Tavi's eyes narrowed. "I'm still mad at you about earlier. Attempting to sacrifice yourself *again* is not the way to get back on my good side."

"You *have* a good side?" I teased, but when her expression turned dangerous, I held up my hands in surrender. "It was just a suggestion. Having options is good."

"Not when those options involve you throwing yourself into danger alone."

I didn't point out that throwing myself into danger alone was pretty much my exact job description. Tavi would not appreciate the reminder. So I did what I did best and changed the subject. "How long until we get to the wormhole?"

"A little over fourteen hours," Tavi said.

"Plenty of time for something to go wrong," Eli grumbled.

"We could add my diplomatic registration to the ship's registry," Liang offered. "But I honestly don't know if it will help or hurt."

"I appreciate it," Tavi said. "We also have a diplomatic registration from Admiral Ohashi, but we haven't used it yet for the same reason."

"If you are planning to add them, you should do it before you get in range of the anchor," Torran said. "The battleship guarding the wormhole won't fire on a diplomatic ship without a direct order, but a ship changing its registration is likely suspicious enough to warrant further investigation."

Tavi tapped her fingers on her terminal. "What would you do?" she asked him.

Torran smiled gently at her. "I would do exactly what you're planning."

She rolled her eyes, but turned to Kee and said, "Please switch the ship's registration back to the correct one and add the diplomatic records—both of them. If they're planning to take us out, let's make it as public as possible."

"On it," Kee said.

"Did Morten say anything else?" I asked. "He was clearly working with Fev, but I'm not sure who was playing who. Was she the one feeding him information about the telepathy-blocking helmets or did he have another mole?"

"He's refusing to say anything at all, other than to curse at us," Tavi said.

I raised my eyebrows. "Are you *sure* he can't have some sort of tragic, fatal accident?"

"Unfortunately," she said with a sigh. "Why don't you go get cleaned up and get some rest?"

She phrased it as a question, but I heard the command underneath. Luckily, I was excellent at ignoring subtle commands. "I'm okay."

"We won't be to the anchor until tomorrow morning. And if something goes wrong, I'd rather have you rested and ready to fight than exhausted and struggling. Don't make me lock you in your bunk."

I grinned. "You *do* know who helped you set up the locks on this ship, right? As if I wouldn't leave myself a way out."

"Lexi," she growled, "go shower and relax. That's an order." Her gaze swept around the bridge. "That goes for the rest of you, too."

Kee stood and saluted with a poorly suppressed grin. "One mandatory relaxation coming right up, Captain!"

"Remind me why I put up with you lot," Tavi said, her voice fondly exasperated.

"Because ejecting us into space would be a lot of work, Captain!" Kee replied with all the boundless enthusiasm of an overeager cadet.

Tavi tried to keep a straight face, but no one could withstand Kee at her most ridiculous. The bridge dissolved into laughter, and it was like a pressure relief valve had been opened. We were far from safe, but it felt good to laugh.

I stood. As much as I didn't want to admit it, a shower would be nice. And Tavi was right—I couldn't do anything except stare at space and worry, so resting wasn't a bad idea, either. "Do you want me to take a watch?" I asked.

Tavi shook her head. "Torran and I will switch off. We'll wake the ship if anything changes, I promise."

AFTER SHOWERING AND CHANGING INTO COMFORTABLE CLOTHES, I returned to the medbay to check on Nilo, only to find Havil awake and sitting up. He blinked at me as I entered. "Would you mind getting me one of the electrolyte drinks from the cold storage? I was just about to attempt it myself, but I'm not sure it's a good idea."

"Of course." I retrieved the drink and handed it to him. "You want me to run up and get you some food? It'll just take a minute." When Havil shook his head, I switched to subvocal comms and connected to Eli. "Havil is awake."

"Don't let him leave," Eli growled. "I'll be right there."

Havil's head tilted, then he turned an accusing glare on me. "You told Eli."

I lifted one shoulder. "He was worried. Now he'll be less worried."

Havil sighed. "He was with Chira." There wasn't any jealousy in his tone, just a kind of gentle longing.

"Look, I'm absolutely horrible at emotional shit," I said. "I can't even tell the person that I'm very likely in love with that I have feelings for him. But, if you want my unsolicited opinion, you and Chira have something special in Eli. So find a way to not fuck it up."

Havil's gaze slid past me to the bed behind me where Nilo was sleeping. "Is it Nilo?"

"Of course it's Nilo," I growled, "but we're talking about *you*."

The medbay door slid open, and Eli rushed in, saving me from more excruciating emotional conversation. Chira lingered in the doorway, and I smiled at her. She smiled back, then her eyes went distant as she communicated telepathically with someone.

Eli pulled Havil's arm over his shoulder and helped the medic stand. Chira slipped into the room and took Havil's other side. They nodded at me, then carefully made their way out through the door, leaving the room quiet.

I sighed and turned to check on Nilo, only to find his eyes open. I blinked at him, then rushed to his side. "You're awake. Why are you awake? Havil just left, I can still catch him."

I turned to do just that, but Nilo caught my fingers, his grip featherlight. "I told him to go."

"Why? He said you'd be out until tomorrow. He needs to check you."

"Havil is exhausted, and nothing is wrong with me that rest won't cure." He met my eyes. "Did you mean it?"

I stiffened. There was only one thing he could mean, but I'd thought I would have another day or more to gather my courage. I swallowed, then whispered, "I meant it."

"Cho arbu chil tavoz," he murmured. *My heart is yours.*

The urge to flee warred with the urge to kiss him. Nilo must've felt my tumult, because rather than pressing, his expression smoothed and he lifted a hand. "Help me up."

"I don't think that's a good idea. Why are you awake so early?"

His eyes glinted. "I know you, *taro.* Porting you at a distance isn't as difficult as it once was, plus Liang added some of his considerable strength to the effort."

I scowled at him even as I helped him sit up. "I told you not to risk yourself for me."

"But you're allowed to risk *yourself* for *me*?" he asked, his voice deceptively mild.

I bit back the affirmative and tried, "It wasn't *just* for you."

"I'm pretty sure Tavi and the rest of the crew would agree with me. Shall we ask them?"

That was a war I definitely would not win, so I said nothing. Nilo nodded knowingly. "That's what I thought." He swung his legs off the side of the bed with a groan, then his eyes settled on my bruised wrist and his expression shuttered. "Why aren't you healed?"

I flexed my fingers. "I am, mostly. The bruises look worse than they are. Havil exhausted himself to help me, so don't complain."

Nilo traced a gentle finger over my wrist. "I can hear your bones breaking in my nightmares."

So could I, but I figured that would just make him feel worse. "Fev paid for it with her life."

His expression darkened. "And nearly yours. If I'd been a fraction of a second slower . . ."

I brushed my fingers across the stubble adorning his jaw. "I knew the risk, and I took the chance anyway. If you can tell me with complete honesty that you wouldn't risk yourself to save Torran and Varro and Chira, then I'll apologize. I won't believe you, but I'll apologize anyway."

Nilo sighed. "I would save them if I could, even if it cost my life."

I pressed a fleeting kiss to his lips. "Of course you would."

Nilo's hands closed into fists, but he didn't reach for me or pull me closer. I tried not to be disappointed.

I failed.

CHAPTER THIRTY

Torran helped me get Nilo upstairs then helped him get cleaned up. I would've done it, but Nilo didn't ask, and I didn't offer. We'd admitted we had feelings for each other, but now things were horribly awkward. Wasn't it supposed to get *easier* once feelings were in the open?

I didn't really have enough experience to know. I traveled so much that most of my liaisons were brief, mutually satisfying, and free of any emotions deeper than desire.

Nilo hadn't asked for me, but I couldn't go to bed without checking on him, so I heated a bowl of leftover curry for him as an excuse. I carried it and a glass of water to his door and knocked by kicking the panel with my foot.

The door slid open, and Nilo froze in surprise in the middle of putting on his shirt. He dropped the cloth, but not quickly enough. Bruises littered his torso, painting his tan skin in shades of purple and red.

"You're hurt." My voice sounded strangely flat to my own ears. He was hurt, and he hadn't told me.

"It's nothing," he said with a grin that didn't quite reach his eyes. "Did you need something?" His expression turned hopeful when he spotted the bowl in my hands. "Is that for me?"

I handed it over automatically, my feelings still in a jumble. "Be careful. It's hot."

He set the bowl and cup on the tiny built-in desk and pulled out the chair. "Thank you."

"You're welcome." The silence stretched taut, until it, like my nerves, snapped. "Why didn't you tell me?"

"Lexi, they're just bruises," he said in an infuriatingly calm tone.

I held up my wrist. "So are these, but you were ready to tear into Havil about them. What is wrong? Why are you shutting me out?"

His eyes glinted as the gold streaks grew. "What do you want?" he demanded hotly. "I told you that you were my heart, and you looked like I was a demon ready to rend you limb from limb! Now I'm giving you space, and you don't want that, either."

His face was filled with frustration and something deeper and infinitely sadder. "You give me hope only to snatch it away again, over and over. That *hurts*. Can't you see that?" He shook his head. "Maybe you can't, and I'm the fool. Or maybe this is some kind of game to you? Well, congratulations, you won!"

The bitter words landed with deadly accuracy. I'd always secretly feared I made people around me quietly miserable, and now I knew. Coming *from Nilo,* it was a wound I wasn't sure I would survive. Agony stole my breath, and I shied away from the yawning pain.

"It's not a game," I whispered, stung. Then pain morphed into anger. *How dare he?* My brain shut down and instinct demanded that I hit back harder, that I make him hurt more. I barely curbed it, but I couldn't quite silence myself.

"I don't know what I want!" I shouted. "I've never been in love before, so fuck me for not knowing how to react, right? I *thought* we'd figure it out together, but since you couldn't even be bothered—" I squeezed my hands into fists and bit off the rest of the sentence before I could say something truly awful.

But the desire was there. The words burned in my mouth, ready to rend and tear and *hurt*.

Just like he'd said. I really was a terrible person.

I silently spun for the door, my heart breaking. It slid open, and I dashed into the hall. Nilo didn't try to stop me. Grief, sharp and raw, nearly buckled my legs.

My room was too close and too small. Tears blurred my vision, but I softened my steps so I wouldn't alert the whole ship and headed for the garden. The grow lights were off for the night cycle, but nightlights lit the path to the arbor in the back corner.

I sank into one of the chairs and tipped my head back, staring sightlessly at the honeysuckle growing overhead. Tears continued to stream from my eyes. I didn't bother wiping them away. Everyone needed a good cry once in a while, even me.

The door opened and I tensed. A moment later, Luna chirped at me before jumping into my lap. I stroked my fingers through her downy coat and chucked weakly. "When Tavi comes looking for you, you're going to get me found."

Luna purred and rubbed her face against my chest for a few minutes before curling up in a warm ball of fluff. Slowly, my muscles unknotted as my tension bled away. My temper cooled, but the hurt lingered.

I was self-aware enough to know that I *might* have overreacted a bit, but Nilo had chosen his tone and words specifically to goad me, so the fault wasn't *entirely* mine, especially when I was already feeling exposed and vulnerable.

But maybe he was feeling the same.

My reaction to his confession had hurt him, and I'd been so wrapped up in my own head that I hadn't noticed. Guilt tugged at me. I needed to apologize. Just . . . not tonight. I still felt wounded. I needed time to let the hurt bleed away.

I could only hope that I wouldn't bleed out in the interim.

CHAPTER THIRTY-ONE

I awoke to Luna chirruping in my ear and repeatedly sending me pictures of her empty food bowl. I was still in the garden and my neck and spine were not improved from a night spent sleeping in a chair.

I groggily scratched the little burbu under the chin, then checked the time. It was barely five. I'd been asleep for nearly nine hours, which explained why I felt welded in place. But with multiple time transitions lately, my body had decided to grab sleep where it could. At least now I would be aligned with standard time again.

I scooped Luna up and stood. The grow lights were starting to brighten, but the arbor was shaded enough that they hadn't woken me.

The ship was quiet as I carried Luna to the galley. I fed her breakfast, then grabbed a cup of coffee from the half-full pot. I slipped into the bridge on quiet feet. Tavi smiled in greeting. "Have you seen Luna?" she asked over the comm because Torran was asleep in his seat.

"She spent the night with me," I responded subvocally. "I just fed her."

"Thank you." Her gaze swept over my face. "You want to talk?"

"Not yet," I said, "but thank you."

She nodded easily. "I'm going to wake everyone in an hour if you'd like to hit the gym or showers while they're empty."

I used a gym more from necessity than desire, since climbing was one of my most useful skills, but exertion actually sounded good this morning. I could work out the lingering knots and soreness. "I'm going to hit the gym. Unless you'd like for me to take watch so you can clean up."

Tavi shook her head. "I showered last night while Torran watched the bridge. Go on."

I left my coffee in the galley for later and grabbed a water bottle. My lounge clothes would work for a gym outfit, so I headed downstairs. The lights in the gym came on as I entered, bathing the area in bright light.

My wrist wasn't completely healed, and I didn't want to undo any of Havil's work, so I'd have to do a lower body workout. I stepped on the treadmill. Maybe if I pushed myself hard enough, I could outrun my problems.

It was a nice thought.

I started with a warm-up walk, then slowly increased the speed until I was moving at a brisk jog. Usually I could run at this speed for kilometers, but my breathing picked up faster than I expected, so I backed off the pace. My body was still recovering, and while pushing myself harder was tempting, we still didn't know what would happen when we reached the anchor.

Staying at a slower pace meant I had plenty of time to think. I needed to apologize to Nilo today. I'd hurt him, he'd lashed out, and rather than apologizing and trying to fix it, I'd shouted at him and stormed away. It hadn't been my finest moment, and regret sat heavily in my belly.

I hadn't meant to make him feel like I didn't want him. And it wasn't a game. I *loved* him.

I blinked in wonder. I loved him, no wiggle words required. Joy and hope filled my chest. Of course I did. How could I not?

The happiness dimmed as reality intruded. I was so used to protecting myself that I kept my emotions locked away. No wonder Nilo was unsure where he stood with me.

Maybe I just wasn't wired right for relationships.

I'd loved my moms, and I loved Kee, Tavi, and Eli, and I was pretty sure they loved me back even though I came armed with knives—both literal and metaphorical. But all of those relationships had grown due to proximity and necessity.

Maybe people only loved me as a defense mechanism when they couldn't escape me.

The kindest path forward would be to let Nilo go, but every cell revolted against the thought. Giving up something precious went against my every instinct. I blew out a slow breath. I would only make him miserable in the end. It would be better to let him go now.

I was deep into a list of pros and cons—pro: Nilo would be happy; con: I would be miserable—when he appeared beside me so suddenly that I missed a step and nearly fell onto the moving tread.

Once I'd caught my balance, he held up a pair of rubber training knives. "Would you like to spar?" he asked, a subtle wariness in his expression.

I nodded and brought the treadmill to a stop. When I stepped off, Nilo handed me one of the knives then turned for the sparring mats before I could apologize.

I toed off my shoes and stepped onto the mats. The memory of his bruises was still fresh in my mind, so I needed to be careful. I spun my right wrist in a circle and there wasn't any pain, but Nilo's eyes darkened at the sight of my own bruises, so I switched the knife to my left hand. I wasn't quite as strong with my off hand, but since I was planning to let Nilo win anyway, it wouldn't make much difference.

Nilo bowed, and I returned the gesture, then he circled to my left. I mirrored him, waiting for him to attack.

"I'm sorry about last night," I said quietly, forcing the words past my tight throat. "And before."

Nilo shook his head, but his eyes didn't leave me. "The fault was mine."

"No," I said, darting forward to test his defenses. He brought his arm up to block in a flash of movement. I retreated without connecting. "I should have handled myself and the situation better. I am sorry. I don't ever want you to hurt because of me."

I love you. The words were there, on the tip of my tongue, but I was trying to let him go, not draw him closer. I swallowed them down and pretended it didn't hurt.

"It wasn't your fault," Nilo reiterated. When I glared at him, he bowed slightly and added, "But I accept your apology. Thank you."

I nodded, and he slid forward, aiming at my ribs. He'd left himself completely open, and I could've hit him in at least three places, all of them likely bruised. Instead, I danced backward, out of reach.

His eyes narrowed. His next attack was blazingly fast. I countered it on instinct alone and ended up with my knife to his throat, his knife on the ground.

Rather than looking upset, he looked pleased. "So you will stop holding back if I push you far enough," he said.

"That's the problem," I muttered, letting him go.

"Defending yourself isn't a problem, *taro,*" he said, his voice soft.

I picked up his knife and held it out to him. "It is when I don't care who I hurt in the process."

His fingers closed around mine, so very gently. "But you *do* care."

I sighed. "Eventually. But that's not good enough."

We reset, and I eyed Nilo. He was wearing his trademark grin, which meant he was up to something. I feinted at him, but he didn't retreat *or* attack. I had just decided to back off when he *did* attack.

He disarmed me and had me pinned on the mats between one breath and the next. Professional admiration warred with wounded personal pride. Admiration won. "How did you do that?"

He grinned as I tested his hold and found it to be solid. "I can teach you, if you'd like," he offered.

The warm weight of his body pinning mine was slowly scrambling my brain, so I nodded eagerly before remembering that I was supposed to be giving him up.

He caught my grimace. "What's wrong?"

"We might not have time before you return to Valovia," I said, fighting hard to keep my voice mild and my body loose and relaxed.

I failed at both.

"We'll have time," Nilo murmured.

I frowned. "How can you be—"

His mouth brushed across mine, stealing the words from my lips. "We'll have time," he said again before he dipped his head and kissed me with a slow thoroughness that shorted out my thoughts.

I licked his lip and he groaned, a sound I could feel in my chest. I used his distraction to flip our positions, then I leaned down and kissed him again. His groin was pinned between my thighs, and I could feel him hardening against me. I rolled my hips and we both hissed in pleasure.

His hands slipped under my shirt, but reason asserted itself at the very last moment. "If we have sex in here, Tavi will make us sanitize the entire room," I gasped.

Nilo's grin was downright wicked. "Worth it."

When his hands found my breasts, I very nearly agreed. But one of the unspoken rules of the ship was that mutual spaces deserved mutual respect. *Starlight* was small enough that the shared spaces were important for crew morale, and fucking like rabbits in one of them was disrespectful to the rest of the crew.

But *hot.*

So hot.

"The medbay is empty," I gasped. "And it needs to be cleaned anyway."

Nilo's power spiked and then we were in the medbay. We'd arrived standing, a trick that my inner ear would never get over. Nilo steadied me while the dizziness passed, then he pressed a tiny kiss to the corner of my mouth. "I'm sorry I didn't understand," he murmured.

I frowned. "What do you mean?"

"I was so delighted when you told Havil you loved me that I rushed you, then I got upset when you couldn't keep up through no fault of your own. I know you're not trying to hurt me. I let frustration choose my words, and I should not have. I'm sorry."

My frown deepened. The first part didn't make any sense, but the second part reminded me that I was supposed to be giving Nilo up, not fucking him in the medbay, no matter how badly I wanted to.

"But I *did* hurt you," I whispered, staring at his chin. "I didn't mean to, but that doesn't excuse it." I swallowed. "You should find someone who won't make you miserable."

Nilo didn't leave, and the aching, lonely part of me clung tenaciously to hope, no matter how much I tried to stomp it out.

"You don't make me miserable," he said softly.

"I will," I muttered, voice dark.

He shook his head and asked, "What do *you* want?"

You. I pushed past the selfish thought. "I want you to be happy."

He tipped my chin up and smiled gently at me. "How convenient that *you* make me happy," he said.

"But—"

He interrupted me. "Why do you think that you will make me miserable?"

I grimaced. "Probably because every time I have to talk about my feelings, I would rather walk into space."

Nilo's smile softened. "That's pretty common, actually. What else?"

He wouldn't let me duck my head, so I avoided his gaze

and admitted, "When something—or someone—hurts me, my first instinct is to hit back harder. I don't want to do that to you."

"We can get professional help—together, separately, or both—to work on healthy communication and coping mechanisms. I could use help in that area, too. What else?"

"Why are you being *so nice*?" I demanded in frustration. "I'm a terrible person, but I'm trying to be kind for once. Escape while you can, because once I decide you're mine, *I'm keeping you.*"

"You're not terrible. And what if I want to be kept?"

My patience broke. If he didn't want to save himself, then I certainly wasn't noble enough to force him. I dragged his head down to mine. He came willingly and his tongue slid into my mouth as if it were meant to be there. Sparks danced down my spine, setting my nerves alight.

"Cho arbu," Nilo whispered reverently. *My heart.*

I shivered. The words had the weight of a vow, but he distracted me by porting away first my shirt and then my bra. When I raised my eyebrows, his shirt vanished, too.

I gasped and touched the flawless skin of his chest. "You're healed."

He nodded. "Havil fixed me up before I came to find you. I didn't want you to worry."

"Was Havil rested enough? For that matter, are you? You shouldn't be teleporting us and our clothes all over—"

Nilo silenced me with another lingering kiss before he worked his way down my neck. But he slipped my pants down my legs rather than porting them, until I stood bare. His eyes gleamed gold on green, and his smile heated the room. "Lie back."

This was the bed Nilo had been on last night and no one

had changed the sheets. I lay back, my legs dangling over the end. Nilo devoured me with his eyes. "Let me share my pleasure with you."

Anxiety threatened to rise, but I trusted Nilo. I nodded before I could psych myself out. A moment later, I felt Nilo's cool presence in the back of mind, but my worry was overwhelmed by a deep feeling of happiness.

Nilo was happy.

He was also burning with desire, but I could make anyone horny. I wasn't sure I'd ever made anyone this *happy* before. I blinked away tears and met his eyes. "Can you feel my pleasure in return?"

When he nodded, I slid my hands up my body, slowly, slowly, until I reached my breasts and tugged on my nipples. I moaned, and he gasped, then his eyes blazed with gold. His fingers traced the same path with even better results, then he wrapped his hands around my hips and tugged me down until my butt was barely on the bed.

He flashed me a stunningly wicked grin, then he knelt, put my legs on his shoulders, and buried his face between my thighs. I arched as pleasure slammed into me. Nilo groaned and fed it right back to me, a wave of delight that ricocheted between us, growing with every pass and every stroke of his tongue.

And he had an *extremely* talented tongue.

Pleasure rose and rose until it shattered into a wave of bliss so acute, it curled my toes and turned my thoughts to static. When I drifted back down to my body, Nilo pressed a kiss to my inner thigh, then carefully moved my legs and stood.

I could feel leashed desire radiating from him, and I wanted to make him just as mindless as he'd made me.

But when I sat up and reached for him, he stepped away. "Touch me and this will be over far too soon, *taro.* And I have plans for you."

I arched an eyebrow at him. "Oh do you, *omazas*?"

Affection and joy spiked at the nickname. He liked it when I played with him. I slid from the bed, relieved when my legs held. I stalked toward him until I'd cornered him against the next bed. "You're wearing too many clothes," I murmured. "Allow me to help."

He stood stock still as I unbuttoned his pants and eased them down his legs. I cupped him through his underwear, then gave him one firm stroke. His hands flexed as his pleasure raced across our connection. "Lexi," he growled.

I slid my fingers under his waistband and *slowly* pulled them down, teasing us both. By the time he was naked, his sleek muscles were corded with tension, but he hadn't moved.

But when I stepped closer, so that my body slid along his, his control broke. He wrapped his arms around me, molding me against his chest, then his mouth crashed down on mine in a blazing kiss that once again set me alight.

I broke the kiss with a gasp. "Someone could walk in at any moment," I whispered.

Nilo's desire burned brighter. "They could," he agreed. "Shall we shock them? Do you have any ideas?"

The question was dangerously close to asking what I wanted, and it took me a second to overcome my innate unwillingness to be that unguarded. Still, I couldn't quite meet Nilo's eyes when I murmured, "Do you think that bending me over one of these beds and fucking me mindless would be shocking enough?"

Surprise, pleasure, affection, and something softer and

warmer all spilled across the connection before sizzling desire overrode everything. Nilo spun me around and bent me over the bed where we'd started. I braced my arms against the sheets, intensely aware of the vulnerable position I was in.

Nilo ran a hand down my back, and I shivered in delight. "You are so strong and brave and beautiful," he whispered. His hand curved around my hip, and then his fingers slid through the slick heat of me, sharpening my need.

He urged me up onto my tiptoes and notched himself against me. "What do you want, Lexi?" he murmured.

You, just you. The thought was loud enough that he caught it, and he surged into me with a groan. I could *feel* his pleasure, and it compounded my own. Then his fingers moved and I moaned in ecstasy as he wound me tighter and tighter.

He hit a spot that made me see stars and I demanded, "Yes, there. Do that again."

He did, and when I groaned in delight, I could feel echoing joy from him. "That's right, demand your pleasure, *cho akinti.* I will give you whatever you want."

"I want you," I gasped as my muscles clenched around him. *So close.*

"You have me."

The words, the pleasure, they were too much and I tipped over the edge into a galaxy of bliss. Nilo groaned and followed me a moment later, sending our combined pleasure even higher.

I let my chest collapse against the bed, and Nilo bent and pressed a kiss to my shoulder. "You okay?"

The movement sent aftershocks skating along my nerves, and I hummed an affirmative under my breath. I was fabulous, and I would tell him just as soon as I could think again.

He chuckled, and I belatedly remembered that he was in my head. The fact that I'd forgotten at all was a testament to just how relaxed I was.

After a few minutes of basking in the warm afterglow, I groaned and pushed myself upright. Nilo helped me stand, then kissed me slowly, lingeringly, until I felt like the treasure he claimed I was.

CHAPTER THIRTY-TWO

After we cleaned the medbay and ourselves, we joined the rest of the crew in the galley for breakfast. The places at the table had shifted slightly since the last time I was on the ship, though my place remained the same. But now Liang sat across from Anja, and Havil had moved closer to Eli and Chira. I sat next to Eli with Nilo on my left.

Tavi didn't usually cook breakfast on the ship, but today she was making pancakes for anyone who wanted them—which was everyone.

Once we all had a pile of food, Tavi joined us at the table. "We're an hour away from the wormhole," she said. "So far, we've been left alone, but we'll see if that holds. After breakfast, I want everyone on the bridge."

"What about Morten?" I asked. "Did anyone remember to feed him?"

"He got a meal bar and a bottle of water, but you'd think

we were starving him by the amount of complaining he did," Eli grumbled.

"Did he accidentally trip and run into your fist?" I asked with a smile.

Eli slid a sly look toward Tavi before grinning. "Not as far as anyone knows."

Tavi sighed in exasperation but didn't call him on it. I'd bet, given the opportunity, that she would like to be the one to deliver a punch or two. Instead, she turned to Liang and changed the subject. "Have you heard anything from your contacts?"

The prince shook his head. "Publicly, I'm still in good standing with the empress. I have a few quiet contacts in the military, and they report the same thing."

Tavi nodded. "Did Siarvez make it home?"

I recognized the name of the fashion designer they'd met on Bastion. Apparently, he and Liang were friends, or at least friendly.

"He did," Liang said. "And there have not been any more attempts on his life, thankfully, but he's hired additional security as a precaution."

Kee let out a relieved sigh. "Good, because he promised me that I could come steal some of his clothes, and I plan to hold him to it." She leaned forward so she could look around Torran and Eli to meet my eyes. "You should invite yourself along," she said. "His designs were incredible, and he said I could bring the crew."

I grinned. "I never turn down free clothes."

"Siarvez is a genius," Liang said with absolute honesty and zero envy. "Every time I ask him to design something for me, he always exceeds my expectations, no matter how high I set them."

The designer sounded like someone I would like to meet. I loved pretty clothes, and I was in desperate need of some new ones. "Kee, let me know when you're planning to go, and I will go with you." I smiled. "You might be too nice to take advantage of his generosity, but I'm not. I'll help you out."

"You're assuming it'll be safe for us to travel to Valovia," Eli said.

I lifted a shoulder. "Safe is relative. But if the empress knows that offing one of us will have embarrassing results, she might think twice. If not, I can get us in and out quietly."

Nilo didn't say anything, but he shifted restlessly beside me. When I looked at him, he wouldn't meet my eyes, and his presence had vanished from the back of my mind.

"What's wrong—" I started, but a warning alarm from the bridge interrupted me.

"The battleship is hailing us," Kee said, checking her comm.

Tavi stood. "Torran, Liang, with me," she commanded. "The rest of you finish breakfast, then join us."

The three of them left for the bridge, their food half eaten. I looked around the table, but no one appeared to want to finish the meal without them. Even Luna looked up from her bowl with a questioning chirrup.

"Let's box everything up for later," I said.

Kee sighed in relief and nodded. The group cleaned up the meal in record time, and we put the neatly labeled leftovers in the walk-in cooler for later—once my stomach unknotted itself, and the Valoffs got past the weird anxiety they felt near the wormhole.

I pulled Nilo aside as the others headed for the bridge. "Are you okay?"

He rubbed his face, his expression unreadable. "Yes."

"Is it the wormhole?"

"That doesn't help," he agreed.

I thought back to the conversation. "Are you mad that I want to meet Siarvez?"

"No," he bit out, then took a deep breath. "I'm not mad." Which was exactly what people who were mad usually said, but before I could call him on it, he said, "We will talk later. For now, we should be on the bridge. I need to know what the battleship wants."

Then he left me standing in the galley, confused and a little hurt.

Clearly we were not going to be able to fuck our way to a working relationship, no matter how nice trying that might be. We were going to have to communicate.

Bleh.

I took a deep breath and slowly counted to ten, then twenty. It didn't make me feel any better, but it gave Nilo time to get to the bridge, so that was something.

By the time I followed him, there was palpable tension in the air, and Liang's jaw was clenched. "I assure you that *Starlight's Shadow* bears my diplomatic registration legally," he bit out in Valovan, his voice ice cold. "Unless you are calling me a liar to my face?"

The sharp-eyed woman on the screen swallowed but held her ground. "I would never insult you, Your Highness. I was merely asked to ensure that you were aboard the ship . . . ," she paused and cleared her throat delicately, ". . . *voluntarily*."

"Who asked you to ensure this?" Liang demanded.

The woman didn't move, but I got the feeling that she

would like to be somewhere, *anywhere,* else. "I am not at liberty to say."

"Tell the empress that while I appreciate her concern, it is unnecessary."

"If you would like to return to Valovia, we have cruisers standing by," the woman tried.

"Standing by to blow us up," Eli muttered over the comm.

"No," Liang said in what I was starting to recognize as his imperial prince voice—cold, haughty, and demanding. "This conversation is over. Unless you have a writ from the empress detaining me, you *will* allow us to pass through the anchor without further interference. I chose this ship for a reason, Captain."

Tavi didn't speak Valovan, but Torran must be translating for her because she didn't look as worried as I would've expected otherwise.

The captain on-screen bowed slightly with her left arm over her chest. "As you command, Your Highness. Have a pleasant journey."

Liang inclined his head, then cut the feed. As soon as the screen went dark, he slumped back in his chair and rubbed his face. "They should let us through, but there will be hell to pay when I eventually make it back to the palace."

"Would they really have sent a cruiser for you?" Kee asked.

"Yes. And then *Starlight* would've had a tragic accident just before making it to the anchor, for the good of the empire."

I shivered and asked, "And you're sure they aren't going to continue with that plan?"

Liang's smile had a grim edge. "Fairly sure."

After that unhappy announcement, the bridge fell into watchful silence. Tavi had put the ship into its active defense state and had the weapons systems on standby. Not that anything we had would really help against a battleship, but it was against Tavi's nature to just give up.

"Here goes nothing," she murmured as she confirmed our course and requested access through the wormhole.

I held my breath and clutched the edge of my terminal. It took the anchor what felt like an eternity to respond, but finally it approved the request and put us in the holding pattern. I checked the screen. There were four ships in front of us.

Four ships and then we'd be back in the relative safety of Fed space.

Four ships and we'd see if the Feds were planning to keep their word.

Luna entered the bridge and paused in the doorway for a moment before turning and hopping up into Nilo's lap. It had not escaped my notice that he'd chosen to sit in a guest chair by Liang rather than sitting next to me.

The first ship in the pattern disappeared through the anchor. Everyone on the bridge was staring intently at the screens, as if we could make it through on willpower alone.

The second, third, and fourth ships disappeared, then it was *Starlight*'s turn. Tavi let the autopilot take over. The massive circular anchor and the strange, bulging piece of space it encircled grew larger on the main screen as we approached.

We were in the danger zone now, which meant the Valoffs could probably get away with killing us and blaming it on a traversal accident. Tavi's knuckles were white where she was gripping the arm of her chair, but her expression was calm.

Then *Starlight*'s engines ramped to full and the ship pierced the plane of the anchor with a shudder. Time compressed and thinned, and the pinprick light of stars spun into dizzying strands of light. I dropped my eyes to the information on my terminal before I lost my breakfast.

A moment later, we were through. The engines continued to run at full throttle until we'd cleared out of the danger zone. I frowned at my screen. There were *far* too many ships around, and several of them sported FHP military registrations. "Captain—"

"I see them," she said.

"Two different incoming communications," Kee said. "Plus a priority vid message from Admiral Ohashi."

"Put the admiral on the main screen."

Kee nodded and tapped her terminal. A woman with gray-streaked dark hair and deep shadows marring the pale skin under her dark eyes appeared on-screen. "Hello, Captain Zarola. I'm not sure when you will get this message, but it will stay on priority loop for as long as possible. The situation has gotten . . . tense. I'm sending three trusted ships to escort you to Bastion. The details are attached."

The admiral stared fiercely from the screen. "There is a faction of the FHP who would rather Frank Morten quietly disappear. Another faction would like him to continue his work even if it means war. So far, Fleet Command is still determined to bring him to trial, but support appears to be eroding day by day. The bounty will be paid dead or alive. Don't risk your crew, but *do not* turn Morten over alive to anyone other than myself. Do what you have to do, and I hope to see you soon."

The vid ended. "Three of the five FHP ships are Ohashi's," Kee said. "Comms are coming from one of them and one of the others. Which do you want to answer first?"

"Put them both on-screen together."

Kee raised her eyebrows but did as requested. A grizzled, older soldier appeared first. His tan skin was deeply lined and his close-cropped hair was solid gray. "Captain Zarola, Admiral Ohashi sent me—"

He was cut off when the second person appeared, a younger woman with pale skin made even paler by a long stint in space. She scowled, presumably at the other captain, who only grunted at her.

"Turn over Frank Morten by order of the FHP Senate," the woman demanded without even bothering with a greeting or introduction.

Tavi leaned more firmly back in her chair. "And you are?"

"Colonel Carina Hampston, deputy director of Counterintelligence."

Tavi looked at the other soldier. "And you?"

"Captain Bruce Boyd. Fleet Command and Admiral Ohashi sent me to escort you to Bastion and prevent outside interference."

"He's telling the truth," Kee said over the comm.

Colonel Hampston's lip curled. "Fleet Command has less jurisdiction than Counterintelligence," she scoffed. "Stand down."

"But we have more guns, Colonel," Captain Boyd said with a smile that was all teeth. "Respectfully, of course."

"Try anything and you'll be court-martialed," she said.

The captain shrugged. "Some things are worth the risk. Do you worst, but if you attempt to approach *Starlight's*

Shadow, you will be deterred by force. Continue and we will destroy your ship. The numbers are on our side, as I'm sure your captain will confirm."

The colonel's eyes flashed before she forced herself to smile at Tavi. "Captain Zarola, you will be well compensated for your help in rescuing Frank Morten. I am prepared to offer you double the bounty that the admiral offered."

I whistled under my breath. Admiral Ohashi had offered Tavi a million and a half credits to return Frank Morten alive. Three million credits was a truly ridiculous number. Someone really, *really* didn't want Morten to stand trial.

"And if Morten is no longer alive?" Tavi asked. "Will you still double the bounty?"

Colonel Hampston's eyes narrowed. "If you turn over the body, we will pay you a million credits." It wasn't quite double the bounty Ohashi had offered for Morten's death, but it was still a stupid amount of money.

"Are you *sure* I can't kill him?" I asked over the comm, only half joking. Tavi slanted a quelling glance my way, and I held up my hands in surrender.

"We will be continuing to Bastion," Tavi said. "And we thank you, Captain Boyd, for your escort. *Starlight* is well armed, but we appreciate the additional safety."

"You're making a mistake," Hampston snarled.

"No," Tavi said calmly, "I don't think I am."

CHAPTER THIRTY-THREE

Tavi conferred with Captain Boyd for a few minutes after shutting off Hampston's vid, then shut down the second vid with a promise to keep in touch. We now had three heavily armed ships escorting us. If Hampston was going to try anything, she'd run into a wall of plas cannons.

"How long to Bastion?" Tavi asked Kee.

"Just under twelve hours if we push it."

"Push it," Tavi confirmed. She glanced around the bridge. "Shipboard duties are suspended today. You're welcome to do whatever you want, but you need to be able to respond quickly in case of emergency."

"Do you think they'll try something?" I asked.

"I hope not, but Ohashi wouldn't have sent an escort if she thought we were in the clear. I've sent her an update, so when I hear back, I'll let you all know what she says."

No one moved, but Havil turned to me. "I can heal your wrist the rest of the way," he offered quietly.

I flexed the joint and shook my head. "Thank you, but if there's a possibility we might run into trouble, you should save your strength. It's okay for now. You did amazing work yesterday."

Havil smiled. "Let me know if you change your mind. Otherwise, once we've safely delivered Morten, I will heal you the rest of the way."

"It's really okay," I tried, but Havil just quietly stared at me until I relented. "Thank you."

He smiled again. "You're welcome."

I stood and crossed the room to Nilo. "Join me?" I asked. Some fragile part of me breathed a sigh of relief when he immediately stood. I led him to the arbor in the garden and sank into one of the chairs.

"This is my favorite room on the ship," he confessed as he sat next to me.

"Mine, too."

I was trying to figure out how to bring up our conversation in the galley when Nilo surprised me by saying, "I'm sorry. I should not have snapped at you earlier." He rubbed his face. "This is more difficult than I expected."

"What is?"

He slanted a glance at me. "Being in love."

I sucked in a sharp breath. He admitted it so easily. "You love me?"

It was his turn to be surprised. "Of course I love you, *taro*. Why would you think I don't?"

"You never told me." I'd been trying for a nonchalant tone, but based on Nilo's frown I hadn't succeeded.

"What do you think *cho arbu chil tavoz* means?" he asked carefully.

"'My heart is yours,'" I translated. When his frown deepened, I rushed to add, "I thought it meant you liked me."

Nilo shook his head. "I thought you knew, and that's why you were upset. But you looked spooked at the mere thought that I *liked* you? Did you truly think that I would sleep with you if I didn't like you? I explained what food meant. You had to know."

"I knew you liked me, but knowing it and hearing it are two different things. If it doesn't mean you like me, what does it mean?"

A tiny, wry smile touched Nilo's mouth. "If I tell you, are you going to run away?"

"I don't run away; I strategically retreat." I blew out a breath when he didn't laugh. "Just tell me. I won't run away, I promise."

"It means I love you," he said slowly, "but it is deeper than that."

My hands tensed on the arms of the chair, but I stayed glued in place. I cleared my tight throat and asked, "What else?"

"It's a vow," Nilo murmured. "That I will always honor and treasure you. That you are my heart, the other half of my soul."

Elation and terror warred for control, stealing my ability to speak. But true to my word, I stayed in the chair.

"So when you made plans with Kee to visit Valovia without even thinking about me, it hurt," Nilo admitted. "I should've explained, but I was afraid I would say something worse."

I chuckled drily. "I understand that problem." I tapped

my fingers and tried to gather my thoughts. "I don't deserve you. I'm . . ." I swallowed. "I'm not a good person. I steal things for a living, and I have a temper, and I don't deal well with emotions. You should find someone better."

Nilo slid his hand over mine. "But I want you. It was you from the moment you arrived at Torran's house, all prickly pride and infuriating skill. I hadn't forgotten you, and fate brought you back. You're the one for me, Lexi Bowen."

Tears filled my eyes, but I whispered, "You hurt more than my pride when you left me in that hotel bar."

"I'm sorry." Nilo stood and scooped me up, then sat back down in my chair. I was sideways in his lap, my legs hanging over the arm rest and my back braced against his arm as well as the chair. "When I returned to the hotel, you were already gone," he admitted quietly.

"You went back?" I asked in surprised confusion. I'd waited for him for far longer than I liked to admit—so long that the bartender had started offering me free pity drinks. The memory burned with humiliation.

"It took me several hours to get in to see Lady Ottiz even with an appointment. It was more than I'd expected, but I needed to know if she was the one leaking information and getting time on her schedule was nearly impossible, so I couldn't leave. Then it took even longer to convince her to give me the job. I was planning to buy you dinner and tell you what I'd done, but by the time I got back, you had vanished. You were so cool and sophisticated, I figured you had been playing with me and had gotten tired of the game when I failed to play my part."

That made me smile. "I was. At first. But you're damnably likable, *omazas*. It's annoying."

Nilo laughed and the sound vibrated through my body. "Then in this case, I'm okay with being annoying."

"I'm glad you went back," I whispered. "Even if I wasn't there. It makes it hurt less."

His arms tightened around me. "I'm sorry I hurt you, *taro.* That was not my intent."

I nodded in acknowledgment and traced my fingers over his chest, gathering courage. Admitting my feelings gave him the power to hurt me, deeply. But *not* admitting them would hurt *him,* so it was a risk I would have to take.

"I love you, Nilo. I know I'm not always the best at expressing it, but never doubt that. Never doubt *me.* You are my heart." I paused for a deep breath and switched to Valovan. *"And my heart is yours."* He turned to stone under me, and I rushed to add, "I mean, if you want it, but if no—"

His mouth crashed down on mine, cutting off the words. "I want it," he breathed against my skin.

"I'm sorry that I hurt you when I was making plans with Kee. It wasn't my intention, either. I'm just so used to being on my own that it'll take a while for me to adjust. And speaking of . . . how will this work?" I waved a hand between us. "I move all the time and you need to be on Valovia to help Torran. I don't know if I can do long distance."

"If Fev was lying to the empress, I may not need to be on Valovia as much, so we could travel. If it becomes safe for you to visit Valovia, then I would like it if we could split our time between there and wherever your jobs take you, because my family is there. Otherwise, I can visit them a couple times a year. And if you need a partner in crime, I might have some skills you'd find useful."

I stilled. "You would travel with me? Even if it was to steal something for a job?"

"Lexi, I would do nearly anything for you," Nilo agreed softly.

I buried my head against his shoulder and hugged him. "I love you," I whispered.

"I love you, too, *cho arbu*."

CHAPTER THIRTY-FOUR

Since Tavi had said that the crew needed to be able to respond quickly, Nilo and I didn't get to spend the day in bed, which was unfortunate. But he *did* begin teaching me how he'd disarmed me so quickly. By the time I'd gotten all the steps in the right order, the gym was full.

We were all antsy, so burning off the excess energy in the gym beat stewing alone. Even Kee was doggedly jogging on the treadmill, and she usually *hated* the gym.

But when Eli and Chira started wrapping their knuckles, all pretense of doing anything but watching went right out the window. Chira was nearly as tall as Eli, but she was long and lean like a runner, where Eli was muscled like a boxer.

But they both moved with the lithe grace of trained fighters.

After a few minutes, it became clear that Eli was holding back, but surprisingly, so was Chira. Then Havil entered the room with a murmured greeting and both fighters had a tiny moment of distraction. Chira recovered faster and put Eli on the mat with a move that was pure art.

Eli grinned up at her and spread his arms. "Aren't you going to pin me down?"

Chira's cheeks flushed a faint pink. "No."

"Then help me up," Eli said, lifting an arm.

Chira, however, wasn't born yesterday. "You can get yourself up." Eli chuckled and her flush deepened. She nudged his ankle with her toe. "You know what I meant."

Eli jumped up with a display of strength and flexibility that was pure showmanship. "I know exactly what you meant," he growled.

Chira snorted, but her expression was fond.

"Eli, if you're done flirting," I interrupted without a drop of remorse, "will you help me practice this disarming move Nilo is teaching me? That way he can watch to see what I'm doing wrong."

Eli mock glared at me before he nodded and we got into position. Nilo adjusted my stance and arm position with light touches that sent shivers down my spine.

"Now who's flirting?" Eli asked, his voice low.

Nilo flashed a grin at him. "Don't feel left out. I'm going to fix your stance next."

Eli looked down at his body with a scowl. "My stance is fine."

"For brawling, sure. But not for knife fighting."

It took nearly an hour, but I got to the point where I could successfully use Nilo's trick to disarm and take down an opponent more often than not, and I'd tried it with nearly everyone on the ship, including Liang, who'd had a surprising amount of training for someone who was apparently supposed to sit around and look pretty.

I had just pinned Nilo for the second time and wasn't in any hurry to get up when the ship's alarm blasted a warning at the same time Tavi shouted, "Brace!" over the comm.

Starlight jerked hard to port and something in the rec room crashed to the floor. Kee pulled out her comm and swore at whatever she saw on screen. "Hampston's ship is firing at us," she said. "The first shot was likely aiming for our engines—or their targeting is terrible—but Boyd's ships are now returning fire." She winced. "With much better targeting."

"Did the colonel think Captain Boyd was bluffing?" I asked. "They're outgunned. What is her plan?"

"They were aligned with where our engine shielding is weakest," Kee said. "If the shot had hit, we would no longer be a problem for the Feds. She saw an opportunity and took it, but I don't know how she was planning to explain why she'd fired on a civilian ship under friendly escort."

"I'm sure the inquiry, if there even was one, would've been swept under the rug," Eli muttered.

"Is everyone okay?" Tavi asked over the comm. When she got back a wave of affirmatives, she said, "It should be safe to move around again. Both of Hampston's ships have been disabled. One of our escorts is staying behind to assist with the emergency evacuation."

"Hopefully they'll lose Hampston in the chaos," Eli muttered, "but I'm sure her cowardly ass will be on the first escape pod."

"Eli, Chira, go check on Morten," Tavi ordered. "The

rest of you check on the ship to ensure nothing is in danger of falling over. Keep Anja informed if there is anything that needs repair."

LUCKILY, NOTHING WAS IRREPARABLY BROKEN, BUT ANJA'S LISTS OF tasks had grown a little after a thorough sweep of the ship. The rest of the trip to Bastion was spent in tense watchfulness, but the other ships within sensor range stayed well out of our way because Captain Boyd had marked our route as a temporary military no-fly zone. It meant ships heading to the FHP–Valovian wormhole from Bastion had to go out of their way, but at least we weren't getting shot at, so that was something.

Morten had fallen and busted his nose, but sadly, not his neck. Eli had patched him up despite Morten screaming insults at him the entire time and then demanding to be healed by "that fucking Valoff." Eli wouldn't let Havil within ten meters of Morten, and I didn't blame him one bit.

It was a relief when Bastion finally appeared on the main screen. We were given clearance to land in a military landing bay that had been cleared out especially for us. If Ohashi was going to double-cross us, now would be an excellent time.

Tavi, apparently, agreed. "I want everyone who still has armor to have it on," she said. "And I want everyone armed. Go."

Nilo helped me strap on my armor while Varro and Kee helped each other, and Liang helped Anja. It looked like the four of us would be leading the charge. The crew had lost so much armor this trip, including several sets of impossible to find Valovian armor. At least the bounty on Morten would soften the blow, assuming Ohashi paid up.

Tavi set the ship down in the middle of the landing bay, and then Eli appeared in the cargo bay with Morten, whose hands were cuffed, but that didn't stop him from running his mouth. "You will all be imprisoned for this," the commodore taunted. "I have the backing of the people who matter, and you have nothing."

"We have you," I said. "And we have video of you torturing an innocent civilian."

Morten scoffed. "Hardly innocent. She was harboring a foreign spy." His eyes cut to Liang and turned speculative.

I didn't care for that look at all, so I changed the subject. "Why was Fev working with you?"

"She thought she was using me. Stupid bitch. But she's got the empress considering war, which works nicely. If the Valoffs break the treaty we can attack with impunity."

"You're seriously talking about starting another fucking war. Why?"

Morten's eyes lit with the zeal of a true believer. "The FHP is starting to run out of the materials we need for our best weapons, and no new wormholes have been found in the last twenty years. The Valoffs refuse to allow us to expand through their territory, probably because they are hoarding those resources for themselves. They refused all of our very reasonable trade deals, and now they're just biding their time before they attack."

"Weapons. Of course it's fucking weapons," I snarled. "People are starving in the streets, but let's go to war to make more weapons."

Morten sneered. "If they want to eat, they can fight. Unless they turn traitor like your so-called capt—"

My fist connected with Morten's jaw with a highly satisfying jolt that was absolutely worth the bruised knuckles

I was going to have. I'd put my whole body behind it, and Morten crumpled to the ground, unconscious.

Kee shook her head in disappointment. "I wanted to do that. Why don't I ever get to punch fascists?"

I waved an arm at Morten's body. "Be my guest."

She actually considered it for a second before sighing and shaking her head. Eli, however, kicked him none too gently. "Wake up. I'm not carrying you, so either you walk or I'm dragging you."

Tavi and Torran entered the cargo bay. Tavi's eyebrows rose at the sight of Morten on the floor, but she didn't even pretend to scowl at us. Torran looked at the commodore like one would look at a particularly annoying insect.

Neither offered to help him up.

"Admiral Ohashi is waiting," Tavi said. "We're going directly to a preliminary military tribunal, so brace yourselves. Kee, do you have all of our information?"

Kee nodded and held up a datachip. "Plus several off-site backups, including one that will release everything publicly in twelve hours."

"Then let's go. Stick together. I don't want anyone wandering off alone."

Eli got Morten on his feet, and Tavi and Torran led the way down the cargo ramp even though neither of them were in armor.

The squad of soldiers lining the wall next to the door, however, *were.*

Admiral Ohashi strode forward as soon as we left the ship. She waved her guard back and approached alone. "Captain Zarola," she said, "I'm glad you made it."

"Did Captain Boyd inform you that we ran into a little problem?"

"He did," Ohashi said. "I apologize for the inconvenience, and I'm glad you were unharmed. I've already initiated the bounty transfer to your account. Well done."

Morten's lip curled. "I demand to speak with Admiral Clark."

Ohashi's smile was as sharp as a blade. "I'm sure you will get to spend plenty of quality time together in prison," she said. "Mr. Clark was found guilty of treason and has been stripped of his rank. And he had plenty to say about *you*."

Morten paled, then rallied. "Then I would speak to Senator Spencer."

"Is there anyone else you would like to contact?" Ohashi asked with an arched eyebrow.

Morten, who'd seemingly just realized that he was outing his allies, clamped his mouth shut, but not before he muttered, "You won't get away with this."

"I might not bring down the entire tree, Commodore, but I'm certainly going to prune as many roots and branches as I can find," she said.

Morten sneered. "You're too weak to do what needs to be done. Sit down and let the true soldiers handle it."

She shook her head. "The tribunal is waiting. This way."

We formed a guard around Morten, less to prevent him from escaping and more to prevent anyone turning him into a martyr before we made it to the tribunal. Ohashi's guards surrounded us, hopefully for the same reason.

We wound our way through the military side of Bastion before entering a small waiting room with a cell built into one corner. Morten was shoved into the cell, which was soundproofed and shielded.

Ohashi turned to us. "Admiral Clark *was* found guilty,"

she said, "but the vote was three to two, even with solid evidence. He has friends in many places, and I'm not sure if the verdict will stick. We need Morten's case to be airtight."

Kee handed over the datachip. "That should be more than enough. Morten had a team kidnap Empress Nepru's grandson in an attempt to either restart the war or blackmail his way through the Valovian Empire's wormholes, and there are orders from the FHP military authorizing his actions. Then his team attacked Bastion, kidnapped two fashion designers, one of them a FHP citizen, and attempted to kidnap Prince Liang. And he tortured me. If that's not enough to put him away, then you've got much bigger problems."

Ohashi sighed. "I've got bigger problems. Fleet Command wants this swept up with minimal fuss."

"You mean without admitting any failure on their part," I scoffed.

The admiral nodded wearily. "Exactly that. I've had teams quietly building cases for months, but the attack on Bastion still took us by surprise. It was a dangerous escalation that we didn't expect, and that's on me. My fear is that they are going to sacrifice Morten and then continue exactly as they have been, just with someone new."

"Then keep digging," Tavi said. "Or 'accidentally' release some of the footage of Morten. Get the public on your side."

Ohashi glanced at Kee with an unreadable expression before returning her attention to Tavi. "I would be fired immediately if any leaks were traced back to me."

Kee grinned. "What if they *weren't* traceable to you?"

"It would have to be exceedingly clear that a third party had acquired the footage without authorization." Ohashi shook her head. "And if the FHP ever found who *had* acquired it, there would likely be criminal charges."

"I'm sure whoever acquired the vid was extra careful not to leave any traces behind," Kee said with a dismissive wave.

The waiting room's inner door opened and a uniformed young man poked his head through. "They're ready for you, Admiral."

We collected Morten, then moved to the next room, which had been set up with a table in front of a trio of vid screens. Two people sat at the table and three more were on-screen. The two men in the room and one of the women on-screen were military. The other man and woman on-screen were civilian, presumably from the Senate.

There were two chairs facing the table. Admiral Ohashi waved for us to stay at the back of the room while she took Morten forward. She shoved the commodore into one of the chairs and stood behind him.

The older man on the left read off a list of charges that started with assault and ramped up to treason. I watched the tribunal members. The man reading the charges was on Admiral Ohashi's side, but the man next to him was more opaque.

The man from the Senate was clearly on Morten's side and looked put out to even have to be here. The civilian woman listened to the charges with growing alarm, so she was probably not in the war camp. The military woman was completely impassive, giving no hint of her thoughts.

So three votes were in play, with no indication of which way they were leaning. Great.

"I demand a lawyer," Morten snarled.

"One will be provided to you prior to trial, assuming

the case moves forward," the speaker said. "This is a preliminary hearing to determine if the case has merit."

I sighed. Of course it was. If Morten's allies had the votes to quash this quietly, then he would walk free today.

Not that I would let him, even in a room full of witnesses. And based on Torran's predatory focus, he wasn't letting Morten walk away, either.

IT TOOK HOURS FOR ALL OF THE EVIDENCE TO BE PRESENTED, ARgued over, and in a few memorable cases, excused. I wondered if the tribunal members knew that they were outing themselves as traitors and just didn't care.

That was a worrying thought.

The older soldier and the civilian woman were on Ohashi's side. The other in-person soldier and the civilian man were on Morten's. Only the female soldier's vote was still in play, and she had remained impassive throughout the vid of the attack on Bastion *and* of Kee's torture at Morten's hand.

It was well after midnight by the time all of the evidence had been presented. Both Tavi and Kee had been grilled with questioning, including questions about how Kee had gotten access to FOSO I in the first place and if that had warranted Morten's subsequent "questioning."

She had smiled grimly and refused to answer.

We were dismissed back to the waiting room while the tribunal members deliberated. Morten went back into the cell, looking entirely too smug, and as soon as the door closed, Ohashi cursed quietly. She turned to Kee. "I'm sorry. They were entirely out of line."

Kee, who was leaning back against Varro, lifted her

shoulder in a tired shrug. "It's what I expected." The big Valoff, however, looked ready to commit murder on her behalf.

Tavi was also wearing the calm, expressionless mask she donned when she was furious, and next to her, Torran looked like an icy, marble statue.

"They can't really believe Kee deserved that treatment, can they?" Nilo asked me quietly.

"Some of them will do whatever mental gymnastics are required to support their position," I said. "Including condoning torture, apparently."

"The outcome likely resides in one vote," he murmured.

"I noticed that, too. As, I'm sure, did Ohashi. Hopefully her investigation will be allowed to continue."

After fifteen minutes, it became clear that we'd be here for a while, so I sat against the wall and made myself as comfortable as I could, considering my armor. Nilo joined me, and slowly the rest of the crew did the same, except for Tavi and Torran who stood in the middle of the room. Their stances looked casual, but they were positioned in such a way that they could each watch a door.

I was drifting in and out of the light doze I used in unsafe areas when the inner door opened and the same young man poked his head in again. "They're ready, Admiral." When Tavi started toward the door, the young man shook his head apologetically. "Just the admiral."

When only Admiral Ohashi left the room, Morten smiled in triumph. "I told you so," he mouthed. Torran glared at him, and the cell creaked ominously, but Morten's smile didn't fade. He was so confident in his allies that a threat from a telekinetic no longer rattled him.

Ohashi returned a few minutes later, her face unreadable. "They are proceeding with the case," she said, her voice quietly furious.

Tavi heard it, too. "But?"

"But the hearing will not be public, and they will not be trying him for treason."

"Are you fucking kidding me?" Eli demanded.

"I wish I was, but my hands are tied. Unless something happens that forces the Senate to step in and demand a public trial, nothing can be done." She very carefully did not look at Kee. "Morten will be held on Expedition until his trial date, which is currently set for a month from now."

"Where on Expedition?" I asked casually.

Ohashi shook her head. "It's classified, but he will be in a maximum-security facility and guarded by people I trust. He will be delivered by Captain Boyd who is standing by."

That was something, but I'd still have Kee hunt down the location for me, just in case I needed it. *For reasons.*

"We can provide bunks for you, or you are welcome to return to your ship," Ohashi said. "I'm sorry this didn't work out the way I'd hoped."

"Not yet," Kee murmured.

"We will return to the ship," Tavi said. She was as wary of the FHP's hospitality as I was.

Ohashi bowed slightly. "I will accompany you, as Captain Boyd is in the same landing bay." She retrieved Morten, who lost some of his smug attitude when she didn't remove his restraints.

"What's the meaning of this?" he demanded.

"You're going to trial in a month. Your lawyer will be in contact shortly, unless you wish to provide your own."

Some of his bravado returned. "I'll provide my own. I'm sure it's already in process," he gloated. "I'm going to walk and there's not a damn thing you can do about it."

Ohashi drew and activated her plas blade in a smooth movement that spoke of long practice. The blue energy blade hit Morten before he even knew he was in danger. He went down with a scream as the nonlethal stun cut his legs from under him. Ohashi hit him again on the way down.

Twice.

"Oops," she said without a hint of remorse. She deactivated the blade and pointed to two of the waiting soldiers. "Help the commodore to the landing bay. Gently, of course."

The taller soldier slung Morten's barely conscious form over his shoulder, then the other soldier helped him stand.

Ohashi led us back through the winding hallways of the base until we reached the landing bay where we'd started. A second ship had joined *Starlight* in the otherwise empty bay, and Captain Boyd was waiting on the cargo ramp.

Tavi and Torran went to greet the other captain and oversee the transfer of Morten while the rest of us headed for *Starlight*.

We waited in the cargo bay while Tavi spoke to Boyd. I doubted Ohashi was planning to double-cross us at this point, but there was no reason to leave the captain on her own, even if she was perfectly safe with Torran at her side.

The group spoke for a few minutes before Boyd took Morten and disappeared into his ship. Tavi and Torran nodded at Ohashi, then returned to *Starlight*.

"This is bullshit," Eli raged as soon as we'd cleared the hatch into the main part of the ship. He stalked toward the galley and the rest of us followed him.

"Yep," Kee said, "which is why we're going to fix it." She started stripping off the outer layers of her armor, and Anja and I followed suit. I didn't regret wearing it, even though we hadn't needed it, but I was certainly happy to take it off. Varro, however, didn't seem to share my sentiment because he kept his on.

Once I'd stripped down to my base layer, I asked, "Can you find where they're taking Morten?"

"It's on my list," Kee said, waving her comm. "But if Tavi quietly asks Boyd, he'll probably tell her."

"They're heading for Titan," Tavi said. "And as far as I know, there's only one military prison in the city, so that's where Morten will be."

I made a mental note to do a little research on the prison's security system, then looked at Kee. "Are you going to release the vids we have?"

"Yes. And I'm going to ask Anna Duarte to release her vid about what really happened on FOSO I and Bastion, as well. I'm going to create a shitstorm so large that even the FHP Senate couldn't possibly ignore it."

"I think you're underestimating their ability to bury their heads in the sand," I said drily.

"We will make enough noise that they'll have to pay attention," Tavi said, her voice quiet but firm. "But for now, I want to get out of this bay, and then we'll get some sleep. Even the Feds won't blow us up right next to their premier space station."

"Hopefully," Eli muttered.

I silently agreed with him.

CHAPTER THIRTY-FIVE

My bunk was closer than Nilo's, and when I tilted my head in invitation, he grinned and followed me inside. As soon as the door closed, I turned and buried my face against his shoulder. He wrapped his arms around me and held me close.

"I've always wanted to break into a prison," he said, his voice light. "When do you want to do it? Before the trial or after?"

I laughed in relief. He knew exactly what I was thinking, even without being in my head, and he wasn't going to try to talk me out of it. "I don't know. It depends on the Senate. If they're not going to try Morten as a traitor, we might as well do it before. Although in that case, catching him after would certainly be easier, because they'll let him walk away with a slap on the wrist."

Nilo rubbed a gentle hand down my back. "What is your plan for the next month?"

I leaned back until I could look at him. "What do you want to do? Do you need to go home? I can find a captain who will take us without asking inconvenient questions."

"You would go with me?"

"We're a team, right?" My voice trembled, so I smiled and added, "I won't let my heart run off into danger alone."

"We're a team," Nilo whispered. "Never doubt that." His fingers rubbed soothing little circles on my back. "But I won't risk your safety yet. My family knows where I am and how to reach me if they need something. And I believe we'll both sleep better if we stick close to *Starlight* until after the trial."

I nodded and some of my tension dissolved. It would be nice to spend some time with the crew—and watch their backs. I pressed a brief kiss to Nilo's mouth, then turned toward the beds. The cabin was outfitted with two individual bunks on opposite sides of the room, but they could be converted to one larger bed.

When I slid out the extra support and started to move the second mattress over, Nilo grabbed the side closer to him with a grin. "Don't you want to snuggle me, *taro*?"

"Maybe I just want to have plenty of room to have my way with you," I countered, shifting the mattress into place. "And we can still snuggle, but now we won't have to worry about one of us ending up on the floor."

The gold in Nilo's eyes expanded. "I like the way you think."

I winked at him. "I thought you might." But even as I said it, a wide yawn cracked my jaw.

Nilo's expression softened. "Go get ready for bed, and I will finish this," he said, waving at the bedding. When I hesitated, he ushered me out of the room, and I went without complaint.

By the time I returned, Nilo had made the bed and disappeared. I changed into my nightgown and slipped under the covers. I was drifting in the calm before sleep when the door opened and Nilo entered wearing a pair of low-slung pants and a T-shirt.

He stripped the shirt off, and I hummed in appreciation. Maybe sleep could wait a little longer.

When he got into bed, I reached for him, and he crawled closer. He slid a hand over my silk nightgown with a lingering caress. "The first time you waltzed into the room dressed like this, I thought I was going to embarrass myself, especially because I'd promised you sleep only. I had to take myself in hand while I was in the bathroom."

I grinned, delighted, and skimmed my hands down his chest before pushing him over onto his back. "Let's see if it still affects you, hmm?" I rose up onto my knees and straddled him.

He made a sound of delight deep in his chest and asked, "Let me feel your pleasure?"

When I nodded, he opened our mental connection, and joy and pleasure and love filled my heart. I leaned down and kissed him, trying to show him how much I adored him, even if I was bad with the words.

His lips parted and I delved into the warmth of his mouth. He hardened under me, and I rocked against him. We both hissed in pleasure.

"How fast can you get naked?" I demanded. His pants vanished with a spike of cool power, and I slid against his warm flesh with a gasp of surprise and delight. "So handy," I murmured. I shifted my hips so that he was notched against me, but I paused before I sank down, teasing us both, just a little. "Ready?"

His hands clenched on my hips. *"Please."*

"You beg so nicely, *cho arbu,*" I whispered. Desire, affection, and love rushed through our connection, and I dropped my hips and took him deep.

We both shuddered at the shared pleasure. Nilo pulled my hips minutely forward so I rubbed against him and stars exploded behind my eyes. He groaned and did it again, driving me toward bliss with nothing but tiny, tiny movements.

But I wanted to take him with me, so we found a rhythm that worked and climbed together. Then he slipped a hand between us and pressed his thumb against me, and my world shattered into shards of pleasure. He guided my hips down once, twice, then locked them in place and followed me into ecstasy.

I slumped against his chest and attempted to catch my breath. "I love you," I whispered against his sweaty skin.

He gathered me close. "I love you, too."

And I could *feel* exactly how much he meant those words.

EVERYONE SLEPT IN THE NEXT MORNING, BUT BY THE TIME NILO AND I managed to keep our hands to ourselves long enough to actually get up and get ready, most of the rest of the crew was already gathered in the galley.

We caught a host of knowing looks, but no one teased us *too* badly—probably because they didn't want to draw attention to their own highly satisfied smiles. The only exceptions were Anja, who looked like she was unhappy and trying to hide it, and Liang, who was completely unreadable.

Tavi entered the room, filled her coffee cup, then stopped next to Liang. "Your ship will be here in thirty minutes." She heroically did not look at Anja. "Unless you want me to delay them."

Liang shook his head. "I must return to Valovia. If Fev was lying to the empress, then delivering Torran's report could make a huge difference to how she reacts to news of Morten's activities."

"But she tried to have you killed," I protested.

"Maybe," he agreed. "But returning is still the best option, and I trust my team. They were going to meet us on Rodeni, but they were delayed, and then my presence on *Starlight* was necessary for you all to return home safely, so I told them to meet me here."

I started to press him to reconsider, but Kee caught my eye and shook her head. "We've already tried," she told me over the comm. "And every denial just makes Anja feel worse."

I winced in sympathy and changed the topic. "Well, if you ever need anything retrieved, you have my info. I'll only charge you a small premium for being part of the imperial family."

A smile finally broke through the mask he'd been wearing, and he raised his eyebrows. "Small like five digits?"

"I *suppose* I could go that low," I said with exaggerated reluctance, "since you helped us out. But that's on top of my normal fee, of course."

Liang laughed. "Of course. If I ever require a recovery specialist, you'll be my first choice."

"As I should be," I said with a smile.

Liang nodded, then looked at Kee. "I would appreciate it if you would give me a few days to return to Valovia before you start leaking information, but I'll understand if you can't."

"We'll wait for word from you," she said. "But if we don't hear anything, then we'll be releasing the footage of Sura Fev threatening you, too. Be sure Empress Nepru understands that our silence depends on your continued health and freedom."

Liang bowed with his left arm over his chest. "I am in your debt."

Kee shook her finger at him. "Nope. We're friends, and friends don't accrue debts."

Liang bowed again, then looked around the room. "Thank you all, for everything."

Anja nodded, then murmured something about checking on the engines and fled the room. When Liang didn't immediately follow, Kee pointed at the door. "Go after her, you dummy," she said.

"I don't think she wants—"

"Just trust me," Kee said. "Go talk to her. We'll still be here when you're done."

Liang nodded, then left the galley. Once he was gone, Tavi sighed. "Do you think that was a good idea?" she asked.

"Yes," Kee said. "They'll work it out or they won't, but at least they'll have closure. And privacy. No one wants to have a painful conversation in front of the whole crew."

Tavi didn't look convinced, but she turned to me and Nilo. "What is your plan? Do you want me to drop you at Bastion? I'll transfer your share of the bounty to your preferred account." She looked at Nilo. "Same for you."

I blinked. "Oh, I didn't expect—"

"You helped retrieve Morten. You get a share," Tavi said, her tone brooking no argument.

I swallowed. Maybe she was giving me a share of the bounty as a subtle way of letting me know the job was done and that I should go, but Nilo and I wanted to stay, at least for a little while.

If she would have us.

Staying required asking, and *asking* meant she could say no, and I wasn't sure if my heart could handle the rejection. In the past, I would've left rather than risking myself, but I'd promised Nilo that I would try to do better.

I smiled brightly to cover my nerves. "Well, I'm not one to turn down free money. Thank you." I hesitated, gathering my courage, and Nilo silently squeezed my fingers. "As for our plan, we'd like to stick with the ship until Morten's trial, if you'll have us." Before she could answer, I rushed to add, "Otherwise, we can hang out on Bastion as I'm suddenly flush with credits."

Old habits died hard, and giving her an out meant that maybe it wouldn't hurt so much if she no longer wanted me aboard. I kept the smile, but Tavi's keen gaze pinned me in place. I couldn't read anything in her expression and my nerves stretched tight. If she said no . . .

The captain crossed the room and pulled me into a hug that made me feel like crying. She leaned back and met my eyes, her face as serious as I'd ever seen it. I braced myself.

"Lexi," she said, her voice terribly gentle, "you're always welcome on *Starlight,* you should know that. You don't need to ask. You don't need to worry. This will *always* be your home, no matter how long you're gone or where your travels take you. You're both welcome for as long as you'd like to stay."

Warmth filled my heart at both her unerring insight and her easy acceptance. I should've realized that the captain knew me better than anyone else. The tension drained away, and I blinked back tears as I whispered, "Thank you."

THE SHIP FELL INTO A ROUTINE. WE ALL DID OUR VARIOUS CLEANING and maintenance duties during the day, had dinner together, and then gathered in the rec room to watch a vid drama that Kee had found.

Kee always quietly ensured that Anja was part of the group and snuggled into couches with the rest of us, but we could all tell that the mechanic was hurting.

A week after Liang had left, Torran received a priority message during dinner. Anticipation and dread tightened nerves at the table until Kee finally exploded. "What does it say?"

"Liang is okay," Torran said, still reading. "And Empress Nepru has reinstated my diplomatic status, as well as my assets and standing. Same for everyone on the team."

Chira sucked in a shocked breath. In fact, all of the Valoffs looked stunned.

"Is it another trap?" Tavi asked quietly.

"If it is, it's a clever one," Torran said. "She's publicly awarding the entire crew a medal of honor for our part in rescuing Cien. We are invited but not required to attend."

"What did Liang *do*?" I asked.

"The empress is distancing herself from both Sura Fev and Morten," Torran said. "She's smart enough to know that trouble is coming, and she doesn't want it touching the crown. Pinning all of the blame on Fev is convenient because she's already dead and can't dispute the claim."

I winced. "My fault, I suppose."

Torran shook his head. "Fev was determined to take

herself out. You just ensured she didn't take the rest of us with her."

"You all could go home," Kee said. Her voice was quiet, but her knuckles were white around her fork.

I stilled. Nilo could go home and just . . . be. He didn't have to roam around the galaxy with me. His hand slid over mine at the same time that Varro murmured to Kee, "I'm not leaving you, *hisi las,* so stop worrying."

"Exactly that," Nilo murmured into my mind. "We're a team. You're my heart. We go together or not at all."

I turned my hand over and linked our fingers. I figured he could feel my love and affection through our connection, but I was trying to get better at the words, too. "I love you."

He squeezed my hand. "I love you, too, *taro.* You are my heart."

"Anyone who wants to stay on the ship is welcome," Tavi said. "But if anyone *does* want to return to Valovia, you are welcome to do that, too." She looked at Torran. "Does this mean we could safely travel to Valovia in *Starlight*?"

He grimaced. "Technically, yes. But I would feel more comfortable if we waited to try it until after Morten's trial. The empress can just as easily change her mind the other way."

"About that," Kee said, perking up. "Now that Liang has told the empress, we're free to ruin the FHP's day, right?"

When Torran nodded, Kee's smile turned gleeful. "The fucking fascists are about to be in for a very bad time, and I am going to enjoy every minute of it."

CHAPTER THIRTY-SIX

Kee barely sat still long enough to finish dinner, then she disappeared into her engineering control room—a glorified utility closet she'd converted into a workspace—to start wreaking havoc on the Feds.

Varro smiled and shook his head. "I'll make sure she sleeps," he said. "And eats."

Tavi dipped her head. "Thank you." She looked at the rest of us. "We don't know how the Feds are going to react, so I'm assigning around-the-clock watches for the next few days. They would be stupid to try something right outside Bastion, but they aren't exactly the best and brightest."

"You think they'll attack the ship?" I asked.

Her mouth compressed. "I hope not, but if they try it, I want to be ready. Each watch period is three hours. Varro and Kee are exempt while she's getting everything set up.

Torran and I will take the first watch, followed by Lexi and Nilo. The rest of the schedule is the duty roster and will remain the same for the next several days. Those of you with an overnight watch may want to shift your hours to accommodate it. Other duties will be limited this week. Questions?"

When we all shook our heads, Tavi nodded and rose with Torran. "We'll be on the bridge if you need us. Lexi, your watch starts at midnight."

I nodded and set an alarm. Tavi and Torran were taking a longer first watch to make the shift changes align with the time. First watch of the day would be midnight to three, then three to six, and so on. It was just one of the million tiny things Tavi did to take care of the crew.

Everyone scattered as those with early morning watches decided to turn in early to start adjusting their sleep schedules.

Nilo and I cleaned up dinner, then he laced his fingers through mine and grinned at me. "What shall we do for the next few hours, *taro*?"

"Watch a vid?" I asked, all innocence. "Read a book?"

Nilo drew me close and brushed his lips over mine. "Whatever you'd like," he promised.

"Cheater," I whispered.

But I took him to bed anyway.

KEE'S LEAK, INCLUDING ANNA DUARTE'S SCATHING ACCOUNT OF what had really happened on Bastion, spread across the galaxy like wildfire. The fashion maven was extremely popular—and extremely powerful. Her contribution ensured that the damning evidence against Morten remained in the spotlight no matter how hard the military tried to brush it aside.

Luckily, the Feds were too busy fighting each other and the media to pick a fight with us, so after five days of extra watches, Tavi reverted the ship to the standard schedule.

But on the first day without watch shifts, I found Tavi sitting on the bridge in the early hours after midnight. I tapped on the door, and she waved me in with a raised eyebrow. "What's up?"

"I could ask you the same," I said, slipping into my usual seat. "Torran and Luna are probably missing you right now."

Tavi's expression softened, and she shook her head with a tiny smile. "When I slipped out, Luna was sleeping on Torran's chest." Her gaze flickered over me, taking in the short robe I'd tossed on over my nightgown. "Why are you awake?"

I lifted one shoulder. "My sleep schedule is destroyed, and I didn't want to keep Nilo up with my tossing and turning."

"He makes you happy," she said.

It wasn't a question, but I nodded anyway. "He does." After a pause, I asked, "You want to talk about what's bothering you?"

She blew out a long, quiet breath. "It's hard, letting go." When I hummed in agreement, she added, "I thought I'd feel different after we caught Morten, but now his fate is no longer in my hands. Kee's doing her best to whip up the public, but what if it's not enough?"

"Nilo's already agreed to help me break into the prison," I said, my voice mild.

Tavi chuckled. "Torran has also assured me that Morten will face justice, one way or another."

I grinned at her. "I knew I liked him for a reason."

"But Morten is just one cog," Tavi said, sobering. "Killing him won't fix the problem."

"It wouldn't hurt," I growled, but I held up my hands when she rolled her eyes. "If you're set on being so damn noble, then help Admiral Ohashi root out the others. You'll have a lot more leeway than she will."

Tavi grimaced. "I don't want to be working for the FHP again."

"I don't blame you, but you'd be working *with,* not for. Ohashi seems like she's actually trying to make a difference, but she could probably use the help."

Tavi stared out at the vast expanse of space, then nodded. "I'll think about it. What about you? What's your plan?"

"Nilo agreed to travel with me, but his family is on Valovia, so we'll be making our way back there occasionally. Hopefully the empress really will let us come and go at will, but I guess we'll find out."

"You're always welcome on *Starlight,*" Tavi quietly reiterated. "For any reason or none at all. This is your home, too."

"Thank you," I whispered. Then I cleared my tight throat and grinned at her. "If you ever need a recovery specialist or a teleporter, you know how to find us. You're our family, and we'll always be there for you."

Tavi smiled and bowed her head in agreement.

OVER THE NEXT COUPLE OF WEEKS, THE PUBLIC OUTRAGE ABOUT Morten and the military's tactics was so loud and so sustained that the FHP Senate was forced to respond.

The Senators mostly made empty promises about rooting out the traitors in the military, but the week before Frank Morten's hearing was supposed to start, they overruled the tribunal's decision and demanded a public trial—and a charge of treason—"in light of the new evidence."

The tribunal members who'd voted against it were quietly fired or retired. The Feds, too, were looking for scapegoats in a desperate attempt to hold onto power.

But a wave of change was coming, and the smarter Senators were starting to get behind it, demanding inquiries and accountability. It remained to be seen if they would succeed, but for the first time in recent memory, I had hope.

Empress Nepru put out a statement assuring the FHP that the Valovian Empire remained committed to upholding the peace treaty. No mention was made of Sura Fev or her part in Morten's plans. The empress also publicly awarded Torran and the entire *Starlight* crew medals of honor in absentia.

Nilo and I decided that we would test exactly how far the empress's hospitality extended. The two of us were best suited to determine whether she was sincere or setting up an elaborate trap, so we planned to return to Valovia on a passenger liner after Morten's trial.

The *Starlight* crew watched the trial along with everyone else in the FHP. Morten's smug little smile won him no supporters, and it was not much of a surprise to anyone—except maybe Frank Morten—when the verdict came back guilty on all counts.

But rather than quelling the rising tide of change, the trial seemed to propel it higher. Admiral Ohashi was appointed to a special military investigation unit and given unilateral authority to investigate instances of abuse of power.

Tavi quietly offered her assistance, and Ohashi immediately found a bounty budget large enough to make me reconsider my life of crime—*briefly*. The *Starlight* crew would be busy hunting fascists for the foreseeable future, and while I was always happy to lend a hand, my skills lay elsewhere.

But change was coming to the FHP, and Nilo and I had been a small part of it.

Snuggled into bed together, sweaty and sated, I traced a finger over his chest and thought about just how lucky I'd been to find him in that hotel bar all those months ago.

It hadn't felt like it at the time, but fate worked in funny ways.

"I love you, too," he whispered, picking up my thoughts. "And I meant to make this a surprise, but I suppose now is as good a time as any: I got a very interesting tip about a certain figurine that one Besor Edfo is desperate to get his hands on."

My eyes widened in delight, and I gasped. "You didn't."

"I very much did. How do you feel about a little recovery job once we get to Valovia?"

My heart swelled with love and affection. No one had ever understood me quite as well as Nilo did. I gave him a slow, wicked grin, then rolled over and showed him *exactly* how I felt.

It was a lesson I'd be happy to keep repeating for a lifetime.

ABOUT THE AUTHOR

Jessie Mihalik has a degree in computer science and a love of all things geeky. A software engineer by trade, Jessie now writes full-time from her home in Texas. When she's not writing, she can be found playing co-op video games with her husband, trying out new board games, or reading books pulled from her overflowing bookshelves.

EXPLORE MORE BY

JESSIE MIHALIK

STARLIGHT'S SHADOW SERIES

THE CONSORTIUM REBELLION SERIES

DISCOVER GREAT AUTHORS, EXCLUSIVE OFFERS, AND MORE AT HC.COM.